Internal Lockdown

Internal Lockdown

Ernie Quatrani

PRODIGY GOLD BOOKS

PHILADELPHIA * LOS ANGELES

PRODIGY
GOLDBOOKS

INTERNAL LOCKDOWN

A Prodigy Gold Book

Prodigy Gold E-book edition/October 2018

Prodigy Gold Paperback edition/October 2018

Copyright (c) 2018 by Ernie Quatrani

Library of Congress Catalog Card Number: On File

Website: http://www.prodigygoldbooks.com

Author's e-mail: equatrani@gmail.com

ISBN 978-1-939665-65-2

Published simultaneously in the US and Canada

PRINTED IN THE UNITED STATES OF AMERICA

ACKNOWLEDGEMENTS

Thanks to my wife, Terry, my first reader and biggest fan.

Thanks to my sons Mike, Matt, and Steve for their encouragement.

Thanks to all of my beta readers for their advice and comments: Vicki Thren, Dom DiDio, Andy Comly, Brian Tice, Judi Quatrani and the many who at least read some of the manuscript and did not tell me to find something else to do.

Thanks to my fellow teachers and administrators and the students I was privileged to teach for inspiring the creation of the heroes and heroines in the novel.

Thanks to the heroes and heroines of real school shootings for inspiring the rest of us to protect our students in any way we can.

Thanks to all involved with The Rosemont College writing events. The knowledge, inspiration, and encouragement was invaluable.

Thanks to Rahiem Brooks at Prodigy Gold Books for his positive reinforcement and for putting me in touch with editors and reviewers and other behind the scenes experts.

Remembrances for all those who have lost their lives in school shootings, including Mike Swann at Upper Perkiomen High School in 1993.

Thoughts for those who have been traumatized by the aftermaths of school shootings.

Hopes that the government, law enforcement, and those charged with protecting our youth can come together to make our schools as safe as they can be.

DEDICATION

Dedicated to my wife Terry for her unwavering support and encouragement.

Internal

Lockdown

PROLOGUE

Mike Zarlapski heard the sirens before he saw the fire engines coming over the crest of the hill. He dutifully pulled over as two pumpers from Stonybrook passed him and headed up route 773.

Zarlapski pulled back into his lane, made the next right and headed the short distance to Vista View High School. He pulled in and found his regular parking spot near the gym just as a few snow flurries fluttered from the sky.

The teacher shuddered as he flung his backpack over his shoulder and headed into the building.

"Good morning," he said to the Student Resource Officer, Carl Manero, who held the door open for him.

"Great baseball weather, huh?" Manero winked.

"Always, this time of year," Zarlapski said. "When are you going to throw batting practice for us?"

"When it gets above 65," Manero said as he went into his office. "Good luck today."

The hall leading to the caf was mostly empty at this time of the morning. Zarlapski had to skirt around a large cart full of bread loaves and rolls that were jutting out into his path. As usual, he could hear the sounds of the cafeteria staff getting breakfast ready for students.

One of the cafeteria ladies popped her head out of the kitchen. "Have you seen the guy who delivers the bread?" she asked.

"Sorry," Zarlapski said. "You want this cart here?"

"I'll get it in a minute," she said and ducked back into the kitchen.

In the main office upstairs, only secretary Darcy Maiden and assistant principal Tom Roth were there. Zarlapski said good morning to both as he headed for the mailroom, where he was surprised to find Megan Speers at the copier.

"Is this some personal early bird record for you?" Zarlapski said.

"Got that right. I hate you morning people."

"Best time of the day."

"Right. I need to run a ton of copies," Megan said. "Had to beat Sue Snider here."

"Depression: an incurable disease?" Zarlapski read from one of the copies. That's uplifting."

Sue Snider bustled into the room.

"How long are you going to be?" Snider asked Speers.

"Fifteen minutes?" Megan said defensively.

Snider turned on her heel to head back to the classroom.

"Good morning to you, too," Zarlapski called.

Snider waved without turning around.

Zarlapski left the office and headed for his classroom. As he turned the corner toward the practical arts area—Maker Space as it was referred to lately—he saw a couple of students come out of the wood shop. He recognized Brandyn Halinski and Anthony Russo. Halinski looked over his shoulder at Zarlapski but didn't acknowledge his former coach. He said something to Russo who glanced back as they turned the corner to the doors leading to the parking lot.

Zarlapski looked through the windows into the wood shop as he passed. Everything seemed OK. He made a mental note to mention something to the shop teacher about those two being in his classroom.

Outside 522, Rachael Megay and Regina Himmelwright were sitting on the floor waiting for their English teacher.

"Morning ladies," Zarlapski said.

"Mr. Z, can you look at our papers to see if we're on the right track?" Rachael said.

Zarlapski let them in and consulted with each of the girls for a few minutes. They then went to their seats to begin revising while the teacher grabbed a stack of papers he needed to finish grading before the first period. He gave an inward groan when Vince Stefanowicz pulled open the door.

"Good morning, Rachael. Regina," Stefanowicz said to the girls, who smiled back.

"Got a minute," he asked Zarlapski.

"No. But that's not going to stop you, is it?"

Stefanowicz finally left five minutes before the first period was to begin after registering his disgust with central administration's seeming sabotage of the gifted program.

"I'll see what I can do, Vince," Zarlapski promised, sighing and shoving the ungraded papers into his backpack.

The halls were now noisy with students opening and slamming lockers shut, pages to and announcements from the office, and the chatter of conversations in the hallways.

Most of Zarlapski's Advanced Placement students were already in the room.

Physical education teacher Tess Bennington carried her daughter's book bag into 522, and Nikki Bennington hobbled in on crutches behind her.

"Feeling better, today Nik?" Zarlapski asked.

"Noooo," Nikki said as she dropped a crutch to the floor and maneuvered awkwardly into her seat.

Tess waved to Zarlapski as she left. "See you at lunch."

"Thanks, mom," Nikki called after Tess.

As usual, the inseparable duo of Matt Bianco and Steve Bennett entered together and nodded curtly at their teacher and coach.

"We playing today?" Bennett asked.

"Afraid of some snow flurries?" Zarlapski said mockingly.

Before Bennett could respond, the day began when the bell sounded, and Tom Roth called for the daily moment of silence over the PA and then started the Pledge of Allegiance.

1

The class groaned as Mr. Zarlapski handed out a multiple choice test to begin the first period of the school day.

"Shuuut uuup." Zarlapski said in mock reproach. "I told you guys this was coming last Friday. Plus, it's posted on the Google Site. Duh."

"I saw it," confirmed Cassie Van Doren.

"See?" said Zarlapski just as Rachael Megay's text alert chimed twice from her purse.

Zarlapski looked at Rachael over his reading glasses and held out his hand. One Z-rule was that if a cell phone distracted during class, he would take it and hold it until the end of the period. Zarlapski could see her blush from twenty feet away.

Zarlapski thought he heard a couple of other text alerts, but no one was acknowledging that it was his or her phone.

Then, another interruption. Isaiah Shue, in a Hawaiian shirt dominated by shades of green, shuffled into the room.

Zarlapski signaled for the class to wait.

"Good morning, Isaiah. Nice shirt," Zarlapski remarked to the portly, bespectacled junior.

"Uh, thanks. Sorry, I'm late," Isaiah said, color rising to his cheeks.

"Not a problem."

Zarlapski placed the questions face down on Isaiah's desk while he lowered his book bag to the floor and settled into his seat.

"Ready?" Zarlapski asked everyone. "Begin."

Zarlapski checked the clock over the door. It was 7:50.

The teacher wrote 8:10 in large numbers on the whiteboard at the front of the classroom and walked around while the fourteen members of the class began to dissect a satirical article from *The Onion*.

Muffled chuckles here and there told the teacher that at least some of the kids were getting it.

Mike Zarlapski enjoyed this class, even if some of them had had their moments this year.

On cue, Carey Ackerman annoyed everyone when his thick bio textbook thumped on the floor next to his bright red sneakers.

"Oops," he said, putting his hand to his face in mock disbelief.

Zarlapski stared Carey down until the pain-in-the-ass went back to the test. Some students shook their heads in exasperation.

Carey generally projected a polite, fawning attitude, but Zarlapski had learned it was a façade. All the "Yes, sirs" and "Thank you for working with me, sirs" were phony. Carey Ackerman was almost a caricature of a sincere, concerned student; his handsome looks helped fill out the illusion. Zarlapski took him with a veteran teacher's "whatever" attitude. Other educators hated Carey, judging from the comments in the faculty room.

Other than Carey, Zarlapski was blessed with one of the best classes he had ever had. A combination of work ethic, enthusiasm, and personality made the class a joy to meet with for ninety minutes every other day.

Zarlapski sat down at his desk and began fiddling with his varsity lineup for today's game against Moreland Prep. The PA chimed as if an announcement was going to be made, but nothing followed. The teacher waved for those students who had looked up to get back to the test. One of *those* days.

He grabbed his phone to check the weather forecast. Highs in the upper forties, variably cloudy. Baseball in early April. He hated coaching in cold weather. Two texts were waiting for him from two other teachers. They would have to wait.

At least the classroom was comfortable this morning. Gray clouds were rolling in over the football field, and it looked like it was still flurrying a bit. Zarlapski sighed aloud, distracting Cassie Van Doren. They locked eyes. Zarlapski tapped his chest. She rolled her eyes and smiled and went back to work.

Cassie played the airhead role too often, probably from a lack of confidence, and she flirted with everyone, but she was a brilliant writer and a diligent student.

At 8:10 Zarlapski called a halt to the test.

"All right. Exchange your papers, sign your name at the bottom. I'll run down the answers, and then we'll discuss," Zarlapski began.

"Ready?"

Isaiah Shue was still looking for somebody to exchange papers. Kelly Keiter reached around Isaiah from behind and took his paper, giving him Nikki Bennington's.

"Thank you, Kelly," said Zarlapski.

"Number 1, D as in Delta."

"Two. A," Zarlapski continued.

Zarlapski ran down the thirteen other answers and then asked if anyone wanted explanations.

John Pagliano put his hand up, "I don't see how ten is C. That's a lot vaguer than 'opulent' in D."

Before Zarlapski could answer, the PA alert dinged again. "Internal lockdown, shooter in the building. Administration. Internal lockdown."

Who to hell was that? Zarlapski thought, not immediately recognizing the voice of assistant principal Tom Roth.

Shooter in the building?

The PA was still live. Was that a firecracker in the background? A scream? Indistinct frantic voices, more firecrackers, glass breaking, a burst of static. The PA went silent.

Eyes locked on either Zarlapski or the speaker next to the clock above the classroom door. Zarlapski froze. He considered urging his students to run to safety, but no words came. Teachers had been told that experts believed that the first best option was to flee the scene of a shooting, if that's what this was, and it sure sounded like it. According to statistics runners have the highest survival rates. The north wing had an exit onto the upper parking lot. Students would have a decent run to get to the tree line on the other side once they got down the three flights of stairs. Or they could turn right and head for the football field, which was the school's rally point for fire drills and other evacuation drills. That would take them behind the north wing. If the gate was unlocked.

The announcement said that the shooter was in the offices? Zarlapski wasn't sure what he had heard. Maybe there was a window of opportunity if there was only one shooter, and not others waiting to ambush them.

But at least three of them would have to stay behind. Isaiah got winded walking two steps and could not be hurried. Nicole Bennington was on crutches. Zarlapski would have to wait with them. Zarlapski knew that tactical thinking mandated leaving those behind that can't keep up. Cold, but practical. Not for Zarlapski. Running was risky. Staying was risky. Lose-lose.

He also knew that police strategy had changed since Columbine. First responders now entered the building immediately and began searching for the "active shooter." Most shootings were over, for better or for worse, in about twelve minutes maximum.

We can hang on for that long, Zarlapski thought. There must be sixty classrooms in the school. The odds were pretty good that the gunman wouldn't find his way to room 522 in twelve minutes if he was in Admin now.

There had been a couple of unannounced practice lockdowns during the year and "shelter in place" procedures had been discussed at faculty meetings. But, for the life of him, Zarlapski could not recall anything he was supposed to do.

With the closed partition separating rooms, his room from 521, 522 had one exit door.

Next to it was a window, three-by-six feet, covered with posters and colored paper. No one could see in—unless they made an effort to peek through little gaps in the paper. The hall was quiet except for the sounds of a key in a lock farther down the hall.

Stephen Bennett finally spoke up, "Well?"

Bennett's voice snapped Zarlapski's brain into gear. Zarlapski pointed to the partition. Most of the students began moving to the only corner of the room that was out of sight from the hallway, as they had practiced a couple of months ago. The teacher grabbed his red emergency binder from his desk and opened to the first page.

Following the procedure, Zarlapski turned out the lights.

Some of the kids were taking places in the corner against the closets and cabinets that lined the wall on that side of the room. Zarlapski motioned palms down, and most of the rest found a place on the floor. Nicole Bennington was propped up in the corner leaning on crutches. Carey Ackerman was still on his feet trying to peer out the door.

"Sit down, Carey," Zarlapski snapped. He gave Mr. Z his this-is-cool grin and sauntered over to an open spot on the floor against the partition.

Zarlapski brisk-walked across the front of the room and taped a green "522" to the window that looked out onto the football field. He also had two red 522's in case immediate help was needed in the room.

The teacher squatted in front of the students and called attendance, to be sure, in a hushed voice from the list in his emergency folder. *Focus*, he implored himself. He had to stop his mind from racing. Everyone answered, "Here," except Carey's, "Hey." Zarlapski noted the asterisk he had placed next to Isaiah's and Regina's names back in September. They were to remind him that, tucked in the pocket of the binder, were multi-paged instructions for each on stapled yellow paper explaining all of Isaiah's and Regina's medical problems and following procedures in an emergency. Like this one.

Isaiah, as his parents had explained in a fall meeting with all of his teachers for the year, had myriad problems including Addison's disease, his adrenal gland did not produce enough hormones. Isaiah's medical issues had caused him to miss about forty days just this year, including all of last week. Any kind of stress could be life-threatening. Isaiah had to hydrate himself and took frequent bathroom breaks constantly. Zarlapski allowed him to just get up and leave without signing out whenever he needed to.

Isaiah needed to be medicated several times a day, pills and shots; the medicine was in the nurse's office in Admin. Unusual stress increased Isaiah's need for medication. Vomiting was a medical emergency. Zarlapski scanned the list of symptoms that would indicate acute distress:

1. DIMINISHED CONSCIOUSNESS
2. DIFFICULTY BREATHING
3. ABDOMINAL PAINS

If Isaiah exhibits any of these symptoms, call the nurse IMMEDIATELY (7709).

Call 911 if you cannot reach the nurse.

During evacuation practices, Isaiah had been escorted down steps by his teacher at the moment, *after* everyone else had moved out of the building. His bones were fragile, and any jostling might result in a fracture. He needed to stay out of the normal hallway rush between periods. During fire drills, Isaiah waited outside the nearest exterior door. Someone, the nurse or a maintenance man, came along in a golf cart and rode him out to the staging area on the football field.

The nurse was tipped off about internal lockdown practice and would have Isaiah sent to her office five minutes before the drill began. Zarlapski had separately asked guidance, the nurse, and the vice principals what he should do with Isaiah Shue if a real internal lockdown occurred.

"We would have a real problem," a guidance counselor had said, giving Zarlapski a sympathetic tilt of her head, but no real plan.

Regina had diabetes. She was diagnosed within the last year, and doctors were still trying to get her condition under control. To complicate matters, Regina was inscrutable. She never changed facial expression, and she never initiated a conversation. Zarlapski would not have been surprised if she had undiagnosed Asperger's.

Zarlapski tucked the sheets back into the pocket, picked up the binder, and walked to the classroom door. He listened for any sounds in the hall. Nothing. He opened the door a crack.

Nothing.

The teacher closed the door quietly and went over to the window and replaced the green 522 placard with the red. He needed to get Isaiah out of here ASAP. There was a space of about three feet between the window and the closed vertical blinds. Students could not see what Mr. Z was doing.

Now that the red 522 was visible outside, the room would be given priority, hopefully.

Zarlapski carried his laptop to the back of the room where he joined his students sitting on the floor.

Isaiah did not look good. He was pale and perspiring. Kelly Keiter had helped Isaiah find his place on the floor, and she was sitting next to him and talking to him in a reassuring voice.

Isaiah was rocking back and forth. Kelly took his hand.

Most of the other students were sitting quietly, some staring, some biting lips, some tearing up. Meredith Clancy's lips were moving like she was praying. Lauren Dougherty was fidgeting because she needed to pee. Ackerman was on his right side, propped on his elbow,

"Awesome. If this goes on for a while, I won't have to take my Calc test," he said.

"Shut up, asshole," responded Matt Bianco who hated everything about Carey Ackerman, from his eyebrow piercing to his red sneakers.

Mr. Z. knew that Carey could be vicious with his peers, especially online. Most of the other students in the room disdained Ackerman. Finding a partner or group for him to work in was problematic, and he usually defaulted to having him work with Kelly Keiter who tried to get along with everybody because it was her Christian duty not to judge.

Ackerman hung around with William Holder, a Vista View expulsion a couple of years ago. He reportedly spent some time in a mental hospital or jail before returning to the community last year.

Carey's in-school friends included some of the most notorious pests in the building, like Anthony Russo who was a bully, a sneaky little vermin who was suspended last year after "accidentally" smashing a girl face-first into her locker. His real forte was cyberbullying, however. Russo had a knack for zeroing in on vulnerabilities. He was a master troll.

Carey and his mother came to the area before Carey's ninth grade year. There were lots of rumors that came with them: his father had abused Carey; Carey had been expelled for, depending on the gossiper: a bomb threat, bringing a weapon to school, pushing a teacher, dealing drugs. Whatever the specifics, he was no angel. Twice in the past month, Zarlapski had seen Carey in Tom Roth's office. Last week the two had been joined by Officer McCaffrey of the Green Hill Police, a former student of Zarlapski's.

Zarlapski was about to warn Bennett and Ackerman when the lights flickered and then went off. There were gasps.

"Damn," John Pagliano muttered.

"What was that?" Rachael Megay said.

Cassie Van Doren tried to stifle a cry with her right hand to her mouth. Kyle Yarborough, sitting next to her, put his arm across Cassie's shoulders.

"Be cool," Zarlapski said, as much to the students as to himself, as he waited for his email.

The next step in the red binder's procedures was to report into guidance, specifically Tricia Belinski. Zarlapski typed in pbelinsk@vvsd.org. In the subject line, he entered "rm 522 all present inc ISAIAH S. and REGINA H.—— ADVISE."

The message lingered on his screen giving no indication it had been successfully sent or was trying to send.

Isaiah was now trying to regulate his breathing by "blowing out birthday candles."

Zarlapski smiled grimly at the unfortunate metaphor. Kelly Keiter locked pleading eyes with Mr. Z as she held Isaiah's hand, their backs against the divider that separated them from 521.

The teacher took the index card out of his shirt pocket that held the test answer key. He wrote, "Alert/Abdominal Pain??—Let me know" and gave the card to Kelly. She read the list and nodded at Z.

Zarlapski saw that his email had been returned as undeliverable. He cursed under his breath and tried again. This time Zarlapski used the address book to make sure that he had Tricia's address correct. He clicked SEND. Same as before.

Maybe the servers were rebooted after the power had blinked. When the lockdown plan had been put together several years it was decided that communication was supposed to take place via email. The plan probably should have been updated by now. However, the odds were very long that the school would ever be in a real internal lockdown. Why waste valuable class time?

Zarlapski got up and walked to the phone hanging on the wall near the door. The usual dial tone was missing. He pushed "0" anyway.

He tried 911 which did not require the prefix "1." Nothing.

He punched in 7503 which was Sue Snider's extension. Nothing.

The students were having better luck communicating than the teacher was. Zarlapski had always figured that, despite the prohibition on cell phone use during a lockdown, in a real emergency the cell phone battle would be a lost cause and he was not about to go to war over it. From the gasps and tears, Zarlapski could tell that bad stuff was happening in some parts of the building

Some students were sharing their screens or whispering the messages to those near them:

"office shot up"

"...machine gun"

"...six people with guns"

"Megan Walls shot."

Cassie crawled next to Zarlapski and sat on his right. Wordlessly she handed him her cell phone; she was shaking. It was a text message from "Levee," Ben Levengood, Zarlapski guessed. The message said, "czar shot CPR 9-1-1 luv u"

"Where is he, Cassie?"

"Math class, Mr. Ric's room."

"Ask him where the shooter is."

Cassie quickly texted.

"IDK," came back quickly.

"Doesn't know."

Cassie was biting her lip trying not to cry again.

"Thanks," Zarlapski said putting his arm across Cassie's shoulders. "I'm sure everything is going to be fine. Keep me updated, OK."

As Cassie crawled back to her seat on the floor. Zarlapski got to his knees so that everyone could see him.

"Yo," he hoarsely whispered a couple of times until everyone, except Isaiah and Regina, was looking at him.

"One, stop the talking. Two, stop sharing the texts unless you have an undeniable fact.

Nobody knows what is going on, including me. If you need to text, fine. But keep it to yourself.

Bring it to me if it's a *fact*. And keep the phones muted. No ringtones."

With impeccable timing, Meredith Clancy's phone started playing "Amazing Grace."

Zarlapski threw his hands up in the air.

"Yes, mom," Meredith whispered into the phone, breaking into tears. She turned her face to the cabinet door and tried to carry on the conversation.

The teacher paused to look carefully at his charges. Some were still showing signs of fear. A couple looked angry. All were concerned. Except for Carey whose thumbs were flying across his keyboard.

Cassie held up an Instagram photo: an adult male on a classroom floor being given CPR by another male adult who was visible only from the shoulders down. Speckles of blood were visible on the floor.

"Mr. Czarnecki," Cassie said tonelessly.

Z took the phone from her and looked at the picture more closely. He handed it back trying to steady a suddenly shaky hand.

"Thanks, Cassie," Z said.

Kelly Keiter still had Isaiah in a relatively calm state, at least outwardly. She leaned in close and whispered something to Isaiah. He nodded. Kelly still held his hand.

"Nothing from the office?" asked Steve Bennett.

"No," Zarlapski said. "I'll check again."

Zarlapski flipped up the laptop. Still no info from the principals. He pulled out his phone and opened texts from faculty friends:

"911 called"

"shooter was in 100 wing"

"anyone have Anthony Russo??? REPLY IF YES"

"OK," Zarlapski told the class, "911 has been called."

Other teachers were replying in flurries to text chains, but there was nothing substantial except that most were hiding and several had called 911.

Tess Bennington texted: "Nicole OK? Tell her to text. Locked in team room."

Zarlapski looked over at Nicole Bennington, now seated awkwardly with her injured right leg extended, crutch held out in front like a rifle. Her head was tilted back, leaning against the partition, eyes closed. Nicole was a warrior. She had sprained a knee playing lacrosse a week ago, and the inactivity was killing her.

The teacher sidled toward her a little bit.

"How you doing Nicole?"

"OK," she sighed, but her lower lip quivered a little bit.

"Want some Advil?"

Nicole shook her head, brushing her auburn hair out of her eyes which were welling with tears.

"Your mom's OK. I just got a text. They're in the locker room. Do you want to text her?"

"I left my phone in the car. Naturally," Nicole said.

Zarlapski's phone began to vibrate in his hand repeatedly. He saw "Tess" on the display.

"Speak of the devil." He poked SEND.

"Yo," he said into the phone.

"Everything OK?

"So far. You? I got your text."

"Great," she said flatly, "Nicole OK?"

Zarlapski answered by handing the phone over to Nicole who immediately burst into tears. She turned her head to the wall and tried to carry on through quiet sobs.

Mike Zarlapski and Tess Bennington went way back, back to when she was Tess Mueller. They had been running partners and close friends for twenty-three years. After school runs were a time to vent about the daily annoyances, aggravations, the vicissitudes of being a public high school teacher and life in general. Outside of the work grind, Zarlapski and his wife Karen hung out with Tess and her husband, Gary.

It was Tess who first told Zarlapski about the murder of Marcus Signe.

As school shootings were becoming part of the fabric of violent America, Theo Spence had walked up behind Marcus Signe and put a bullet through his classmate's head at 8:13 on a bright, sunny May morning nineteen years ago in room 205 just as twenty-two students were moving toward their stations for a biology experiment.

Brain matter, scalp, and hair splattered onto the dropped ceiling as gangly, 6'3, mortally wounded Marcus Signe fell face first onto a desk and then onto the linoleum tile floor. The much smaller Spence had shot from his Magnum at an upward angle. Blood spread across the center of the room. Several hours later, after the detectives were done, two high school janitors with strong stomachs volunteered to clean up the mess. They needn't have hurried. The room was not used again that year.

A Pennsville police officer found Spence sitting under a tree forty-five minutes later and arrested him without incident.

Several years later, Zarlapski came across a newspaper's archive about the shooting. One of the headlines caught his attention: **Shooter Thought about Massacre in Cafeteria**. In the article, Spence claimed that his original plan included killing the principal and taking out as many as possible in the caf study hall before killing himself. After shooting Signe, however, he "kind of lost interest" and "felt tired."

In the years since that incident, Zarlapski's mind had imprinted several scenes from that day: hearing the gory details from Tess, walking the halls, looking into classrooms and seeing the frozen stages of everyday high school life.

In the succeeding years, Zarlapski still involuntarily grimaced when earnest students asked, "Do you think that could happen here?"

"It already did," he would tell them, and then give a capsule summary designed to, well, scare them.

Most of the teachers and administrators who were in the building on the day of that ancient shooting had retired, or died, or moved on. Only five remained.

Besides Nicole Bennington, a few of the other kids were on their phones, apparently with their parents, including Rachael Megay who had retrieved her phone from Zarlapski.

Matt Bianco had turned to face the partition, his forehead resting against a poster featuring Shakespearian sayings. He was trying to keep his voice low, but he could not hide his exasperation, "I know mom" he kept repeating.

"I love you too," Meredith Clancy said several times into her phone as she nervously patted the bun of dirty blond hair at the back of her head.

John Pagliano was patiently recounting the events of the day in chronological order to his father.

All of the conversations were being conducted in hushed voices with nervous glances in the direction of the hallway.

Despite the violation of lockdown regulations, Zarlapski let the conversations continue.

Isaiah was still hanging tough, but now Regina Himmelwright was rocking back and forth ferociously, her face a mask. Rachael ended her phone call and got nose-to-nose to say something to Regina. The rocking slowed somewhat, but Regina continued to look past Rachael's left shoulder.

"I gotta go to the bathroom, like now," Carey said pleadingly, bending his left knee inward for visual effect.

"Sorry, man. You can't leave the room. Hang in there," replied Zarlapski.

"Why not? Nobody's out there. I can sneak down to the lav and come right back."

Z had grown to hate that sing-songy whiny voice Carey used when he argued.

Zarlapski wouldn't have been surprised if Carey was looking for a way to get out of the room and wander around.

"Sorry, Carey."

"I have to go, too," said Lauren Dougherty, standing and hopping from foot to foot. Zarlapski figured her request was legit. Just about every day she got up to get the pass before 8:30. Some condition qualified her for unlimited bathroom privileges, according to a note from guidance.

"Hang on a minute," Zarlapski sighed as he weighed options.

During the lockdown discussions and drills, Zarlapski had pondered the bathroom problem. If they couldn't leave the classroom for an extended period what was he going to do with kids about going to the lav?

Zarlapski grabbed the plastic wastebasket near the door and jogged diagonally to the far back corner of the classroom. As quietly as he could, he pulled a few desks forward, and then rolled the large green, portable closet to the corner, leaving a small space between the cabinet and the wall. He put the wastebasket in the space.

"Lauren. You first," he whispered across the room.

"Me first what?" she said, alarmed.

"Shh. Use the wastebasket."

Lauren gave Zarlapski an incredulous stare.

"Either that or hold it," Zarlapski said.

"This sucks," she said, still in the same spot, weighing the pros and cons.

"Hey, I asked first," Carey said.

"Be a gentleman," Bennett said acidly.

Carey waved him off but sat down and was quickly absorbed in his phone.

"Dan," Zarlapski called. "That cabinet you are leaning against. There should be a roll of paper towels."

Dan Streeter rotated on his butt and opened the door. Zarlapski used his thumb to indicate that he should give the roll to Lauren. Dan gave a short overhand toss.

"Lauren, if you are not going to go, give the roll to Carey."

"I'm going. I'm going."

"Leave the roll there when you are done."

Lauren repositioned the closet for more privacy.

Zarlapski caught the faint sound of sirens approaching from Main Street. Finally, this was going to end soon. Right? Zarlapski was not happy with himself for the way he was performing under pressure. Action, not hope, was necessary.

"Steve, Matt, Kyle, Dan come here; let's move this table and desk against the door.

Zarlapski and the boys quickly cleared everything off the tops of the furniture. Steve and Matt slid the massive gray desk across the entrance to the room. Kyle and Zarlapski overturned the wooden table, placing it on top of the desk. Zarlapski took a couple of plastic chairs and put them on the table so that it could not be climbed over easily.

It would now be difficult for someone to enter the room directly without taking the time to move the obstacles. It also made it difficult to get out in a hurry. Students might still be vulnerable in room 521 —the room next door.

Steve Laird, a social studies teacher, did not have a class period 1. Laird usually stayed in 521 during his prep period, but not today. If it wasn't locked, a shooter could stroll in and fire blindly through the hollow divider. There would be little cover in 522. The folding access door through the divider was at the far corner of the room, near the makeshift latrine.

It was the last of five interlocking panels and could only be opened from Zarlapski's room.

Lauren Dougherty emerged from behind the cabinet and briskly moved in a semi-crouch along the divider back to her seat on the floor.

Carey got up and sauntered nonchalantly across the back of the room.

Among some of the students sitting on the floor, some texting was still going on, but phone calls had ceased, except for Nicole's.

"Anything new?" Zarlapski quietly asked the group, crouching in front of them.

"Don't know. Phone's not working," Rachael said.

"Nobody knows anything, anyway," offered Cassie.

"Everybody's doing what we're doing," Kyle Yarborough added.

Zarlapski studied Isaiah for a few seconds. Kelly shook her head slightly.

Damn, Zarlapski thought. He fruitlessly checked for replies on his computer. He needed his phone back.

He was interrupted by Carey's sing-songy voice proclaiming, "Lauren's having her period."

Lauren bit her lip, embarrassed. Several students shot him killer looks.

Steve Bennett looked incredulously at Zarlapski and then sprang to his feet. "Shut the fuck up, asshole," Bennett growled, clenching his fists at his side.

Ackerman had the good sense to come to a halt several feet from Bennett.

"Did you hear that?" Carey asked Zarlapski.

"Yeah, I did. Take his advice and while you're at it, sit down. Don't open your mouth," Zarlapski hissed as loudly as he dared.

Ackerman sulkily dropped to the floor next to Cassie, who slid a couple of feet away. Bennett remained on his feet staring at Carey. Zarlapski cleared his throat to get Steve's attention and motioned to him to sit. He complied while attempting to glare a hole through Carey.

"My mom wants to talk to you," said Nicole, holding the teacher's iPhone out at arm's length.

"What's happen…" a loud boom interrupted Zarlapski's question, and a shudder seemed to run through the building.

Rachael Megay screamed out, "Oh my God."

Students reflexively ducked their heads and held their breaths, listening for what came next.

"Tess?" Zarlapski spoke into the phone.

There were no sounds at all. For Nikki's sake, Zarlapski said, "OK, good luck," into the dead phone.

"She's fine. Had to go," Z lied.

Meredith Clancy slid over to Rachael and put her arm around her in a tight embrace.

Bennett and Bianco got to their feet eager to do something, anything.

Regina's jeans turned darker, spreading blue as she continued to rock. Cassie noticed and looked away.

"Was that outside or inside?" Zarlapski asked the class.

Shoulder shrugs, head shakes.

Two seconds later, the piercing shrill of the fire alarm blasted the room and the strobe light starting blinking rhythmically.

Everyone froze and stared at the light until Carey jumped up and said, "I'm outta here."

Others started to get to their feet.

"Hold it. Hold it," yelled Zarlapski over the din of the alarm. "We're not going anywhere."

"What?" responded an incredulous John Pagliano.

"In a lockdown, we are to sit tight even if the alarms go off."

"Why?" Pagliano asked, forever the inquisitive one noted Zarlapski.

"We were told in our training that there was a school shooting down South a few years ago. Kids pulled a fire alarm and then picked people off as they left the building," said the teacher.

That gave the class a few seconds of pause.

"Yeah, what if there is a fire?" Matt Bianco asked. "We just heard an explosion."

"Then we will have to leave," said Zarlapski. He wanted to add, "I guess." He could feel his panic rising inside.

Isaiah was attempting to lurch to his feet, and Kelly got up to steady him even as she urged him back to the floor.

The alarm was cycling through a loud bell followed by a brief pause. The strobe was pulsing. Ominous sounds like firecrackers came from somewhere, intermittently audible through the cacophony of the alarm. Below? Then another loud blast unmasked by the fire alarm seemed to shake the room. Then there was another and a few seconds later another. People were screaming downstairs. Zarlapski and his students were frozen, listening.

Brrring-Pop-pop-pop-Brring

More screaming.

Another pop-pop-pop.

A faint odor of acrid smoke drifted through the room.

The noise, the smell, the fear was overwhelming. Kelly had Isaiah back on the floor. She was praying in a low voice. Meredith was sobbing now. Nikki was working hard not to cry openly, but a gasp or two escaped. John Pagliano was repeatedly running his left hand through his thick dirty blond hair. Others were hugging. Some had eyes closed, fists clenched, and tears streamed down cheeks. The only one who seemed unconcerned was Carey Ackerman. He locked eyes with Zarlapski, his face a mask.

"Good call," Bennett said to the teacher.

Infrequent muffled bursts of gunfire continued.

"We safe here?" Bianco asked.

The teacher shrugged.

Zarlapski thought he smelled a different type of smoke, like something, was on fire. Students were now sticking their noses in the air and sniffing. The smell was coming from outside, a hint of gasoline in the air.

He decided to risk a look through the outside window to see what he could see. Maybe they were going to have to make a run for it after all.

"Sit tight," raising his voice above the racket of the fire alarm. "I'm going to look out the window and check next door."

The little window alcove facing the football field provided a partial view of the south end of the campus. Zarlapski could see thick, black smoke from the area of the loading dock being carried out across the north end zone. The smoke engulfed a police vehicle, but he could not tell if the SUV was on fire. Zarlapski stared, entranced at the unreality of it all. There seemed to be a separate column of smoke coming from a source hidden to Zarlapski's view. At least it looked like the explosion had been outside the building. Good news for Tess he hoped. A helicopter was moving closer to campus from out over the reservoir. Media or police? Zarlapski couldn't see any clear markings.

The teacher called Bennett over to the side of the room.

"I'm going to check next door," he said over the alarm. "No problems with Carey. Got it?"

"No problems," Bennett said.

"Should only be a minute in case anyone misses me."

Zarlapski turned his attention to the panel in the partition that would give him access to 521. He pulled up on the floor latch that held the door in place, rotated the door slightly, and cautiously peeked into room 521. Empty and dark. Zarlapski moved into the room and started to jog along the partition.

Zarlapski hesitated at the outside door. He took a deep breath and began picking at the tape holding a poster over the glass in the door. As slowly as he could, he peeled back the poster and got a limited view of the hallway. It looked empty. He held his breath and listened as best he could between alarm wails.

Zarlapski opened the classroom door and looked right. The door was adjacent to the north stairwell. The two gray doors at the top of the steps were closed as usual. As he started to look left, the alarm stopped. The relative quiet startled him. He could hear the chop of the helicopter and more sirens from outside.

Zarlapski pushed open one of the hall doors. Indistinct sounds came from below. Zarlapski closed the gray door as quietly as he could and then cursed himself when he found that the door to 521 had locked behind him. He quickly fished his keys out of his pocket and let himself back in. Z took three steps into the room, turned and reopened the door to check to see if he had relocked it.

Zarlapski jogged back to the divider and signaled for Bennett and Bianco to come into 521.

"Grab the desk," the teacher said pointing to the oversized industrial strength behemoth in the far corner of the room.

"Block the door." Zarlapski remained to straddle the opening, surveying the scene in his classroom while supervising Bennett and Bianco.

He called Cassie, John Pagliano, and Dan Streeter over to 521. "Pile up the table on top of the desk and turn some desks over. Put some on the table and the rest on the floor. Hurry, but be quiet."

The kids did their best, but there was still noise. Speed was more important than stealth, and the four students were working rapidly.

"Let's go. That'll do," Zarlapski said from the open divider panel.

The sound of Rachael's agitated "Knock it off," came from 522.

Zarlapski was the last through the partition door, re-latching it quickly.

Kyle Yarborough was standing menacingly close to Carey Ackerman.

"Problem?" Zarlapski said to Rachael, stepping between Ackerman and Holder.

"He's Snap-chatting," Rachael said, "Like this is some party."

"End it. Delete it," Zarlapski said, turning to Ackerman as Bennett moved behind him.

"It's my phone," Carey countered.

"And I'll take it from you."

"You can't do that."

"Watch me."

"If he doesn't, I will," Bennett snarled at Ackerman.

There was some hesitation before Carey acquiesced.

"Fine."

"Show me the files," Zarlapski said.

Carey turned his phone around so Zarlapski could see where the video was stored.

"Make sure he deletes it," Zarlapski said to Bennett.

"Gladly."

"Don't kill him," Zarlapski whispered to Bennett as everyone else took their places on the floor except for Dan Streeter keeping vigil at the door.

This whole mess was spiraling out of control: no direction from the office, kids crying and pissing themselves, smoke, gunshots, the alarm, the blinking light, Carey, and, worst of all, everyone's imagination.

A couple of parents had called their children's cell phones again, but reception was getting worse. No doubt word was spreading through the community, and phone usage was climbing. Some students had tried unsuccessfully to call home or their parents' work.

Isaiah slumped to the floor, on his side, eyes open but glassy. Kelly was trying to get him to sit up.

"Kyle, Kelly, put Isaiah in a rescue position in case he vomits. And keep an eye on him. Be very gentle. His bones break easy." Zarlapski knew that Kyle Yarborough was a lifeguard and would know first aid and CPR.

Zarlapski moved to the closet next to his desk and pulled out a blanket. He tossed it to Kyle. "Make sure he doesn't get shocky."

Yarborough told Kelly how to help, and they got Isaiah on his side with a knee bent, chin to the ground.

By that time Bennett was satisfied that Ackerman had erased the video and defiantly flipped the cell back to Carey who caught it and sat back down.

When Isaiah was stable, Zarlapski addressed the group. "The explosion was outside. Probably around the loading dock. The building is not on fire."

"What exploded?" Steve Bennett asked.

"Looked like a dumpster," Zarlapski lied.

Bennett looked incredulous.

With an active shooter in the building, doing nothing was not an alternative. In school shooting after school shooting, people who had frozen and tried to be invisible merely made themselves easy targets and victims. Flight or fight were the only two options and, given the sounds from downstairs, flight was out of the question, at least temporarily. If the shooter came to 522, everyone had to be ready to fight. At least some of them might survive.

Propped near the closet was Zarlapski's first defensive option, an aluminum baseball bat, 34 inches/34 ounces, gripped with orange tape, used as a classroom attention-getter. He felt a comforting reassurance working the bat in his hands as if he was heading to the plate.

"All right listen," he stage-whispered over the ticking of the strobe light. Most eyes turned toward him. "We are going to arm ourselves."

"With what?" asked Yarborough.

"Lauren, open the cabinet you're sitting against. There should be a couple of spray bottles. Get whatever is there."

She hesitated.

"Now."

"Rachael, start running the hot water and then fill those two coffee cups. Keep the water as hot as you can."

Lauren held up Windex and a Clorox spray.

"Good, prime them."

She gave Zarlapski a quizzical look.

"Pump the handle until some stuff comes out." He pantomimed the motion for her.

"If any of you have keys, take them out and put them in your fist. Have the longest key sticking out between your fingers," Zarlapski said to the class. "Use your pens like knives. Anybody have anything else weapon-like?"

Cassie Van Doren pulled a nail file out of her purse.

"Good"

Rachael had filled two oversize cups with hot water.

"Mr. Z." called Kyle Yarborough. Isaiah had gone into a scary-looking seizure and was now on his back.

"Damn. Put the blanket under his head. Wait 'til it stops."

Out of the corner of his eye, he saw Regina Himmelwright leap up and move to the door. She threw a desk to the floor before John Pagliano wrapped his big arms around her from behind and lifted her off the ground. She continued to air-walk toward the door as John wrestled her away. After a couple of seconds, she went limp, and the color drained from her face. John placed her prone on the floor. He rolled her to her side. She had not uttered a sound the whole time. Meredith Clancy slid over to her and started rubbing Regina's back as she curled into the fetal position.

"Thanks, John. Everybody else OK?" Zarlapski asked. He swept the room with his eyes.

There were a few nods. *Yeah, everybody is great*, thought Zarlapski.

Within a few seconds Isaiah's seizure stopped, but a bluish tinge was creeping in around his mouth. Kyle saw it too. He locked eyes with Zarlapski who crouched next to Kyle. "OK with rescue breathing?" Zarlapski asked.

Kyle nodded. The teacher walked over to his first aid kit-a ziplock bag and grabbed the breathing shield.

"Here," he said to Kyle. "Keep checking for a fever too. Thanks."

After a minute, the classroom grew relatively quiet. Zarlapski noted the absence of sound from the hall, or down below, or outside, save the distant thrum of a helicopter and the ticking of the light in the classroom.

Zarlapski tried the nurse's cell phone. It went right to her full message box.

He punched in 911. He immediately got a recording saying the system was overloaded and the call would be taken as soon as possible. Zarlapski held the phone in front of him staring in disbelief.

Cassie came over and stood close to Z trying to be discreet. "Mr. Czarnecki is dead," she reported matter-of-factly. Zarlapski froze.

"What?" was all he could say.

Tears started to well in Cassie's eyes. Zarlapski reached out squeezed her arm and put his index finger to his lips. Cassie nodded and went to sit down. Zarlapski tried to remember how, Rob Czarnecki—his former assistant baseball coach—looked. He couldn't remember.

Kelly Keiter had heard Cassie's somber announcement and gasped. Several seconds later she made a run for the makeshift bathroom. Zarlapski remembered that Czarnecki was good friends with Mr. Keiter, and they served together as deacons in their church.

Zarlapski signaled with his thumb for Meredith Clancy to check on Kelly. Meredith had to step over the legs of Ackerman who was again oblivious to everything going on, thumbs flying across his smartphone.

Intermittently, other information was now coming in from outside and being reported.

"My mom says police are all over the place."

"The windows in the office are blown out."

"We're on the news."

"There is smoke coming from the gym."

Zarlapski glanced at Nicole Bennington who didn't say anything. Her eyes were closed.

"Nicole, take my phone, call 911, and wait until they pick up if you have to. Tell them you are in a classroom, and the teacher needs to talk to the police."

Nicole hobbled over and took the phone. Zarlapski uprighted a plastic chair for her to sit on.

Meredith helped Kelly resume her place on the floor with Isaiah.

"Give me your phone," Matt Bianco said to Cassie Van Doren.

"Why?"

Matt thrust out his hand emphatically, and Cassie gave him the phone. He saw that she was in the middle of texting Ben Levengood. Bianco swiped the screen and touched "Phone."

He tapped in the number for the Pennsville police department. Matt's father had been a policeman, the type of cop who was never off duty. The scanner in the house had been the soundtrack of Matt's youth. A couple of years ago, Matt had helped out in the Pennsville police radio room. He still remembered the phone number.

That line was busy.

"Keep hitting 'redial' until you get through," Matt said as he handed the phone back to Cassie.

"To who?" asked Cassie.

"Pennsville police."

"Where's your phone?" Bianco asked Lauren Dougherty.

She reached into her left hip jeans pocket. He signaled for the phone. She flipped it to him.

Matt slid it open and dialed the number for Vista ambulance. He had that number memorized, too. After seven rings, he handed the phone back to Lauren.

"Keep listening. It's Vista ambulance."

"What do I say?"

"Just tell them you're in a classroom in the high school, and the teacher wants to talk to the police."

A suddenly excited Carey Ackerman relayed a text he had just received from a friend who was in room 512 on the floor below Zarlapski's classroom.

"Brandyn Halinski says a lot of people got shot. He said bodies are lying in the hall and that Baltz is dead."

"God," muttered Kyle Yarborough.

"Where's Halinski?" Zarlapski asked Carey.

"Baltz's room."

"How many shooters?"

Carey hesitated and then typed the question.

"He thinks two. But he didn't see anyone."

"Are they alright down there?" Zarlapski asked.

"Except for the dead people," Carey deadpanned.

A couple of silent seconds ticked by.

"I need somebody to take one of the spray bottles and guard that side of the door," said Zarlapski still staring at Carey who held Zarlapski's gaze until the teacher looked away. "Volunteer?"

John Pagliano raised his hand.

"Thanks, John."

Lauren, phone still at her ear, handed him the bottle of Clorox and John went to the corner where the closet met the front wall of the classroom. He crouched on his haunches, butt against the wall, Clorox in his right hand.

Zarlapski instructed him, "Stay out of sight as best you can. Somebody else over there, please. Carey?"

Carey shook his head without looking up.

"I got it," Matt Bianco said. Zarlapski opened the middle drawer of his desk which was still barricading the door. He took out a letter opener and handed it to Bianco as Matt moved across the door and stood with his back against the closet.

"Good. Listen," said Zarlapski. "If a bad guy comes through the door, Matt, you tackle him around the knees, and John, spray that stuff in his eyes. Got it?"

They nodded. Bianco knew how to tackle. He was a starting linebacker on the football team.

At the far end of the hall, the sounds of the stairway door at the top of the steps being opened were unmistakable. Maintenance had not gotten around to eliminating the squeak.

The classroom froze and strained to listen past Isaiah's labored drawn-out breathing and the metronome tick-tick-tick of the flashing light and low voices on cell phones and muted sirens and noises from outside.

"Hang up." Zarlapski hissed to the people holding phones. "Except you guys waiting for the police."

Bianco, who was standing on the immediate right of 522's door whispered, "I think I heard a classroom door open."

"Hopkin's room?"

Matt shrugged.

Mr. Gary Hopkins taught three doors down from room 522. He usually had a period 1 class, but Zarlapski vaguely recalled him saying something about going to the library today.

Between Hopkins' and Zarlapski's rooms were rooms 523 and 524, but that was one large classroom. Clark Lewis, a social studies teacher, and Vince Stefanowicz, team-taught three classes. They always kept the divider open. Zarlapski knew there was a class of about thirty kids in there now.

Zarlapski went over to where Matt was standing next to the door and whispered,

"Matt, if you see a gun, go for it. Break thumbs."

Bianco nodded

"Dan, give me the bat," Zarlapski ordered.

Streeter reached behind him and held the bat out by the barrel.

"I'll use this," Zarlapski continued in a whisper. "The rest of you be ready to jump on. Hit him in the groin. Make him hurt."

"Steve, anymore sounds?" Bennett shook his head.

"Are we going to get out of this?" Lauren asked.

Zarlapski was caught off guard by the question. "Well, we made it this far. And the more time goes by, the better it is for the police, I would assume," Zarlapski said. "Maybe it's over already."

"I don't think so," Carey said from a few feet away.

"Why do you say that?" Zarlapski asked.

Carey shrugged and went back to focusing on his phone.

Zarlapski paused, debating whether to press Carey about his statement when he felt a tug on his right pants leg. Kelly Keiter pointed at Kyle who had Isaiah prone on his back as he knelt over him monitoring his breathing. Kyle shook his head at Zarlapski indicating he could not detect any, but at that moment Isaiah gave out a gasp and took in a deep, rattling breath. The class held its collective breath as Isaiah struggled for his.

"Nikki?"

She shook her head. 911 was still on hold.

"What are we going to do?" pleaded Kelly, tears welling.

At the same time all of this was going on in room 522, teachers in the special education wing located over the office were wondering the same thing. The department chair, forty-eight-year-old David Manning, and most of his department were hosting Dr. Alphonso Gerrits of the state education office who was updating the group on the latest unfunded state mandates.

Just as Zarlapski had, the teachers froze at the words of the announcement.

"I don't know," Manning said in response to questioning stares. "Let me call Roth."

The other teachers checked for text messages or calls. They put the phones on the desks.

Roth did not pick up. Manning tried the other assistant principal, Judy Buckwalter. The call went directly to voicemail.

"I've got to get out of here," Gerrits said. "I have to be at North Hills by ten."

"I wouldn't advise leaving, sir," Manning said as he now tried the principal's office.

"I'm parked right out in front."

"Sounded like the action might be right below us," Manning warned.

"I'll take my chances," insisted Gerrits snapping his briefcase shut and heading out the door without further discussion.

"Those state guys are morons," Manning observed, holding his phone to his ear.

"Can't get hold of the principal either," Manning announced as he tried his email.

"So, what *are* we going to do?" asked Sherri McCrudden.

Various viewpoints were expressed with most desiring to flee rather than hide. The conversation went quiet when Rick Heimbach brought in a student he had been giving speech therapy to.

The kid was wide-eyed and trembling.

"Know anything, Rick?" Manning asked.

"Definitely a shooter in the building according to a couple of texts I got."

"Why don't we all go down to 306," Manning suggested. "It's close to the stairwell if we have to go. I don't think we should use the one in front."

The teachers moved briskly but cautiously out of the room. Heimbach took his student by the hand.

———

Also at the same time, in room 214, Tori O'Connell had been intensely focused on getting her website project updated. She had started a fictitious dog grooming business and was in the process of uploading some brushing tips she had videoed with her dog on Saturday.

Then the internal lockdown had been called.

Tori didn't have far to go to take her place on the floor under the whiteboard; she dutifully put her computer to sleep as the class had practiced during a lockdown drill. Tori's best friend squeezed in next to Tori on the floor. The room was lit dimly now by the narrow window midway on the outer wall that faced onto the small courtyard with picnic tables.

Twenty-four students were shoulder to shoulder in a U around the front of the room. Faith Stennis was the last to find her place. By design, the corpulent sixteen-year-old junior always sat at the first computer station just inside the door. The easy in, easy out was practical. Today, however, she had to navigate the narrow aisle between the edges of the tables and the closets that lined the wall closest to the hallway. Faith turned herself sideways at each table. Her breathing became more labored and wheezy as she struggled toward the back of the room. Finally, on a chair, she used the inhaler she carried with her.

In a couple of minutes, the class had nervously settled in hoping this was just an amped up drill. Tori felt somewhat secure behind the numerous tables, but they were extremely vulnerable. A shooter coming in the door would not have a clear shot and would have to navigate the narrow aisles. However, if a perp was determined, there was no way for the students to flee.

Some of the students were using their phones. A couple of the students was rocking back and forth. One student was squirming like he had to pee.

2

County Dispatch received the first 911 call from the high school almost at the same time the lockdown announcement had been made and notified Pennsville police chief Barry Greco who raced to the building.

Greco heard County Dispatch reporting shots fired, people shot, pleas for help from inside and County had quickly gone from Code Orange to a Code Red alert. A County Incident Response Team (CIRT) was scrambling to a predetermined rally point.

Code Red meant that all county municipalities were to contribute manpower and equipment. State police were to give priority to the scene. Target time to get to any site was thirty minutes; that was going to be tested because Vista View High School was the northwesternmost district in Montgomery County.

The CIRT commander of the day was forty-year-old John Mann, ex-Army sharpshooter and currently the lead detective in the Hopewell PD. He would assume the role of co-commander along with the local jurisdiction, in this case, Greco, once he arrived on the scene.

State police were already responding but had been in the middle of a shift change, and, at best, it would take fifteen minutes for the first cruiser to arrive from the Dublin Barracks.

Two Green Hill police officers arrived ahead of Greco and Pennsville Police per the boroughs' mutual aid agreement.

Greco was eager to get men into the building. Police tactics had evolved from the wait-and-negotiate approach at Columbine to active shooter tactics that sent the police after the killers as quickly as possible. The goal was to minimize casualties by pressuring the shooter and disrupting the twisted scenario he had planned. In a large number of the cases studied, shooters took their own lives when confronted by police.

Green Hill patrolman Jason Laessig made a fast drive past the front of the school calling in "bullet holes and shattered glass at the front of the building." He proceeded to the upper lot and parked, got out and radioed McCaffrey who had gone to the back of the school.

"Take the back near the football field. Going to investigate the front," Laessig said.

McCaffrey parked parallel to the loading dock in front of a bread truck backed up to the platform. *Bad luck for that driver today,* McCaffrey thought.

The twenty-four-year-old officer got out of his car and first checked the outside locker room door to the left of the loading dock area, the same door from which McCaffrey, as captain, had led the Vista View Blue Devils football team out to the field just a few short years ago. It was locked.

He cursed as his radio came to life too loudly.

"Be advised we've had reports of multiple gunshots inside. Both of you go in as soon as possible, stay together. Active shooter tactics. We'll be there shortly," radioed Greco. "Any shooting now?"

"Negative," replied both Green Hill officers.

"I'll come around to you, Mike. Do you have an entryway?" radioed Laessig.

McCaffrey drew his gun, hopped on the loading dock and tugged at the door on the left. Locked. He sidled past the delivery truck and pulled at the other door. Locked. The officer climbed down three steps and started checking the bread truck. Both front doors of the truck and the sliding door in the back were locked. Out of the corner of his eye, he noted two of the high school's maintenance men running toward him.

He held up his hand in a stop sign. They froze about twenty feet away.

McCaffrey cautiously hopped up on the passenger side running board of the truck and peered inside. His eyes widened.

The truck blew up in a fury of metal and smoke and fire.

McCaffrey's flaming, dismembered body was thrown up against the wall outside the gym. The truck's doors had been blown out, but McCaffrey's detached left hand was still gripping the large rear view mirror.

Laessig came running calling frantically for 23-2 on his radio as he moved toward the inferno until he saw McCaffrey's body lying distorted grotesquely on the walkway.

To his left, Laessig saw that one of the maintenance men was decapitated. The other lay in a heap, bleeding profusely.

As Greco was pulling onto the high school property, he simultaneously saw the oily black smoke rising behind the gym and heard Laessig's frantic "officer down" call on the radio. Followed closely by the other two Pennsville patrol cars, Greco sped across the South Parking Lot toward the back of the building.

Greco directed his two officers to assist behind the school and headed there himself. A jagged piece of steel was lodged in the abdomen of the surviving worker; he was unresponsive. One of the cops dragged him behind Greco's car and put him on his back to check for breathing and a pulse and began CPR.

Greco crouched behind his car sweeping the building with his eyes. He heard alarm bells cycling in the building.

One of Vista View's pumpers squealed to a stop at the mouth of the driveway that led behind the school.

Procedurally, the scene should have been declared secure before the firefighters were allowed near the building, but he didn't want the building going up in flames and gave the go-ahead.

Greco could still hear fire alarms going off, but no one was coming out of the building, at least as far as he could see.

Greco ordered Laessig to follow him, and they jogged to a pumper. The chief got a first aid kit off the rig and gave Laessig some gauze to press against the bleeding scratch on his face and then went over to the maintenance guy, who was now breathing on his own.

"Let's get him over here," Greco said, noting the last name "Painter" sewn onto his work shirt.

The two of them hauled the victim behind the pumper. Newly arriving paramedics took charge.

"Give these guys cover," Greco told his officers. "I'm going to set up by the tennis courts." He asked for updates from County.

"Calls from the school indicate possible multiple shooters. Descriptions are vague, but all are males, headdress, dark clothing, long gowns or coats, appear to be on the move, current 10-20 unknown. Maybe fatalities in office on the west side of the building. A caller reported a teacher shot and in need of immediate care in room 115 which is on the floor below the office. A call from inside the school also reports shots fired in the last minute on the second floor of the north wing. Possible casualties."

"10-4. We have a working fire here and a police fatality. Internal fire alarms are going off, but no people exiting. We will be attempting to enter the building ASAP. ETA on CIRT?

"Thirty minutes. We are also dispatching all available units from other municipalities. We are Code Red."

"I'm going to establish the command post near the tennis courts. Inform incoming units to look for an orange cone on top of my car," Greco told County.

Long gowns? Head coverings? Was this a terrorist attack? Greco asked himself.

3

When the fire alarm went off, the twenty-four juniors in Room 513 prepared to do what they had practiced every month since the school year began, evacuate through the parking lot to the football field.

"Can I get my coat? My locker's right there," said Missy Fahey, as she rose to her feet.

John Baltz, her sixty-four-year-old social studies teacher, ignored her as he struggled to his feet. As usual, he was angry. Baltz had started the day pissed at the slowness of his laptop, and got pissier when only half of the worksheets he had assigned for homework were turned in. Then his quiz was interrupted.

"Probably some half-assed attempt at 'realism,'" he muttered.

John Baltz never did anything he was supposed to do, and he got away with it.

Baltz rarely followed up on email or read directives and procedures, as in, for example, what to do when the fire alarm goes off during an internal lockdown. "Guess they forget what it's like in the classroom," he would complain about the trio of building administrators.

In addition to Baltz' room, two of the other four classrooms on the second floor were occupied during period 1. The classes at each end, 511 and 515, were not.

In 512, Tara Robbinson had organized her twenty-two Honors English 10 students in the back of the classroom and had barricaded the only door with her massive teacher desk.

Robbinson grabbed the handbag from the back of her chair and brought it back to her place beside the door along the wall. She took her phone out.

In 514, Lauren Chapman had done the same with her twenty-one Academic English 10 students.

"What now," Chapman had texted Robbinson.

"Sit tight. Arm yourself."

"Pray," Robbinson added.

When the fire alarm went off immediately after the explosion outside, Robbinson quickly texted Chapman to "STAY IN ROOM" even as her students had started to rise from the floor.

"Stay," Robbinson commanded the class, holding her left hand out in front like she did when she was training dogs on the weekend.

"We stay here unless told otherwise."

"Why?" Caleb Stoltz loudly demanded.

"One, because I said so, and two because that's the procedure."

Stoltz glared at the teacher. She glared back, her usual half-smirk on her face. Just the other day, Robbinson had remarked to Lauren Chapman what "a belligerent little prick" Stoltz had become lately.

The kid fell off a cliff academically. His dominant personality traits had shifted to anger, arrogance, and disrespect. The teacher suspected that some traumatic event had taken place or drugs were involved or both. She had started the process of having him evaluated by the school's Student Assistance Program.

The face-off with Stoltz was interrupted by pops and screams from the hallway. Robbinson had no doubt shots were being fired.

When the alarm sounded, Chapman was confused for a moment by the connection between her phone vibrating in her hand and the alarm going off.

Chapman read Robbinson's text and put her left hand out as her friend had done. "Sit."

Baltz' Academic Social Studies 11 class was the only one of the three occupied classrooms on the second floor to walk into the ambush.

Two shooters, one with an AR-15 assault rifle, one with a Glock 22 Semi-Automatic .40 Holder and Wesson, stepped out of the stairwell. They had on military-style jackets and poorly tied turban-like things on their heads.

The shooter with the rifle began spraying bullets down the hall.

The initial rounds were high and missed most of the group, but not the two students at the front of the line. A boy and a girl were cut down instantly with shots to the upper torsos and heads, and they died within seconds of each other.

Some of Baltz' students froze, but Baltz' aggressive instincts, honed in Vietnam, kicked in. He sidled quickly along the wall grabbing kids by their clothing and pulling them back toward the classroom. A few students set into motion by Baltz' tugging ran away from the shooter and scrambled back into the classroom joining their classmates. Some were standing cluelessly at the front of the room; two girls were on their knees against the wall sobbing.

The incompetent shooter paused and then started firing again, succeeding only in obliterating several white ceiling tiles. The shooter's sidekick grew impatient with the ineptitude and ordered him to give up the weapon. The respite gave Baltz time to pull more students toward his room. He noticed the shooters' diverted attention and decided to make a move on them.

The old teacher limped within ten feet of the shooters. Shooter #2, much more skilled, calmly pivoted, raised his Glock, and dropped Baltz with one shot to the middle of the chest. Screams echoed down the hallway as Baltz convulsed on the floor. Shooter #2 exchanged weapons with his partner. He trained the AR-15 down the hall and picked off seven of the nine students who were still outside of the classroom. The other two turned into the boys' bathroom.

The first shooter walked over to Baltz and fired three shots into the teacher's twitching body.

"Fuck you, Baltz."

The gunman took a couple of steps down the hallway.

"Let's go," his partner called. "You can come back for them. They're not going anywhere."

"But…"

"Maybe you'll learn to shoot by then."

A couple of students tumbled into 513 over Missy Fahey who had slipped on blood at the classroom door. Robbie Quinn grabbed her by the belt in her jeans and dragged her into the room. Injured crawled across the threshold, blood and tears streaking their faces. The hot scent of ammo permeated the air as students sought refuge in this corner and then that corner or under a desk, some whimpering at the futility of the situation.

"We got to fight. We got to fight. We got to fight," Theo Iacone kept yelling, punching awkwardly at the air to emphasize his point.

"Theo, I need you to be quiet," Quinn said calmly. He had seen meltdowns before. "Theo. Look at me. Be quiet."

"We got to fight," repeated Theo, his face scrunched up, tears streaming down his face.

"Theo, come over here with me," Quinn said in a monotone. "I need you to help me with this table. You will pick up that end, and I'll take this end. Theo? Answer me."

"OK." They picked up the table and put it in front of the door. Robbie stayed with Theo as they worked together.

A couple of other students got the idea and started piling up overturned desks with the legs splayed in many different directions. It reminded Robbie of the Omaha Beach pictures Baltz had shown the class during the World War II unit.

'He's right," Missy said behind Robbie. "We have to fight."

"With what?"

"Anything."

Iacone looked around the room. "Theo, get the fire extinguisher. Bring it here."

"Baltz always has an umbrella in the closet," someone said. "I'll get it."

"That's good, Theo," Quinn said. "I know you know how to use these things from that shop thing last year, so you stand here and stay ready. If somebody tries to get in, blast them in the face."

Theo nodded grimly and assumed an exaggerated fighting stance.

"Everybody have something you can throw or stab with," Quinn urged.

A rattling noise, someone was trying the classroom door, interrupted the weapon gathering. Quinn put his hand on Theo's arm and a finger to his lips. Those not pre-occupied with their situations held their breaths and stared at the door.

Knocking began, audible between cycles of the alarm.

After a few seconds, Quinn shrugged his shoulders. "I'll look."

Robbie crawled past the desk-obstacles and under the table blocking the door. He picked at the tape holding the construction paper in place over the glass strip in the door. He peeled the paper back slowly and gasped. Staring back at him was the bloody face of someone. He turned the doorknob and pushed the door open, hitting the shoulder of the person outside the door.

"Move the table," Robbie said over his shoulder.

"Theo, stay ready. Wait for me to tell you." Robbie straightened up on his knees and opened the door wider.

"I can't," was all the girl could say before she passed out. He grabbed her pullover sweater at both shoulders and pulled her swiftly into the room.

"I think that's Candi Gresham," Missy Fahey wailed. "Oh my God. Is she alive?"

"She's breathing. Give me a hand; we'll turn her over," Robbie ordered.

The intestine was leaking out of a tear in her stomach.

Missy did not make it to the sink before vomiting.

"Keep them moist," Iacone instructed matter-of-factly. "Get some wet paper towels."

No one moved.

"I'll do it. God." An irritated Theo put down the fire extinguisher and wet several towels.

Theo pulled the girl's sweater up higher. He fought off a wave of nausea at the sight and smell, extended his arms and dropped the wet towels the last six inches onto the wound.

"I'll call 911," Missy Fahey said, but several attempts were futile.

Others pulled out phones, but they could not get through either.

The unconscious Candi Gresham breathed irregularly on the floor. Robbie Quinn pushed her body gently up against the wall, away from the obstacles.

Theo handed the fire extinguisher to a classmate and became the watcher of wet paper towels. He took out his gaudy red handkerchief and pressed it against a small hole that was leaking blood near a gash on Candi's cheek. Her eyes fluttered for a moment.

Muffled crying and an occasional gasp or moan in the room mingled with the sounds of the alarm.

Robbie stood up and addressed the other eight students over the noise.

"I say we stay here. I don't want to walk into an ambush, and I don't want to go out there and see all those bodies. Everybody have something to fight with if anybody comes? Everybody rush him if they come in. Bite, kick punch, stab, whatever. Otherwise, we don't have a chance. Got it?"

No one said anything except Missy. "I'll keep trying 911."

Next to Baltz' room, Robbinson was straining to hear what was happening in the hallway when an "Oh my God" brought her attention back into the room.

Stoltz had reached into his backpack and was straightening up clutching a gun in his right hand.

Cheap little Kel-Tec P3AT, Robbinson thought. She dove and rolled under a table as Stoltz was bringing the gun up. He fired wildly into the whiteboard. Her instincts kept her moving as Stoltz sidled along the back wall. Cowering students slithered out of the way.

She wanted to tell her class to run. But to where?

Robbinson matched Stoltz's moves and tried to close the distance between them subtly. He was a rank amateur with a gun. Her play was to try and surprise Stoltz by rolling into his legs, and bringing him to the floor, and/or grab the gun. Maybe she could jam the slide with her hand.

But as big and doughy as he was, Stoltz was still light on his feet as many surprised wrestling heavyweights had found out.

He stepped back and shot as Robbinson was rising. The bullet went through her raised left hand and spun her to the floor.

Stoltz didn't need to be an expert marksman to step forward and shoot her twice in the head, scattering blood, brain, and bone on the back wall and students nearby.

Two male students lunged at Stoltz from his right. He pivoted and shot one in the chest.

A girl began screaming at the top of her lungs.

"Shut up," Stoltz yelled without turning around to see who it was. "Shut up."

The wounded student gurgled as he tried to draw breaths. The other nineteen students in the room tried to shrink to invisibility; those closest moved away from the dead teacher.

Two doors down in 514, Mrs. Chapman, was texting furiously to her husband and her child's daycare teacher, without much success, when a terrified, "Oh my God" made her look up.

Chapman froze when she saw Hosni "Little Ahmed" Afarini struggling to steady a large handgun. In Arabic his name meant "Much Praised" and that motivated him this morning.

"What are you doing, Hosni?"

"We need to go outside," Hosni almost pleaded in a quaking voice.

"There's shooting out there," Chapman said, her voice quivering.

Peripherally, Mrs. C could see Chloe Genter moving stealthily closer to the gunman. Chapman was mentally rooting for her, but Afarini turned to his left and fired at Chloe—the second bullet penetrated her skull. Blood was everywhere, students screamed and moved away.

Chapman instinctively moved to tend to Chloe now rolling back and forth on the classroom floor. Afarini fired, catching Chapman in the left bicep. The impact spun Chapman to the floor where she landed hard on her elbow. She wailed in pain. Hosni stood over her while he played the gun over the terrified students in room 514.

"Silence, silence." Hosni fired two shots toward the ceiling, shattering a light.

Whimpering replaced screams.

Hosni stepped back and looked down at Mrs. Chapman who was curled on the floor. He cautiously walked backward, grabbed his backpack, and slumped in a desk on the other side of the room, the gun on the desktop.

Chapman painfully crawled to the back of the room to be near Chloe, eyeing Hosni every few feet. The teacher accepted several paper towels from nearby students and tried to stem the flow of blood from Chloe's head.

Hosni watched impassively and the room settled into a stalemate.

The fire alarm finally went silent. It was quiet in the hall.

4

At the same time the events on the second floor of the 500 wing had been playing out, the lights in the entire physical education wing went dark including in the team room. Despite the two walls that separated the team room from the loading dock, the detonation of the truck had been loud, and the place had shaken.

It took the gym teacher, Tess Bennington, a long, panicky minute to collect her wits and find her phone which had fallen out of her hand as she finished the call with her daughter, sheltering with Mike Zarlapski in 522.

Forty-seven freshmen and sophomores were in various stages of terror. Tess' teaching partner for mod 1, Mike Falcone, was trying to be heard above the alarm and the crying and the moaning.

"Anybody hurt?" he shouted. "Anybody hurt?"

He held up his cell phone and used the flashlight app to survey the room.

Some students turned on their flashlights after groping for phones in lockers.

"We're getting out of here," Bennington shouted into Falcone's ear.

There were two exits. The closest door led out to the fields but would put them in the general proximity of the explosion. *God knows what is going on out there*, Tess thought.

"Through the locker room," Tess said to Falcone. "I'll lead. You make sure everyone gets out."

"Hey," Mrs. Bennington yelled above the din. "Follow me." She said making an overhead, sweeping motion with her right arm to the class. "Let's go. Let's go," she yelled emphatically.

Bennington opened the door separating the team room from the PE class changing room. The emergency light was functioning here.

Quickly, Tess decided the best route was through the gym to the double doors on the other side, and then into the hallway, fifty feet to the doors leading out to the parking lot.

There was sufficient light from the windows near the ceiling to maneuver through the gym safely.

Mrs. Bennington turned to the closest students in line. "I'll hold the door. Go left and run. When you get to the outside doors, put your hands in the air, and run toward the tennis courts. Got it?"

Several nodded.

"Ready?"

Mrs. Bennington opened the door and stepped out into the hallway. She emphatically signaled the first two students in line to go. They sprinted to the doors before bursting through and throwing their hands in the air and running toward the tennis courts.

"That everybody?" Tess asked when Falcone got to the hallway.

"Yep."

"Let's get to hell out of here," she said.

Chief Greco was finishing up his conversation with dispatch when he saw the class coming at him. He started toward them while he scanned the rooftop of the PE wing.

"Keep an eye on the roof," Greco said over his radio to his men.

Greco signaled the out of breath students to get behind him as the two teachers caught up to their class.

"Yours?" Greco asked.

"Yep," Falcone said.

"All of them?"

Falcone looked at Tess. "Think so. We were in the team room, and we just ran."

"Give me a minute," Greco said to the teachers.

County radio had been calling for Greco several times, and he took a few seconds to tell them to stand-by until he called them.

Two state police cars rolled up to Greco's car, and two troopers got out.

"Glad you're here," Greco said before filling them in on what was going on.

"Line them up and eyeball them for weapons," Greco told the troopers. "Ask each one if they know anything."

Several of the out-of-shape students were struggling to catch their breaths. One girl was using her inhaler. Many were shivering, arms across their chests trying to stay warm.

Greco found a couple of blankets in the trunk of his car and handed them to the nearest students. The troopers did the same.

Greco told the two teachers to escort the class to the Memorial Field parking lot, another fifty yards away from the command post, and to keep them there until he figured out what to do with them. Greco told the teachers to write down the names of the students on a legal pad he handed them,

It took the troopers just a couple of minutes for their cursory inspections and questions. None of the students knew anything.

Bennington and Falcone led the class to the parking area for the fields. There were no cars on the lot this morning.

"Call the Davenport Bus Company," Greco told County over the radio. "Tell them to roll some buses to the Memorial Field parking lot ASAP."

"10-4," County replied. "We have multiple calls from room 115 about a teacher with gunshot wounds. We also have a teacher on the line from 522 who has a critically ill student. Do you want the contact numbers?"

"Text me the numbers. I'll call both in a minute."

Greco called up the high school's floor plan on his unit's computer and found room 115 first. He saw that the room was almost directly across from the cafeteria.

Green Hill chief Greg Hawthorne was arriving in his unmarked Chevy Impala followed by Sean McCarthy in a marked Green Hill cruiser.

"Who was the 10-79 for?" Hawthorne asked Greco as soon as he got out of his car.

"I'm sorry, Greg. It was McCaffrey. Never had a chance. The truck blew up."

"Damn. Damn it," an angry Hawthorne replied. "Where is he?"

Greco pointed to the back of the gym where smoke was still rising. Hawthorne and Greco stared into each other's eyes for a few seconds.

"Bomb?" McCarthy asked

"Looks like it."

"We'll be back," Hawthorne said as the two Green Hill cops started off toward the loading dock area.

Greco told John Abrams and Whitey Fallon, two of his men, "Get pry bars and put your vests on. Go in through the gym entrance. You have a straight line down a hall to a T-intersection. Priority is the shooter or shooters. Find them and take them out if you can. The second priority is room 115, on the other side of the caf. We have an injured person in that room. Get on Tac 2. You're Team 1."

"We got it," said Fallon a Vista View alum. "I know the layout."

Greco went over the descriptions of the shooters.

"Terrorists?" said Fallon.

"One way or another," replied Greco.

"When McCarthy gets back, take him with you," he said.

The two Pennsville officers were almost done gearing up when an angry McCarthy came from viewing the carnage behind the school.

Abrams explained the plan to McCarthy.

"Active shooter protocols," Greco called after them as they sprinted for the gym entrance.

"Careful."

5

After deliberating together in the corner of room 522, Steve Bennett and Matt Bianco approached Mr. Zarlapski.

"Matt and I will take Isaiah to the nurse," said Bennett.

Zarlapski hesitated, looking into the eyes of Bennett and then glancing at Isaiah Shue, still being tended to by his classmates. Cassie had dampened a paper towel and was gently wiping some drool from Isaiah's increasingly waxy skin.

"I can't let you do that, but thanks," said Zarlapski still eyeing Isaiah.

"He's gonna die in the next few minutes," Bianco said matter-of-factly.

"You don't know that," Zarlapski said while admitting to himself that they were probably right.

"He looks like my grandfather did right before he passed," Bianco said.

"How do we know the shooter isn't right outside?" Zarlapski continued.

"I'll check," said Matt Bianco, starting for the door.

"Whoa. Whoa. I'll check," said Zarlapski. "Give me a hand."

Bianco and Bennett moved some of the desks that formed the barricade just enough for Zarlapski to get to the door. He turned and motioned for the class to be quiet. All eyes were on him as he gripped the door handle.

The teacher took a deep breath and listened outside. For the first time, he thought about his wife, Karen, and their three kids. Did she know what was going on? He made a mental note to call her ASAP. Up to this point, he'd done an excellent job of keeping his emotions in check. But now the teacher couldn't stop his internal narrator, somewhere from the back of his mind, it was saying: Hey. This might be the last thing you ever do.

Focus, he thought, with the same emphasis used on his team when games were going badly. His senses began to sharpen. He noted the sweat, urine, stale perfume, smoke, vomit now polluting the atmosphere of his classroom.

So, this is what fear smells like, he thought, recalling a prompt he used during a poetry unit.

The teacher signaled Bennett and Bianco to move back. Zarlapski could feel his heart rate picking up.

Zarlapski paused to listen into the hall—and say an abbreviated Act of Contrition.

He pushed the handle down as slowly as he could, but it still clicked. The teacher held it in place for a second and edged the door open. The top hinge squeaked. Zarlapski pushed a little more until he could peer straight ahead into the hall, straining all the while to listen.

Nothing.

He opened the door a little wider and eased his upper body through.

The sound of the hall door had come from the left. Look left.

The hall was clear. But was that a voice from down the hall?

Zarlapski swiveled his head right.

Clear.

"Mr. Z," a voice whispered behind him causing him to flinch.

Zarlapski caught his breath and then waved his right arm downward in a "be quiet" motion. He looked over his shoulder at Nikki Bennington holding the phone out in front of her.

Finally. 911.

Zarlapski retook a look at both ends of the hall and eased his upper body back into the room.

"Nikki," Zarlapski said, "tell them what's going on. I'll be right back. I need to get a stretcher. Keep them on the line."

"Tell them where we are Nik," said Matt Bianco.

The 911 system was overwhelmed. Dispatchers asked professionally but tersely: "Are you in the building?" and "Do you have information about the shooting for the police?" If the answers were no, they were advised that the lines had to be kept clear and then disconnected.

When Nicole told the dispatcher that she was in a classroom in the high school, her call was passed along to a supervisor who took a professional but motherly approach.

"What's your name, hon?" the dispatcher began as Zarlapski closed the door behind him. The teacher's goal was to cross the hall to the elevator "lobby," a small cavity where students could wait for the elevator. A couple of tables, with swiveling chairs attached, were bolted to the walls on each side. Across from the elevator door was a four-foot high metal cabinet that contained a stretcher type device that could "walk" downstairs.

Four unnaturally long strides on tip-toe brought Zarlapski to the cabinet. He maneuvered the stretcher from its container.

Holding the folded purple and green contraption in his left hand, Zarlapski edged toward the intersection with the hallway. He caught his breath when he heard a door open off to his right.

Zarlapski put the stretcher on the floor gently and moved against the wall, still in the elevator alcove. Sucking in his breath, he inched his face around the corner of the wall.

Vince Stefanowicz was poking his head out of 523, looking down the hall. Their eyes met. Stefanowicz opened his mouth to say something, but Zarlapski waved him back into the room. Stefanowicz nodded and eased his door shut.

Zarlapski waited a few seconds and then picked up the stretcher and moved across the hall, not looking, either way, this time. He hurried back into his classroom.

Isaiah's infrequent, pained gasps sounded like they might be his last. But at least he was still breathing. For how much longer?

Nicole Bennington was still on the phone with Montgomery County Dispatch, and they wanted to talk to Zarlapski. Pennsville and the ambulance had not picked up.

"Hold on," he said to Nik.

Zarlapski laid the stretcher out on the floor and started to unlatch the hinges. Fully extended it was more like a rolling chair than a stretcher.

Kyle Yarborough crouched at Isaiah's head, and Steve was standing at the feet.

"Kelly, you support his neck and head," directed Kyle, waiting for everyone to get into position.

"We lift on three. Ready?"

They nodded.

"One, two, three."

Bennett and Bianco quickly strapped Isaiah in. His head lolled off to the right. He looked and sounded ghastly.

Bianco grabbed the head end of the stretcher and Bennett stood at the foot.

"Ready?" Steve said to Matt.

Zarlapski held up his left hand. "Hold it. Let me talk to 911 first," he said to Steve and Matt. Both grimaced with impatience.

"Nicole," he said gesturing for the phone.

"My name's Zarlapski," he told the dispatcher, who had been handed the call by the "motherly" dispatcher. "I'm the teacher in room 522."

"We need to verify the information we got from Nicole Bennington," was the reply.

"I don't have time for that right now. I've got a medical emergency here, and I've got to get a kid to a hospital NOW."

"Understood sir, your best bet though is to remain in your classroom."

Zarlapski felt a flash of anger.

"No, it's not. I need to talk to a policeman or paramedic on the scene," he hissed at the dispatcher.

"What is the nature of your medical emergency?"

Zarlapski let out a sigh through clenched teeth.

"I have a sixteen-year-old with severe breathing problems who needs his medication which we keep in the nurse's office."

Zarlapski looked around at all the students listening to him. "He is going to die soon unless we get him out of here."

"Stay on the line, sir. I'll call the command post."

Isaiah's breathing was coming in more rapid audible rasps, now the only sound in the room beside the incessant ticking of the flashing light.

"Anything, Dan?" Zarlapski said quietly to Dan Streeter, who was stationed to the left of the door.

Dan shook his head.

"Mr. Zarlapski?" came a voice from the phone.

"Here."

"Chief Greco will call you on your phone." The dispatcher read back Zarlapski's number from her caller ID. Zarlapski verified the number and poked END.

The phone buzzed a few seconds later.

"Mr. Zarlapski?"

"Yes"

"This is Chief Greco. County said you had a critically ill person with you."

"Correct. He's having trouble breathing, and he's turning blue. He has a lot of medical problems. His meds are in the nurse's office."

"Where are you, Mr. Zarlapski?"

"Room 522. North Wing. Top floor."

Zarlapski could hear the chaos of orders shouted, questions asked and answered, and the impatient growling of idling emergency vehicles. Zarlapski had met the chief a few times. Barry Greco had been in Special Forces and saw action sometime late in the Vietnam War. That perpetual half-grin on his face was probably saying "being a policeman in a small town is nothing compared to what I've seen."

"Here's the situation, Mr. Zarlapski. We have reports of several people shot on the floor below you. We are not sure where the shooter is. We have unconfirmed reports that the exit doors are chained shut. In short, there is nowhere to go."

That gave the teacher some pause. He looked at Bennett and Bianco.

"Mr. Zarlapski?"

"Well, give me a suggestion. This kid isn't going to make it much longer."

A couple of seconds of silence. "Give me a minute, I'll call you back."

The call ended before Zarlapski could reply.

While Zarlapski was on the phone trying to get help for his students and the chaos in the 500 wing was taking place, the Special Ed teachers were still on the third floor with some students.

Dave Manning, who had taken charge, had managed to finally get through to 911 while two of his colleagues were on their knees trying to defuse two separate student meltdowns.

The group had reached a consensus that they were going to try and flee, but first, they had to get their kids under control. A couple of teachers had wanted to shelter in place but were talked out of it.

"Think the state guy made it out?" asked Sherri McCrudden. "What was his name? Gerrits?"

"Yeah, Gerrits," Manning confirmed. "I don't know. I guess he did, or he would have come back."

"Or he's dead," McCrudden said.

Her observation proved to be prescient when the group of student and teachers finally got moving.

Manning, in the vanguard of the procession, saw Gerrits' body as soon as he turned the corner toward the stairs that would lead them to the front of the building. The corpse was on his back, in a pool of blood, across the exit doors. He had a death grip on his briefcase, which had two bullet holes in it.

Manning stepped back around the corner and ordered the group to retrace their steps and head for the back stairwell which would take them to the cafeteria level and then to the gym exit—if they could get that far.

6

Outside, more and more police were arriving at the scene and gathering at the temporary command post near the tennis courts, including off-duty officers from Pennsville and Green Hill. Greco was trying to keep up with developments in the building by listening to the two walkie-talkies on the roof of his car. Simultaneously, he was trying to brief the incoming officers and form teams to send into the building.

"Active shooter protocols," he reminded all the cops. "Get into the building and find the gunmen."

The chief went back to scanning the floor plans while he monitored calls.

Besides finding and neutralizing the shooters, Greco was prioritizing rescuing Isaiah Shue and getting to the injured teacher in a classroom near the cafeteria, and, of course, leading as many students to safety as possible.

But, first and foremost, they had to get to the bad guys. At least the fire behind the school had been doused by the fire company.

Greco's radio came to life. "We're approaching the T-intersection at the cafeteria," reported Pennsville PD's John Abrams over the radio.

Emergency vehicles of all types were queuing up outside the main entrance, dutifully being checked in by fire police. A few of the fire policemen had also set up checkpoints at the other two driveway entrances/exits to the school grounds and were trying to keep a perimeter around the entirety of the property to keep out parents, the curious, and the media.

Some borough maintenance men from Green Hill had arrived in a pick-up and were supplementing the fire police.

Green Hill police chief Greg Hawthorne walked up to Greco. "What do you want me to do?"

"Round up all the agencies coming in. Stage them up on the grass where all those ambulances are," Greco said just as Abram called in.

"We have some students here. Bringing them out," Abrams reported.

The students and teachers from the special ed wing of the building had made their way to the hallway leading past the caf and had run into Abrams and the policemen with him. The police reversed course and hustled the students past the gym and into the parking lot and Greco's command post.

"I got them," Greco called. "Is that all of them?"

"Yes," Abrams said over his shoulder as he hustled back into the building. "He's in charge," Abrams added pointing at teacher Dave Manning.

"Can you take all your people over there, please?" Greco said to Manning.

"How bad is it?" Manning asked Greco in a low voice.

"We're working on finding out," the chief responded. "Did everyone get out of your wing?"

"Yes. Except some guy from the state was here. He's dead."

Greco shook his head. "We need you to take care of your students and help us get them home safe."

"Got it. Everybody OK?" Manning called as he turned to face the contingent he had just led out of the building.

Some teachers nodded in reply.

"We're good," Dave Manning said. "Good luck."

State police lieutenant Frank Larabee maneuvered his car as close to Greco's as he could.

Greco gave an inward sigh. Larabee could be a royal pain in the ass, a smug superiority complex was a prominent feature of his dealing with local cops.

"The County team will be here in thirty," Larabee said. "You got people inside?"

Before Greco could reply, Team 2 called in.

"Team 2 to 27-1. Unable to gain entry so far," reported Keller. "Door might be chained. One more to check."

Greco brought Larabee up to date as calls continued to come in from the teams now trying to enter the school and County updates. Communication was getting difficult as radio traffic trampled on simultaneous calls.

John Abram's agitated voice crackled out of the radio: "Team 1 has an officer injured. We are coming back out."

Greco grabbed his radios, and he and Larabee ran toward the gym doors, signaling for other officers to join them.

Abrams was half-carrying a bloodied, stumbling cop through the doors.

"What happened?" asked Greco running up to the men.

"Bomb, in the dropped ceiling in the hallway," Abrams related. "Knocked us down. Whitey here was closer. Another one went off farther up the hall a little after the first one."

Larabee made eye contact with Greco.

"IED's," Larabee said.

Greco used his radio to put out a warning to the men trying to gain entry into the building.

"Be advised the building may be booby-trapped. Careful of ceilings."

Greco made sure every team checked in to acknowledge receipt of the message. As they did, he asked each group about its progress. Multiple teams were unable to open the solid metal exterior doors, even with pry bars, because they seemed secured from the inside.

"Keep trying doors for now. He can't have chained all of them," Greco told the teams.

Larabee sidled up beside Greco.

"You want us to take over command, Greco?" Larabee said, hands on hips.

"I got it," the Chief said, failing to keep the irritation out of his voice. "You have a bomb squad coming?"

"Should be if we're Code Red. You know technically the State Police can…"

"When they get here, check all the cars in the parking lots," Greco ordered.

"Start forming your people into contact teams as they get here," Greco told him. "We got to get in there."

Larabee eyed Greco for a couple of seconds. "Okay," Larabee said and started for the three clustered state cruisers twenty yards away.

Out of the corner of his eye, Greco saw four buses caravanning down Montgomery Avenue toward the high school.

Greco waved to get the attention of a fire policeman, signaling that the buses should be directed to the parking lot across the street from the tennis courts where the escaped gym class and special education teachers and students were congregating.

"Tell them to park and just shelter the kids for now," Greco yelled.

Greco walked over to the paramedic treating Whitey Fallon for his injuries from the booby-trap.

"Lots of stitches coming, maybe a concussion. We're going to transport to Carbon Valley," the paramedic said in response to Greco's query.

"Hang in buddy," Greco said bending down to pat Fallon on the shoulder as he was being placed on a stretcher and loaded into Medic 43.

The chief turned and sprinted back to the temporary command post: his car and a long table.

7

In the hallway on the second floor of the 500 wing, where Mr. Baltz' class had been ambushed, a bloodied Katie McPhee raised her head to peer over the body of a fallen classmate who was crosswise on his stomach in the hall, three distinct holes in his back leaking blood, his left arm grotesquely bent behind his body. Katie knew the boy but could not recall his name.

Katie waited for another half-minute and then rose to her knees facing the North Parking Lot. She saw two fallen, entangled bodies farther up the hall. Her teacher, Mr. Baltz, was sprawled face down, motionless against the lockers. Katie gasped and covered her mouth with both hands as she rose to her feet. She backed away from the horror in front of her and tripped over another body behind her. Eyes still open, the face was frozen in disbelief.

Katie stifled a sob and got to her feet again. She did not want to look behind. She started walking toward the door that led to the parking lot. Katie averted her eyes from Baltz' corpse but had to look down to avoid tripping over the bodies of the entangled couple in the middle of the floor. She recognized and knew both. She could not think of their names, either.

Katie got to the door and saw the chains but kept pushing on the doors. She was baffled as to why they would not budge even an inch. She put her shoulder to the doors, but they would not open.

Katie noticed blood streaked on the bottom of her left arm. Her yellow spring blouse with a floral print was stained with blood as were her new jeans. She felt at the bloodstains. Am I shot? Katie felt no pain.

She stumbled through the stairwell doors to her right and went down a flight of stairs before sitting on the bottom step to fight off a wave of nausea. She tasted the bitterness at the back of her mouth.

Katie decided to go upstairs and see her tennis coach in 521. He would help. Katie started up the steps when she heard a door open and muffled voices above her. She hesitated and then went back to sit on the same step.

She didn't know what else to do.

8

Zarlapski surveyed his students in 522. Isaiah was a shade of blue that Zarlapski had only read about in CPR manuals. He was drooling and incontinent.

Steve Bennett and Matt Bianco gave inquiring, impatient looks to Mr. Zarlapski who held up one finger.

Dan Streeter was still poised at the door, holding the Clorox bottle at his hip.

Regina Himmelwright was still rocking on the floor.

Nikki Bennington had assumed a position behind Dan staring off into space.

Meredith Clancy had crawled her way to the "lav" in the corner of the room and vomited into the wastebasket.

Kyle Yarborough was crouched trying to console Cassie who was silently crying, clutching her nail file like a dagger.

Lauren Dougherty was seated, staring at the cell phone that had gone dead before anyone at Vista Ambulance had answered.

John Pagliano, squatting with his back against the door, was still on the line with his father who was in Boston. No one talked.

Kelly Keiter was kneeling a few feet from Isaiah praying silently.

Carey Ackerman was sitting apart, texting or playing a game; he had Beats headphones on.

Rachael Megay was rerunning hot water, her vibrating cell phone inching along the counter. She was still disturbed by something Carey had said to her a few minutes ago: "Ahmed sends his regards. Hopes to see you soon."

Ahmed was William Holder. Rachael had been befriended by Holder's group, a clique that included Carey Ackerman, shortly after moving to the district two summers ago and taking a job at a local restaurant. Will had trained her and been the complete gentleman the whole time. Eventually, they began dating, even though Will was a couple of years older. For a few weeks, things had gone OK until Holder wanted to take the physical relationship farther and would not take no for an answer. She made a harrowing escape from a deserted park and told her mother about the incident and avoided Holder and his entourage for the rest of the summer.

Rachael, in retrospect, shook her head at the willful blindness she had suffered. "Was I that desperate for acceptance?" she asked herself. They were cruel people. Rachael realized that Holder's group of friends was more like a cult. Holder had some mesmerizing effect on them that led to unquestioned loyalty, almost like a Charles Manson.

From a couple of conversations Rachael had overheard, Holder had a fascination with white nationalist philosophies and terrorism techniques and, at times, made Ackerman and Russo call him "Ahmed," like he was a jihadist or something.

There were a few girls who hung out with the group, too. Donna Slowick practically worshipped Holder and was miffed at his attraction to Rachael, who tried to befriend Slowick and defuse the hatred, but to no avail.

When school began, members of the cult, especially Carey Ackerman, Anthony Russo, and Donna Slowick, spread rumors about Rachael's "skankiness." It took Rachael over a year to shed the stereotype. William Holder, meanwhile, got himself thrown out of Vista by shoving Miss Spears into a locker and threatening to kill her. He was placed in an alternative school for troubled teens somewhere upstate, and, after he turned eighteen, he managed to earn a six-month sentence for robbery. From what Rachael gathered around town and in school, that only increased the awe Holder's cult had for their leader.

And now Rachael had heard the rumors that he was back in town.

"Give us a hand here, will you, Rachael," Matt Bianco was saying to her, breaking into her thoughts.

Bianco grabbed the head end of the stretcher and Bennett stood at the foot as Rachael moved obstacles out of the way.

"Ready?" Steve said to Matt.

"Wait a minute. Wait a minute. What's the plan here?" Zarlapski asked as his mind raced. He had only two bad choices.

Steve Bennett must have been reading his mind.

"Look, Mr. Z. My uncle was a Navy SEAL. He'll kick my ass if I don't try to do something."

"Maybe so. At least you'd be alive to get your ass kicked. We have no idea what you might be walking into."

He turned to his classmates. "Mr. Z doesn't want us to go, but we are disobeying. If anything happens to us, it's not his fault."

"Great," the teacher said. "That's not what I meant."

"We're going to take him down the steps and out to the parking lot," Steve said, turning back to Zarlapski.

"Yeah? Just ignoring the fact that shots were fired below us a few minutes ago? What are you going to do if you run into the shooter?"

"We won't," said Matt.

Zarlapski rolled his eyes.

Isaiah was vomiting on the stretcher. Kyle steadied him and kept him on his side.

Zarlapski, and everyone else, guessed that Isaiah might have only minutes, seconds, to live.

"We'll be careful. If it doesn't feel right, we'll come back up," Steve assured his teacher.

Zarlapski raised his hands in tacit approval.

The barricade was moved aside by Rachael and Lauren.

Zarlapski wrote his phone number on an index card and gave it to Bianco. "I'll be back in a minute," the teacher said to the rest of the class. He preceded the stretcher bearers into the hall, waved them forward, and led them to the right.

At the doors to the steps, Zarlapski peered carefully through the small window. The lights were out in the windowless stairwell.

He opened the door slowly, walked a couple of steps, and looked over the landing. Two flights down, he could barely make out the door that led to the parking lot.

He waved behind him for Bianco and Bennett to bring the stretcher.

Still, on his side, Isaiah was a small, blue, motionless lump.

"Don't be martyrs," Zarlapski said.

Bennett led the way as they started down the steps.

Zarlapski watched them make the first turn and descend into the darker unknown. He heard hurried footsteps in the hall behind him. The teacher turned and slipped behind the open door in case he needed protection.

"Mr. Z, Mr. Z." He stepped around the door and into the hall.

"Hurry. It's Regina," Rachael exclaimed in a half-whisper.

He heard a sound from the stairwell below, but Rachael was tugging him forward by the sleeve. They jogged the fifty feet to the door of 522 and slipped inside.

Regina was seated on the floor shaking uncontrollably, her hands to her head pressing against her temples.

Zarlapski knelt in front of her and took her pulse at the neck as best he could. Regina's heart was racing, somewhere close to two hundred.

"Rachael, bring that red folder over. Quickly," Zarlapski said, pointing to the emergency folder.

Rachael handed it over and Zarlapski located Regina's 504 Plan for her diabetes.

"If blood sugar is below 80, Regina should report to the nurse."

"If she needs a snack or drink, Regina should report to the nurse."

"In the event of an emergency evacuation or shelter-in-place situation, the nurse will oversee all diabetic care."

Great, great, and great, thought Zarlapski.

He searched in the folder again for the sheet with protocols for hypoglycemia.

"Regina, do you have any sweets with you?"

No response. She was in her own world. Zarlapski noticed a sheen of sweat on Regina's face. According to the chart in his hand, Regina was heading for insulin shock.

"Look in her bag, Rachael. Anything to eat there?"

Rachael immediately turned the bag over and emptied out the contents. Nothing helpful. No juice or milk or soft candy or soda.

"John," said Zarlapski, "Check through the cabinets. See if there is a bag of candy or a juice box in there somewhere."

Zarlapski ignored the buzzing in his pocket.

John jumped up and found a juice box in the first door opened.

"Toss it."

Zarlapski caught the box and quickly inserted the straw. Now he held it to Regina's lips. She did not respond.

Rachael sat beside her and put her mouth next to Regina's ear. "Regina," she shouted urgently. "Regina." Rachael shook Regina's shoulder violently.

That snapped Regina out of her stupor. She looked surprised to see Zarlapski right on top of her holding the juice in front of her face.

"Drink it, Regina," Zarlapski commanded.

Regina drew the hand holding the carton to her face and began to drink the juice.

"Good girl. Finish it up," Zarlapski said.

When the box was empty, he asked Regina how she felt.

She did not answer.

Rachael got right next to Regina's ear.

"How do you feel?" she said as loudly as she dared.

"Better," Regina said without looking up. She still did not look well.

"Anymore in there in case we need them, John?"

John held up three fingers.

Pagliano got back on his phone and explained what had just happened to his father.

Zarlapski heard him finish by saying, "I'm running out of charge Dad, I call back when I can. Love you."

The teacher gave him a thumbs up and fished his phone out of his pocket. It was his wife's name on the "Missed Call" notification. He texted her: "OK...will call later." He hoped.

Z took stock of the room. Something was amiss.

"Carey took off," Nicole informed him, noting his puzzled look.

Zarlapski raised both hands quizzically.

She shrugged in reply.

"Anybody know where he went? Is he coming back?"

"Didn't say," sneered John. "Not that I care. As soon as you went out, he got up, and watched you go down the hall and then took off that way." John was pointing to the left of the door.

"Did you try and stop him?"

"I said, where you going, and he flipped me off."

"Great."

Zarlapski considered what to do about Carey's *escape*, but there was nothing really to do. The teacher was not sorry that he no longer had to deal with Carey today. Whatever, Zarlapski concluded as he grabbed a can of room deodorizer from his desk drawer and went into the latrine spraying a path through the acrid stench and trying to hold his breath. He grabbed the white trash bag lining the can and knotted it up and saturated the can with more deodorizer. Then he took the bag into the far corner of 521 which was behind the teacher desk.

"Sorry, Mr. Laird." Laird always kept a bag of ground coffee in a desk drawer. Zarlapski found a fresh, unopened bag. He sprinkled some of the coffee on the white trash bag and left the open coffee bag on Laird's desk before going back to 522.

The fighting force was still at the ready. Dan was to the left of the door, cocking the spray bottle in his right hand. Kyle was standing just behind John, his belt wrapped around his fist.

Zarlapski's phone buzzed with an incoming call from Greco. He stepped to the corner of the room at the latrine.

"Zarlapski here," he said into his phone.

"Sorry. We had a situation." Greco said. "Can you sit tight? We're having problems getting into the building, but your room is a top priority," Greco assured him.

Zarlapski brought Greco up to date on all that had gone on since he first talked to county dispatch: Bianco and Bennett taking Isaiah on a stretcher, Carey's desertion, Regina's seizure.

"We need to get her out of here soon, too," Zarlapski emphasized.

"Hang on Zarlapski. I have to get on the radio." By his tone, Zarlapski could tell that Greco disapproved of his decision.

Greco got back on the phone after updating his officers with Zarlapski's news.

"Zarlapski."

"I'm here."

"Can you contact these boys?"

"I have their numbers, but we left it as they would call me."

"I need to know where they are," Greco said.

"Do you think it's a good idea to try and call or text them? It might tip off a hiding place or something. I'm sorry, Chief. I know I probably should have kept them in the room, but they wanted to try. I know that's not an excuse, but the Shue kid is either going to get help, or he's going to die. Soon."

"You did what you thought you had to do. Let's make sure it turns out OK. Try a text first. Find out where they are. OK?"

"OK."

"What about the other kid?"

"No idea where he went. I don't have his number."

"All right. If any of the kids call, and they're in the building still, tell them to find a safe place and stay put. We've run into some booby-traps."

"Booby-traps?" The class was listening to Zarlapski's side of the conversation, and there were gasps when he repeated Greco's words.

"Yeah, stuff in the ceiling. Call me when you hear from those kids. I have to go. Good luck." Greco ended the call.

Zarlapski shook his head as he slowly moved the phone from his ear.

"What's wrong?" asked Nicole, alarm evident in her voice.

"Nothing except we have a shooter in the building," Zarlapski lamely joked while attempting to put on his I'm-in-control-teacher-face.

"You did the right thing, Mr. Z," Nicole told him. "Isaiah wouldn't have lasted two more minutes. My mom showed me all the crap he has. She said she was a nervous wreck when he had gym."

"Thanks, Nicole. Let's hope for the best. Have you heard from your mom?"

Zarlapski regretted the question as soon as he asked it. Nicole shook her head, tears welling.

"Don't jump to conclusions. We have to ride this out. Everybody is going to be fine."

Zarlapski sarcastically congratulated himself for cornering the market on lame platitudes.

"I think you did the right thing, too," said Rachael. "What booby-traps?"

"Oh, the police are concerned about the possibility. They're just trying to cover their bases," Zarlapski lied.

He decided that a text needed to be sent to Bianco and Bennett.

"Hallways booby-trapped. Careful. Where are you?" he tapped out on his phone.

Zarlapski gave Nicole a reassuring squeeze on her shoulder and walked over to the door where John Pagliano was still standing guard.

"Anything?"

Pagliano shook his head.

Mike Zarlapski had been at Vista for twenty-four years and at age fifty-five, and every day was still a joy. He had a reputation as one of the best teachers in the school, not only because of his methods in class, but also because he seemed to be at every extra-curricular event. He was also a successful varsity baseball coach, as league and district championship banners in the gym testified.

As a resident of the school community, he and his wife had the credibility of having put three kids through district schools. The youngest, Stephen, had graduated just three years ago and was working his way through college.

Some students trusted Zarlapski enough to confide in him about issues outside of the intricacies of taking an AP test or the nuances of *The Scarlet Letter*.

Cassie came across as an outgoing, social, airhead who was reaching a little too far by taking an AP class. From numerous tutoring sessions at lunch and after school, Zarlapski knew her as a desperate perfectionist about her writing, although she didn't process what she heard in class quickly. Cassie would revise a paper a dozen times if that's what it took to get an A. Zarlapski also knew that her extrovert qualities hid the pain of having a mother slowly losing her battle with breast cancer. Zarlapski figured that she kept herself as busy as possible to try and keep the future at bay.

Zarlapski squatted in front of Cassie, who was still sitting on the floor with Lauren Dougherty, shoulders touching, nail files ready.

The two girls had been friends since middle school when they met on the cheering squad. Lauren was a fierce defender of cheering as a sport, not just an activity. Her last persuasive paper was on the topic, and God help the person who expressed the opinion that cheering was a trivial activity.

Lauren, 5'8" with long flowing chestnut hair when she let it down, lifted weights three times a week and ran track in the spring

She was also Cassie's chief defender in class. "Good point, Cassie," Lauren might exclaim when the eye-rolling started after one of Cassie's "dumb" questions. Then she would go on to explain what Cassie meant to say.

"Thanks for all your help, Kelly," Zarlapski said as he took a seat on the floor beside Kelly Keiter. "Feeling OK?"

She shook her head grimly. "I'm trying to pray for Mr. Czarnecki, but I can't remember any prayers." A tear trickled down her right cheek.

"Well, that can come later. Try to stay in the here-and-now. Heck, we don't even know if anything we're hearing is true."

Kelly nodded, her eyes still watery.

"Doing OK, Regina?" Zarlapski asked, leaning in front of Kelly. Regina grimaced without looking up.

"She'll be fine," Kelly said.

While he was getting to his feet, Zarlapski felt his phone buzz in his pocket. Susan Snider was calling.

As usual, Snider skipped the preliminaries.

"If you're near kids, go to a corner or something."

9

Frustration mounted for Pennsville officer Ray Keller and Green Hill officer Jason Laessig after unsuccessfully trying three outer doors.

"This place is like a prison minus the razor wire and guard towers," Keller said.

The accessible windows were mere slits in the wall. The solid steel doors they had tried to pry open with a crowbar were tightly bound from the inside.

"Security," Laessig said with unintended irony as they tried the black doors that led into the arts wing at the front of the building. Behind the doors was the hallway that divided the music rooms from the back of the stage in the auditorium.

Laessig took the pry bar from Keller and worked it into the opening between the doors.

He was surprised when the doors started to give with a painful screech. He repositioned the bar and leaned all of his one hundred and eighty-three pounds into it until the latches at the top and bottom broke free, and the door swung open.

Both men flattened themselves against the wall, guns drawn. Why this door was able to be pried open, and the other was not was a question worth considering.

Keller contacted Greco to explain what was happening.

"Careful that you're not being funneled into an ambush," Greco advised.

The Pennsville chief redirected a couple of his teams to support Keller and Laessig and had Frank Larabee take some of his state police troopers to the entry point.

Larabee gave a piercing whistle to get the attention of four officers who had just pulled up in the county's AWV, a lightly armored Advanced Weapon Vehicle, that carried M4 semi-automatic rifles, shotguns, and stun grenades among other items. They were putting on Kevlar vests.

"Get over here," Larabee shouted, waving his arm at them.

On his tablet, Greco called up a map. He pointed to the door breached by Laessig and Keller, and then to the rooms on each side of the six-foot-wide hallway.

"We're in a hurry to get to these two areas," Greco said as he pointed out the 500 wing and room 522 to Larabee. "Shots were fired on the floor below about fifteen minutes ago."

"Active shooter protocols, shooters and then injured," Greco told them before going back to the map of the arts wing. The floor plan showed six rooms and an interior hallway that would have to be checked on the left; on the right, backstage, the auditorium proper, and two bathrooms. Greco sketched out a quick game plan on a yellow legal pad.

"The only descriptions of the shooters we have are males in dark clothing, long gowns or coats, may have headdresses on. Questions?"

"As in terrorists?" asked one of the troopers.

"What I told you is what was reported to County," Greco responded.

"Let's go," Larabee ordered, as snow flurries fell from scudding dark clouds.

The men sprinted single-file to the other end of the building, joined up with the officers already there.

The officers evenly divided the men and split up as Greco had advised. They would execute a room-by-room search, including the auditorium, classrooms, bathrooms, closets, offices and meet at the T-intersection on the other side of the wing.

The men nodded at each other, handguns at the ready, .40 caliber Glocks for the troopers, .40 caliber Smith and Wesson for the local officers.

Trooper Matt Weiss positioned his men as they moved into the backstage area of the five hundred seat auditorium. Battery-powered emergency lights gave minimum illumination. The black backdrop curtain was fully extended across the stage. Weiss futilely flipped the six light switches on the inside wall.

Another trooper tried the dressing room door while another peeked around the side of the black curtain, holding his breath and relying more on his ears than eyes to determine that the stage was empty. The main curtain was open and as far as he could see in the dim glow of two emergency lights over the back exits; the seating area was also empty.

At the other end of the stage was a half wall that ran about ten feet toward the audience and separated the stage from a storage closet and small bathroom.

Both men sidled along the wall until they got to the edge of the stage. Weiss listened for a few seconds before peeking around the corner. He decided to risk his flashlight and shined it around the wall toward the bathroom.

Weiss noticed red droplets on the wooden floor making a dotted line toward the bathroom. Weiss pointed to the blood and hooked his thumb toward the bathroom and pointed to himself.

Weiss moved closer to the bathroom door, flattened himself to the wall and listened. He leaned and pushed the bathroom door open with his left hand which held his flashlight, gun in his right. The solid wooden door moved noiselessly inward to about halfway open, but then it hit an obstacle and would not go farther. Weiss shined his light into the room and then onto the floor where he saw two legs, toes down, the torso behind the door.

Weiss wedged himself through the door and shined his light around the room.

Blood and bloody paper towels coagulated in the white sink and there was a red streak down the front of the porcelain. An adult male lay on his stomach in a pool of blood on the floor.

The trooper checked vainly for a pulse and then patted down the body. He pulled a thin wallet out of the right rear pocket. Weiss recognized the name on the license. Charles Ekelmeyer had been the choir director for twenty years, ran all sorts of musical groups in the district and beyond, and did some singing of his own in a regional choir. He was a revered figure in the Valley's music community.

Weiss went back out to the hall where the other team was waiting. He called in a report to Greco and then set his team as they prepared to search the rest of the stage, and the various little rooms and storage areas around it, the auditorium proper, and the "crow's nest" overlooking the seats, a nice perch for a sniper.

Green Hill's Jason Laessig was left to maintain security in the area just searched.

The policemen began to move up their aisles shining lights into each row of soft blue seats while Weiss swept the entire auditorium with his eyes and gun.

One team had just passed the halfway point of the aisles when a flash illuminated the auditorium, and a loud bang sent everyone diving to the floor.

Several seats near an aisle in the row were shredded. The closest officer, Pennsville's Ray Keller, was thrown halfway into the opposite row by the blast and now lay draped across a seat.

For a second many of the police thought they were bleeding but quickly realized that the sprinklers had come on and were soaking their position. Weiss picked up his handgun and holstered it and promptly took the M4 off his shoulder, sweeping the room for a threat.

Keller appeared to be trying to steady himself and was staggering aimlessly up the aisle before falling.

Out of the corner of his eye, Weiss detected movement on his left. He swung his gun around quickly. It was Laessig on the stage.

Dumb ass, Weiss thought.

Laessig stopped on a dime when he saw the rifle pointed at him.

"Get back outside," Weiss hissed at him. "We're pulling back."

"How is he?" someone yelled.

"Alive."

"See if he can move."

Weiss went to help Keller to his feet.

"Team 3 to 27-1," Weiss called into his radio. "We have an injured officer. Some kind of explosion. We will return to your position. Leaving now. Auditorium is not secure."

10

Working as a team, Steve Bennett and Matt Bianco maneuvered the stretcher down the stairs to the first landing below.

The two had been best buddies since kindergarten, playing together, hunting together, hanging out together, attending camps together. Bennett batted fourth and Bianco fifth on the baseball team, Bennett was a catcher, Bianco a pitcher/first baseman. In football, they played side-by-side as linebackers, and they were both forwards on the basketball team. They were closer than twins.

On the second floor, they put the stretcher down cautiously. Isaiah's breathing was shallow and irregular.

Movement on the stairs arrested Bianco's attention. He tapped Bennett on the shoulder. A girl was sitting on the bottom step, against the wall of the intermediate landing heading to The Dungeon. Bennett made a "Now what?" motion with his hands.

Bianco signaled that they should each take a side, and they started creeping down the stairs. Within a couple of steps of the girl, they heard snatches of a prayer being said. They noted the blood on her blouse.

Bennett stopped on the step immediately behind the girl, poised to grab her if necessary. Bianco came around in front of her. The girl gasped and turned to the wall, head to her knees.

"You OK?" Bianco asked.

The girl shook her head.

"We can't stay here. We're trying to get to the nurse."

"What's your name?" Bennett asked.

"Katie."

"All right, Katie, we have to get moving. Where were you before?"

"Social studies."

"Second floor?"

Katie nodded.

"Can we get out that way?" Bianco asked.

Katie teared up as she shook her head.

"There are dead bodies in the hallway," she said in a monotone.

"Can we get to the parking lot?"

Katie shook her head again.

"Katie, come with us," Steve Bennett said as he lifted her by the arm.

Bennett peeked through the small window in the door to the second floor. He could see only five or six feet down the hall. To the right, he saw that the door leading to the parking lot was secured tightly with a thick chain and heavy-duty padlocks.

"No go," he said over his shoulder to Bianco. "Chained."

"Left?" Bianco whispered.

"Down."

The next flight of stairs took them into The Dungeon, the bottom floor of the north wing. Only three classrooms were used in The Dungeon; two sat unfinished.

At the bottom of the steps, they lowered the stretcher to the floor. Steve looked through the hall door's glass and then slowly turned the handle and stuck his head into the corridor far enough to inspect the hall. It was empty.

Bennett turned to Bianco and motioned toward the left.

"No choice, bro," he whispered.

Bianco held the door open with his foot as they maneuvered the stretcher into the hall. Katie helped open it wider and then took her place beside the stretcher as they walked. The first classroom, 501, was noiseless. However, Bianco could hear muffled sounds from 502. Room 503 was dark and quiet. The glass strip in the door was uncovered, but no one was in sight.

In the center of the hallway, on the group's right, was the elevator alcove, same as the other floors in the wing. But there were also doors in the wall, a singleton next to the elevator and a double door directly across from the elevator.

At the far end of the hall was a double door leading outside to a driveway that went past the gym and loading dock to connect with the South Parking Lot.

At the end of the hall, to the left, stairs were leading back to the first and second floor. On the next level, there was also a hallway that led into the Arts and Vocational Center, and further down that hallway was the auditorium on the west side of the building.

As they neared the exit doors, Bennett could see they were also chained tight.

"Now what?" asked Bianco.

"Is he breathing?" Bennett asked in alarm, looking down at Isaiah who was ashen and still.

"I don't think so," Katie said.

"Back," said Bianco and they retraced their steps to 503. Bianco was about to try the knob when he came eye to eye with Ms. Snider surreptitiously peeking into the hall. Snider's students were in 502 where Snider had been helping the substitute English teacher, Barbara Knaul. Snider had gone back to 503 to retrieve her laptop.

"Open up, Ms. Snider," Bianco said. "We have a sick person."

Snider had no qualms about letting Bianco and Bennett into the room; she knew both of them well. Not only was Snider a respected science teacher, but she was also the athletic trainer. She had been on the sidelines for every game the two boys had participated in during high school. The veteran trainer had enjoyed every minute of watching two of Vista's best athletes.

Snider had guided Bennett through a knee rehab after a football injury two years ago. Not only had Bennett been able to avoid surgery, but he was also one hundred percent by the time baseball season rolled around. Steve Bennett had thanked the trainer by cutting Snider's grass for free all summer.

Snider held the door open for the stretcher bearers and Katie to enter. "Holy crap," she said when she got a look at Isaiah.

"Get him on the floor back there." The teacher knew Isaiah's backstory. She had the same folder as Zarlapski and Bennington.

Snider immediately began an assessment.

"He's breathing. Barely. Get my coat out of the closet, Matt."

Snider did a pulse check at the carotid artery and noted that Isaiah's Shue's heartbeat was tachycardic.

Snider put her trainer's jacket over the unconscious Isaiah and gently rolled him onto his side in case he vomited again. He was as stable as he was going to get.

"Trying to get outside with him?" Snider asked.

Bennett gave a quick recap of what was going on upstairs, their encounter with Katie, their journey down to The Dungeon. Only about five minutes had gone by since they had left 522.

"How you doing, Katie?" Snider asked. "Are you hurt anywhere? Is that your blood?"

Katie shook her head slowly.

"Any ideas?" Bennett asked.

"I know there are medicines for Isaiah in the nurse's office. If you can get up there, maybe you can get them."

"Yeah, but how?"

"How about those doors across the hall? The one on the right is a huge storage area. Maybe there is a way out at the other end," Snider said.

"Key?"

Snider shook her head. She went through a couple of desk drawers and came out with a heavy-duty letter opener and a long screwdriver.

"Never know what you'll find in here," she said, as she moved toward the door.

"Stay with him," Snider said to Katie. "Be right back."

Snider held the door open and signaled for the boys to move across the hall. Bennett tried the doorknob. Miraculously it turned, and the door opened. Was that good or bad? Bennett signaled Bianco to wait.

Steve sank to his haunches and opened the door wider so he could duckwalk. A blinking light on the opposite wall kept a silent vigil. The rest of the room was weakly lit by a few battery-powered emergency lights located around the perimeter of the room. The only sound was of dripping water at the far end of the darkness. Steve found two light switches and flipped them up. Nothing. A large cardboard box was on his right, and he rolled behind it to present a moving target just in case. Holding his breath, he listened hard for a couple of seconds. Nothing.

Bennett opened the door again and signaled Bianco to come on.

"What are you going to do?" Snider whispered.

"See if we can find a way out up there," Bennett said pointing his chin at the far end.

"OK. Careful." Snider said as she gently closed the door to the storage area and cautiously headed back to 503.

"Any change?" she asked Katie in a whisper.

"I think he's going to die," Katie said matter-of-factly.

Kneeling beside the sickly Isaiah, Snider felt the erratic pulse at his neck. She was helplessly stuck here with a kid who needed an ER staff. The unglued Ms. Knaul in the classroom next door was going to have to survive without her for the moment.

Isaiah's gasps were less forceful, now. His eyes fluttered open briefly as Snider stroked his hair and held his hand.

Across the hall, Bianco's first thought when he surveyed the storage room was "airplane hangar." The area spanned the entire width and length of the 500 wing and the industrial arts area. The section near the doors was shelved and held all of the school's athletic equipment. The remainder of the room seemed to contain the ancient remains of Vista View's prior civilizations.

Bennett signaled Bianco to take the other side of the room, and they both started walking toward the far end. Aisles were artificially formed through miles of extra desks, boxes of ceiling tiles, dusty display cases, upended broken tables, paint cans, an old bingo call board, artificial Christmas trees, porcelain toilets and sinks. Deeper into the bowels of the room were props from drama club productions: palm trees from "South Pacific," champagne glasses from "The Importance of Being Earnest," rows of footwear including Dorothy's ruby slippers. Against the back wall, a formally dressed silhouetted cardboard couple danced the years away.

Bennett noted a door and an elevator in the rear wall. The door opened into some control room; an instrument panel glowed with red lights.

Next to the elevator, a key dangled from the access panel to the right of the door. Bianco turned it, but nothing happened.

"Hand me that screwdriver," Matt said. From his back pocket, Bennett pulled the tool Snider had given him. "Does the door open from the right or left?" Matt asked.

"Our right."

Bianco pried open the door a couple of inches. The two boys each grabbed and strained to pull, opening the door enough to squeeze into the shaft.

"Where are we here?" Bianco asked.

"I'm guessing this is the elevator that comes out right by the nurse's office," Bennett replied. "This door must open into the 100's," he added, pointing at doors across from their position.

A muffled boom seemed to flow down the elevator shaft.

"What was that?" Bennett asked.

Bianco shrugged.

"Let's get moving," Bennett said.

The floor in the elevator shaft dropped off a couple of feet. Bianco shined his flashlight app toward the top of the shaft.

"Is that the elevator up there?" Bennett said.

"I guess."

Below the elevator car, the boys could make out the doors that opened next to the health suite.

"I can climb up there," Bennett said.

"And do what?"

"Pry open the door, what do you think?"

"Why don't we go through these doors?" Bianco said, pointing straight ahead.

"Because the nurse's office is up there. It'll be easier just to sneak in, grab the meds, and get back."

"Didn't you hear the shooting over the PA which is in, you know, the office? And what if the elevator starts moving?"

"It won't. The power must be out. Remember, never use an elevator in an emergency," Bennett remarked grimly.

"What if…"

"What if we don't try anything and Isaiah dies?"

Bianco held his friend's eyes for a second.

"I saw a ladder back there," Bianco said.

Matt returned in a few seconds with a step ladder, but when they put it up inside the elevator shaft, it was a few feet short of the doors that open into the office area.

"Shine your light up there," Bennett commanded. "See those bars going out to the side. I can get a toehold and use the cables to climb to that ledge in front of the doors."

Bennett swiftly got to the top of the ladder. His hand slipped off the cable at first grab, and he tottered on the top step before grasping a less greasy spot to steady himself. Gingerly he tested the metal piece that supported the vertical bars that ran the height of the shaft to stabilize the elevator. The piece was about an inch off the wall and Bennett would have to bring his knee up about chest high to reach it.

As he shifted his weight-bearing to his arms and the cable, both boys heard a loud creak from above.

"Go, go." Matt urged Steve from below.

But the elevator didn't move, despite the ominous sound.

Bennett used the cable and the toehold to hoist himself up to the ledge under the exterior door. His chest was at floor level. Steve put the screwdriver on the ledge, which protruded only a couple of inches into the shaft, and repositioned as best he could so that he could get some leverage to pry the door.

Bennett pushed as hard as circumstances allowed and felt some give as the door opened a few inches. He boosted himself all the way up, stuck his right arm through the opening, and braced himself until he got his feet safely under him. Bennett put his body weight against the door, and it slid away from him enough until he could get his body through.

Steve emitted a loud gasp before he could stifle himself.

Two feet away was the school nurse curled into a fetal position, her open, terror-stricken eyes staring right at Steve, a small puddle of blood drying at the edges under her.

Bennett fought off his shock and darted past a blood splatter on the wall and into the darkened nurse's office to his right, a couple of steps away. He listened for a few seconds; it was weirdly quiet except for the ticking of the emergency light. Bennett stuck his head out of the doorway and surveyed the area.

Straight ahead was a hallway that bisected classrooms on either side. The T-intersection fifty yards down the hall led to the library on the right; the left went to the 300 wing or led to the stairway that brought students to the caf, 100 wing, and TV studio.

A body lay crumpled at the intersection outside room 213 where another hallway went off to the right to the science labs. Bennett observed the inert form for a few seconds hoping to see movement, but there was none. He couldn't tell whether it was an adult or student.

On Bennett's right was the hallway that ran between the guidance suite and the offices of the principal and assistant principals. Several of the floor-to-ceiling panes of glass were shattered or were missing huge chunks. Most of the glass had fallen into the offices as if the damage had been done from the hallway.

Bennett took a quick look around at the shelves in the nurse's office but did not see any medicines. In a room off the office, he saw a refrigerator labeled "Medications" and opened the door. One of the large freezer bags said ISAIAH SHUE in large red letters. Steve grabbed the bag and returned to the elevator. From a squat, he called for Bianco.

He showed the bag over the shaft. "Matt. Got it. Ready?"

When he saw Bianco put his hands up, he dropped the bag.

"Get it to Snider," Bennett told his partner.

"You coming?"

"I'm gonna look around."

"Seriously?"

"Go."

Bianco held Bennett's eyes for a moment, shrugged, and took off through the storage area. He sprinted to Snider's classroom and tapped lightly on the glass, glancing alternately over his shoulders until he felt the knob turn in his hand.

"Got it," he said to Snider holding the freezer bag aloft.

Over Snider's shoulder, Bianco saw Isaiah's inert form on the floor, his shirt open, chest still, eyes closed.

Katie McPhee was sitting in the opposite corner. Her face turned toward the wall.

Snider put her phone down, took the bag and put both on her desk. She braced Bianco at the shoulders.

"He stopped breathing almost as soon as you guys left. I've been giving him CPR and tried calling 911, but no answer."

Bianco was staring at the body as Snider removed her hands from the junior's arms.

"Sorry, nothing else we could have done," Snider said firmly before giving Bianco time to process the news.

"Where is Steve?" she said after a moment.

"Upstairs. He wanted to look around," Bianco said as he finally took his eyes off the jacket draped stretcher.

"Not a good idea, Matt."

"I'm going back up there."

"That's not a good idea, either."

Matt shrugged.

"You guys can't be wandering around the building. Suppose the cops mistake you two for shooters?"

Matt shrugged again.

"Call him. See where he is. Don't tell him about Isaiah. Tell him we need help back here. Which we do."

Bianco thought for a moment and reluctantly took out his phone. He noticed a text from Zarlapski: "Police say halls booby-trapped. NO CHANCES."

He went to his favorites and tapped Steve's name.

11

Sue Snider's name popped up on Zarlapski's phone.

"Go ahead," Zarlapski whispered as he stood against the blinds in the "latrine."

"The boys brought Isaiah down here," said Snider. "They couldn't get out of the building. Isaiah is dead. I tried, but he went quick. Nothing we could do."

Zarlapski rubbed his hand through his hair from front to back but didn't say anything. He took the phone from his ear to read an incoming text.

"Got it," said the reply from Steve about the booby-traps.

Zarlapski put the phone back to his ear.

"You there?" Snider was saying.

"Yeah. I was reading a text from Bennett."

"Bianco's here. Bennett is still up in Admin, I guess. Bianco is texting him to come back.

I'll keep them here. The sub next door is a mess. I'm trying to help with her kids."

"Know anything, Sue?"

"Not much. Sounded like some shots were fired on the second floor right after the fire alarm went off. Must be some fire behind the gym. Lots of rumors from the kids I'm with. Did you hear that Czarnecki was shot?"

"Yeah."

"You know anything?" Snider asked Zarlapski.

Zarlapski's phone signaled another incoming call.

"I'll text you, Bennett's calling. Stay safe, woman."

"Go ahead, Steve. Where are you?"

"In the nurses. She's dead. Shot." His voice was quivering. Zarlapski heard him take a deep breath.

"Get out of there now. Go back to Snider or come back here."

"I don't think anyone's here. I can get out the front doors, maybe. The doors in the 500 wing are chained."

"Listen, Steve, like I texted, there are booby-traps in the halls. The cops couldn't even make it through. They're making plans to come back in now. They might think you are a bad guy. Get back the way you came, now."

"But, I think..."

"Don't argue with me, Steve. Now. I'll tell the police what you told me. And I'm telling them you are on your way back. Got it?"

"Yeah."

"Text me when you get back. You OK?"

"Yeah."

"I got a call coming in from the police, got to go. No chances."

"OK."

12

Steve heard sneaker squeaks in the hall coming at him. Good guy or bad guy? He stepped into the darkness of the inner office and crouched beside the door, right fist cocked.

The footsteps stopped in front of the door to the suite. There were no sounds for a couple of long seconds until the faint tinkle of jewelry and then a low whistle. Steve heard the distinctive click of a cell phone photo being taken followed by silence again until the squeaks started off in the direction of the offices.

After a few seconds, Steve risked coming out and sidled to the door leading to the hallway. The nurse's dead body had been half-rolled, her open eyes now staring at the ceiling.

The footsteps were still receding, and Steve took a look around the corner. A person dressed in all black, except for incongruous red sneakers, was standing along the wall staring into the guidance office. He was wearing a scarf wrapped around his head like terrorists did; only his eyes were showing. He was carrying a backpack in his left hand, a gun in his right. There was something very familiar about the figure when he walked.

The terrorist gave a long, low whistle as he put the backpack and gun on the floor, took a phone from his pocket, and snapped a couple of pictures before, apparently, texting. After picking up the backpack and gun, the figure in black went into the office, emerging several seconds later engrossed in whatever was on his phone, laughing to himself. He did not have the backpack anymore, but he still had the gun.

Every fiber of Steve's being wanted to do something. He was surprised he was not afraid. He was angry that this clown was dictating his life at the moment. Bennett briefly considered attacking the rat bastard; he could wait until the terrorist's back was turned and then level him with a satisfying rib breaking tackle.

But he heard Zarlapski's voice in his head saying "Be careful."

Bennett shook his head as he watched the figure start up the hallway. The mannerisms and movements were familiar. He had seen those red sneakers lately. Where?

Suddenly, the figure fired a short burst of gunfire in the hallway, and Bennett hugged the wall as he heard wood and glass splinter.

In the business classroom at the other end of the hallway, Tori O'Connell heard the same noises and pops Steve heard. Sometimes there were a couple of pops. Sometimes there was a staccato burst. Kids gasped, prayed, and cried. The teacher admonished the class to be quiet.

After a time there were no more pops, but Tori could not relax. People were trying to hang onto their emotions. She glanced at the clock over the whiteboard. It had stopped working.

Lockdown drills usually lasted about fifteen minutes. Tori assured herself that this was just an unusually realistic drill. Right?

A louder pop, muffled.

This was a very realistic drill. Tori glanced at the clock. It still said 8:13.

I have to finish this website, she thought. *Let's get this over with.*

A scream. Maybe a cry.

The teacher's laptop beeped.

Tori strained to hear outside. Noises in the room were becoming distracting.

"It's weird that you can hear people holding their breath," she thought idly. She heard stifled crying and sniffling and sharp intakes of breath and a fart.

"Idiot," she thought. None of the boys laughed.

"Oh God," Tori implored. "Please don't let anyone be out there."

She listened carefully.

Tori pushed herself off the ground with both hands and got on her knees. She looked for Mrs. Bartkowski and found her sitting on a chair on the side of the room a few feet from her desk. She was rubbing the large bump under her blue dress, grimacing once in a while, or biting her lip trying to stay strong. She looked pale.

What if she's in labor? Tori thought in a panic.

Suddenly, fragments of the classroom door exploded inward. Four blasts blew splinters into the room and chipped paint and plaster off the wall above computer station twenty-six. A girl nearby screamed, loudly. Without thinking, Tori scrambled over and covered the girl's mouth. Dust danced around the four head-high holes that horizontally lined the door.

Another burst behind them now. Maybe the library.

Meanwhile, Steve Bennett had crept deeper into the nurse's office at the other end of the corridor.

The sounds were moving away from him.

After an eternity of stillness, Bennett cautiously peered out of the nurse's suite. Indistinct sounds filtered through the haze twisting slowly in the empty hallway. Was that moaning from down the hall? Bennett saw that three bullet holes traced a horizontal path head high across the wooden door of room 210. He surmised that the gunman had blasted every classroom door in the hallway. He was either trying to cowl people in the rooms to cover his escape. Or, he was a stone sadist intimidating people for his amusement. *Probably both.*

Steve considered Zarlapski's admonition to head to the 500 wing right away, but he just couldn't. Bennett thought about checking the classrooms in case people needed help, but that was too risky. Ninja-boy could be waiting to pick people off from the other end of the hallway. Or he could come back. Steve focused hard on the far end of the hallway trying to detect movement. He didn't see any.

At the least, he could find out if the backpack was in the office and maybe figure out what was in it. If it was a bomb, he could report it to Zarlapski, who could report it to the police.

This is so surreal, he thought.

Bennett stealthily started toward his right, ducking below the small square windows of the stairwell doors and then crossing over to hug the wall on the guidance side of the hallway. He stayed close to the wall until he got to a position where he could see into the office.

Blood sprays covered the walls and furniture, the bodies of three students in front of the counter where the secretary greeted visitors. Steve recognized the prone form of Amy Keller. The girl next to her was probably her identical twin, Eve. The bodies were dressed alike in plaid skirts and blue sweater tops. The mischievous pair knew that most people could not tell them apart and sometimes wore the same outfit just for the fun of messing with people's heads. Eve had her left arm draped across her sister's chest.

They were two of the most intelligent people Steve had ever met, but they were also very patient with those who did not get the concepts they saw immediately. Amy and Eve were planning on enrolling in the same college as education majors.

Now they were dead.

The third student, a male, was lying up against the counter in the fetal position. Broken eyeglasses were resting a few feet away.

Tom Roth, the principal who had called the lockdown, had his head and hands resting on his desk like he was taking a quick nap.

Behind the counter Bennett glimpsed arms and legs splayed on the floor.

In addition to the human carnage, the PA console, the bell controls, and a few other electrical-looking boxes had been annihilated. A quick impression went through Bennett's head: a gunman with an automatic weapon standing in the center of the room pivoting 270 degrees.

Steve took a deep breath and remembered red sneakers' backpack. A quick scan of the floor failed to locate it. Steve dismissed the idea of going into the office to search.

In the guidance suite across the hall, the scene was similar except only one body was visible. Someone, a female, was lying across the threshold of the guidance office, legs sticking out into the guidance reception area.

Steve suddenly felt very alone and vulnerable and sick. He gathered his wits with a deep breath and listened. It was quiet. He made his way back along the wall, stopping at the hallway intersection to check for the ninja. The haze was still hanging outside the classrooms.

After a few seconds, Steve hustled to the elevator shaft. Fortunately, the partially opened door had not meant anything to the terrorist. Bennett paused to close Nell Langley's lifeless eyes but thought better of leaving any sign that he had been there. He made the Sign of the Cross as he went around her. Steve left the elevator door open.

The ladder tottered as Bennett descended, and he fell the last couple of feet to the floor but managed to steady the aluminum ladder before it clattered against the wall. He held out his hurting arm as he froze in place until he was sure there was no reaction from above.

Bennett moved the ladder away from the shaft and started to run back to room 503. He would give Zarlapski a call when he got there.

Halfway through the vast storage area, a connection finally clicked in Bennett's head. Carey Ackerman was wearing red sneakers today.

"Bastard."

He regretted not punching the snot out of him in 522.

13

While Bennett and Bianco were on their mission, two huge vehicles arrived at the high school, creating a stir among the media and spectators. A desert-camouflaged Mine-Resistant Ambush Protected (MRAP) vehicle, inherited from the military, rumbled to a halt at the edge of the parking lot.

The smaller Montgomery County Mobile Command (MC2), a forty-foot vehicle designed to help streamline communication for authorities at a major crime scene, stopped near Greco's car at the edge of the tennis courts. The four-person crew introduced themselves to Greco and began setting up.

Helicopters belonging to Channel 8 and Channel 4 were now hovering in the airspace near the high school, adding to the ever-growing media presence and contributing to the background noise. The incident had pre-empted morning programming on all local stations and was garnering attention on national news outlets and global social media.

John Mann, in command of the MRAP and the county response teams, and his lieutenant, Antonio Garcia, shook hands with Greco. Mann had decision-making authority at the scene but was OK leaving that authority with Greco, whom he had known personally for several years.

"I see the vultures are here," John Mann said, hooking his thumb toward the news vans.

Greco gave him the basic outline as they walked into MC2. There were curt nods and waves of acknowledgment. Mann took in the scenes on the monitors quickly coming online.

Neighboring and distant first responders were arriving with more equipment and manpower. Greco asked the local fire chiefs to take charge of staging the vehicles by function and getting a list of names and call signs.

Greco addressed the newcomers a few minutes later in front of MC2.

"The assault began in the main office in the front of the building. The panic button was pushed in the office at 8:11 and a lockdown was called. There has been no contact with building administrators. The landlines in the school are not working. We're thinking the worst for office personnel.

"Shortly after we got here, a truck at the loading dock blew killing one of our guys, Officer Michael McCaffrey of Green Hill Police."

"Sorry, Chief," Mann interjected, turning to Hawthorne, who nodded in reply

"Two maintenance guys were also killed," Greco continued. "A third is critical.

"Who were the maintenance guys?" Hawthorne asked.

"Russ Conrad was one of them," Greco said. "Not sure of the other. One was here on a service call for the air conditioner. Truck's parked over there."

"Bad luck for that guy," Mann said.

"What about the truck?" Larabee asked.

"Bread truck, delivering to the caf we assume," Greco said.

"Know anything about it?"

"Nope," Greco said.

"We'll get a detective on it when more get here," Larabee said.

"A gym class ran out of the building. They're over there," Greco continued, indicating the buses over his shoulder. "Another group from the special ed wing also made it out. As far as we know, they are the only ones who have gotten out of the building. They don't know anything helpful"

"We sent a team in through those doors," Greco said, indicating the gym entrance. "They think a bomb went off in the ceiling down the hallway. One guy was hurt. They retreated."

"Two other teams are on their way back from the auditorium. They got hit with an explosion also. One guy hurt. They reported finding the body of a teacher. They also said that they think the doors are chained from the inside. Reports from people inside say the same thing."

Mann let out a low whistle.

"I talked to a teacher in this area," Greco said pointing to room 522 on his tablet. "He had a severely sick kid in his room. Two other kids took him out on a stretcher. The sick kid died. One of the other two kids is up near the offices. Here," said Greco pointing.

"He reported seeing one dead body. The other kid is in 503.

"Several 911 calls reported a teacher shot and bleeding out in this room," Greco continued indicating 115.

He paused to let people process the information.

"Those are the basic facts that we know. I'm afraid it is going to be much, much worse than that," Greco said.

"Agreed," added Larabee.

"What's next?" said Mann.

Before Greco could respond, the teams who had been sent to get into the building finally appeared around the corner of the physical education wing. Paramedics ran to help, and Keller was placed gently on a stretcher and loaded into Medic 89.

Matt Weiss came up to the commanders.

"Everybody else OK, trooper?" Larabee asked him.

"Yes, sir."

Weiss gave a quick recap of the chain of events in the auditorium.

Greco had already asked the personnel in MC2 to contact the Feds, including Homeland Security.

Another large vehicle maneuvered into the parking lot. The Hazardous Device and Explosive Team (HDET) vehicle carried two other troopers, their bomb suits, a robot, or "wheelbarrow," bomb blankets, x-ray units, and other tools of the trade. Sgt. Eugene Diehl hopped out of the HDET vehicle and checked on his group.

Two bomb detection dogs arrived separately with their handlers. The bomb disposal truck was still on the way.

Greco was handed a page of notes taken inside the command center.

"Couple of other things I left out. We have only vague descriptions of the perps, but consistent reports have them wearing head wrapping and long coats."

"Terrorists?" Larabee interjected. "Is this a terror attack?"

Greco shrugged. "I have the guy in there contacting the Feds."

Larabee nodded, and Greco continued with the descriptions of the perpetrators. "White, male, high school age or early twenties, tall and short, lots of contradictions. Last shooting reported was about thirty minutes ago in the 500 wing, which is at the other end."

"Maybe they killed themselves," Mann offered.

"Hope so," Larabee muttered. "Bastards."

"Well, we have to assume that they are alive and active. Be aggressive, but be careful. Even if they are dead, we still have IED's to worry about," Greco warned before doling out responsibilities.

"Not all the outside doors are chained right?" Mann asked. "Not here at the gym. Not by the auditorium, right? What specific doors?"

"Don't know," Greco said. "I'll try to pin them down."

The group noticed that it had become much more comfortable to hear. The drone of the media helicopters had receded. They were much higher and looked to be farther away.

"Johnny, you guys handle all the inside stuff. I'll give you Laessig as a liaison," Greco said. "He knows the building pretty well. You should have the floor plans on your computer on the Code Red site. Coordinate with Larabee on the bomb squad guys. Careful in the halls."

Greco turned to Larabee, "Set up around the building. Anybody comes out, you got 'em. Cover innocents if need be. Escort everyone except suspects over there by the buses. Set up quick interrogations."

"OK. That's still going to take a while," the state police commander warned imperiously.

"Do the best you can," Greco said evenly.

Larabee whistled and signaled for a meeting at the MRAP with his troopers.

Pennsville Council President Tim Petit came walking up to Greco, worry etched on his boyish, round face, but he did not interrupt.

Greco turned toward Hawthorne.

"OK, I'm going to have the local guys help on the perimeter. No one sets foot on school property. No media, no parents, no concerned citizens. Got it?"

"Got it."

"Also, Greg, have some guys ready in case we have to transport prisoners. We'll take them to our house if need be," Greco said.

"Let's hope they put up a fight," Hawthorne responded.

"Greg, I know how you must feel, with McCaffrey being killed, but none of that stuff, OK?"

"Just saying."

"Hey, I'm not telling you not to defend yourselves, but let's not provoke a firefight if we can help it."

"I hear you. I'm good," Hawthorne responded testily.

Greco wasn't convinced as he watched Hawthorne walk away. He could understand the anger.

MC2 personnel used Twitter Advanced Search and other methods to find postings from students inside the building, adding it to the intelligence they received from 911 and phone calls. Pictures, videos and narrative tweets increased as Marilyn Archer, of the MC2 crew, hit on the right search words. An index card in front of her reminded her to try to determine the # OF SHOOTERS/ID/LOCATION. Archer's notebook was filling with scribbled notes.

A scenario was emerging of multiple shooters mostly in the 100, 200 and 500 wings, multiple casualties in those areas, and hundreds of terrified students. One blurry, shaky Snapchat showed a shooter in a long coat or garment running through the stairwell doors from the first to the second floor in the 100 wing. There were pictures of students holding hands, huddled against a wall, sitting against barricades. There were lots of entries pleading for help. A few saying goodbyes to loved ones. #vistaview #schoolshooting #help were trending.

An upload looked like it came from a GoPro camera. The soundless footage showed the camera-wearer coming out of a room into a hallway. Two classrooms are emptying, the students coming at the camera. Most of the students' freeze, staring in the direction of the camera and then a couple fall, entry wounds visible. A girl's head blows up in a haze of red. Students turn and run back to the classrooms. Or attempt to. Red wounds open on their backs, legs, heads. *Lambs to the slaughter.*

"Where is that from?" Mann asked.

"My guess would be the second floor of the 500 wing. We've had multiple reports of victims in hallways and 911 calls," answered Rita Salvatore, one of the cops working MC2.

"Who sent it?"

"It's from a high school Twitter account that students can post to. #VVStudentSection."

"Student shooters? Let's get these pictures and videos copied," Mann urged.

Outside MC2, Greco turned toward the council president. "What can I do for you, Mr. Petit?"

"My son and daughter are in there, Chief," Petit said in a shaky voice.

"You know where?" Greco asked, putting his hand on Petit's shoulder.

"Macie had gym. I haven't heard from her. Brendan called from Mr. Pisker's class, 150 something I think he said. He's OK for now. They're hunkered down."

"Well, the gym class is over there on one of those buses," Greco said, pointing. He hesitated before adding, "And we haven't had any reports from that part of the 100 wing."

"I'll be right back," Petit said, moving as quickly as his heavy frame could take him toward the buses. "Thanks," he called over his shoulder.

Greco hoped Mr. Petit was not confusing "115" with "150." Room 115 had a teacher with gunshot wounds. There was no 150.

Dozens of buses were now in the Memorial Field Parking Lot. Greco was going to have to decide what to do with those kids if he didn't hear from the school district administration soon.

It was troubling that central administration had not been in contact with police. Greco learned that the superintendent and her assistant were at a two-day conference in Philadelphia.

Greco doubted that they would be much help, anyway. He decided to act on his own.

"County," he said into his radio, "Call Dr. Danielle Bedford at the Vista Middle School. Tell her we are busing kids to her auditorium. Tell her we'll announce that to the media when we get the chance. Parents can go pick up their kids there."

14

Miss Snider used a damp towel to wipe the blood off Katie McPhee's hands and face and helped her out of her blouse and into a blue training room polo shirt Snider kept in her closet.

The teacher had tried asking her about the blood, but all Snider could get out of her was that she had been in social studies.

"When Steve gets here, we'll all go next door," Snider said to Bianco.

Bianco kept watching at the door. Bennett emerged from the storage area, and they each checked the hall in both directions. Bianco pointed to room 502.

"Steve's here," he whispered over his shoulder.

Room 502 was a clone of room 522: two rooms down from the stairwell, separated from its sister room, 501, by a divider. Both rooms paralleled the back driveway and the football field. The classroom sat below the floor where the gunfire and bomb blasts had come from. The room had a much more feminine touch than Zarlapski's room, primarily because of all the little shelves and knickknacks that decorated the light blue walls, newly painted in the fall by some volunteer NHS members. A ceramic cat and a William Shakespeare bust lay in pieces on the far side of the room.

Snider grabbed McPhee by the arm and hustled her along. There was too much noise coming from inside the room, especially a loud voice complaining about being "trapped like rats."

The door was propped with a thick English anthology. When Bennett came in from the hallway, Barbara Knaul, subbing in the district for the first time, screamed.

"Get a hold of yourself," said Snider, marching up to Knaul and grabbing her arm. "Why is that door propped?"

"Kids had to go to the bathroom."

Snider shook her head.

"Close that door," she ordered Bianco.

"You want me to go get them?" Bianco asked kicking the book into the room.

"No," Snider said as she gave Knaul a reproving stare. "I told them not to leave the room. I'm not risking your ass too."

Snider saw that the twenty-three seniors she had brought over from her anatomy class were still seated along the wall on the floor, exactly where she had told them to sit. Some of them were staring off into space. Some were texting or watching on phones. Some were quietly comforting each other.

"Sit with them," Snider directed Katie.

Some of the twenty-seven sophomores in Knaul's charge were seated on the floor obediently.

A group of five was sitting in desks in the center of the room watching media coverage of the shooting on a tablet, looks of horror on their faces. A couple of boys were standing in the corner talking. Another boy-girl group was seated in the front of the room oblivious to the danger they were in if somebody burst through the door.

A few seniors couldn't conceal the disdain they felt for Knaul and the underclassmen she had feebly tried to control when Snider was out of the room.

The teacher put her head down on the desk and began to sob.

The locked door handle rattled and then came a knock. The room went quiet.

"Open up, open up. It's us," pleaded a female voice.

"Must be the people from the bathroom," someone said from the other side of the room. "That's them."

Snider moved to the door. "Who is it?" she asked.

"Donna Slowick, Mary Halstead, and Brian Maslow," said the female voice.

Snider opened the door a crack, and it was quickly yanked open from the outside. The three sophomores hurled themselves into the room and headed for the group with the iPad.

Snider intercepted them. "Sit up against the wall over there," she said, pointing. "And keep your mouths shut. And that goes for the rest of you," she said threateningly.

Bennett and Bianco were appalled that no defensive preparations had been made in the room, as Mr. Zarlapski had done upstairs. The two didn't need any prompting to take charge.

"Everybody over here," Bianco said to a group that was in the direct line of sight of the door. He pointed to the area where the seniors were already seated.

"Now," he reiterated angrily when they were slow to react.

"Do what he says," commanded Snider.

The designated students throughout the room began to get up.

"Faster," Snider said to the slower moving boys. One oversized mop-haired male made sure he moved as slowly as he could.

"Double up. You," Bianco said pointing to a tall, thin blond girl, "sit here." The rest of the sophomores got the idea and sat down inches in front of the seniors in the most protected part of the room. Only Knaul stayed in the front of the room.

Seconds after the last boy finally sat down, Bennett, who had been guarding the door, said in a low voice, "Quiet, I hear talking." He put his finger to his lips for emphasis.

Everyone held their breaths and went wide-eyed, straining to hear anything.

Ms. Knaul could not hold back a loud sob.

Bennett and Bianco had the same thought simultaneously. They each grabbed an arm of Knaul's teacher chair and carried her to the back of the room. Snider took the sweater off the back of the chair and held it up to Knaul's face so she could cry into it.

Everyone heard the hall door close with its unique click. Then came indistinct conversation and laughter.

Bennett and Bianco took up positions on either side of the door. The footsteps were moving past the room when a country and western ringtone went off in the room. A beefy girl with a rose tattoo on her wrist pawed frantically through her purse as a couple of nearby girls pleaded with her to find the phone and mute it, which she did after a few agonizing seconds.

Now there were no sounds from the hall. A few seconds more went by, and then the door handle on the entry door moved slightly.

Bennett and Bianco made eye contact. Steve pointed at Matt and held his right hand horizontally head high. He pointed at himself and made the same motion but knee high. Matt nodded.

"You know, you're not supposed to be making noise in there," came a mocking voice from outside.

Bennett looked at Bianco and then Snider who was standing next to Knaul. Snider applied severe pressure to Knaul's right arm to distract her from starting to sob again.

"Someone with a gun…"

There was laughter from a different person in the hall.

"Someone with a gun might shoot you, you know."

More laughter.

"Oh my God," someone wailed from the back of the room.

Three people responded with "Shut up" at the same time.

"I'll be back," said an artificially deep voice just outside the door.

Laughter.

"I know where you live," said a different voice.

Kellie Frazier and Donna Slowick, sitting next to each other on the floor, simultaneously turned and looked at each other. Slowick shrugged and put her fingers to her lips. Snider noted the exchange.

Ten seconds went by without any noise on either side of the door. Then there came the clicks and squeaks of the hall doors at the other end of the wing opening and closing.

The sounds provoked a flood of pent up emotions. Many could not stop tears from flowing. A slightly built male grabbed the nearby wastebasket, but all he could muster was dry heaves.

"Shut up," Bianco hissed to the class. "They might still be out there."

More people started crying.

Snider released her grip on Knaul, who was catatonic, staring straight ahead.

"What happened here?" whispered Snider coming up behind Bennett.

"What do you mean?"

"You have a pretty good cut," she said, touching his left arm. "Hold still."

Snider grabbed the room's emergency bag off its hook next to the closet and used a couple of gauze pads and tape to patch up the wound expertly.

"I think they left," Bianco said.

"Where's Isaiah?" Bennett asked.

Snider involuntarily glanced at Bianco.

"Dead," she said. "Nothing, you guys, could have done differently."

Bennett held Snider's eyes for a few seconds before shaking his head.

"We can't stay here," Steve said.

"Agreed. Where to though?" Snider asked.

"We can't get outside," said Matt.

"You think those assholes know about the storage room?" said Steve.

"The door was unlocked," Matt reminded him.

"So?" asked Snider.

"Well, who unlocked it?" Matt said.

"Could have been left open by maintenance. They were down here before school," Snider noted.

"We can't stay here," Steve said again.

Snider agreed that they could not hang around and be sitting ducks. The storage area was the best, if not only, option at this point. They couldn't be wandering the halls looking for a haven.

"And if we can't find a way out, we can defend that area better. Maybe," Bianco added.

"Let's think this through for a minute," Snider said.

The three of them planned in the center of the room, interrupted by Snider having to walk over to a knot of three tenth graders conversing too loudly.

"I'll check the door," Bennett told Bianco.

Steve gave an OK sign to Snider after listening hard for thirty seconds.

"OK. Look at me," Snider said to the students in the room. "We are going to move across the hall, fast. Follow Matt and Steve. Line up behind them. Wait until I say go. And be very quiet."

Snider called to two of the bigger boys from her anatomy class. "When I say so, each of you grab an arm of the chair. I'll stay…"

The muffled sounds of an explosion reached the room and froze everyone in place again.

Sprinkles of dust fell from the ceiling caught by the gray light in the slitted windows high in the wall.

Snider felt a stab of fear but put it aside quickly.

"Let's go. Let's go," she said to everyone. "Follow these two guys," she ordered as she moved behind Knaul.

Ms. Snider nodded at Bennett. He opened the door a crack and listened. He stepped into the hall and held the door wide and signaled Bianco to go. Bianco used the same hand gesture to signal the class.

"Follow me. Move."

Bianco got across the hall quickly and held the black door open while herding students and occasionally glancing down the hallway.

"Go to the middle of the room and wait," he repeated every few seconds.

About half the class had made it across the hall when another boom reverberated through The Dungeon. All of the classroom doors on the floor rattled; dust floated in the hall. There were screams from the storage area, and for a second Bianco thought the explosion had come from there. He looked in. Most of the students already in the room dove for the floor. A couple of boxes containing football equipment had toppled from a shelf, and a few smaller items fell in other places in the vast room.

Once the last reverberation had passed Snider gathered her wits and the rest of the students.

"Go," Snider said from the classroom. Those who still needed to get to the storage area started moving again. Todd and Ed shuffled the chair across the hall. Snider was the last to leave the room, closing the door behind her. She didn't bother to look left or right but bolted for the entrance to the storage area.

Bennett and Bianco were waiting inside the door, and once Snider got into the room, they closed the door.

"What to hell was that?" Bianco said.

"Bomb," Bennett said with certainty.

"Can we secure this door somehow?" Bianco asked and then walked off without waiting for an answer. "Let me see if there are any chains or something around here."

"You said we could get to the front from here," Snider said to Bennett.

Steve summarized what he and Bianco had found in their trek through the room a little while ago. He also gave a recap of what he had seen on the second floor and in Admin including Carey Ackerman.

Snider was aghast. "I'm sorry you had to see all that, Steve." She suddenly felt very sad. Every name Steve had mentioned, Sue Snider knew very well. The Keller twins were the best students she had ever had in AP Chemistry. She sometimes ate lunch with the guidance counselors, and Tom Roth had been in the science department for several years before becoming an administrator.

Bianco had returned with a long length of rope and had caught Carey Ackerman's name at the tail end of the conversation.

"What a douche bag. How did he get out of Zarlapski's room?"

"Probably was part of this all along. What are we going to do with that?" Bennett said, indicating the rope.

"How about we tie this from the door handle to the beam up there?" Bianco said, indicating an exposed I-beam in the ceiling.

"You know how to tie a knot?" Snider asked.

"Not really," Bianco said.

Bennett shook his head. "No."

"Any of you guys Boy Scouts?" Snider called to the group.

Two boys put their hands up.

"Come here," Snider called.

"I'm going to call Mr. Z and tell him what I saw. Does he know Isaiah died?" Bennett said.

"I told him," Snider said.

Bennett went to an empty corner of the room and took out his cell phone. He punched the wall a couple of times between attempts to reach room 522.

The Scouts, after a couple of aborted attempts, succeeded in tying the rope off with two half hitches.

"Nice job, men," Bianco said, patting them both on the back.

"Can't we get that undone in a hurry if we have to?" Snider asked.

Both Scouts nodded.

"OK, good job. You guys stay here and guard the doors. Let's get everybody against that far wall," Snider suggested to Bianco.

Snider scanned the room for a couple of faces.

She found who she was looking for.

"You two," Snider said, pointing at Donna Slowick and Kellie Frazier, "Come here."

Frazier got up right away. Slowick glared at Snider with her right eye. Her jet black hair covered her left. She got up as slowly as she could. Snider headed toward a "private" place in the room between two racks of drama costumes and signaled for the two girls to follow.

Most students arranged themselves by classes subdivided into cliques or friends. A few of the "different" students were inadvertently isolated in their little spaces. Some students began arranging boxes, and furniture and whatever else was there as cover in case the bad guys walked in. Others sat and stared listlessly. Some looked at their phones. One girl, sitting alone, began reading and taking notes from her biology textbook.

Bianco reminded the room to mute phones. Some did double-check.

Slowick and Frazier sauntered over to Snider. Kellie Frazier stood behind and to Slowick's left. Slowick was a head taller than Snider, but the teacher got inside the girl's personal space to make sure everyone knew who was going to control this conversation.

"You recognized those voices in the hall didn't you?" Snider said.

Slowick took a step back and turned toward Frazier who dropped her eyes. After a few seconds, Slowick shook her head.

"Who were they?" Snider asked.

"We don't know," Donna Slowick said meeting Snider's intense eyes defiantly.

"That true?" Snider asked Frazier.

Snider had to repeat the question.

"Yes," Frazier said after glancing at Slowick.

"What's your name again?"

"Kellie Frazier."

"You?"

"Donna Slowick."

"OK. Donna, why don't you go and sit down over on that stool over there. I'll come over, and we'll talk some more in a minute. I want to talk to Kellie."

Donna hesitated before slowly taking her leave, looking over her shoulder three times at Kellie.

Snider grabbed Kellie's arm and guided her to a space thirty feet away behind two tall unused freezer units.

Snider eyed Kellie Frazier, a pretty brunette who had not done an outstanding job of covering up an acne outbreak. Her eyeliner was overdone for Snider's taste, and the lipstick was a little off. The jeans were a bit too tight. Snider saw fear in Kellie's eyes.

"You know, this whole thing is really, really bad. Worse than you think. Do you know Isaiah Shue?" Snider asked.

"Yes. We were in the Reading Olympics together. Why?"

"His dead body is lying in room 503 right now." Snider succeeded in shocking Kellie.

"Lots of other people are dead, too. Do you want to be accused of protecting a murderer, Kellie? You could go to jail."

The young girl started crying, eyeliner liquefying on her cheeks.

"He wouldn't kill people," Kellie gasped.

"Who?"

"I'm not sure it was even him."

"Who, Kellie?"

She looked around to make sure no one was in earshot and lowered her voice even more.

"It sounded like Anthony Russo, but I'm not one hundred percent, you know."

"You know him?"

"We hang out sometimes."

"What about the other voice?"

"I don't know. I swear to God."

"Did you know about this, Kellie? Did you know Russo was going to do something like this?"

"No. God no."

Snider patted Kellie's shoulder as the sophomore struggled to hold back more tears, putting her bitten-down nails against her lips.

"OK. You did the right thing. Don't tell the other girl you said anything. I am going to talk to her now, but I won't tell, either. I believe you."

Snider gave Kellie Frazer her best reassuring smile and tissue from her pocket. "Clean your face up before you go back to the group."

Snider left Kellie between the freezer units and walked into the middle of the storage area.

Knaul's English class on the left, the anatomy class to the right.

Ms. Knaul was more with it now and sat watching the students move to the wall. Her left arm draped over her stomach.

Snider gave the OK sign to the boys at the door, and they did the same back to her.

She went over to Donna Slowick and pulled up a stool next to her. Slowick slid back a little on her stool.

"Kellie said she didn't recognize the voices from the hall. I'm just wondering why you guys looked at each other the way you did."

"I don't know. We just did," said Slowick defensively. Her black eyes dropped to the floor as she spoke.

"Come on. You know who it was."

Slowick shook her head defiantly, her black hair falling over her eye again. "Why don't you believe us?" she said challengingly. "Kellie wouldn't lie. She goes to church."

"Uh huh," snorted Snider.

Slowick crossed her arms and shuddered like she was cold.

"Did you know this was going to happen?" Snider said with her prosecutor tone. "Anything on Facebook or that other crap?"

"No. Why would I?"

"Just don't want to see you get in trouble. If you did know, helping now would save you some trouble down the line," said Snider.

There was the briefest of hesitation, but Slowick defiantly proclaimed that she didn't know anything as she met and held the teacher's eyes.

"Fine. Go. If you change your mind, we can talk," Snider said to Donna Slowick's back. She shook her head as she watched the teenager go.

"I'm sorry," Barbara Knaul said when Snider came up to her. "I'm OK now. I took this job at the last second this morning," the substitute teacher said wistfully to Snider. "Should have ignored the text."

"Yeah, well, we can take the next month off," Snider replied.

Bennett came back to join Bianco and Snider.

"No answer. I tried Z, Kyle, Lauren. Nothing. I sent a text out."

For a few seconds, each pondered what the lack of contact might mean.

"You guys haven't told anybody about Isaiah, have you?" Snider asked.

Bennett shook his head.

"I didn't," said Bianco.

"Good. Don't," Snider warned. "Let me call Z. I have something to tell him anyway."

Snider walked away a few feet and tried a couple of times to reach Zarlapski to no avail.

She came back to the Bennett and Bianco.

"We'll try again in a minute," Snider said.

Snider noted that Slowick was now sitting on the floor next to Kellie. The former was doing all the talking. Kellie kept shaking her head.

15

"You believe in God, right?" Raven Bartholomew whispered to Mandy Holder as they sat on the floor in the far corner of room 212.

Mandy held up her gold cross necklace.

"Do you think there's a heaven?"

"Yes, I do," Mandy said in a low, emphatic voice.

"We used to go to that Calvary Church because of my mother," Raven continued. "After my parents got divorced, I stayed with my dad. He doesn't go to church anymore."

"That's a shame," replied Mandy who wondered why this girl was even talking to her. Mandy couldn't recall the girl's name if she ever knew it. Mandy wanted to be left alone.

Maybe the girl had heard her reciting the psalms during the all the shooting out in the hall ten minutes ago. Mandy had been sure she was going to die.

Raven was undeterred that Mandy had turned away from her. "I was ten when the divorce happened. I can say The Lord's Prayer and a couple of others, but that's about it."

"Well, I don't think you have to say the prayers to talk to God. God will listen to anything we say," Mandy retorted, hoping the girl would get the hint.

"That's a nice idea," Raven said with a cracking voice.

Mandy turned her head and took a good look at the girl for the first time, her attitude softening when she saw a tear trickle down

Raven's cheek. Something clicked in Mandy's memory. Randy something. No Raven. Rumors about a breakdown or abuse teased at Mandy's thoughts.

"We were in the same gym class in middle school," Raven said.

That did not ring a bell with Mandy. There must have been sixty people in that class.

"I hate gym," Mandy said.

"I kind of miss it. I can't fit it into my schedule because I go to vo-tech."

"For what?"

"Cosmetology."

That seemed about right to Mandy, now that she had taken a closer look at Raven. She was everything physically that Mandy wasn't. Raven had makeup on, maybe too much. There was a red streak in her jet black, styled hair. She wasn't hiding anything with her black yoga pants and skin-tight black v-neck top.

"I know The Serenity Prayer," Raven said after a moment of quiet.

"God, grant me the serenity
To accept the things I cannot change
The courage to change the things I can
And the wisdom to know the difference."

"That's a good prayer," Mandy said. "Never heard it before. Did they say that at your church?"

"Family group meeting."

Mandy wasn't sure what that was, but let it go when Raven bowed her head, and more tears smeared her make-up.

"I'm sorry. I'm not usually like this," Raven said. "Sorry if I'm bothering you."

"Not at all," Mandy said, truthfully now. "I'm Mandy."

"Yeah, I know."

A loud bang in the hall commanded the room's attention, and they joined the rest of the twenty-one fearful students and teacher in holding their breaths and straining to listen.

After a minute of noiselessness, Raven whispered urgently, "Do you think if we pray hard enough, God will get us out of this?"

"I'm sure it will help," Mandy said. "We'll be alright."

"How do you know there is a God?"

"I just believe it."

"Yeah, but…"

"It's called faith," Mandy whispered. "You can't be sure, you know."

"I wish I knew if there was a heaven."

"Well, think of it this way, if there is no afterlife, you'll never know. I think it's safer to assume that God is waiting for us."

"Yeah. Maybe."

The hall was quiet again.

The two fell into the silence of their thoughts and prayers.

16

"Everything OK?" Greco asked councilman Tim Pettit who had walked back from the buses with Tess Bennington, his daughter's PE teacher.

"Macy was over there," the mayor said. "Thank you. Any word from inside the building? You think I should have heard from my son by now? Other kids...."

"I'm sure he's fine. Calls have been spotty. We'll be sending teams in a couple of minutes. Get this thing over with, I hope," Greco said.

"Everyone accounted for?" Greco asked turning to Mrs. Bennington who was biting her lip.

"Yes," Tess said.

"You OK?"

Bennington nodded.

"Mr. Petit, how about going out on the perimeter and help us keep people calm?" Greco said, turning to the council president.

"Calm? *I'm* not even calm. I'd rather..."

"Exactly. You know how people are feeling. Better to talk to you than some twenty-five-year-old cop from Green Hill, right?"

Petit gave a reluctant nod. "You'd tell me if you knew anything. Right?"

"I'll make sure you are updated on what's going on." Greco patted him on the arm. "I have your number."

Petit started toward the perimeter of the property. A ragged line of people had formed beyond the fields that separated the high school itself from the nearest houses several hundred yards away.

Greco grabbed Bennington by the arm. "I need some help here, Tess," Greco said, guiding her into the command center.

Several video monitors were now online. One of the bigger monitors was quartered into the feeds of four local TV stations covering the shooting. Another showed the body cams of two of the County Incident Response Teams squad leaders as they approached different areas of the property. The computer monitor at the police workspace showed the feeds from five of the seven outside security monitors.

"Where'd you get these?" Greco asked pointing to the security camera pictures.

"Internet," said Rita Salvatore, one of the police operating MC2.

"Anybody can see it?" Greco asked.

"If they know the IP address."

"Is the security footage recorded?

"Might've been, in the office or someplace. I can't get to it now if that's what you're asking."

"What about interior cameras?" Greco inquired.

"Trying. That address is not cooperating," Salvatore said.

Another of the MC2 personnel was getting a recap from County Dispatch of the 911 calls originating from inside the building, and he was setting up a quick and dirty database, organizing the calls by their points of origin from within the building.

Greco went to Tess, "We are trying to figure out where the heaviest concentrations of students might be," he said. "Can you give us a quick estimate?"

"I'll try."

The total enrollment of the high school was 1,153 in four grades. Factoring in off-campus vocational students and the average absentee rate, Greco figured there were approximately nine hundred students in the building. The high school had seventy-two faculty members, eight aides, four special education teachers from the intermediate unit who worked with the severely handicapped, three administrators, three guidance counselors, the nurse, the athletic director, the IT specialist, five secretaries, four maintenance workers, six cafeteria workers, the school resource officer, and whoever else might have had the misfortune to be in the building at the time.

"Let's start with this end of the building," Greco said, indicating the athletic wing.

"Mrs. Bennington got her...how many many kids?"

"Forty-seven."

"Forty-seven kids out of the gym. Any other classes down there?"

"There was a fitness class in the weight room, here," Tess said pointing at a location down the hall from the gym, "and Lifeguarding in the pool, here."

"How many kids?" Burke asked.

"Um, maybe twenty in each class."

"Anyone in the caf?" Greco asked moving his finger down the floor plan.

"Cafeteria workers. No kids, usually."

"How about these classrooms?" Greco indicated the 100 wing. "We've gotten several calls from that wing. We know that we have an injured adult here," he said, pointing to room 115.

"Who? Paul Ric?" Tess Bennington asked.

"Don't know. We are trying to get to him or her," Greco said as he checked off the rooms identified as being occupied.

"What's the average class size, you think?"

"They're mostly math classes, so maybe twenty-five," Bennington said.

"So about two hundred, two hundred fifty," Burke said as he wrote on his spreadsheet.

"What about this side?" Burke asked.

"Um, language classrooms, computer lab, small classrooms," Bennington said pointing at the floor plan. "I doubt the language classes have more than twenty. This is a special needs room. Kids in wheelchairs."

"That could be a problem. Give your guys a heads up," Greco said to Mann before turning to a new page: the administrative wing and the 200 classrooms.

"How many people in the offices?"

"Fifteen, twenty, I guess," said Bennington.

"These classrooms?"

"Mixed bag: some science, English, computers, health, business."

"Three hundred?"

"Somewhere in there, I guess."

"Library?"

"Depends. Sometimes teachers take their classes there. Sometimes it's empty. No idea how many it holds."

"What rooms did they get calls from?" Greco asked Salvatore.

Salvatore ran down a list of nine rooms.

Greco added to the check marks.

"300's?" Greco said to Tess Bennington as he turned to another floor plan.

"I thought they all got out," Tess said.

"Right, right. My bad."

"We know the music wing and auditorium are empty," Greco said as he turned to another page. He deliberately left out the adult male body in the stage area. "How many kids take shop?"

"Twenty maybe," Tess said. "I don't know; I'm guessing."

"This whole area has been the most active since we've been here," Greco said, indicating the 500 wing.

"Same for 911 calls," Salvatore said looking at the spreadsheet.

Greco noticed that Bennington was beginning to tear up. Then he remembered. "This is where your daughter is."

"Yeah, 522."

"OK, we can take it from here," Greco said to her. "You've given us a good…"

"I'd like to stay," Tess interrupted. "I've talked to her. She's fine. I hope. Mike will keep her safe."

Greco thought for a couple of seconds and then squeezed Bennington's shoulder.

"This wing is a little different. Three floors, five classrooms per floor, all on the outer walls. Reports of gunfire on the second floor after the fire alarm went off. Might have been an ambush."

Bennington started at that information but did not say anything.

Greco continued, "We have a large storage area here, bathrooms and an elevator. The outside doors might be chained. This is our highest priority area, this and 115. Plus we have a couple of students from 522 trying to get a sick student on a stretcher some help."

"Isaiah Shue?" Bennington said.

"Know him?" Brown asked.

"Lots of issues," the PE teacher responded.

Using the approximate numbers, Greco, Larabee, and Mann formulated a plan that would send the five-member County Incident Response Teams into the building areas most heavily occupied, four teams to different areas. All of the teams were to hunt for active shooters, evacuating immediately life-threatening injuries if possible, and evacuating everyone in immediate danger.

"Remind your teams to be wary of booby-traps," Greco told Mann. "Go on your signal."

On one of the monitors, a fire in the North Parking Lot lit up the screen. One of the fire companies was calling in that several cars were aflame.

"Wow," Brown said flatly as he watched flames leaping several feet above the cars on two monitors.

The explosion had originated in a Ford 150 pickup that had been parked in the third row, four spaces in. A Honda Civic and a Chevy Equinox parked on either side of the pickup were less heavily enveloped in flames. Stonybrook's pumper began fighting the fire in the pickup. The second Stonybrook truck maneuvered to the other side of the conflagration.

On the feed from camera number one, Stonybrook's pumpers came into view and stopped about one hundred feet from the burning cars. Two firefighters started working with a hose to tamp down the flames; other firefighters stood by with pry bars and chemical extinguishers, ready to pop the hoods when the fire died down. The second truck quickly got to work on the other cars.

Larrabee ordered his men to space themselves out around the building and to watch for possible perpetrators using the car fire as a diversion and attempt to escape. He was also concerned that the shooters were luring targets. The troopers were ordered to keep a close eye on windows and rooftops just in case. Three state troopers took up positions at the outer edge of the parking lot.

"Car bomb?" Greco asked in MC2.

"Maybe," Mann responded.

"Planned," Larabee weighed in.

"Why?" Greco asked.

There was a pause.

"What is the plan?" Greco asked Larabee again.

"Ambush. Attention-getting. Diversion. I have my men looking for snipers."

The quality of the video was degrading and freezing up every couple of seconds; it was more of a slide show than a video, but it looked like Stonybrook had gotten a handle on the situation, the flames from the pickup looked significantly less intimidating. No fire was visible in the other two cars.

A voice crackled out of the speaker. "We have the fire..."

There was a loud roar and nothing but static on the radios for a few seconds and then came agonizing screams wailing through Larrabee's radio. Someone's microphone was open in the North Parking Lot. Somebody started repeating, "Oh my God, oh my God" over the radio.

The video coming into MC2 was wavy, pixelated, and useless.

Greco tried the fire chief's radio but got only static.

The frantic voice of a Stonybrook fireman came over the radio. "We need help up here. Another car blew up. People hurt."

"On the way," replied Salvatore. who sent three medic units and another pumper to the North Parking Lot. "Use caution," she advised the units.

Larabee ordered the bomb squad to begin checking the cars parked in the three lots around the school. Eugene Diehl, the driver for the Hazard Device and Explosive Team, pulled wide of the fire and began rolling the robot out of the back of the truck while others were double-checking their protective gear.

The second bomb had been planted in a dark blue Chevy Impala that was now a smoking chassis. The car had been angled into the space and overlapped the one in front of it. The open area gave maximum range to the shrapnel: nails, bolts, ball bearings, screws, and car parts that erupted in an outward ring of destruction heralded by the blastwave, and followed by the supersonic shock wave and fragmentation which clobbered the three closest firefighters, including the company chief and two state troopers providing protection, killing them instantly.

Three other troopers and two firefighters from Stonybrook were bleeding and or unconscious but still alive. One of the troopers was gasping audibly as he struggled to breathe with the "blast lung" caused by the shockwave of the explosion.

Truck 65-11 was between its firefighters and the explosion and took the brunt of the shrapnel that flew in all directions. The blast bent the apparatus, shattered windows, and peeled metal, but the doomed fire engine had prevented the immediate deaths of the four firemen near the rig and a state trooper standing with them.

"All units responding to the North Parking Lot," radioed Rita Salvatore. "Treat the scene as unsafe. Remove victims ASAP. Transport to triage. Repeat: remove victims from the scene."

Amid the squawking of car alarms, paramedics raced from their units to assess the victims. Uninjured fire and police personnel helped yank stretchers from the rear of the medic units. Drivers stayed behind the wheels, engines running, nervously glancing at potential bombs parked in their spaces. The rapid assessment of victims focused on whether or not the patients' heads, necks, or spines had to be stabilized.

If they did not need stabilization, the victims were put on stretchers and wheeled or carried to units.

The dead were left where they had fallen.

Paramedic units were pulling out and transporting to the triage area at the baseball field.

One victim, a fireman, could not be moved. His burned head was lolling grotesquely off to the side as if it was no longer connected to his spine. Blood was running onto the blacktop. A paramedic applied several gauze pads to the neck wound as gently but firmly as she could. Charred skin slid off under the pad. Nancy Crowley could hear the fireman's tortured attempts to breathe even over the rumble of the various apparatus. "Hatton" was printed in magic marker on the left breast of his Stonybrook fireman's coat.

"What do you want to do?" Crowley asked her captain who had walked up to her.

Jack Debarge shook his head after bending down to get a closer look. "I'll get a backboard. Keep the pressure on the wound."

"No pulse," Crowley shouted. "Starting CPR."

"Don't," Debarge said. "Nothing we can do."

"But…"

"Get a blanket," Debarge shouted to another paramedic, pulling Crowley to her feet.

Debarge threw the blanket over Hatton's now still body.

The media helicopters were showing long overhead views of the North Parking Lot and its blackened "cavity" in the middle of the lot, a car fully involved with fire, the pumper still in position, and bodies scattered around the perimeter of the blast zone.

"I'm going up there," an enraged Greco said heading for the door.

Larabee cut him off. "I got it. My men," he said, bolting past Greco who stepped outside MC2. Black smoke was visible above the school. Greco knew that most run-of-the-mill school shooters if there is such a thing, lost their desires or drives to kill fairly quickly. A political terrorist group would have much more motivation to sustain the terror as long as possible.

Greco took a couple of deep breaths and went back inside.

Larabee's fury grew into a rage in the North Parking Lot where the sight of two dead state police officers left him clenching and unclenching his fists as he walked from body to body, pausing to pay a few seconds of respect at each corpse.

He ordered that blankets be brought to the parking lot to cover the bodies. While he waited, the state police lieutenant noticed part of a license plate propped against the curb and went over to get it. The four remaining digits on the Pennsylvania plate were GT62.

Larabee recited the number to the command center. He took out his cell phone and began taking photos of any plates, or fragments of plates, he could find in the vicinity of the burned out cars. He began relaying them to Burke who typed the numbers into the statewide database.

"You need to get out of the vicinity, Frank," Greco called over the radio. "Suppose another car goes off."

"OK," Larabee responded as he kept moving through the rows of cars taking pictures of license plates.

Inside MC2, a call from inside the school to 911 had been routed to the command post and was now on speaker. Everyone paused as Rachael Megay told 911that gunshots were coming from "right next door."

"We have people on the way, Rachael. Just sit tight."

"We can't wait. We're going to die. Do something."

The sounds of popping sounds came distinctly through Rachael's phone.

"Are you out of sight?"

No answer.

"Are you out of sight, hon?"

"Yes, yes. We are out of sight."

"Is your teacher there?"

"Yes."

"OK. Do what you are told."

Muffled shouts came out of the speaker.

"People are being killed next-door. When are...."

A loud bang interrupted the call. Multiple screams. Crying. Silence

"Hello? Are you still there? Rachael?" the dispatcher said after a few seconds.

"I'm here," Rachael reported.

Sounds of people moving around and voices came over the call.

"Rachael?" the dispatcher called several times before the phone was finally picked up.

"It's over—for now," Rachael growled. "People are probably dead next-door. Thanks for your help."

"Rachael, we're getting..."

The call ended.

"Where was that?" Greco inquired.

"Room 522."

A sob escaped Tess Bennington who had been standing in a corner.

17

Before the explosion that killed the first responders in the parking lot, Mike Zarlapski and his class had reached a relative state of calm. Zarlapski had sent a quick text to his wife: "safe for now. everything OK. still in the building with my class. don't worry. Love." He deleted "for now" before sending.

Then, he did a check on his 4News app. It took an eternity to load, but, finally, Zarlapski saw: BREAKING NEWS, "Shooting at High School" in red letters with black outlines. The first seven stories underneath had to do with Vista View, but Zarlapski could not open any.

He noticed that the battery level of his phone was under thirty percent, and his charger was out in the car. He quickly flicked away all his open apps to conserve energy.

The ten remaining students in the classroom were composed. Regina had her head up and was looking around the room.

Zarlapski signaled for attention.

"Listen up. I'm sure you are all anxious and scared. Me too. But we're safe, and the police have the situation under control. It's just a matter of time until they get to us," Zarlapski said in a stage whisper.

"Steve and Matt are downstairs with Miss Snider. Isaiah is there, too. They were able to get his medicine. They are going to stay in The Dungeon and help with the classes down there."

"How's Isaiah?" Kelly asked.

"Stable," Zarlapski said, too quickly.

John Pagliano, still guarding the door, pumped his fist. Kelly let out a sigh of relief.

Rachael, however, was looking at Zarlapski with an almost accusatory look on her face. Did she know?

Rachael was relatively new to the Valley, moving in from Kentucky just before tenth grade began. Innate shyness and a slightly alien twang to her speech did not help her assimilation. This year she had become more active in co-curricular: girls tennis, part in the play, writer's club. That had gained her a wider circle of acquaintances and a couple of friends, like Regina, another outsider.

AP English was intimidating to her at first, but it did not take long for Rachael to impress with her writing. Rachael also went out of her way to take on tasks in group work which earned the respect of the solid citizens of the class.

Zarlapski had noticed that she had an edge to her lately, though. On a couple of occasions, there was a caustic bite to some of her comments. That was new.

The only person who did not get along with Rachael in class was Carey Ackerman, who always seemed to have something snide to say to her or would roll his eyes when Rachael was making a point. But Carey was that way about a lot of people, and his behavior toward Rachael ironically endeared her to the people who despised Carey.

Early in the year, Rachael and Carey had been in the same workgroup with three other people and Carey's comments on the GoogleDoc they were producing might have qualified as bullying: "that is the dumbest comment I ever read ," "do you ever get tired of being a brownnoser?" "no wonder boys hate you." Zarlapski angrily lectured Ackerman and made sure that he never worked with Rachael again. He had also passed Ackerman's comments on to guidance and administration. Rachael shrugged off the whole episode, but Zarlapski got the impression that she was hiding something.

He asked around among the teaching staff if anyone knew of any problems between Rachael Megay and Carey Ackerman. Megan Speers, a health teacher, related a story about an incident in the caf last year when Carey had sat down uninvited at Rachael's table, which she was sharing with two other girls, and put on a show for his friends a few tables away. He mimicked the way the girls were eating, pantomimed conversation, generally made them very uncomfortable.

Speers knew about the incident because Rachael had come to her class after lunch upset about something. Rachael wouldn't talk but her friends had, and Carey was banned from the caf for two weeks after Speers had a conversation with assistant principal Tom Roth.

"Wish I had known about that," Zarlapski barked to Roth when he had gone to the office to discuss Ackerman's comments to Rachael.

Roth had put his hands up and shrugged.

"Off the record next time?" Zarlapski had urged.

"Got you," the vice principal had said.

As if reading his thoughts, Rachael now approached Zarlapski in 522. "Can I talk to you for a minute?" she said.

They stepped to a "private" corner, and Rachael related Carey's comment to her and went into the background of her association with Ackerman, William Holder et al., including the latter's "Ahmed" moniker and fascination with white supremacists.

"The cop I was talking to a little while ago asked if I knew any Ahmed's in school," Zarlapski said. "Anything else?"

"Yeah, yeah. Some guy named Lutz, I think it was. He is supposed to be this, quote, 'lit psycho' who knows all about bombs."

"Never heard of him. Student here?"

Rachael shrugged.

"Never had the Holder kid, but him I know. Dropped an F-bomb on me in the library. Anything else?"

Rachael shook her head, "I tried to forget all that stuff."

She paused, and her face changed. "Oh my God," she blurted. "Oh my God. Do you think he's after me? Carey knows I'm here. Oh, God."

"They're after all of us," Zarlapski said. Not a very comforting thought. Rachael's hypothesis alarmed him and further convinced him that they needed to relocate.

"Let me call the police and see if I can get an update," He squeezed Rachael's arm.

"We'll protect you Rachael if that's the case. We're all in this together."

Rachael nodded and took a couple of deep breaths while Zarlapski found Greco's number.

"I'm good," she said and walked back to her friends.

It took three tries to get a ring out of Greco's phone, and he didn't pick up anyway. Zarlapski summarized Rachael's info in a voice mail.

He had barely ended the call when Zarlapski and the class heard some faint noises from the hall.

The boys guarding the door moved back a step and tensed up. Those on the floor squirmed a little closer to the wall. Kids tightened their grips on their weapons.

Zarlapski grabbed his bat from the corner and moved behind Kyle Yarborough.

The noises were moving at a quick pace toward 522, but they went past the room and came to a stop at the end of the hall.

Everyone seemed to be in control of their emotions, although Meredith Clancy was biting her lip, a tear running down her left cheek.

A voice and an excited giggle broke the silent standoff. Zarlapski exchanged glances with the guards at the door and made sure everyone else in the room saw him with his fingers on his lips.

What were they doing?

Then a boom shook the room. Lauren's scream must have been audible in the hall before Cassie could put her hand over Lauren's mouth. Zarlapski urgently signaled for quiet; fear-filled eyes turned to him.

Another explosion. Less violent, but not less scary. Lauren's bladder let go as she put her head on Cassie's shoulder and sobbed.

The voices in the hall couldn't contain their glee at whatever they were watching. Someone clapped a couple of times.

Zarlapski heard the door to his classroom's left, room 523, open. Someone shouted, "Hey" followed a few seconds later by a couple of loud popping sounds, a scream of pain, footsteps running past the room, a door slamming, the sound of the door to 522 being rattled, cursing, two more pops, breaking glass, screams from the classroom next door, more pops, several in rapid succession, more screaming.

Many of the students in Zarlapski's room were cringing in fear, hugging the floor or each other. A couple of more bladders went.

Kyle Yarborough and John Pagliano were flattened against the closets on either side of the classroom door nervously maintaining their vigils.

Room 523 needed help, but Zarlapski would not risk his students' lives. They were not commandos. Selfish or prudent?

Could bullets come through the wall? They seemed thin enough.

"Get on the floor. Lay on the floor," he ordered those still standing.

That was when, calmly, Rachael called 911. Miraculously, the call was answered right away.

"Rachael Megay. We're in room 522, and somebody is shooting right next door. You have to get us out of here. Now."

She listened for a second.

"We can't wait. We're going to die. Do something," she said, her voice rising more in exasperation than fear drawing the attention of others in the room even as ominous sounds from the ongoing havoc next door continued.

The conversation went on like that; Rachael expressing the desperation of their situation, the 911 operator trying to calm her down and reassure her.

"Really?" Rachael said at one point before holding her phone in the air for a few seconds. "Hear that? Doesn't sound like everything being OK to me. You need to get guns up here, now."

On the floor, Zarlapski's students were unsuccessfully trying to help each other stay quiet.

From next door, there was shouting and crying and the occasional shot. Things crashed against the common wall separating the two classrooms.

"People are being killed next door," Zarlapski heard Rachael plead.

Running in the hallway, another shot; ceramic tiles breaking and shattering on the floor immediately outside Zarlapski's classroom. The boys closest to the hall instinctively covered their heads. Everyone else froze in place.

Then, there were no more sounds in the hall. There were noises coming from 523, though.

"Hello? Are you still there? Rachael?"

In the chaos, Rachael's phone had somehow been switched to speaker. She sat up calmly, switched modes and put the phone to her ear.

"It's over for now," Rachael said into the phone. "People are probably dead next door. Thanks for your help."

She defiantly punched the end button and gave the phone the finger.

The teens in the room sat immobile for a time. Listening. Staring. Silent. John Pagliano got up first, and then other students rose shakily off the floor.

Kelly got the paper towels, rolled them thickly around her right hand, and wordlessly began sopping up the small puddles and wet streaks on the floor. Nicole and Meredith helped.

Pagliano ran to the latrine.

The third floor of the 500 wing was now as quiet as a typical Tuesday school day in early spring.

18

Under the direction of Green Hill's Greg Hawthorne, personnel had fanned out to keep concerned parents from rushing the school and or command post. Also to keep everyone else, especially the media, off the school property and at a safe distance. The crowd was growing, so two officers had been assigned to the bus staging area.

On the reservoir side, Hawthorne assigned only one officer. It would be practically impossible for anyone to come in that way. Just in case, though, a couple of fire police were tasked to help the officer. John Mann had also sent a sharpshooter to the press box atop the home side of the stadium.

Each of the ten classrooms occupying the second and third floors had two slits. White vertical slats blocked the views in most windows. A red 522 hung in one of the windows on the top floor. Mann had called it in.

All police were instructed about students exiting the building.

"Make them put their hands up; pat them down and get them over to the buses. Have them sign their names and a parent phone number," Greg Hawthorne had instructed. "Bus drivers will have paper."

Media members were constantly clamoring for more news and complaining about access to official information while interviewing as many parents as possible. Mothers and fathers pleaded with police, especially the local area cops they recognized. Some were tearful; some were angry. All were afraid.

One mother of two boys, a junior and a senior, collapsed at the feet of an officer on the perimeter as she tearfully begged the trooper to let her find her sons. The obese fifty-year-old crumpled in mid-sentence, dropping to the ground before the cop could react to break her fall.

While that was going on, a red-faced citizen named Jerry Mamo confronted a couple of officers about thirty yards farther up the perimeter line.

"What are you guys doing here? Get into the school. You guys have any balls? I'll go myself," he yelled before trying to shove aside a Darby cop who took him to the ground. A SIG Sauer P226 pistol fell onto the grass.

Three officers in the area drew on him.

"Let's go, Jerry. Backseat," Greg Hawthorne commanded. "Stepped in it again, didn't you?"

Councilman Petit continued to try and reassure his neighbors and constituents.

"The police are doing everything they can," he must have said fifty times, in the same voice that was often the calming influence at rancorous borough meetings. He had to work at submerging his anxiety as he gave hugs or shook hands or squeezed shoulders.

A woman Petit did not know stepped out of the crowd and grabbed Petit's elbow

"Your kids out?" she asked bluntly.

"One is. Macy's over there," he said indicating the buses across the street.

"Can I go over and check if mine is there?"

Petit hesitated. He did not want to start a stampede of parents.

"I'm sorry. We have to wait for the police."

The woman bit her lip and fought back tears.

Petit walked on. He gave a few more hugs and shook some hands before hurrying back to the command center.

The mayor of Pennsville, Ray Buffkin, also was walking the perimeter.

Buffkin had been taking his dog for a walk when several emergency vehicles had whizzed by him. The defiantly proud non-owner of a cell phone, Buffkin had to wait to get home before calling Barry Greco who did not pick up. Buffkin saw he had a message and pushed play to hear Tim Petit telling him that Green Hill police were responding on Pennsville territory.

"That little prick," Buffkin fumed.

He tried Greco again and then started walking to the school, arriving minutes before the fatal explosion in the North Parking Lot.

"What's going on boys?" Buffkin said to the group of old-timers who ate together every Wednesday at the Pennsville Diner. Buffkin sometimes joined them.

"You tell us, Ray," said Dieter Dieckman. "If you know."

"Of course I know, Dieter. Just can't talk about it. You know."

"Say the word Ray, and we'll go home and get our guns. End this thing in ten minutes," boasted Dieckman.

"Who is that guy?" a Channel 4 reporter asked a local newspaper reporter.

"Ray Buffkin, the illustrious mayor of Pennsville."

"Mr. Mayor, Mr. Mayor. Do you have any comments?" the reporter called waving her microphone in the air.

Buffkin strode over to her, flattening his hair. Several other reporters rushed over, and now Buffkin was holding a press conference. At the stations, graphics assistants scrambled onto Google to get his name correct. Boom mics formed an arch over Buffkin's head.

"Do you know of any fatalities inside?" the reporter began.

"Well, I gather there must be dozens," Buffkin stated.

"Dozens?" she said, taken aback. "Did you get that from the police?"

"Well it stands to reason, doesn't it?" Buffkin replied.

"So you don't know for sure?" the reporter asked as she took notes, adding "IDIOT" in the margin.

"How many shooters are there?" chimed in another reporter.

"Well, I would say given the size that building that there has to be three or four otherwise we would be in there by now."

"Are you saying police have not gone into the building yet?" said a reporter for Channel 35 On the Spot News.

Buffkin's face had popped up almost simultaneously on the four newsfeeds being monitored in the command center.

"Shit," said Greco as he turned up the volume on one of the feeds in MC2 and then headed for the door.

"Excuse us," Greco said to the reporters twenty seconds later. "We have a situation."

Once they were several feet away from the reporters, Greco admonished the mayor. "They are going to run with every single thing you say, and you don't know crap, so take my advice and shut up and find something else to do unless you want to look like more of a country bumpkin than you already do."

Buffkin shook himself free and waved at Greco in disdain as he walked away.

Reporters called after Buffkin for some more comment. He waved his hand over his head again as he ambled toward Tim Petit who was pacing outside the command post.

At that point, the explosion in the North Parking Lot erupted followed by secondary explosions.

19

Unable to get through on the jammed up 911 system, a few students had called into TV stations to find out what was going on. Some able to get through, found themselves thrust into the roles of reporters and eyewitnesses.

Nobody knew anything, but hearing students who were fearing for lives had an emotional impact on the audience.

"We heard these loud bangs," a student identified as Tori said on air, "but we kept on working on our lab. Then the principal came on the PA and said we were on lockdown, so we went to the back of the room and sat down."

"Do you feel like you are in any danger now?" asked Channel 13's, Rebecca Williams. Updates crawled from right to left across the screen in front of her navy blue sweater over a white blouse.

"We're all scared," Tori said. "We think we heard an explosion a little bit ago."

"Where are you in the building?" Williams asked.

"Room, um, what room is this? Uh, 203."

"And where is that?"

"Second floor. Kinda between the office and the library."

"Is your teacher there with you?"

"Yes."

"Is it a male or female?"

Williams' stage manager rolled his eyes and gave her a "get moving" sign with his right hand.

"Man," Tori said.

"Did you see the shooter?"

Tori paused before answering. "There *is* a shooter? Are you sure? Oh my God."

Viewers could hear Tori spreading the word to other people in the room.

Williams bit her lip.

"Did you see anything outside of the classroom, Tori?" Williams asked.

"No. Well, just a lot of running and people shouting," Tori said in a shaky voice.

"Wrap it up," Williams' producer was saying in her ear.

"OK, Tori. You stay safe and listen to your teacher," Williams said.

"OK," Tori said doubtfully.

Channel 4 had several calls queued up for morning news anchor Raymond Cove. When he got his cue, Cove brought the ever-increasing viewership up-to-date, reading from the teleprompter with a gravitas not normally displayed on the peppy, news/entertainment hybrid he anchored with Sally Scott every morning.

"This is what we know about the incident at Vista View High School," Cove began. "The school was placed on lockdown about thirty minutes ago when gunshots were reported inside the school; that has not been confirmed officially. What is definite is that there is a fire behind the school. Students were seen fleeing the building and running across a parking lot. And, of course, there has been a massive response from law enforcement and emergency personnel."

A live shot from the Channel 4 helicopter appeared on screen as Cove narrated under a hastily labeled map done by a graphics producer who had Googled the area.

An eyewitness from inside the building was on the line.

"Stephanie," a voice cued him in his ear. "Student. Go."

"On the phone, we have Stephanie who is a student at the school," Cove told his audience as shots from above continued on screen now mixed with video culled from an uplinked camera feed to the station.

"Stephanie is it safe for you to talk?"

"Yes," she said in a hoarse whisper.

"Tell us what you experienced this morning, Stephanie."

"I was in my math class, and Mrs. Nagatura had started to go over homework when there was this yelling in the hall, and she went out to check. Then there was this noise like something fell, and someone screamed, and Mrs. Nagatura ran back in, and she had this horrible look on her face, I'll never forget it," Stephanie said, her voice cracking. "She closed the door and told us to get to the back of the room and sit, and then she gets her phone out of her purse and calls 911 and says that we need help at the high school. Someone's been shot."

Stephanie could not continue at that point, her crying audible over the air.

"Stephanie?"

"Yes?"

"Are you OK, Stephanie?"

"Yes."

"Who was shot?"

"I don't know."

"Do you know how badly they were shot?" Cove mentally kicked himself for the awkward phrasing of the question.

"No"

"Is your teacher there now?"

"Yes."

"Will she talk to us?"

"She's busy right now."

"Doing what?"

"Somebody is having a meltdown. She's trying to calm him down."

"A student is having a meltdown?"

"Yes. Are the police here yet?" Stephanie asked Cove.

"Yes, Stephanie. There are many police on scene. Where are you?"

"Room 109."

"Where is that?"

"Um, we're kinda near the caf."

In his earpiece, Cove's director told him to wrap-up and summarize.

"OK, Stephanie. You stay safe. We want to talk to you again when all this is over."

"OK." Stephanie started sniffling again.

Cove began reading a summary of events, "for those just joining us," that had been loaded into the teleprompter.

The search on social media had begun to pay off for the news outlets. Regular staffers and interns had been scouring various sites, just as law enforcement had. Posts, tweets, video, pictures, and selfies were available from students locked down in the building. Producers ordered albums compiled. Faces were blurred out. Most of the outlets held onto their clips, exercising prudence based on legal advice. The more generic shots from inside, however, were posted online to media web pages.

No one had come across any clues as to who the shooter might be. Media staff kept digging.

As TV vans arrived scrambling reporters scoured locations for stand-ups and grabbed anybody who wanted to talk.

There were "eyewitness" accounts of fires inside the building, a claim that "a police officer friend" said the siege would be over within the hour. Some angrily questioned why the police had not stormed the building. A seventeen-year-old could not stop crying as she clutched her six-week-old baby to her bosom. "My boyfriend is in there," she wailed. "They won't let him come out even though he said he wants to." A fortyish woman was side-by-side with her son, a junior at the high school, who had the good fortune of having an orthodontist appointment at 7:45. They were now standing on the perimeter "hoping and praying for Sean's friends and all the people in the building."

The boy was a particularly desired subject as reporters grilled him about possible perpetrators if he had "heard" anything that might have tipped this off. Were there gangs in the school? Had he ever been bullied? Did he know of other students being bullied? Was he in contact with any friends still in the building?

"What a bunch of morons," he said to his mother as they walked away.

Several people reported seeing a woman wearing a headdress in the area. Others stated it was more than a headdress; she was wearing a burka. A couple of people said the unidentified person had gone into the school "just before this all happened."

A retired line worker for a power company related a rumor that a bunch of foreigners had bought a house on Benedict Street recently and had "paid cash for it."

"Foreigners" became "Arabs" when he spoke with NewsRadio. The number of people living there doubled to ten by the time he talked with CNN.

He never did make it on air live, but most reporters filed away his information. You never know.

20

Mike Zarlapski almost missed the phone buzzing in his pocket as he tried to calm the class after the chaos next door in 523.

"I hear you had a rough time up there," Greco said to Zarlapski. "Everyone OK?"

"In here. I don't know about next door. Chief, you got to get us out of here," Zarlapski said quietly into the phone.

"We have a team trying to get into your end of the building now."

"Well, tell them to hurry," Zarlapski replied. "What was that explosion anyway?"

"A car blew up in the parking lot," the chief told him. "We got some people hurt."

"Wow," Zarlapski said quietly. "All right look, have you ID'ed any of these guys yet?"

"The shooters?"

"Yeah."

"No, we haven't."

"I might be able to help you," Zarlapski told him.

He related his conversation with Bennett about suspecting Carey Ackerman was the person who had shot up the 200 wing, and he summarized what Rachael Megay had revealed about William Holder.

"And I just thought of this," Zarlapski said. "At the very beginning of this whole thing, a teacher put out a message asking if anyone knew where Anthony Russo was. Did you get my voicemail about these guys knowing each other? At least, according to one of my students."

"Thanks," Greco said. "That all helps."

Zarlapski also relayed what Bennett had told him about the administrative wing: the bodies and the shot-up interiors.

"And he said that Ackerman left a backpack in the office, maybe," Zarlapski warned Greco.

"Thanks. I'll notify the team about to go in. Tell your boy not to go on any more excursions. He's lucky he didn't get killed."

"Yeah, well, we're all going to be lucky if we don't get killed," Zarlapski said a little too loudly.

Nicole Bennington heard him and began to cry.

"Hang in there," Greco said. "We'll be there soon, God willing."

Zarlapski sighed and went over to comfort Nicole. "Come on, Nic. It's the pessimist in me. You know, always expect the worst. I need you to be strong."

"Oh, by the way, everybody gets a 9+ on the multiple choice test today."

Nobody even smiled.

"Anybody have any info on what's going on elsewhere?" Zarlapski asked after an awkward pause.

Before anyone could answer, Rachael interjected. "Are we going to help next door?"

"What do you mean?" Zarlapski asked.

"It could be that people might be hurt. Are we going to help or not?"

"Too risky. We were told to stay put."

Rachael and Dan Streeter looked at each other.

"I'll go," Dan offered.

"I'll go, too," Rachael said defiantly.

"Me, too," chimed in Cassie Van Doren

Everyone was looking at the teacher now. Zarlapski shook his head.

"I would hope they would help us if we had been attacked," Kelly Keiter said. "I'll go too."

Zarlapski paused for a couple of seconds and walked toward the door. Another situation with no right answer.

"Anything?" he asked Pagliano.

Pagliano shook his head.

"Who wants us to help?" Zarlapski asked his class.

Everyone except Regina put their hands in the air.

The teacher shrugged his shoulders. "Stay put for a minute."

Zarlapski moved a couple of desks to the side and peeked into the hall. To his left, he saw the body of Vince Stefanowicz crumpled in the fetal position outside of room 523.

"God," Zarlapski gasped.

Stefanowicz moaned. Zarlapski took a deep breath and moved beside his fellow teacher. There was a puddle of blood underneath Stefanowicz.

"You all right, Vince?"

Zarlapski checked up and down the hallway again.

"Do I look all right?"

"Good point."

Stefanowicz moaned again, pulling his knees tighter to his chest.

"Look we got to get out of the hall. You OK if I drag you into my room?"

"Got to be. Or not to be."

"Was that a Hamlet allusion?"

"Damn right."

Always the wise ass. Good sign, I guess, Zarlapski thought.

"OK, here we go."

Zarlapski put his right hand inside Stefanowicz's shirt collar and dragged him to the door of 522 as quickly as he dared. Stefanowicz began moaning in pain and left a blood trail on the floor.

Streeter held the door open. Pagliano and Kyle Yarborough came out to help and dragged the injured teacher to the far wall, near the windows. Streeter closed the door.

The sight of the bleeding Stefanowicz brought a new round of dismay to the AP students in the room. More than half of them had had Stefanowicz in the ninth and tenth-grade gifted humanities which meant they had been exposed to the manic brilliance of Mr. Stefanowicz every day for two consecutive years.

"Is he going to be all right?" Cassie asked aloud to no one in particular.

Rachael grabbed a roll of paper towels and tried to stop the bleeding from a wound through Stefanowicz' rib cage. Kelly joined her.

"Keep the pressure on, Kel," Rachael said, handing wad after wad of paper towels.

Yarborough got a blanket from the closet and tossed it to Cassie. "Put it over him," he commanded.

Zarlapski punched up Greco's number but got no signal this time.

"Anything?" he asked Pagliano who was trying to listen through the door. John shook his head.

Zarlapski took a deep breath, opened the door, and again stepped out into the hall.

In rooms 523 and 524, Stefanowicz and Clark Lewis never closed the divider. Essentially 523 and 524 were always one classroom. Zarlapski opened the door to 523 a crack and looked in. Desks were overturned, pieces of the dropped ceiling had landed on the floor or desks, books were strewn haphazardly all over the place.

"It's Mr. Zarlapski," announced the teacher in a hoarse whisper. "I'm coming in."

"Over here. Over here," a male voice to Zarlapski's right said.

The door clicked shut behind Zarlapski. Against the wall closest to the hallway, dead center in the length of the room, several students were clustered around Mr. Lewis who lay unconscious on his side on the floor.

"Is he breathing?" Zarlapski asked one of the boys kneeling near Lewis.

"Yes."

"Was he shot?"

"I don't think so. He fell pretty hard. He might have hit his head."

Lewis' skin was pale and cool to the touch. Zarlapski reached behind him and took Stefanowicz's coat off the back of a chair and covered Lewis.

As he did so, Zarlapski felt the vibration of his phone. Greco was calling.

"Mr. Zar…"

"I'm in the room next door now. I have a bleeding teacher over in 522 and here, unconscious teacher and about…" Zarlapski did a quick count. "…about 20-25 students."

"Any other injuries?"

"Hang on, I'm checking."

"Anybody hurt?" Zarlapski asked the group.

Several hands went up.

Eight students had been injured in the melee, but none were life-threatening. One of the most severe injuries appeared to be a long, horizontal gash across a girl's back. Blood was leaking through the tear in her black Vista View long sleeve shirt. Another serious injury was to a girl's eye.

Zarlapski went to the bleeding girl first as he narrated to Greco. A male student was using his sweatshirt as a compress on her back. The girl was crying.

"She OK?" he asked the male.

"I guess."

"Did somebody stab you?" Zarlapski asked the girl after taking a closer look at the wounds.

The girl gave a tearful nod. "I think so."

"Yeah, the little douche bag pulled a knife and started chasing after people," said the boy stemming the blood flow.

"How many attackers were there?" asked Zarlapski.

"Two," said the bleeding girl.

"Did you know them?"

"I think it was that Russo kid. Douche bag was dressed like he was a terrorist."

"Hang on a minute."

Zarlapski asked Greco if he had heard that exchange. The Chief had.

"All right look," Greco said. "I promise you we are doing everything we can do to get there as quickly as possible. We're frustrated, too. I would suggest you move everybody into your room. I'll call you back."

Zarlapski patted the boy holding the sweatshirt to the girl's wound. "Good job. Thanks. Keep doing what you're doing."

The teacher moved to the eye injury.

"You OK?" Zarlapski asked a girl in a blood-spotted yellow dress who was covering the left side of her face in obvious distress.

The girl shook her head. Another student, who had been trying to console her injured friend bit her lip as new tears formed and ran down her cheeks.

Zarlapski gently pulled the hand away and saw that a cut ran across the bridge of the girl's nose and her eyelid. The eye had swollen shut.

"We're working on trying to get out of here," Zarlapski said. "What's your name?"

"Ann-Marie Regan."

"Hang in there Ann-Marie."

Lewis was moaning.

"Are they coming? The police?" asked Margie Sweeney, crawling up to Zarlapski from her position along the wall. The teacher knew Margie from last year's journalism class.

"They're working on it, Margie. You OK?"

"Yep. You?"

"Good question, as usual, Margie. I'll have to think about it."

"What does 'working on it' mean?"

"The police said they will be here shortly," Zarlapski lied.

Margie accepted the clarification and knee-walked back to her position along the wall.

"Stay put. I'll be right back," Zarlapski said to the students. "Stay quiet." He put his fingers to his lips.

The teacher moved toward the door and did his routine.

"It's Zarlapski," he said as he opened the door to 522.

"How is he?" he asked Kelly, who was kneeling beside Stefanowicz.

She shrugged her shoulders.

"I'm good. I'm good," Stefanowicz said. "What about my room?"

"Couple of minor injuries. We're going to bring everyone over here," Zarlapski told him.

"What about Clark?"

"Unconscious. Kids said he hit his head."

Zarlapski stood up. "Let's clear some space back there," he said, indicating the area in front of the divider. The largest class he had ever housed was twenty-eight. Now there would be around forty people in the room.

"I'm going to bring them over in a couple of groups. Everybody OK?"

He got some nods in return.

"Give me that blanket," Zarlapski said to Cassie.

"Want help?" Streeter asked.

"You guys stay here and keep everything in order. If I get stuck over there because the shooters come back, have everybody fight like we talked about."

Streeter and Pagliano looked wide-eyed at each other and then nodded.

Back in 523, Zarlapski gave the blanket to the boy closest to Lewis. The injured teacher was quiet and motionless on the floor.

"You guys. Come here," commanded Zarlapski pointing to two boys standing nearby, watching.

"OK, we are very gently going to get this blanket under Mr. Lewis so we can drag him over to my room."

"Come here, Margie," Zarlapski signaled Sweeney. "Kneel at his head.

"We have to keep Mr. Lewis' head in line with his body in case he has a neck injury," Zarlapski explained. "So, we are going real slow. Can you do that?"

"I'll try," Margie said.

"More than try, Margie."

"OK. Got it," she said taking a deep breath.

The two boys knelt in front of Lewis, who was still in a rescue position. Margie and Zarlapski, at his back, put the blanket under Lewis.

"Ready?" Zarlapski asked.

Margie stabilized Lewis' head as she had been taught while Zarlapski and the boys slowly rolled him face up onto the blanket. They paused. Lewis seemed to stir a little bit. His eyelids fluttered but did not open. His breathing sounded normal.

"OK," Z said to the class. "We are going to go over in two groups. Injured first. If you are hurt, come up here by the door. Hurry up."

All the injured students were ambulatory, although Ann-Marie Regan needed help. Eight gathered to the left of the door.

"Wait for me," the teacher said.

Zarlapski checked the hall.

He signaled the group to come on.

The injured made the short walk to 522 with Zarlapski monitoring the hallway.

The rest of the students in 523 had gathered behind Zarlapski, eager to leave the trashed rooms.

Once the first group was safely into 522, Zarlapski turned to the other students.

"Everybody here?" Zarlapski asked. He took a quick scan around the messy room. How is it no one had gotten killed?

Zarlapski checked the hall and then had everyone file past him.

John Pagliano held the door to 522 while the students shuffled into the room. The AP students helped the other kids find places on the floor, dispensing hugs, asking if they were OK.

The last boy in line made it just inside the door before starting to wobble and then collapse. Streeter caught him before he hit the floor. Pagliano moved to help and together they put the boy on the floor under the whiteboard. He regained his senses within a few seconds but was a pasty white.

"Sorry," he muttered to no one in particular. Streeter patted him on the shoulder and went back to the door.

"I'll keep an eye on him," Nikki Bennington said.

Zarlapski, Lewis and the three students were the only ones left in 523.

"OK," Zarlapski said. "We have to kind of crouch or walk on our knees and go real slow while we pull the blanket. Boys, grab a corner at his head. When we start, pull slowly. Margie keep his head steady. OK?"

Zarlapski opened the door but heard a noise at the other end of the hall. After an eternity, everything seemed quiet again.

"On me. Count of 3. 1-2-3," Zarlapski whispered.

They moved at Margie's pace. She was kneeling on one leg at Lewis' head and going forward as best she could. Zarlapski was behind her coaching and scanning the hallway.

The group stopped outside of 522, and Z tapped on the door. "Zarlapski," he said.

Lewis was pulled into the room.

The phone in Z's pocket began to vibrate. Zarlapski didn't even look. First things first.

The crowded room was stifling again with body heat and other unpleasant odors.

Rachael had taken charge and positioned the newcomers at the back of the room. Lewis was placed beside Stefanowicz.

Some of the injured were starting to feel more intense pain as the adrenaline rushes subsided and reality began to set in. The girl with the eye injury was crying in gasping sobs now.

The teacher's phone buzzed again. He did not recognize the number.

"Zarlaspski," he said tersely.

"Mr. Zarlapski, this is Dr. Newhall," said a female voice. "Chief Greco asked me to call and see if I can give you advice on the injuries you have."

Zarlapski knew of Dr. Danielle Newhall. She was part of the Valley Medical Group that Zarlapski saw for primary care, but he had never had an appointment with her.

"Yeah, thanks doc," Zarlapski said. "Where do you want me to start?"

"Anything life-threatening?"

"Maybe," the teacher said as he moved near the "latrine" and turned his back to the students. "I have two teachers who are in the worst shape. One is bleeding from the chest, but is conscious and seems to be holding on. The other is unconscious. Moans once in a while. Kids said he hit his head."

"How is the bleeder's breathing?"

"Seems to be in pain sometimes when he breathes. Sometimes struggles to get a breath. Sounds wheezy."

"Can he talk?"

"Yes."

"Was he shot?"

"I assumed he was. Do you want to talk to him directly?"

"Yeah, that's a good idea."

Zarlapski walked over to Stefanowicz and crouched over him. He explained that Dr. Newhall wanted to talk to him about his injuries and handed the phone to him. Zarlapski made sure the conversation got started and then went over and opened the door into 521. The barricades were still in place.

Z deliberated for a few seconds and then made the decision that some people were going to have to move into 521. Those who were injured or ill could stay put in 522. They totaled eleven, including Regina who was slumping again. Rachael, Cassie, Nikki, and Lauren could remain as "nurses." Guards would have to be placed at both doors.

The teacher's thought process was interrupted by a student from Stefanowicz's class bringing Zarlapski's phone back to him.

He nodded thanks to the kid who looked terrified. Zarlapski patted him on the shoulder.

"Zarlapski"

"He did get shot, but from how he described his wound, it might have missed his lung and exited out his back. We have to guard against shock. Sounds like you are doing that already. What about the unconscious teacher?"

"Same. Still out. Doesn't seem to have any other injuries."

"Breathing?"

"Seems normal except for the occasional moan."

Zarlapski ran down the other injuries sustained in 523. The bottom line was that, under normal circumstances, several of these people needed to be in the hospital as soon as possible. Dr. Newhall assured Zarlapski that the teacher was doing all he could.

A sound from the hall garnered everyone's attention, and the room held its collective breath.

"Got to go," Zarlapski said, ending the call.

The hall door near 525 had clicked shut. And then the classroom door to 523 opened. There was no sound of the door closing.

Pagliano and Streeter flattened their butts against the wall and tensed into semi-crouches on each side of the door, arms flexed in front of them as if in a wrestling match. They had already worked out that Pagliano would go high and Streeter low. The AP students quietly got to their feet—weapons at the ready. The other students looked on in tense confusion.

Zarlapski put his finger to his lips and made sure that everyone saw him. He motioned to Margie to put her hand over Lewis' mouth if he started to moan.

Someone on the outside tried the knob to 522. Twice. Seconds passed, and the squeak of a sneaker or shoe was audible from the hallway.

Zarlapski signaled for quiet again and moved to the open panel in the partition, standing with a leg in each room. Someone tried the knob on 521's door. It was also locked. A few seconds later, the hallway door squeaked open and close, the latch clicking into the strike on the other door.

Decoy? Did they want us to think they had left? Was that a reconnaissance mission? Zarlapski continued to strain to hear.

21

Baby Doll—it's 9:15. we should be in Mod 2. i think. i hate this. It's kind of quiet now. r u in school i didnt see u in the caf. i hope your not. this sucks weve been sneaking looks at the news on peoples phones. mancuso keeps yelling at us to put them away. i hate him. You think he'd be a ltlle more sensitive. Were all scared and cranky. I saw some stuff on mary's from outside. wierd its like im here but im not here u no. fire engines and cop cars and helicopters. i dont have my phone or Id text. Not "responsible enough." i don't even know if youll get this email. The computers here suck but this guy tommy i was telling you about brought in his own laptop. He's lettin me use it. I think hes trying to get in good with me. i want to go home. i forgot to eat breakfast. (i know what ur thinking. Not true). im gonna go canibull. mancuso keeps telling us it won't be long but hes lying. He dont know shit. saw him sneak a couple of pretzels out of drawer. pig. think he'd share. its cold on this floor and i got to go pretty bad. My head starting to hurt. Everybodies saying that. i hope we don't die.some people are saying they herd kids were killed. maybe a teacher. I can believe it. I think we heard gunshots a while ago. im not scared now. Just tired. I wish i had an emoticon that was a pile of poop :(Audrey

22

"I need a second, Chief," Officer Tara Scofield said over the controlled chaos in MC2, the command center.

"Quickly," he said without taking his eyes off the monitor.

She handed him a note: "Shooter talking to Channel 8."

Scofield held up her phone. "I have them on the line now."

Chief turned to Rita Salvatore. "Tell Detective Donahue and ask her to step inside."

Tara spoke into the phone. "Stay on the line, Phil. I don't care, Phil. Stay on the fucking phone."

Salvatore quickly located Donahue giving instructions to a group of newly arrived detectives. She showed Donahue the note. "Greco needs to see you right now."

Donahue held up a finger and made a radio call to Detectives Harrison Knoll and Will Clancy, calling them to the command center.

Donahue and Scofield went to a relatively isolated corner of the Command Post.

"Get them to have the shooter call us directly," Donahue said.

"Tried. Shooter said no."

"Do they have the number?"

"No. Blocked."

"Who's he talking to?"

"One of their reporters. I'm talking to the executive producer, Phil Barlow."

Greco moved closer to the group, but kept his eyes on the monitors, as Knoll and Clancy joined Donahue and Scofield.

Harrison Knoll looked like he stepped out of a 1950's police procedural: black, big shoulders, ill-fitting suit, white shirt, black tie, crewcut. He looked much older than his thirty-five years. Nothing riled Harrison Knoll. He seemed to have a knack for getting perps to talk to him confessionally.

His partner, Will Clancy, was a year younger with a much better fashion sense and a more excitable demeanor. He also had a slavish devotion to his partner Knoll with whom he had worked for five years in the art of negotiating with scumbags.

"I'm going to give you Detective Knoll of the state police," Scofield was telling Barlow on the phone. "I don't care, Phil," Tara was saying into the phone. "And none of this gets used or attributed to 'unnamed sources'. Clear? You can have your scoop later."

"Clear?" Scofield repeated more forcefully.

Knoll took the phone and introduced himself while Clancy produced the standard negotiating checklist from his backpack and began to fill it out as Knoll relayed Barlow's answers.

The male caller electronically distorted his voice. He called Channel 8 shortly after the explosion in the parking lot. He was talking to Melissa Craig, a well-respected veteran reporter. She had asked if this was a terrorist attack and was told: "Don't you know the definition of terrorism?"

Donahue reluctantly excused herself to take a call from a detective at the buses.

"Keep me posted," she said to Clancy

"Ask him where he is," Knoll told Barlow.

"We did. Won't say."

"Name?"

"He said to call him Ahmed."

"How does Ahmed sound? Accent? In control? Emotional? Angry?"

Knoll could hear Barlow relaying the information.

"She said he sounds unemotional, in control. Used 'we' several times. No accent."

Knoll repeated what he was being told for Clancy's benefit.

"Any personal info?"

"Nope."

"Are you sure this is legit?" Knoll asked Barlow. "Not some prankster?"

"Pretty sure."

"*Pretty* sure?"

"Can we make sure, please?"

"How?"

"What's your reporter doing now?"

"Waiting. She's been on hold for five. I guess he's back. She's talking again."

"Well, then, have her tell him you don't believe he's in the building. Prove it."

Knoll was uncomfortable with this whole set-up. He needed to strike up a conversation and gain some trust from Ahmed. This relaying back and forth was not going to work.

"You there, Knoll?"

"Yeah."

"Ahmed said that if you haven't already, you'll find an adult body around the stage area, and he also has a request," Barlow said.

"Go ahead," Knoll said while he wrote, **ADULT VICTIM FOUND IN STAGE AREA,** and handed the note to Scofield. She took the note to Greco.

"He wants the American flag hung upside down from the flagpole in front of the school."

"Why?"

Knoll waited.

Barlow came back on. "This is what he said. Quote: 'That's a distress signal. I would say this country is pretty distressed, don't you think? Especially for white people.' End quote."

"Tell him we need a show of good faith in return. What will he do for us if we hang the flag?"

Knoll recapped the conversation to Clancy. Scofield returned. She had written "CONFIRMED" on the paper Knoll had given her.

Barlow was back on. "He hung up before I got to the good faith idea," Barlow said. "Said he'll call back when the flag is up. He said that the cops shouldn't be walking around in the building, because they have lots of bombs around. He also said to stay out of the 500 wing or hostages will be killed."

23

In the basement, Sue Snider spotted Kellie Frazier sitting alone after Donna Slowick had headed for a group of people deeper in the room. Snider saw a chance to find out what Frazier knew about the shooters and gestured for the girl to come over. Frazier hesitated but got up, glancing nervously in the direction of the bathroom.

Snider called Steve Bennett over for a quick conversation.

Steve nodded and walked over to Matt Bianco.

"Come over here," Snider said, grabbing Kellie's arm and maneuvering behind a stack of boxes.

"We never got to finish our conversation," Snider said genially. "Is there anything else you want to tell me about what's going on?"

Frazier looked around nervously. "I, I don't feel safe here. Do you know that big kid with the beard? I think his name is Crawford."

"What about him?"

"I think he is one of them. One of the shooters."

"Why do you say that?" asked an alarmed Snider.

"I saw him talking to Anthony Russo in the parking lot."

"Kellie, are you saying you're sure Russo is involved?" Snider asked.

She nodded.

"Is he in this room?"

Frazier nodded.

"Where?"

"He was sitting farther up against the wall from where I was."

"Does this Crawford kid have a gun?" Snider asked.

"I don't know."

"Anything else about him?"

"I don't know. He acts like he's waiting for something. Keeps checking his phone but doesn't use it like everybody else is, you know texting or looking for video."

Bennett stepped into the meeting and gestured over her shoulder. Snider nodded.

"OK, Kellie. Steve here is going to walk you back to where you were sitting. You had to help him move some boxes. Got it?"

Kellie Frazier nodded nervously as Steve led her back to where Donna Slowick was glowering impatiently.

"Thanks for helping with the boxes," Steve said to Kellie and walked away. Slowick glared after him.

Snider waited a minute and then walked back to where Matt Bianco and Steve Bennett were waiting.

"Either of you know a kid named Crawford?" Snider asked. "Big kid. Beard."

"Brian Crawford?" Matt Bianco said. "I know what he looks like."

"Good. See him? Don't be obvious."

Bianco scanned the room. "I see him. Red hunting coat over against the wall."

Sue Snider took a couple of steps into the center of the room and made a pretense of checking the contents of a box while she sized Crawford up.

He stood about 5'11", stocky bordering on obese. Wisps of a blond beard sprouted in patches on his round face. His hair was a dirty blond, unkempt, the ends curling up. In addition to the red plaid hunting coat, Crawford was wearing baggy tan pants and work boots. There was a bulge in the right pants pocket.

Snider recapped for the boys what Kellie Frazier had revealed, and they came up with a plan to neutralize him if he did have a gun.

"Right pants pocket, maybe," Snider warned.

Bennett went to enlist one of the Boy Scouts for their mission.

The three boys grabbed boxes and started toward the elevator. As they passed Crawford, the Boy Scout "tripped" and spilled books on

Crawford. Bennett and Bianco pounced on the target immediately and forced his face down on the floor, each pinning an arm.

Students nearby jumped to their feet and moved away.

Bianco went for the right pants pocket with his free hand and extracted a phone, a thick wallet, and an index card. Bianco crudely patted down the rest of Crawford's body.

"You have a gun, pal?" Bianco asked menacingly.

"No." He wheezed.

The index card looked like a phone number but was one digit short.

"What is this?" Bennett asked, holding the card in front of Crawford's face as Snider joined the group.

"Phone number."

"It's missing a number."

"Yeah, I know. Guy was gonna text me the number if he wanted me to call. Can I get up? I can't breathe."

"What guy?" Bennett asked, tightening his grip on Crawford's left arm.

"I don't know his name." Crawford was starting to cry.

"Why did he want to talk to you?" Snider asked, signaling Bennett not to get carried away.

Crawford didn't answer but yelped as Bianco twisted his arm.

"There's a text on the phone," the Boy Scout said. He showed it to Snider, Bennett and then Bianco.

It was sent by "NO ID" and read "6-9." The text was time-stamped fifteen minutes ago.

"Why two numbers?" Snider asked without revealing the numbers.

"The first number will be the place in the order."

Bianco studied the phone and number.

Snider tried Crawford again. "Why did he want to talk to you?"

Crawford shook his head.

"Don't even think of trying that number," Snider ordered Bianco. "Suppose it sets off a bomb?"

"Good thought," Bennett said. "But suppose it disarms a bomb?"

"Not likely and not worth the risk," Snider said.

"Yeah, yeah, I know," Bianco said. "What do you want me to do with his stuff?"

"Give it to me," Snider said.

"What are we going to do with him?" Bennett asked.

"Tie him up. Get the Boy Scouts to help you. Put him in a corner somewhere. We'll let the police deal with him," Snider said.

"Pretty cowardly for a Nazi," Bennett said.

"What do you mean?" Bianco asked.

"You didn't see the swastika tattoo on his wrist?"

Kellie Frazier came up to Snider. "I want to stay with you," Frazier said, glancing over her shoulder.

"Not a problem. Does Donna have a weapon?" Snider asked Frazier.

"I don't think so," Kellie said alarmed.

"Is she talking with the shooters?"

"I don't think so."

"We'll keep an eye on her," she said, motioning to Donna Slowick who was now sitting alone against the wall, arms wrapped around her legs.

24

Alpha team studied floor plans behind the Mine Resistant Ambush Protected vehicle, parked in the front lot. Bobby Matheson, the Alpha team leader, had been examining the office area with binoculars. He saw broken glass, overturned furniture, a body draped over a desk but no sign of movement.

Below the office were the visitors' doors. On the wall was a buzzer with a built-in camera and audio link that fed to the receptionist's desk.

Behind the doors were two sets of stairs. To get to the office, one climbed the steps to another set of doors, went through the doors and turned right into the administration suite. Those steps also continued up to the 300 wing of the building where many of the special ed teachers were located. There were also bathrooms, a storage closet for the janitors, elevators, and a locked door that led to a storage loft and the roof in the 300 wing. The descending stairs led down into the 100 wing.

"What do you think?" Matheson asked Andy Fitzgerald, a Franklintown cop.

"If we can't get in through the doors, maybe we can squeeze somebody through those windows if we can get up there."

Matheson was about to call the rest of his five-man team over when the explosion went off in the North Parking Lot. The Alpha team couldn't see much from its vantage point. Mann ordered all the teams to stand-by at their positions.

A couple of minutes later, another explosion had everyone ducking. Mann warned all teams to be on the alert for any activity in case the blast had been a diversion.

The Alpha team covered emergency personnel headed up the driveway and then received the go-ahead to proceed with their mission. Charlie team, however, was re-tasked to the North Parking Lot.

Matheson gathered his team around him.

"We're going in through this door; it opens outward," Matheson said, pointing to the floor plan he had been given in MC2.

"Down the steps, past the bathrooms, 108 is the third classroom on the left. Two people per room, three for immediate threats, he reminded them."

The team performed a jump check to make sure that all their gear was properly secured and then lined up behind Fitzgerald and Matheson.

The door that Alpha was about to enter opened a crack.

Fitzgerald yelled, "Door." and the men ducked for cover.

A white Philadelphia Phillies rally towel appeared through the opening and waved around for a few seconds, and then the door opened wide, and an adult poked his head out.

"Show your hands," Matheson yelled across the driveway.

"Teacher. We're coming out."

He stepped sideways to open the door and students started pouring onto the sidewalk, some running toward the mine-resistant vehicle, some fast-walking, some shuffling in a daze or carried along by their peers. One limping boy trying to run went down in the crowd and took three people to the concrete. Terrified students ran around them. Two of the students who had tripped over the boy with the limp helped get him to his feet, and they rejoined the flow of the pack.

"Damn. Get their hands up and get them over to the command post," Matheson yelled to his men and the three troopers who had been assigned to support Alpha.

"Hands up. Hands up." Fitzgerald yelled as the rest of the men kept their weapons trained on the students. The policeman redirected the flow of kids toward the command center.

"Alpha 1 to command center. We have students exiting the building. Front door."

"10-4. Use caution. Hustle them to the buses," John Mann replied.

Three cops ran toward the students coming out of the building, meeting them in the driveway. Other state troopers stayed in a crouch behind their cars scanning for an ambush.

Matheson and Fitzgerald worked past the flow of the exodus and into the building and stood covering the second-floor landing in case a shooter appeared. The policemen eyeballed the fleeing students and teachers as they crowded up the steps, focused on getting to the door and safety. The two cops noticed bloodstains on the clothes of some of the teens. Several students had facial wounds.

One teacher was covered in blood.

"You OK, sir?" Matheson asked Paul Ric.

Ric shook his head. "Not my blood," he said as he walked up the steps behind his class.

Matheson redirected the stream toward the command post.

"Hands behind your head," he yelled several times as he stood in front of the line.

All students did as they were told and awkwardly ran.

"Hands up. Stay in line. Hustle it up," the Alpha team told the students repeatedly. "If you are injured, step out of line."

Teachers stayed with their classes, spacing themselves along the line of students. Two officers ran beside a class at a time, asking the teachers if everything was OK and then moving back to the next group. Other police and paramedics came hustling up to the group from the command post, and the police team handed over the students and circled back to the door.

The six paramedics helped those who had stepped aside and culled the injured or struggling who had tried to stay with the group. EMT's began impromptu triage. Students with blood on their clothes were pulled from the line and examined. Some had been cut by debris, some had fallen or scraped against something, some had the blood of others on them. Those deemed ambulatory were grouped and walked across the parking lot to the "ER" behind the baseball field. A few of the students needed time to catch their breaths. Inhalers were produced for those who needed them.

The last person to climb the steps was Bryan Mueller, the math teacher in 111. Fitzgerald followed him out. The evacuation had taken about three minutes.

"Everybody out?" Fitzgerald asked Mueller as the rest of the Alpha members listened.

"Except for the dead," Mueller said flatly.

"How many?"

"Two teachers, five students that I know of."

Fitzgerald and Matheson exchanged glances.

"You OK?" Matheson asked

"Seen it before. Iraq. Still…" Mueller said, pausing for a few seconds. "Go ahead."

"How many shooters?" Fitzgerald asked

"One that I saw."

"No sign of him now?"

"Not since about thirty minutes ago."

"Did you know him?"

Mueller shook his head. "Had a headdress and mask; long jacket; maybe six foot."

The police asked rapid-fire questions and got a decent description of the shooter.

"Gun?"

"Tek 9."

"Did the shooter say anything?"

"No."

"What rooms were you guys in?" Matheson asked.

"All the rooms on this side. The math teachers texted each other, and we decided to go after the explosion. Was that a bomb?" Mueller asked.

"We don't know. Came from the parking lot up there," Matheson said, pointing at the north lot.

"So all the math teachers are out?" Fitzgerald continued.

"The ones in this wing," Mueller said. "And one Spanish class."

"Where are the bodies?"

"Uh. Rob Czarnecki is in 108. He's a teacher. Was a teacher. Another teacher is in 112, Megan Speers; she's dead. The students are in 108 also. They were shot in the hallway. We dragged the bodies in before we ran. I didn't recognize any of them," Mueller said, his voice wavering at the end.

"Anything else you can tell us, Bryan?" Matheson asked after a brief pause

"Sorry. We were sitting tight most of the time."

"Thanks. Officer Fitzgerald here will help get you over to the command post."

Fitzgerald and Mueller trotted toward the South Parking Lot where the teacher was handed off to another policeman for the rest of the escort.

Matheson related to the command center what Mueller had told him. Mann acknowledged and told him to enter the building as planned.

Matheson signaled his men with a twirling motion and made sure everyone was ready to go. They all nodded.

The team members went through the same doors the evacuees had used and headed down the steps toward the classrooms that had just been vacated. At the bottom of the steps, there were three choices: straight ahead to the classrooms, to the left steps, next to the elevator, which led to the auditorium lobby, to the right to a hallway with classrooms on either side, located directly under the office.

The corridors were dark except for emergency lights at each end and light from a small opaque window in the faculty room at the very end of the hall.

Matheson indicated straight ahead with a chopping motion of his right hand.

With practiced precision, the men began a room by room search starting with the side-by-side lavatories on the left. Matheson and Vito Abbonizio took the boys room, Steve Brown and Sean Davidoff the girls. Fitzgerald returned to cover the hall.

The lavatory doors were closed. The four officers took out their bright tactical flashlights and carried them in their non-dominant hands, outside of the body frame and above head high. They held their handguns in their dominant hands. The officers moved the light at random angles.

The entrance was a dangerous funnel to enter. A shooter had a natural aiming zone and would be able to shoot in the direction of the police even if blinded by the light.

Outside the boy's door, Abbonizio got into a crouch, gun in his right hand, flashlight in his left. Matheson stood behind him ready to open the door. Brown and Davidoff were doing the same routine at the girls' bathroom.

A scream came from the girls' room, and Abbonizio and Matheson pivoted into the hall.

A male voice pleaded, "Don't shoot. Don't shoot," from inside the girls' lav. Brown had surprised one male student and two female students in the bathroom. The flashlight revealed one of the girls sitting on the floor with her back against the wall ashen and unresponsive, blood matting her blonde hair and trickling onto her gray Vista View field hockey sweatshirt.

The other female, an African-American girl in a dark sweater and jeans, was also seated on the floor, holding the victim's left hand while the male was trying to stem the flow of blood from the blond girl's head wound using some tampons from the pried-open dispenser on the wall.

Brown checked the stalls. Davidoff began assessing the injured teen. Abbonizio stayed at the doorway eyeballing the other students while Matheson and Fitzgerald covered the hall.

"What's your name?" Brown asked the boy whose Pittsburgh Steelers black tee shirt and blue jeans had blood stains.

"Jason."

"You did good here, Jason," Brown said as he and Davidoff prepared to carry the injured girl outside. Brown scooped her into his arms while Davidoff stabilized her head and neck.

"I'm Dawn Green," the African-American girl said, unprompted.

"Are you hurt?" Matheson said eyeing the red streaks on Dawn.

"No. This is Catherine's blood."

"Are you OK?" Matheson said turning toward Jason.

"Yes," he said absently. He was shaking.

"OK. We'll take you two outside. Stay with me."

Fitzgerald waited in the hall while Abbonizio went through the girl's lav one more time.

"Why didn't they leave when everybody else came out?" Fitzgerald asked Brown, who shrugged his shoulders.

"I don't know. Maybe they were too afraid to move."

After a minute, Matheson sent Abbonizio and Fitzgerald into the boys' room while Brown and Davidoff prepared to search classroom 107.

As soon as Abbonizio turned the corner around the inner wall of the lav his foot slid. He went into a crouch and played his flashlight around the room. Two bodies were on the bloody tile floor. He quickly moved past them as Fitzgerald came around the corner. Abbonizio used his foot to nudge open the four stall doors while Fitzgerald covered him.

"Clear," Abbonizio said quietly and moved to check the bodies.

"Careful. Booby-traps," Fitzgerald reminded his partner.

Both bodies were facedown on the floor. The blonde haired boy had curled into the fetal position. The black student had left the bloody handprint on the white porcelain sink. He, too, was deceased; part of his skull lay in the corner of the room.

The two officers shook their heads at each other.

Farther down the hall the rest of Alpha team was still checking classroom by classroom.

Room 107 had been turned into a fortress with desks piled near the door. Books and other belongings lined the walls where students had been seated.

Outside of room 108, several blood trails led from the hall into the classroom. Three distinct, bloody handprints testified to the desperate crawl the victim had made into the messy room. Bloody paper towels and shirts littered the floor. Desks were shoved away from the congealing blood pool that made the vinyl tile floor slippery. Czarnecki's body was lying neatly in the corner, arms crossed on the chest. A folded, bloody towel covered his face. It was evident that Czarnecki had taken a bullet or two to the gut.

Five dead students, two females and three males, had been dragged to the front corner of the room. Fitzgerald and Abbonizio had to take only cursory looks to confirm they had expired.

Alpha moved methodically down the hallway.

Rooms 109, 110, and 111 had been spared bloodshed. Remnants of a normal day: worksheets, math tests, calculators, textbooks, laptops, mingled with feeble barricades and personal belongings strewn haphazardly around the classroom.

Room 112 was an exception. Desks were neatly arranged in groupings of four to facilitate student collaboration. An article entitled "Depression: an incurable disease?" had been placed on each desk awaiting the second-period class. Posters on various health topics hung neatly on every wall except for the back wall which supported a full-length bulletin board that announced achievements of various Vista View students through "Shout Outs." or newspaper clippings or selfies that had been printed in hard copy.

The setting was spoiled by a blood splatter on the back wall behind the teacher desk and the body of Megan Speers crumpled in the corner clutching a crucifix from a now broken necklace. It looked like the young teacher had been shot in the back of the head at close range, and if Matheson had to guess, he would have said she was on her knees at the time of her execution.

25

Barry Greco was calmly juggling several events at once. In the last several minutes, bombs had gone off in the North Parking Lot, detectives were in the midst of interviews, students had been evacuated from the building, three teams were hunting in the building and team Bravo had found students hiding in a shed, police were on the way to a suspect's home, a shooter was talking indirectly to negotiators.

"What do you think?" Greco asked about the order to hang a flag upside down.

"It'll buy us some time," Harrison Knoll said.

"The media will have questions," John Mann worried.

"Why don't we tell the media what's going on? I'll let Channel 8 break the story and then brief the rest of the media," said Tara Scofield. "I'll put it out on social media. We'll sell it that we're protecting the hostages at all costs."

Greco and Mann looked at each other. The latter shrugged.

"OK. Send someone out in body armor to fly the flag. Make sure he's covered."

"John," Greco said as he walked over to the monitors at the command table. "Tell your teams to be careful about bombs, and, for now, keep everybody out of the 500 wing."

Tara punched in Barlow's number, "We're going to do the flag thing. You guys get it first but don't report it until it's happening.

Then I'll send it to everybody else. Bare minimum, Phil. Don't reveal too much."

"Any luck on linking Ahmed to this Will Holder guy?" Greco asked Scofield.

"Nothing yet. Still digging."

"What is that?" Greco asked, pointing to an indistinct image moving in the upper right corner of the feed from MC2's elevated camera.

"Don't know," said John Mann after several seconds of staring at the image. "Let me zoom in."

Mann sat at the keyboard and repositioned the camera, moving in as close as he could. Whatever it was, it appeared to be over the North Parking Lot, the scudding white and gray clouds made it hard to see the white object distinctly.

As the two men leaned in toward the screen, the hazy image suddenly rose out of the camera's view.

"Was that a drone?" Greco asked.

"A drone? Some moron is flying a drone over the high school. Now?" said Rita Salvatore who had joined the group.

"I'll replay it, see if I can get a good screen grab," Salvatore stated.

"You know Chief, I've been wondering about those booby-traps," Mann said, steely blue eyes still on the monitor.

"What do you mean?"

"Well, how come those bombs go off when our guys are in close proximity?"

"I don't know. I figured they were hitting trip wires or having bad luck."

"What if the bad guys are watching our movements in and out of the building?"

"With a drone?"

"And what if they've tapped into the security cameras somehow?"

"Is that possible?"

"Just thinking out loud."

Greco stared at the monitor for a few seconds.

"That's pretty sophisticated stuff."

"Well, if these guys are real terrorists…"

"Yeah, this certainly isn't a spur of the moment deal, but it's looking like it's kids. Unless they were recruited somehow," Greco mused.

Greg Hawthorne came through the door. "The guys are arriving at Bleaker Street."

"Thanks," Greco said. "Keep me posted. How close do you have to be to fly one of those drones?"

"The controllable range for cheaper ones, about three hundred yards. But, if you know what you are doing and have money to spend on equipment, you could go for miles," Salvatore responded.

"How do you know?" Greco queried.

"I own two. You thinking someone is taking video or pictures? I'm also thinking somebody close by has to be controlling it," said Salvatore.

"The operator has to have an unobstructed path from controller to drone, but you can program it to return to base, so to speak, or even have a flight system that will take it home automatically if the connection is lost."

Larabee, flushed with anger, came into MC2 and stood scanning the monitors.

"Salvatore," Larabee called. "Here's my phone. I took pictures of license plates. Upload them. Let's get them checked out ASAP."

"Like I was saying," Salvatore said after she had walked the phone over to a technician, "somebody close by might be controlling it. What do you think?"

"Maybe," said Greco.

Larabee asked what they were talking about.

"We should shoot the bastard down," he pronounced when he was told.

"Can we?" Greco asked

"Screw it. We can apologize later."

"Yeah, maybe. But not just yet. Ask your guys if they've seen that drone, if that's what it is. If there's someone on the outside controlling that thing, maybe we can find him."

Larabee rolled his eyes but made a radio calls to the state police who were outside of the building.

"Looks like we have people on the roof," Mann interrupted.

"Where?" Larabee asked.

Mann pointed to Monitor 3. "Approaching the 300 wing."

"Delta 1 to Command Post," came Tom Morgan's voice over the radio. "We have several of the cafeteria workers. We are taking them out of the building now."

"I'll check with the media about the drones," Salvatore said while Greco was talking to Morgan. "Make sure it's not one of theirs."

"Probably belongs to some neighborhood asshole," Larabee opined.

Greco called Bravo One, "We have kids on the roof above your twenty."

There was a pause in the communications.

"10-4. We are evacuating students from this area now. We'll check it out in a minute."

"Rita, get Charlie to send a couple of people to the arts area to help Bravo," Greco ordered.

"Got it."

After completing her radio call, Salvatore walked over to Tara Scofield.

"Let's be careful what we say," said Rita. "If we ask if anyone is using a drone, we might set off a drone-chase by the media, if it isn't one of them in the first place."

"How about we just put out a general warning not to use drones?" suggested Scofield.

"Makes it sound like we know who was flying the drone," agreed Rita.

Salvatore and Scofield started making calls and sending texts to news producers and posting on the designated Twitter account that was sending out "Official Police Updates."

Salvatore got an update on what was coming out on social media.

"Videos are on the Internet, but no drone footage," she reported to Greco and Larabee.

"Couple of my guys noticed the drone about a half-hour ago," Larabee said after checking with his men. "Figured it was the media or us. Mostly hung over the back end of the parking lot. They haven't seen it for awhile."

"Tell them to let us know as soon as they see it again," Greco said not taking his eyes off the monitors.

"Already did."

"Great," Greco said. "If it shows up again we follow it. I'll start a couple of cars back toward this development," he said, pointing on a map tacked to the wall. "Maybe we'll get lucky and spot the thing."

"And if we don't, we'll use it for target practice," Larabee said.

Mann reminded Greco to call Zarlapski. Greco nodded as he finally connected with the teacher.

"I don't know if you want to send uniforms to search for the drone," Salvatore said, coming up behind John Mann. "Have anybody who doesn't look like a cop?"

Mann paused for a few seconds. "Maybe. Let me think about it."

"What were you saying about tapping into the security cameras a minute ago?" Greco asked Mann.

"I don't know, it just seems mighty fortuitous that the bombs went off at the exact time men were in the area."

"Can they tap into the cameras?"

"This is a wireless feed. Don't know if it is encrypted. Anyone you can ask?"

"I wish I could. Haven't been able to get hold of the SRO. Any way we can block the feed?"

"Not sure. I have been trying to get access. Hell, for all we know these guys might have set up their cameras."

Mann though for a moment. "I'm going to tell my guys in the building to take out any cameras they see."

"Hate to see the repair bill when this is all over," Larabee said.

"When this is all over, they're going to plow it under to make a memorial park and start over someplace else," Mann said ruefully.

26

Steve Bennett, Matt Bianco, and Miss Snider huddled in the storage room and discussed their next steps.

"So you think that Ackerman kid might be involved in all this? You told Mr. Z?" Snider asked.

"Yeah, he knows," Bennett told her.

"Think the backpack had a bomb in it?"

"That's what I'm thinking," Bennett said. "That's why I didn't hang in the office too long."

Bianco noted, "Could have been what we heard."

"I don't know. I thought the sounds came from outside."

Their phones vibrated at almost the same time.

The boys reached into their pockets and checked. They had both gotten the same text from Zarlapski, asking if they were still OK.

"He sent that ten minutes ago," said Bennett, noting the time stamp.

Snider's phone vibrated. She saw the same text on her phone.

"I'll answer," said the teacher.

"In storage room still. Things cool," she typed. "You?"

"How about if Matt and I see if we can get out through the front of the building?" Steve said. "If we can, we'll get everybody out that way."

"I don't know, Steve. After what you told me that doesn't sound too safe. Maybe we just better wait here."

"Yeah, and what if those guys come back."

The conversation was interrupted when a couple of girls came up to Snider.

They glanced at Bennett and Bianco before turning to the teacher.

"We have to pee," said one of them.

Snider sighed.

"We'll set something up," said Bianco. He and Steve headed to the far corner on the right, grabbing items that would have utility for a makeshift lavatory.

They stacked up some boxes against a wall and rigged a sheet over the "entrance."

Bianco and Bennett christened two buckets before they left the new lavatory.

"All yours," said Bianco to the girls, tossing them a roll of paper towels.

Snider led the girls to the back corner and waited outside until they were done and then used the facility herself.

Several other students, male and female, were heading Snider's way. She stayed to regulate gender traffic, checking her phone while she waited. No reply from Zarlapski.

While Snider was preoccupied, Bennett and Bianco continued to debate the merits of staying put versus seeking a way out.

"You want your life to depend on these people putting up a fight?" Bennett said as he motioned toward the two classes arranged in the room.

Bianco snorted. "What then?"

"We go up to the second level again."

"Why?"

"Why what"?

"Why not the first floor?"

"Because I already know what it looks like at the office, and I think that they won't come back there."

Bianco finished the thought, "Nobody else to kill."

Bennett nodded. "Exactly."

"But, you said there were still people in the classrooms," Bianco said.

"Yeah. Good point."

"And what if that was a bomb in the backpack. What if that went off while we were up there?"

"Well, then what do you suggest, Matt?"

"We go out through the 100 wing."

"Why?"

"Well, for one thing, we don't have to climb up the elevator shaft," Bianco said, pointing to Bennett's laceration for emphasis. "And, maybe the killers concentrated on Admin because it's Admin."

"What to hell does that mean? Remember Cassie told us that Czarnecki had been shot in Ric's room? Isn't that right near the caf? In the 100 wing?"

"Then maybe they're done down there too. Then what?" Bianco countered.

The two friends were getting exasperated with each other. Their voices had risen a level, and some of the other students heard part of the conversation.

Jill Markos, a junior in Snider's anatomy class, got up and stood across from the boys. Jill, a field hockey player, traveled in the same social circles as Bianco and Bennett. Many of the junior male athletes protected her like a sister, not that she could not stand on her two feet, as she was doing now.

"What are you guys talking about? What about Mr. Czarnecki?" she asked, her eyes hinting fear.

Bianco looked past her and saw the eyes of several students fixed on them, breaths held, trying to hear the conversation.

"You OK?" Matt said in a lowered voice signaling they should turn to the wall.

Jill started to nod, but then shook her head a couple of times. Tears began to well.

"What about Mr. Czarnecki?" Jill repeated.

Bennett and Bianco eyed each other. Bennett shrugged.

"We heard that he had been shot," Bianco told her. "May or may not be true. That's all we know. Swear to God."

Jill wiped away her tears. "I'm supposed to have him this period."

The three sat in silence for a moment.

"Are we just going to sit here? Shouldn't we be trying to… escape?"

"Well, that's what we've been discussing," Bianco said.

"Don't stop on my part. I'm game."

Snider was walking up to them when the sound of boxes filled with books crashing to the floor diverted their attention.

Ms. Knaul had tried to stand. A futile grab at the shelving behind her only served to make matters worse when she tipped a partially filled box of old hardbound math books. When Snider got to her, the box still partially covered Knaul's head, her left cheek pressed against the concrete floor. Knaul was unconscious and pale.

"Did she hit her head on the floor?" Snider asked a girl closest to the scene.

"I don't know. She got up and then kind of fainted or something. I didn't see her hit the floor. I was ducking."

"She did hit her head pretty hard," Kellie Frazier said. "And then the box fell on her."

As Snider was assessing Knaul's prone form, the substitute teacher returned to semi-consciousness.

"Are you OK?" Snider asked

A red lump was quickly swelling under Knaul's mussed hair.

"Are you OK?" Snider asked again, getting closer to Knaul's ear.

The response was a prolonged sigh and a fluttering of the eyelids.

Snider activated the flashlight on her phone and put it in her left hand and examined Knaul's eyes. She saw a difference in the size of the pupils. If Knaul's brain was bleeding, minutes, seconds were going to count. Instinctively she tried to call 911, but she could not get a connection after two separate dialings.

"Shit," she said audibly.

"What are you doing?" Bennett asked.

"Calling 911."

"They can't get in, remember?"

"Try 911 with your phone," she said to Bennett.

Same result. Same result when Bianco tried his phone.

Snider worked to make sure Knaul was stable. Bennett and Bianco moved the students nearest to Knaul and helped them get situated farther down the wall. Bianco checked with the two boys guarding the door.

"We haven't heard anything," one of the Boy Scouts, Thomas Perry, said as Bianco eyed the knot that was keeping the door "locked."

"You're sure that's gonna hold?"

"Pretty sure."

"I think I read somewhere that you can wrap the door closer up there a certain way and it won't open," Bianco said, pointing to the top of the door.

"Maybe a belt?" Perry said taking a thick black belt off his hips and holding it up.

"Nice," Bianco said. "Try it."

Perry brought a chair over and wrapped the belt as tightly as he could around the closer.

"Looks good," said Bianco

Bianco patted him on the back and went to join Snider and Bennett squatting next to Knaul who was moaning in and out of consciousness.

"You guys really think you can get out of the building?" Snider said to the two boys without taking her eyes off Knaul.

"Yes," Bennett answered for both.

"You're not going to take any stupid, macho chances are you?" Snider said, looking up.

"Of course not. What could go wrong?" Bianco said.

Snider arched an eyebrow at him.

"Seriously. We're not getting killed, and she needs help now, doesn't she?"

On cue, Knaul went rigid with a seizure that fortunately lasted only a few seconds before subsiding. Snider bent over Knaul's face to listen for her breathing which resumed with a gasp and continued fitfully.

"Just be very, very careful," Snider said to Bennett.

Bennett signaled for Jill Markos, who had gone back to her place with her friends after the commotion, to join them.

"We're going to borrow Jill," Bennett said.

"For what?" said Snider.

"She is going to stay at the elevator doors and help us listen. She can report back to you if, when, we make it," Bennett explained.

"You OK with that?" Bennett said looking at Jill.

"Sure," she said uncertainly.

"You don't have to Jill," Bennett said.

She looked Bennett squarely in the eye. "I said 'sure' didn't I?"

"Good luck," Snider said. "Get people here as quickly as possible, but don't take any chances."

"First or second?" Bianco asked Bennett as they approached the back corner of the room.

"Second," Bennett decided.

Bennett explained that the two of them were going to climb up to the second floor,

Bennett first. Jill would have to steady the ladder for Bianco.

"Be ready for what you are going to see," Bennett said to Bianco, glancing at Jill.

"What's he going to see?" asked Jill.

"We'll explain when we get back," Bianco said.

"Once we get through the doors, go back and tell Snider we made it. If these phones ever start working we'll text. Then come back here and hold the ladder if we have to get back down. If anything else happens, go warn people," said Bennett.

"Like what?"

"You'll know if it happens," Bianco said.

"You guys are scaring me."

"That's because this a scary situation," Bianco said. "OK?"

Before Jill could respond, an explosion shook the room knocking the three of them off their feet as the room seemed to physically sway. Loud noises emanated from the other side of the elevator entrance door. The elevator car itself started sliding down the shaft. Bennett was just able to pull his feet out before the car toppled the ladder and crashed the rest of the way to the floor. There were rumblings and creakings from the floor above and dust was everywhere.

27

In 522, Zarlapski snapped his fingers three times to get attention.

"Listen up, Gifted Humanities," he said in a stage whisper from the middle of the room. The teacher went over the same defense strategy he had discussed an hour ago with his AP class. As he spoke, some kids began digging into their pockets to inventory "weapons."

"I need some of you to go next door," Zarlapski said gesturing to 521, "in case someone tries to get in. Kyle, you mind being in charge over there?"

"Got you," Kyle Yarborough said.

"I'll go with him," volunteered Rachael Megay.

"Go," Zarlapski assented. "Nothing stupid."

Rachael rolled her eyes.

Kyle began recruiting kids from the Humanities class. Zarlapski followed seven volunteers through the partition opening and made sure they were strategically positioned.

"What about the gun Mr. Lewis had?" asked a tall blonde-haired boy standing in 521.

Everything stopped.

"What gun?" Zarlapski asked.

"I saw Mr. Lewis grab the gun out of one kid's hand. Then there was a loud noise, and I got knocked to the ground so I don't know what happened to the gun."

"Anybody know?" Zarlapski asked.

Several heads shook.

Zarlapski went back to 522 and asked about the gun.

"We were all ducking," a dark-skinned boy said.

"I didn't see a gun," a girl said.

"Was it a handgun?" Z asked.

"Yes," said the blond boy.

Zarlapski went over and patted down Lewis' pants pockets. No gun. He deliberated about the merits and risks of going back to 523 and searching for the gun.

The issue of arming teachers surfaced periodically, especially after serious incidents in schools. Zarlapski was adamantly opposed to the idea for many reasons.

Gun advocates claimed that armed employees could have prevented casualties. There were good arguments on both sides of the issue. Wouldn't a would-be shooter avoid a place where somebody could shoot back? Common sense says yes. As an NRA spokesman had put it, "The only thing that stops a bad guy with a gun is a good guy with a gun." The NRA recommends that School Resource Officers, at least, be armed.

After the Sandy Hook Elementary School shootings, Missouri districts were given the option of sending employees to a forty-hour training program. The person becomes duty-bound to respond to a threatening situation. The identities of the men and women carrying weapons would be known to only a few district personnel.

Oklahoma legalized arming teachers with a law passed in 2015. The school district in Harrold, Texas has allowed employees to carry concealed guns, with requirements, since 2007.

On the other hand, statistically, the chances of being killed in a school shooting are less than the odds of being hit by lightning. There is no definitive evidence that having armed security cuts down on violence in schools.

Gun battles are not video games. In New York City, nine bystanders were hit by gunfire from police firing at a bad guy near the Empire State Building. If police can be that inaccurate, imagine a firefight in a school cafeteria or a crowded hallway or a classroom full of kids. Studies show that environmental factors, such as lighting, affect depth perception. The reaction time of an individual is a factor; some people are more athletic than others.

Gunshot wounds, in the vast majority of cases, do not incapacitate instantly unless the bullet hits the brain or spinal cord. The shooter may keep coming for minutes until the internal damage takes its toll.

Zarlapski had read about professionals who reported brain distorting experiences similar to what happens during a car wreck: events slow down, distances and spaces exaggerate, survival response overcomes decision making. Many police do not remember making conscious decisions but responding automatically based on extensive training. If this happened to regular police, what would it be like to a novice in a gunfight, no matter the level of training?

Today, barricaded in his classroom with frightened teenagers and two injured colleagues, Zarlapski had a different perspective on the debate. He had little to lose. Maybe there are students in his room who have experience with guns.

"I'm going to see if that gun is still next door," Zarlapski told Streeter. "Hold the fort."

The teacher started his door opening routine, but froze and then closed the door as quickly and as quietly as he could, his heart leaping into his throat.

"What?" Pagliano asked, alarmed.

Zarlapski whispered, "Two with guns at the end of the hall." The pair, hoods pulled up over their heads, were standing outside of 524, weapons slung casually over their shoulders, apparently having a conversation.

The teacher put his back to the inside of the classroom door in 522 and urgently signaled for everyone to be quiet. He mimed two people with guns.

"Cassie," Zarlapski whispered. "Tell them next door. Everybody quiet."

Cassie crawled to the door in the partition from her position on the floor and disappeared into 521.

As quietly as possible, Zarlapski lifted the desks that had been moved to clear a path out of the room and put them back in the barricade. Streeter and Pagliano joined in.

"Be ready to fight," Zarlapski whispered to the class. He grabbed his aluminum bat.

Nail files and keys protruded through the clenched fists of Zarlapski's AP students. The kids from the gifted class picked up on what they were doing.

Without her crutches, Nikki stood shoulder to shoulder with Pagliano at the door, massaging the trigger on a spray bottle of bleach bathroom cleaner.

A brief burst of gunfire erupted from the hall. Audible gasps escaped from terrified teenagers.

Another burst, closer.

Then silence, like the gunmen were listening for reactions.

Several seconds later, the faint whine of a classroom door being opened raised the level of tension even more.

Another burst of gunfire. The bullets sounded like they were hitting the wall that separated 522 and 523.

Zarlapski urgently signaled everyone to stay close to the floor.

Silence again.

Someone started pounding on the classroom door. A male voice pleaded, "Let me in. Let me in. Hurry."

Streeter stood up and moved aside a desk to get to the door. Zarlapski grabbed Streeter's arms and pulled him into the corner near the closet a second before two gunshots were followed by a scream and then a moan. The door handle was shaken violently, and then someone outside said, "Let's go."

There were no more sounds from the hall as Streeter shook himself free from Zarlapski's grasp. The teacher felt a wave of nausea again. Should he have opened the door? Was a defenseless kid just slaughtered? Did he save those in the classroom?

He heard sobbing behind him.

Streeter was looking at him with…what? Disbelief? Disdain?

Sounds from 523-524 came to them: the crunching of broken glass, a desk being moved, a closet door banged shut.

"Now what?" Zarlapski said to himself. Actually, he hadn't said that to himself. Rachael, returning from 521, had come up to him and asked the question.

Some of them could be dead in a couple of minutes, and they probably could not do anything about it. Maybe they could overwhelm the shooters with superior numbers. Eventually. But how many would die first? And how many would run toward firing weapons instead of cowering on the floor in paralyzed fear until they were all dead?

Rachael was about to say something else until Zarlapski held up his hand.

Something was being dragged on the floor outside. A couple of seconds later the door handle shook again. Someone in the hall said, "Get back."

The next sound from the hall was a loud musical text alert.

He hoped the text was important enough to change their plans. The guards at the door remained at the ready to pounce, but many of the students behind him were already folding into fetal positions on the floor trying to make themselves invisible.

No kids were getting left behind this time. Zarlapski was determined to die first.

Seconds ticked by.

Then the footsteps ran away from the room and the banging of the push bar on the hall door was audible at the other end near 525.

Zarlapski hustled to the open partition door and checked on his group in 521. Cassie had stayed with them. He put his fingers to his lips and tried to encourage them with an OK signal. Many of the kids were wide-eyed with fear.

What was that all about? The teacher wondered as he tried to control his shaking hands.

As Zarlapski was ducking back into 522, muted thunder rumbled through the walls and down the corridor and some dust shook loose from the ceiling tiles above the classroom.

28

Green Hill's Sean McCarthy led two state police cars to 1171 Bleaker Street in the Green Hill section of the Valley with orders to knock and talk first. If they were denied permission, the troopers were to enter anyway. The commanders didn't think they would have a problem arguing exigent circumstances if a search warrant could not be obtained rapidly.

McCarthy had been to the Russo residence a few times in the last two years, for both the boy and his father. The old man was an abusive drinker who had hit his wife and his youngest of three boys, Anthony. He had managed to avoid jail time when his spouse refused to testify.

Officer McCarthy waited until the troopers were deployed around the house and then he and Trooper Larry Thompson went to the front door. McCarthy banged loudly on the windowless blue door and yelled "Police."

McCarthy waited a few seconds and repeated.

He tried the knob which turned freely, but the deadbolt was on.

"What about this?" Thompson said, pointing to a combination lock box hanging over the mailbox.

McCarthy flipped open the cover of the lock and tried the default "0000." The key compartment popped open.

"Lazy people," Thompson noted.

"Police," McCarthy yelled into the house. "We're coming in."

McCarthy spotted a news van parking down the street.

The officers could hear the hum of a refrigerator off to the left. The foyer was clear, the steps to the second floor straight ahead, the living room to the right.

Thompson radioed for two of the other troopers to join them while he and McCarthy worked together to check the downstairs. Thompson pointed to an American Furniture Classic gun rack in the corner of the family room. Three of the slots were missing rifles, and one of the drawers was slightly open.

Thompson snapped a photo of the rack with his phone.

Everything else appeared in order, if "in order" meant dirty dishes strewn on the counter, congealed food in pots on the stove, clothes tossed on the furniture, and unopened mail piled on a table.

Thompson sent two officers to check the basement. Thompson and McCarthy went into the garage.

The four re-formed and started cautiously up the stairs. Thompson used hand signals to indicate that he and McCarthy would take the master bedroom.

As he opened the door, Thompson caught a whiff of something out of the ordinary. Deer processing popped into his brain. The odor of alcohol hung in the air also. McCarthy's eyes were wide. It was semi-dark in the room, dark curtains drawn across the two windows.

Work clothes were piled on the floor in a promiscuous heap or partially draped over the sides of a clothes basket at the foot of the bed. A half-finished bottle of Jack Daniels sat upright in the basket— a white sock curled at its base.

Thompson felt for a light switch and flipped it on. The blood-spattered spread was pulled up to the mahogany headboard. A lacerated open hand at the end of a bare, hairy arm was protruding from the covers, a congealing puddle of blood on the gray rug.

McCarthy pushed open the bathroom door and stepped inside. It was empty. The bathroom was oddly neat. Clean towels hung on the rack, the floor, sink, and countertop were spotless.

McCarthy and Thompson grabbed the spread at the top and whisked it down.

Frankie Russo was a bloody mess, stab wounds from his stomach to his face. His white tee shirt was tattered and bloody. A slash in his neck had saturated the sheets and mattress. His bloodied right hand reached for an empty bottle of Rebel Yell Bourbon at the edge of the bed. The bottle of bourbon had a small crack in it that Thompson surmised was going to match up with the bruise on Frankie's right temple.

Thompson radioed the command center from the landing while the other officers began securing the crime scene.

29

A dozen students huddled close with a teacher trying to stay warm and quiet. Art instructor Katie Barr had taken in the panicked students from Cyril Weidner's remedial reading class. They had fled as the portly Weidner wrestled with a gunman in a long coat in the corner of the classroom.

Mrs. Lynn Stiles and Barr had decided to move their students to the loft above the art rooms after scary accounts had started proliferating on texts.

Barr had been the last one out of her classroom, or studio, as she preferred when Weidner's students came running toward her screaming about a gunman. The three students walking with Barr froze at the sight of the fleeing students. Two shots exploded from Weidner's room.

"Here, here," Barr said, keeping her voice as low as she could and pointing to room 402 which looked out onto a courtyard still waiting for its spring spruce up. Fallen leaves, storm-damaged pine branches, brown plants, food wrappers, and overturned chairs and picnic tables littered the landscape. A storage shed sat in the northwest corner.

"Into the courtyard," Barr ordered as she fumbled through her keys to find the one for the large shed.

On the third try, Barr stabbed the key into the padlock, swung the two doors open and hastily moved a wheelbarrow out of the way. *Thank God Stiles is a neat-freak*, Barr thought. All the implements needed for the courtyard's upkeep were either hanging or vertically stacked in corners.

Barr closed the doors, and after a moment of getting adjusted to the darkness, some began to sit on the floor.

A couple of phones gave light here and there as screens lit up with notifications and faded off.

"No phones," Barr warned. "And mute them for God's sake."

"Is Mr. Weidner OK, you think?" asked a student.

"He probably is upstairs," Barr responded.

Noiseless minutes ticked in the damp, cold, darkness until a voice from outside the shed yelled, "This is the police. Do not make any sudden movements. Open the doors of the shed. Do not step out of the shed until we tell you."

Eyes looked to Mrs. Barr.

After a few tense seconds, both doors opened simultaneously. A dozen terrified students blinked in the light, some with their hands in the air already.

Police team Bravo, led by Jon Butler, had retraced the steps of the police who had searched the arts area forty-five minutes ago moving through a hallway heading east past the wood and electrical shops and courtyard.

"Walk slowly toward the officers with your hands behind your heads," Butler told the group. "Single file."

Each student was quickly patted down.

"These all your kids, ma'am?" Butler asked Mrs. Barr.

"Some. The rest of my class went with Mrs. Stiles. There's a loft above the office in there." Barr pointed to 402.

"Show us," Butler commanded.

Lynn Stiles had been hell-bent on getting her kids out of the building until she saw the chained doors at the end of the hall.

"God almighty. This is real," she had said aloud to herself.

She made the snap decision to hide in the loft over the art rooms. It was dusty and crowded with random supplies, but there would be enough room, she hoped, to hide out until this blew over. Plus they could get out onto the roof if they had to.

"Get going," Stiles yelled. "Everybody upstairs. Hurry. Find a spot and be quiet. Move."

Her class started climbing as Stiles had gone to find Barr. "Bring your kids over here. We're going into the loft."

Most of Barr's class had made it to Stiles room before the loud report of two shots unnerved everyone. The remaining students scrambled to get up the ladder, those below firmly pushing on the butts of those in front as they ascended.

Stiles noted a lone figure run down the hall outside the classroom.

"Quiet," she whispered. The figure bypassed the room.

Stiles was the last one up the ladder. She flattened on her stomach and looked down, waiting for Barr to appear, but after a minute, she and a student had brought the ladder up toward them.

That was when the odor of vomit hit her. She felt her gorge rise as she scrambled through the students in the narrow aisles carved through the boxes of supplies, unused equipment, old projects, tables, chairs and other debris.

"Let's get to the roof," she had yelled, praying the door was unlocked. It was.

Now Butler and his unit were standing below that loft.

The Bravo leader pulled the ladder down and began cautiously ascending. After determining that the loft was empty, Butler came down the ladder a couple of steps and signaled for McGinn and Martin to follow him back up.

The command center called to tell them about the students on the roof.

"We are in an attic above the classrooms. Stand-by."

Two girls screamed as a policeman with a gun, and then another emerged through the door to the roof. Mrs. Stiles was on the roof with about thirty students huddled around her as they stood twenty feet from the edge that looked out over the front driveway and the administrative parking lot. They were standing over the auditorium lobby in the shadow of the 300 wing.

"It's the police," Stiles yelled, trying to calm her class.

"Hands where we can see them." Jon Butler ordered as the police team approached. "Don't move."

"Mrs. Stiles?" Butler said, turning his attention to the teacher after the police checked the group.

"Yes."

"We're going to go back down through the art rooms and take you out through the doors by the music rooms. Is everyone OK?"

"I think so," said Mrs. Stiles who still had her paint dappled art smock on.

The group paused at the distant sound of automatic weapons. A police helicopter climbed rapidly out of its hover over the scene and headed away from the school.

"All units be advised of gunfire from the third floor, east side of the building," came a call from the command center several seconds later. "Proceed with caution."

Butler was about to advise command that they were moving back into the building when a boom shook the roof.

Those closest stumbled into the attic creating a pile-up. Everyone else flattened on the ground or tried to. Debris from the 300 wing hurled outward catching several of the art students at the end of the line.

30

The Lifeguarding students hiding in the walk-in storage closet in the boy's locker room were shivering from fear and wet bathing suits.

Some of the swimmers, a few with VV swim caps still on, were hugging to stay warm. Others were blowing into their hands. Others were in a sitting fetal position on the floor.

There had been no sounds for over an hour, and instructor Lori McCutcheon was considering letting the kids get their clothes when the door swung open, and somebody yelled, "police."

"Don't shoot," responded McCutcheon.

"Hands in the air," ordered Delta's Tom Morgan.

"It's students," said McCutcheon, her hands in the air.

After a quick search of each student and their lockers, officer Morgan allowed the males to get dressed.

A female officer escorted the girls to their locker room where they waited outside while the locker room was searched. Then the teens were allowed in to change before being lead past the command center to the buses, where detectives interviewed them.

The rest of the Delta team moved on. Thomas Morgan organized his team's search in the food prep area. A row of half-made sandwiches was waiting on a countertop, a microwave periodically beeped impatiently, stacks of milk cartons were beading with condensation, but there was no sign of the staff until Morgan opened the walk-in refrigerator and freed six very cold adults.

"Delta 1," called Greco. "Ask them if they know where the driver of the bread truck is."

"They did get a bread delivery this morning," Morgan responded after a couple of minutes, "but the trays were left in the hall. No one saw the driver."

"10-4, Delta 1. Bring them out."

31

While police teams were on the roof and in the arts wings and the caf, students were getting antsy in the 200 wing. Since the pandemonium in the wing earlier, tense waiting had mingled with distant but ominous sounds that seemed to creep out of the walls.

"For the millionth time, I'm telling you, she was shot," Shannon Zimmerman said irritably when her friend again asked about Deanna Lansing.

"I don't believe it."

Shannon grabbed her friend by both arms and knelt in front of her. "Believe it or not. I saw her fall to the ground."

Both of them began crying.

Shannon pulled her in for a hug. "I'm sorry. We're all scared."

The two girls were sitting on the wall in 212 with the twenty other students and their English teacher.

The room was more stable now. The teacher wasn't exactly a disciplinarian, and some of the kids had ignored him when he told them to put away phones and computers.

But the three shots fired into the room had shut everybody up.

Shannon dabbed her eyes as she leaned back against the wall.

"Did you hear that?" Raven Bartholomew asked no one in particular.

"Someone's out there," Shannon said a couple of seconds later.

Eyes turned instinctively to the teacher who sat immobile under the whiteboard, a deer in the headlights.

The classroom door swung outward, and a helmeted head peered into the room. Alpha's Steve Brown and Sean Davidoff moved quickly into the room without a barricade—SIG Sauers level. Brown went left, and Davidoff took a couple of steps into the room on the right scanning the students for any threat.

"Police. Hands in the air," he ordered as Brown moved along the wall. "Stay where you are."

Davidoff used his radio to call Bobby Matheson into the room from unoccupied room 213.

The three rapidly assessed the room and determined no threats.

"Anyone hurt?" Matheson asked the teacher.

"I don't think so."

"Line your kids up along the wall," Matheson ordered. "Wait for us."

The students and a pregnant teacher in 214 had already been vetted and were lined up waiting for evacuation.

Matheson intended to search the rest of the corridor before shepherding the students to safety until his earpiece crackled to life.

The Alpha commander strained to hear something about shots fired at a police helicopter.

"Everybody out of here, now," Matheson said to his officers. "We'll come back for the other rooms. Back steps, the way we came up here. I'll notify."

"You and Fitz take 214," Matheson directed Brown. "Vito, you help Davidoff."

"What about the body?" Brown asked.

When they first entered the hallway, Matheson had checked the prone figure. The girl, lying face down, right arm awkwardly under her stomach, was wearing a Vista View black lacrosse sweatshirt. On the back was the name Lansing and the number 15, both in gold vinyl.

He had shined his flashlight into her face revealing half-opened eyes and skin a terrible shade of blue. The light also caught the glint of a wire attached to the body's right hand and running toward her abdomen. The Alpha commander moved away from the body.

"Wire," he had warned his team.

Fitzgerald retrieved a blanket he saw in 214 and gently covered Deanna Lansing's head. He also took a piece of ruled paper and wrote: "Do Not Move—Alpha" and left it near the body.

Matheson positioned himself in front of the body and directed his men to start the evacuation process between 212 and 214.

Shannon Zimmerman put both hands over her mouth when she saw the blanket-covered body on the floor outside of room 213.

"Don't look, keep moving," Bobby Matheson ordered the students coming out of 212 and 214.

The English class and the business class merged and mingled as Alpha herded them toward the hallway that would take them downstairs.

"That's Emily," Shannon said pointing to the body.

"Oh my God. Are you sure?" someone said behind her.

Shannon nodded tearfully.

The classes began their trek out of the building.

Matheson waited until everyone had turned the corner and was about to follow when voices in the parallel hallway, on the other side of the 200 wing, attracted his attention.

A male adult put his head around the corner at the far end of the north-south hallway. He and Matheson locked eyes. Matheson trained his Glock on the man.

"Police. Hands in the air and step out into the hallway. Slowly."

The subject froze. Matheson moved to the other side of the hallway for a better visual angle and more protection.

"I'm a teacher," said the man. "Coming out. Don't shoot."

"Who else is with you?"

"My class, and two other classes."

Since the rest of his team had already descended with the evacuating students, Matheson was alone, and this was not a one-man operation. It seemed unlikely, but he could be walking into a set-up.

Matheson jogged toward the teacher. He slowed when he got close. The man was shaking. Suicide bomber crossed his mind.

"Keep your hands in the air." Matheson reminded him leaning out into the hallway while keeping the teacher in his peripheral vision.

Matheson saw sixty to seventy students huddled in the dark, dusty hallway, several doing their best to stifle coughs.

"Put your hands down," Matheson said to the teacher after patting him down. "Move them into the stairwell. Let's get out of this mess. Wait there."

The teacher signaled the students to move forward. Another teacher, Shannon Gibbs, stood behind the group, urging everyone to move quickly while dragging a student who had gone limp with fear, coaxing her toward the stairwell.

The door of 203 opened and a white towel clipped to a yardstick appeared through the crack.

"Coming out," came a male voice.

"Stay there," Matheson said.

He went over and cautiously opened the classroom door wider with his foot and peered into the room.

A couple of dozen students were lined up along the wall. Matheson eyeballed them and then turned to the teacher and told him to evacuate to the stairwell with the other classes.

Three members of Charlie and the returning Alpha team appeared in the hallway.

"Here," Matheson called.

Matheson directed officers to search the rooms along the hall quickly.

The door to classroom 200, a computer lab closest to the stairwell, opened and students from the room started joining the procession down the stairwell.

Matheson hustled three members of Charlie Team to the students coming out of 200.

Matheson stepped into room 200 and saw the teacher talking into a cell phone.

"My wife," he said to Matheson.

"Later," said the police officer.

"I love you," the twenty-something instructor said as he disconnected.

"All your students accounted for?" Matheson asked.

"Yes."

"Stay with them. Wait in the stairwell," Matheson ordered.

He held the students until Steve Brown got to the front of the line and could lead the way.

"Everyone out of your rooms?" Matheson asked Mrs. Gibbs.

Before the teacher could answer, screams reverberated from the other end of the hallway.

Students from a physics class were running out of the corner lab at the office end of the hall. As the teens emerged from the room, they caught sight of some of the carnage that had occurred in the administration area, including bodies and parts of bodies.

The physics teacher was trying to at least partially shield her twenty-three students from the view by holding up her red emergency folder.

"This way, hurry. Don't look," she said repeatedly.

The police guided students toward the stairwell where the others were still waiting.

"Everyone out?" Matheson asked the teacher.

"Yeah. I think so. I'll check. We were all in the back closet. Took a while to get the door open. Was that a bomb?"

"Don't know," Matheson said. "We're going to take you out of the building."

The stairwell was full of fidgety teenagers and their anxious caretakers.

"Get everybody out of here," Matheson yelled. "We'll finish the search and meet you outside."

A boom from the front of the building prompted kids to begin screaming. Matheson scrambled into the alcove outside the library and looked toward administration where smoke and debris were pouring into the hallway. A second explosion rocked the building, and vibrations seemed to roll through the floors and walls. Tongues of flame licked at the air near Admin and then receded.

"Let's go. Let's go," Matheson screamed. "Move everybody, now."

32

The sounds of the explosion on the roof re-ignited panic in 522. Regina Himmelwright started screaming at the top of her lungs. Kelly Keiter moved to the floor and embraced her firmly. "Quiet Regina; quiet."

Regina sobbed, "Leave me alone" and rose. Kelly took a painful shoulder to the chin. John Pagliano rushed over to help as Regina continued screaming, "Leave me alone." Pagliano put his hand over Regina's mouth and got kneed in the groin for his trouble. He doubled over with a groan as Regina started tearing at the barricade, flinging desks out of the way.

The other students in the class were mesmerized at this meek girl's transformation.

Zarlapski bear-hugged her from behind, but Regina's twisting and turning brought them both to the floor with the teacher taking the brunt of the fall on his left shoulder.

Kyle Yarborough rushed in from 521 through the partition to check on the commotion.

Yarborough darted to Regina and put a choke hold on her before she could get to her feet.

Every time she tried to get away, Kyle tightened his grip just enough to cause some pain. Regina started crying, but much of the fury was gone, and after a minute, she went limp and rolled into the fetal position under the whiteboard after Holder cautiously released his grip.

Rachael went to help Zarlapski who was trying to clear his head and sit up.

"A little dizzy," he said as Rachael tried to pull him to his feet. "Give me a sec."

"You OK?" he called in a whisper to Pagliano who was still curled up on the ground.

"No. Bitch."

"She didn't mean it," Rachael scolded Pagliano.

"You?" he said to Kellie who was holding her chin. She nodded tearfully.

Yarborough moved to the door and listened. He waved his hand in a downward motion at a group of gifted kids who were trying to console a girl who was on a non-stop monologue about all the things she wasn't going to be able to do now.

"Quiet," Zarlapski hissed at the girl. She glared at Zarlapski and then starting to cry quietly into sweatshirt-covered arms on raised knees.

Kyle was listening at the door. The hum of helicopters and idling fire engines and distant sirens were now merely a part of the setting, like the unregistered hum of fluorescent lights. After twenty seconds Kyle shook his head at Z and made an inquisitive pulling motion.

A loud moan from the other side of the classroom caused Yarborough and Zarlapski to jump. Mr. Lewis had regained consciousness and was grabbing his head as he rolled into a sitting position.

Rachael went over to Lewis, got his attention and put her finger to his lips. He shook his head as if to clear it and then nodded at Rachael. He looked around in bewilderment at his surroundings and shrugged at Rachael who put her fingers to her lips again. Lewis spotted Stefanowicz laying on the floor a few feet away and moved over next to him.

"Welcome back," his fellow teacher whispered to Lewis.

Zarlapski moved past Yarborough at the door. "I'll take a look."

The hall was empty.

Zarlapski came back and crouched in front of Lewis.

"Kids said you picked up a gun?"

Lewis stared at Zarlapski. "I did?" He said after a couple of seconds. "If I did I don't remember. How did I get in here anyway?"

"Do you remember anything about what happened in your classroom?"

Lewis again gave a long stare over Zarlapski's shoulder. A look of concern grew on his face.

"No. I don't. What happened?"

"I'll tell you later. Take care of your partner here," Zarlapski said, motioning at Stefanowicz.

Zarlapski moved back to the door and asked Kyle if he heard anything in the hall.

Kyle shook his head, and Zarlapski went into the hall cautiously.

The body of a male student lay near the elevator where he had crawled after being shot moments ago. The teacher did not recognize him. Zarlapski tried to push away the horrid reality that his decision to not open the open had cost this kid his life. He felt sick and was dizzy again for a moment and then soldiered on sadly.

He poked his head into 523, stepped into the mess of a room and closed the door. The drawers of both teacher desks had been pulled out; some wrenched entirely from the desk, contents strewn. Maybe someone else had the same idea to look for the gun.

The cabinets and drawers along the wall had also been opened, but the contents of the closets were mostly intact. Maybe the explosion had aborted the search. Zarlapski decided to check more in-depth into the closets and ignore the drawers. If the gun had been there, it would be gone anyway.

Do these guys throw anything out? Zarlapski thought as he reached into crevices and cavities behind books and boxes and magazines and stacked folders. He found nothing.

The teacher shook his head to clear it and started a slow scan of the room from right to left, ending at the wall that separated 523 from his room. He was about to turn to go back to 522 when something familiar caught his eye, familiar but out of place, so out of context that he did not recognize it for a couple of seconds. It should have been on his deck at home.

Underneath the whiteboard was a beige propane tank partially hidden by an overturned desk. Black and red wires were running from the connector down behind the tank.

Zarlapski spied another tank with wires in the corner, along the outside wall.

"Oh my God." He felt rooted in place. His legs were not obeying his brain. The teacher finally got moving by wrenching his eyes from the homemade bomb, and he raced out the door without checking the hallway first.

Yarborough, Streeter, and Pagliano, who were closest to the entrance to 522, were startled when Zarlapski ripped open the door and burst in without warning.

Streeter got into a crouch and made a move toward the "intruder."

"It's me. It's me," he said before Streeter could tackle him.

"There is a bomb next door. We need to move now."

"Where to?" asked Streeter amid the gasps and cries from other students.

Zarlapski pointed his thumb to the right, toward the North Parking Lot, "We'll try to get out to the parking lot. If we can't, we head for The Dungeon. Dan, open up the divider so we can move. Fold it back. One section will be fine."

"Kyle, organize some people to carry Mr. Stefanowicz."

"Can you walk, Mr. Lewis?"

"I think so."

Streeter had the divider open into 521.

"Kellie, can you help Regina?"

"I'll try," she said, still rubbing her chin.

"Nikki?"

"I'll be good."

"Let's go," Zarlapski ordered. "Bring any weapons you can carry. Same thing we talked about before. If a bad guy shows up, fight. Swarm him. Everybody by the door over there. Wait before we go into the hall."

Lewis was pushing himself gingerly off the floor and tried to brace with a hand on a desk but wobbled into a couple of his gifted students who caught him and held him up. Lewis used the students to steady himself until he gained his equilibrium and then signaled he could stand on his own. He took a couple of tentative steps.

"I'm good."

"You OK to lead?" Zarlapski asked.

"To where?"

"Parking lot. If we can't get there, to The Dungeon, that storage area down there."

"What about Vince?"

"We'll carry him."

Zarlapski grabbed his baseball bat.

Kyle was already standing at Stefanowicz's head instructing Pagliano and three gifted students on how to lift and carry the injured teacher as soon as Zarlapski gave the word.

Uninjured students paired up with those needing assistance.

"Thanks," Zarlapski said to all of them.

Out of the corner of his eye, Zarlapski noted Kellie was helping a passive Regina to her feet.

"Get going," Zarlapski said to Lewis. "I'll stay at the end."

Zarlapski felt the pressure of time pounding in his head again. The bombs could blow any second.

And what if this was a ruse to flush them out into the open, and they would get ambushed in the stairwell or downstairs?

Two bad options again. No choice.

Lewis led the group out of 521, taking the same stairwell Bennett and Bianco had used a couple of hours ago. The group followed Lewis in pairs, some holding hands, some gripping the cold, gray steel railing.

Lewis paused at the first landing and leaned out to peer down. The sharp turning of his head caused a wave of dizziness, forcing him to close his eyes and steady himself with the railing. The episode passed, and he ventured onto the top step of the next flight. The doors to the second floor were in front of him. Behind them was the exit to the parking lot.

The group carrying Stefanowicz was at the very back of the line. Zarlapski stayed with them.

"Come on, come on," he pleaded silently to Lewis. Those bombs could go off any second.

Finally, the line began moving again.

Lewis gently opened the gray doors to the second floor and saw immediately that the doors to the parking lot were chained tightly and locked with the kind of padlock one would need a diamond saw to cut through, the same thing Bennett and Bianco had discovered. The gust of air from the hallway carried a fetid odor that caused Lewis to gasp and cover his nose as he turned to look to his left. He felt dizzy again as he tried to take in the horror show of strewn bodies.

A few students still in the stairwell immediately behind Lewis caught a whiff of the hallway. Some gagged, desperately trying not to vomit. Lewis took a deep breath and pushed on the chained parking lot doors tentatively with his right hand and then put his shoulder to the door and used his legs to shove futilely against the doors.

At the top of the steps, Zarlapski breathed in a slightly diluted version of the tainted air, but it was enough to raise the hairs on the nape of his neck and caused him to cover his nose. Kids up and down the stairs were reacting, some panicking at the scent.

Zarlapski chanced a step back into the third-floor hallway to check. He could hear the ticking of the bomb. His stomach leaped until he realized it was the fire alarm light still pulsing.

They finally started to move again. Looking over the landing railing, Zarlapski could see Lewis was leading them down to the first floor.

The line halted again as Lewis checked the first floor. The sound of someone retching on the stairwell behind Lewis made everyone wince and brace for the additional odor of fresh vomit.

The trip down the stairs was not helping Stefanowicz even though the kids carrying him were keeping him as stable as they could. The stricken teacher looked like Isaiah had before he had left 522, eyes glazed and, most ominously, quiet and unaware of what was going on.

Zarlapski decided to give Snider a heads-up.

Amazingly, she answered on the third ring.

'What?"

"We're on our way to The Dungeon, be there in a minute. Let us in."

"Yeah well, I don't know if we are safe here."

"Great. We'll talk about it. See you in a minute."

Zarlapski ended the call and tried Greco again. The line started to move when the stairwell doors leading to the second floor burst open behind Zarlapski. The teacher dropped his phone and braced for the worst, gripping his bat with two hands as he turned. Two female students came through the door. One was propping up the other whose shirt was so soaked in blood that Zarlapski could not tell the original color. The other was trying to press a formerly white blouse against a scalp wound that was sporadically dribbling blood through drying, caked, darkening scarlet stains.

"God," Nikki said from the stairwell. She hobbled up to help steady the pair. The bloody girl raised her eyes and started crying when she saw Zarlapski.

Zarlapski put his fingers to his lips, and the girl nodded under matted hair.

"You OK?" Nikki asked the helper student, a diminutive girl named Chrissy with Oriental features who was wearing only a bra above a black skirt. Her torso and the white bra had streaks of blood stains in several places.

Zarlapski unbuttoned his dark blue button-down and gave it to Chrissy who was slumped against the wall shivering violently. Nikki helped her put the shirt around her shoulders and then turned back to tending Debbie.

Most of the line was still moving toward the basement behind Lewis, who had reached the door to the storage area.

The injury contingent, which now numbered thirteen, had stopped on the steps when the girls came through the doors, the only ones left in the stairwell.

"You guys, OK?" Zarlapski said to the group tending Stefanowicz. Pagliano answered in the affirmative.

"Pick him up and get going."

They started awkwardly down the last of flight sidestepping the vomit on the third and fourth steps from the landing.

"Let's go," he said to Nikki, who gave out a gasp as she put too much pressure on her injured leg and felt the pain ride up her thigh.

"Put your arm around my neck," Zarlapski said as Nikki tried to hop down the stairs. He braced himself with the bat.

INTERNAL LOCKDOWN

Chrissy was steadying Debbie as best she could as they took one step at a time ahead of Nikki and Z.

On the ground floor, they picked up their hobbling pace toward the storage room door.

33

In room 104, ten Spanish V students were huddled together inside a fortress they had made out of the teacher's desk, student desks, chairs, and a rolling blackboard.

Senora Dora Vasquez was reading another short story, *La Carretera Sinuosa*, in Spanish, forcing the students to concentrate by asking questions and sometimes handing off the reading.

She almost had the three boys and seven girls thinking it was an average class day when the classroom door clicked open and brought them back to the reality of the moment.

Vasquez stopped reading and put her fingers to her lips.

A cop leveled his gun at the "fort" while another announced their presence.

"We're here. Spanish class," Vasquez called from inside the barricade.

Students and teacher followed Tom Morgan's directions to come out slowly with hands visible.

Once they were on their feet and checked out, they were led out of the room and building, and the team moved on to check the Specialized Needs area which sat in the corner at the end of the hall next to the stairway that led to Admin.

There, two teachers and four aides spent every minute of the school day with six severely physically and mentally challenged teenagers.

INTERNAL LOCKDOWN

Four of the students, three of them females, were wheelchair-bound because of severe neurological problems or catastrophic head injuries that severely limited their abilities to communicate at the most basic level. Two of them required special feeding techniques, and one was incontinent.

The other two students had brain disabilities that harshly limited their functioning, intellectually and socially. They were physically able to get around the building, but one young man also manifested Oppositional Defiant Disorder by randomly falling to the floor and refusing to budge. Sometimes he became an obstacle in the halls during the change of classes.

Before leaving Mann's briefing at the command center, Bobby Matheson and Morgan had been given a heads-up about Special Needs.

Morgan studied the corner for a few seconds. There was one door into the suite. He noted an empty motorized wheelchair blocking the entrance way. He thought he heard noises, maybe crying, coming from behind the door.

The Delta commander was about to force entry when command notified all teams that shots had been fired from the third floor of the 500 wing.

A minute later, there was a loud explosion, and then another and the administration wing started to come down on top of them.

34

Detective Carol Donahue was used to high-pressure situations. A nineteen-year veteran of the state police, she had been in on several high profile investigations, including the murder of a well-known political couple that had originally been ruled a murder-suicide. It was the work of a political rival. The case had made national headlines, and the forty-three-year-old detective was now working on a book about the case that had made her career.

At the bus staging area on the Memorial Field parking lot, Donahue gathered eight other detectives from various area police forces and briefed them on what Greco had told them and gave them guidelines for witness interviews.

"Get their names, asked them where they were, and if they saw anything. If they did see something worthwhile continue the interview.

"Try to find out if anybody had any foreknowledge of this. Something they saw on social media. Rumors. Whatever. Something we can use right away. Fill out a logbook in the command post. Questions?"

The explosion in the North Parking Lot had disrupted the moment. The detectives watched as a column of smoke rose over the building.

"Stay here a second," Donahue ordered while she went to check with Greco.

Then the students in the 100 wing had poured out the front door. The detectives rushed to help with the initial search of those kids, checked their names off, and got them situated on buses.

Donahue got a recap of teacher Bryan Mueller's observations about the carnage in the 100 wing. She made a mental note to ask if any of the high school counselors had gotten out of the building and could help on the buses.

"Be in control," she yelled after the personnel now fanning out through the parking lot.

Then there were other explosions and other escapes and the reports from the Russo home. Permutations of crises were multiplying exponentially.

Parents had gathered as close as they could to the buses sheltering kids. Police kept everyone back and informed parents that a pick-up place would be designated soon. Parents signaled their children to call on their phones. Many of the kids were already on their cell phones, several crying through conversations. Some belligerent parents wanted their kids NOW, but the police held firm.

Each class was assigned to a different bus with their teacher on board and a police officer. Tess Bennington filled in on Czarnecki's bus 145. Reality was starting to set in for the students who had begun the day expecting another high energy, productive day of studying geometry. Czarnecki was always overjoyed to see his first mod class. The period zoomed by as Czarnecki got everyone involved in the lesson of the day, pulling props like cones and spheres and cubes out of his closet to illustrate concepts, all the while mixing in puns that had the class groaning or laughing or both.

The finality of Mr. Czarnecki's death and the trauma of watching him die was apparently on the minds of the students who were sitting on bus 145. Mrs. Bennington fought her own emotions and anxieties and walked down the narrow aisle of the bus consoling students as best she could, hugging those who reached their arms out to her.

The police were able to piece together some useful information.

Students agreed the shooter came down the stairs from the office and then went through the doors at the end of the hallway, the same hall that Alpha had explored. The descriptions of the shooter ran the gamut from average height to 6'8. Most agreed that the assailant was wearing a head covering that also wrapped around his face. "Like a terrorist," said one girl. He was dressed in dark jeans, or dark sweatpants, or dark cargo pants under a long coat: he had a rifle, machine gun, "one of those short things," and or a handgun. Some witnesses said he was aiming at specific people; some said he was firing at random.

The detectives agreed to go with teacher Bryan Mueller's description of a 6' male in a head covering and a long, dark jacket.

A few people were out in the hall when the shooter appeared. Some students had been elsewhere in the building and were trying to get back to their rooms even though, during the drills, they had been instructed to go to the nearest classroom. Some paid for their choices.

Witnesses did agree that the gunman fired into the boy's lav, and he did fire down the hallway killing some girls. A couple of witnesses also saw Czarnecki get shot. Two of the students had followed him out into the hall after they heard some popping noises and some screams and one of the fatally wounded girls had been thrown up against Czarnecki's classroom door. As soon as the teacher was out the door, bullets tore into his body, and he fell in the hallway immediately bleeding profusely and seizing on the floor.

Paul Ric had risked his own life. Running into the hallway, he had grabbed Czarnecki under his arms and dragged him into his classroom—a task made easier by the lubricating blood leaking onto the floor. After the initial shock, some of the students in Ric's room had reacted nobly. Many busied themselves trying to help.

Ben Levengood, who later texted news of Czarnecki's death to Cassie Van Doren, brought Czarnecki's students to Ric's room while the teacher tended to Czarnecki. Ben had the students barricade the door and clear space around Czarnecki who was writhing on the floor, screaming in agony from his stomach wound.

"Call 911," Ric had instructed Ebony Davis, a student who was standing near-by. "Now."

Ric and a couple of his braver students worked to stem the flow of blood using, first, a towel they had found in the closet and then sweatshirts and T-shirts donated by students. But the blood kept on coming.

Davis couldn't get through to 911, and Czarnecki's cries soon faded to moans as he went into shock and then he drifted into unconsciousness and then rasped a couple of breaths and went still.

Many of the students in the room cried but tried to stay quiet. Ric crossed himself and said a quick prayer before once again grasping Czarnecki under his arms and gently dragging the body to the back corner of the room. Ric folded Czarnecki's hands across his chest and covered his upper body.

The bullets must have been .40 caliber or better, Ric speculated. Even immediate help would not have saved Czarnecki's life.

On the bus, Ric made sure he sat for a moment with each of the students, leaving each with a hug or a pat on the back or a shoulder squeeze.

In the command center, Rita Salvatore coolly steered radio calls to the proper monitoring station and kept track of the cascade of events. Greco was handed notes on small index cards on a priority basis. Tara Scofield stayed at Greco's side as another set of eyes and ears. Another member of the command center team, Jim Olin, sat calmly at his station monitoring the command post's computers, video feeds, and internet access. Mann placed a call and asked for mass casualty buses from Philadelphia and Harrisburg.

Salvatore wrote on a notecard that the two bomb-sniffing dogs were almost finished the car-by-car search in the South Parking Lot and in front of the school.

Then she called the Pennsylvania Criminal Intelligence Center to get them working on digging up whatever they could find on Ackerman and Russo.

"And see if you can dig up something on an Ahmed. Not sure of the spelling. We had a couple of witnesses say they heard one of the shooters being called Ahmed," Salvatore told her contact at Intelligence Center. "Could be the same person as a William Holder."

John Mann wrote a note for Scofield. "Bread company contacted? Driver? How did bomb get inside? Trace route for the day." The company might not even be aware that one of their trucks was a smoldering wreck at the loading dock of Vista View High School.

Evacuations were going smoothly, and hopes were rising as each student was escorted to the buses. The perimeter was under control; the media was at arm's length. A police helicopter had arrived from Philadelphia, and the pilot and the two other officers aboard were asked to do a reconnaissance of the building.

The IED's set off in the 100 wing hallway and the auditorium and the fact that some doors were inaccessible from the outside catalyzed a slow-motion discussion between Greco, Larabee, and Mann about alternatives to building entry as each man attended to incoming calls and situation updates.

"Are we sure the doors are chained that tightly?" Larabee asked.

"Looks like it," Mann responded. "We got a look at one chained door from some of the video that was pulled off the internet. Looks like the chain and padlock are high-quality cut-resistant stuff."

"Men to the roof with the ladder truck?" Larabee suggested.

"Access to 500 wing from the roof?" Mann chimed in.

After consulting the building plans, Greco replied, "Not directly. Closest is over the arts wing."

"Cut through the roof?" Mann asked.

"High ceilings. Forty-foot drop to floor."

"Ram with the tank," Larabee suggested, referencing the mine-resistant vehicle.

"Doors?" Greco responded.

"Or wall."

"Structural integrity?" Mann interjected.

"Find out," Larabee urged.

Greco called Salvatore over and asked her to contact engineers or architects or contractors who might be able to tell them if the building could be breached without catastrophe.

Dr. Danielle Newhall stayed in the command center at Greco's request to advise him on injury reports and to talk to those who needed guidance.

Greco got another phone call from Dr. Gilmore, the superintendent. He handed Gilmore off to Tara and let her deal with the woman.

Then there was the shot at the helicopter.

"All units be advised of gunfire from the third floor, east side of the building," Mann broadcast to his teams in the building. "Proceed with caution."

The helicopter had been grazed on the undercarriage but flew unscathed to a safer range.

"At least we know where a shooter is," Greco said. "That must be from room 525. It is…"

Rita Salvatore's "Oh my God" brought Greco's attention to the monitors in the room. Explosions lit up the monitors from various angles, and the top of the wall of the 300 wing over the office appeared to fold in on itself.

"Get everybody out," Greco screamed at Rita who had already begun transmitting an evacuation order.

At that moment a bright flash erupted from the office and debris and remains spewed into the driveway in front of the school. The 300 wing listed a little more to the left and the front of the 200 wing.

Some of the police in the building checked in via radio but verbal traffic was so heavy, most of it was useless garble.

A call from Bravo sounded like the team was reporting from the roof, where the explosion had occurred.

Firefighters were trying to decide on a response to the fire. Was there going to be another explosion, like there had been in the North Parking Lot? On the other hand, people were in imminent danger, may be trapped. The fire had to be kept from spreading.

"What do you want me to do?" fire chief Scott Brown asked Greco.

"Get some water on the fire."

There were now eighteen pieces of equipment on the high school campus, not counting the two pumpers that had been damaged in the two explosions in the North Parking Lot.

Brown directed two to the front of the building.

"Stay behind the MRAP and start pouring water from the parking lot," Brown ordered.

The ladder truck and yellow pumpers of the two fire companies drove across the grass. At Larabee's suggestion, a firefighter geared up in borrowed protective armor and manned the hose at the top of

Mainville's ladder. The pumpers parked at the maximum range of their high-pressure hoses.

Led by the police, students from the 200 wing started to emerge through the gym entrance. Once the students had been handed off, the Alpha team ran back into the building.

Students from other wings soon joined those from the 200's. As they made their way to the buses in the parking lot, several teens stared in shock or began to cry when they saw the injured building they had exited a few minutes ago.

35

In the storage area, after the explosion on the roof, Steve Bennett, Matt Bianco, and Jill Markos had stumbled back to the group pursued by powdery debris generated by the blast. Except for Jill's right knee, which banged hard on the gray concrete floor, the three were unhurt. Sue Snider ran toward them.

"What happened?"

"Don't know," answered Bennett. "There was the boom, and things started coming down like a cave-in."

"We're not getting out that way," said Bianco.

"Why is this happening?" a tearful Jill said as she rubbed her knee.

"Don't know. Don't know," said Snider, half to herself.

"I'm sick of this," Bennett declared emphatically. "I feel like we've been playing defense the whole time, and we're getting our ass kicked."

Bianco nodded his agreement. "We've got to get out of here."

"We're safe here," Snider asserted. "Who knows what's going on everywhere else."

"Are we?" Bianco's anger was becoming manifest in his clenched fists and scowling visage. "We only have one way out of here now. Are we just going to wait for those fuckers to show up, knock politely, and then waste all of us?"

Snider was taken aback, "I'm sure the police will be here soon, Steve."

"They probably can't even get in," chimed in Bennett. "We saw the chains."

Snider looked over her shoulder at the rest of the people hunkered down in the storage room. Some kids were sitting silently on the floor, arms wrapped around their knees as the dust settled on them like light snow. Others had gotten to their feet and were hugging friends or standing close for comfort. To their credit, the boys guarding the door were standing at attention.

"I have to get back to Knaul," Snider said. "You OK, Jill?"

Markos was sitting on the ground, rubbing her painful knee.

"It hurts. I'll live," Jill said tearfully. "I can still walk."

"Matt and I and maybe a couple of other guys will find a way out of here, and take out the shooters," said Bennett so matter of factly Snider let out a little laugh.

"Really? How are you going to do that?"

"Weapons. Something. Anything," said Bennett as he scanned the room.

Bianco walked over to a box labeled "FH STICKS" written in blocky magic marker. He held one aloft.

"Good enough," Bennett said.

"The best thing would be if we can get one of them alone and get a gun or two," said Bianco. "Do some real hunting."

"This isn't a movie," snapped Snider. "You could end up dead doing something stupid."

"Same if we stay here," countered Bennett. "Suppose more of that ceiling had come down."

Snider felt her phone vibrate in the pocket of her white lab coat.

"What?" she said without checking who the caller was.

Bennett and Bianco heard her say, "Yeah well, I don't know if we are safe here."

"Z is on his way down with his class," Snider said. "Have the door opened up."

Bennett and Bianco hustled over to the boys guarding the door.

"Untie the knots," Bennett commanded, just as there was a knock from outside. "Hurry."

The Boy Scouts worked quickly to get the knots undone while Bennett unwrapped the closer.

Bennett pushed the door open, and he and Bianco stepped into the hall. Lewis held the door open as the students from the third floor filed in.

Bennett and Bianco went past Lewis and stood guard, looking each way down the hall. Some of their classmates from AP gave them fist bumps or pats on the back. A tearful Meredith Clancy hugged Steve. He put his arm around her and walked her to the door of the storage area before going back out to the hall.

Lewis sought out Snider. "Vince is hurt. You got to take a look at him."

"Where is he?" Snider asked.

"Coming."

When Bennett and Bianco saw the walking wounded, coming out of the stairway, they rushed to help.

"Take them over there," Snider directed as several other students began helping the injured.

Stefanowicz was carried in, gray and unconscious.

Zarlapski came through the doors last and hurried into the storage area. He put his back to a wall, closed his eyes and breathed a sigh of relief. He propped his aluminum bat in the corner before Snider gave him a brief hug. "Where's your shirt?"

Z pointed to the girl he had given it to.

"I got a hospital going over here," she said as she turned and ran back to the hurt that now included Knaul, Stefanowicz and the injured students from upstairs.

"I'll give Greco a call," Zarlapski said, patting his pockets to find his phone.

With growing alarm, he redid the search through his pockets before he thought back to the last time he had the phone. He was going to call Greco from the stairwell. Where was the damn phone?

36

The command center kept trying to raise Bravo, but Jon Butler was too busy to answer as his team scrambled to get students off the roof of the arts wing before it collapsed.

Flying debris had caused mayhem. Several students had been bloodied. Two were sprawled on the flat roof, unconscious or worse.

"Check them," Butler called to his men who had somehow avoided injury.

Butler guided ambulatory students back through the attic. The other students who had been on the roof had evacuated down the ladder, frightened, but unhurt. There they were met by Mrs. Stiles and two police officers, Angel Huertas and Karen Bancroft.

"Keep going; you guys are doing great," encouraged Butler as the students reached the ladder.

As the last student descended, Butler started back for the roof and called John Mann.

"We are evacuating students from the roof. We still have two victims on the roof. Assessing now. All Bravo units OK."

"Coming up," police called from below.

One of the students, a male, who had been knocked out had regained consciousness but was dazed and unable to respond to Butler's questions.

"Can he walk?" Mrs. Stiles asked.

"Going to have to, I guess," Butler said. "We can't stay here."

Flames were licking out of the special ed wing.

"You feel the roof swaying?" Angel Huertas asked.

"I don't," Karen Bancroft said. "But you're right, we can't stay here. How are we going to get him down the ladder?"

"I'll go first and guide his feet rung by rung if I have to," Huertas said.

The female victim was even more problematic. A deep head wound was still running blood at an alarming rate from under the handkerchief Butler had pressed against the unconscious girl's scalp.

"Get a big box from that storage area. Cut it up so we can use it as stretcher to slide her down the ladder," Butler ordered. "Get somebody else up here to help."

They gently turned the girl onto her back, stabilizing her head as best they could. Huertas held the girl's head steady and aligned with the neck as the others carried her through the door and to the top of the ladder and then to the floor of the art room.

"How is she?" Stiles asked.

"Breathing. Bleeding has slowed down. I don't know if that is good or bad," Butler responded.

Butler called the command center.

"We have two injured. Need paramedics at this location."

"Negative, Bravo 1. Outside area is unsafe."

Butler shook his head in exasperation.

"We're coming out."

37

In the Special Needs Suite, aide Tobi Yount completed her third cycle of CPR on Chloe Phipps and, exhausted, ordered teacher Deirdre Brady to take over.

Brady had used Chloe's heavy, motorized wheelchair to barricade the main entry door.

Yount grabbed the dangling end of Chloe's IV, but could not find a vein to put it in.

Brady was about to start another round of CPR when the room shook, and dust floated to the floor. She protectively covered Chloe.

"Keep trying," Yount ordered after a few seconds of listening.

Three other aides in the room were trying to deal with the other severely challenged children in the activity room area of the suite.

Several minutes later, Delta, which had ridden out the explosion intact, loudly knocked on the door and pushed it open, only to be stopped by the wheelchair.

"Police. Move the barrier," Delta's Thomas Morgan called.

The aides looked toward Yount.

Morgan repeated his order.

Yount knee-walked across the floor and released the brakes on the chair before moving it aside.

Morgan and Kyheim Winters hustled past the woman and into the activity room. Others took up positions inside the door. Skye Keaton guarded the hallway.

"Hurry," Mrs. Brady said to Morgan. "She needs a hospital."

The building gave a groan, and some debris floated to the floor.

"Get that," Morgan said to Winters, pointing out a stretcher propped against the back wall.

"On three," Yount said to Brady. "One, two, three."

They moved the stricken girl onto the stretcher.

The teachers and aides had the rest of the students in the wheelchairs, except for an overweight boy who had refused to stay in the chair and had sat on the floor, arms crossed in protest.

"Not now, Kyle," Dierdre Brady pleaded. She threw up her hands.

"Keaton, get in here," Morgan called.

Skye Keaton rushed into the room as a muffled pop went off in the distance.

"Think you can pick him up and help me get him in the chair?"

"I'll help her," Brady said. "He's not going to cooperate."

With Brady and Keaton on the other side, they began lifting and carrying Kyle to the wheelchair. He kicked his feet, and a flailing arm escaped Brady's grip, and she got popped in the cheek. She regained her grip, and the three managed to get him in the chair. They pinned Kyle's arms while Tobi Yount tightened the seat belt.

"Cuff him to the chair," Morgan ordered Keaton as he used his cuffs to secure Kyle to the bars. With Brady holding down Kyle's arm, Keaton did the same as Kyle wailed.

Keaton looked down both corridors. "Let's go."

The caravan headed for the parking lot.

38

"Ahmed's on the line again," Phil Barlow, Channel 8's executive producer, whispered over the phone to Tara Scofield. "He has a new demand."

"Yeah," said Tara angrily as she waved her hand to get Detective Knoll's attention. He poked his head outside to get Will Clancy. "What happened to the old demand?"

"He said the cops moved too slow. He called a couple of minutes ago, after the explosion."

"Great. Hang on."

Scofield recapped her conversation for Knoll and Clancy and then gave her phone, now on speaker, to Knoll.

"Here's Detective Knoll."

"What does he want now?" Harrison Knoll asked Barlow.

"Well, first of all, he said he has classrooms full of hostages, and he will, or they will, I'm quoting here, 'detonate the vests we're all wearing,' end quote. Later he changed that to shooting people one by one."

"Any indication where these hostages are?"

"No. We asked."

"What's the demand?"

"He wants a bus, a tour bus parked in the North Parking Lot, up against the curb, outside the shop, bus door closest to the building, with the engine running. He'll be quote 'generous' and give you until 11:15. Hang on."

Knoll threw up his hands. "What to hell?"

Tara Scofield leaned over Knoll's shoulder. "Phil," she said to the phone. "Tell your reporter to call Ahmed, 'Holder'."

"What? Why?" Barlow said.

"Just do it, Phil. And take your phone with you so we can hear this conversation."

The cops listened as the reporter "accidentally" called Ahmed, Holder. Unfortunately, they could not hear the reporter's phone clearly.

Barlow came back on the phone, shaken "Did you hear that? Was that a gun?"

"We couldn't make it out."

"Sounded like we hit a nerve. Ahmed got angry," Barlow said. "He said, he still wants that flag up, too. Last thing he did was fire a gun, I think. We heard screams in the background. He also said that connectivity is, quoting here, 'shit,' and if he can't get through it's not his fault. Then he hung up. Who's Holder?"

"Nobody," Tara said and went to tell Greco of the latest demand.

Knoll wrote on his legal pad, "SEE IF ANYONE HEARD SHOTS FROM THE BUILDING," and showed it to Clancy.

Knoll said to Barlow, "Did he sound any different?"

"What do you mean?"

"More confident, scared, rushed?"

Barlow asked his reporter.

"Melissa says no, sounded the same as the first call. And, before you tell me, she tried to convince Ahmed to talk directly to you guys. She also warned him that these demands take time. He didn't respond."

"Did you get his number?"

There was some hesitation. "No."

"Anything else?" Tara Scofield asked Knoll, who was writing notes. He shook his head. Tara picked up her phone and thanked Barlow, but again warned him about leaking any information.

"Is that prick lying to us about the number?" Knoll asked.

Scofield shrugged. "Usually he's trustworthy."

Greco joined the group.

"I don't get it," Scofield said. "A bus? That's just weird."

"Anything we can do to buy time, we'll do it," Greco said. "We're working on getting the bus here. Maybe we can put a cop on board as the driver, and we'll have it rigged with a camera."

"Don't you think Ahmed will anticipate the cop-on-board thing?" Clancy asked.

"Maybe, maybe not."

"Don't like it," Clancy said. "They can't be that stupid to think they can get away in a bus. Something else is going on here."

"Couple of guys in the parking lot said they heard a shot, maybe, from the 500 wing a couple of minutes ago. Sounded close to their end," John Mann called to the group

"That doesn't help a whole lot," Knoll said. "We already figured they were in the 500's."

39

In The Dungeon storage room, the best Sue Snider could do was try to keep Barb Knaul and Vince Stefanowicz comfortable and monitor their breathing. She had them on the floor lying on doubled up towels somebody had found in a box, and she blanketed the injured with draperies used in "Around the World in 80 Days."

A nauseous Lewis sat up against the wall, keeping vigil at Stefanowicz' head.

Zarlapski had risked retracing his steps in the hallway looking for his phone, even opening the stairwell door to peer up the first flight of steps. Nothing. He cursed himself again for losing the phone. He thought about going back up the steps, but a distant bang dissuaded him, reminding him that the bombs in 523 still had not gone off. He scrambled back to the storage room.

"It's Zarlapski," he said through the door to get someone to un-band the door closed and let him in. They had dispensed with the ropes.

"Thanks," Zarlapski said as Bennett stepped up to him.

"Matt and I are going to find a way out of here."

"Oh?"

"We're sitting ducks here," Bennett said. "That door is the only way out now."

"Too risky."

"No disrespect Mr. Z, but we're going to go. We're ready."

"We have weapons," said Bianco, displaying the hockey stick arsenal propped against the wall.

Bennett showed Zarlapski some screwdrivers and a hammer he had found in a desk drawer.

"We'll see if a couple of guys want to go along," Bennett said.

"I'll go," said Rachael Megay who had been following the conversation.

Bianco and Bennett eyed one another.

"I don't think so," Bianco said. "You're like, what, 110 pounds?"

"So?"

"So, I was thinking like Smitty over there or Zach," Bianco said, moving toward two stocky senior linemen from the football team.

"Stay here and help Miss Snider, Rachael," Zarlapski said.

"Screw you," Rachael yelled after Bianco as she turned on her heel and headed for Snider.

"What about Pags or Kyle or Dan?" Bianco asked.

"If things go bad here, they're probably going to be needed. Can't leave this place defenseless. There's got to be a couple of guys in here who will man-up," Bennett said.

Zarlapski went to check on Lewis and Stefanowicz and the other injured.

Hydration was becoming an issue. Snider had sent a couple of her anatomy kids on a hunt for bottled water or other drinks but to no avail so far.

"I don't think she's breathing," Zarlapski heard an alarmed Rachael say to Snider.

"Let me see," said Snider as she knelt by Knaul's side and put her ear close to Knaul's mouth. Snider was about to start a rescue breath when Knaul gave a gasp and resumed her labored breathing.

Snider squeezed Barb Knaul's hand hard but got no response. Snider looked at the fingernails for telltale blue. She noted a small diamond engagement ring on Knaul's slender finger. *She would have made a beautiful bride*, Snider thought, gently brushing golden hair from Knaul's forehead.

"Good job, Rachael," Snider said. "Keep monitoring her."

"Anything I can do?" Zarlapski asked Snider.

"Call 911 and tell them to get the hell in here," Snider said.

"No phone," Zarlapski said.

"I'll call," Rachael said taking out her phone.

While she waited for someone to connect on the other end, a thought occurred to her.

"Where's Isaiah?"

Snider and Zarlapski locked eyes.

"He didn't make it," Zarlapski finally said.

"I tried," added Snider, "but there was nothing anybody could have done."

"He was a good guy," Rachael said after a minute, turning and bowing her head as she listened on her phone.

Snider patted her on the shoulder.

"How's he doing?" Zarlapski asked Snider, looking toward Stefanowicz.

"Not good. But he seems to be breathing OK. He keeps drifting in and out."

"Can't get a signal," Rachael said. "Anybody's phone working?" she called to the group of students nearby.

A few hands went up including Lauren Dougherty's. Rachael walked over and sat next to Lauren on the cold gray floor and took the phone and tried 911 again.

"What's his story?" Zarlapski asked, noticing the trussed up Brian Crawford for the first time.

Snider explained Kellie Frazier concerns and the subsequent "interrogation."

"I don't think he's stopped crying the whole time," Snider added.

"You going to let those kids go?" Snider asked Zarlapski, nodding toward Bennett and Bianco who were talking to a group of students on the other side of the room.

"What do you think? Maybe I should go with them," Zarlapski rambled. "I don't know. I wish I could talk to the police, but if they're not going to get here soon, we may have no choice."

Stefanowicz groaned loudly, painfully.

Bennett and Bianco came back.

"They always were a couple of wusses," Bianco was muttering to Bennett. Two football players had declined to join their two teammates on the hunt for the shooters. Bennett had asked a couple of the other athletes but received only head shakes in return.

"No takers?" Zarlapski asked as Rachael glared at all of them.

"Nope," Bennett said.

"I don't think just the two of you should go out there," Zarlapski argued.

"We're going."

"I'll go," said JenMar Neris, rising from a sitting position on the floor.

"Me too," offered Joseph Ma.

Both were students from Knaul's class. Both were good-sized kids.

"Sure?" Bennett asked both of them.

"Yep. What do you want me to do?" Ma asked.

"Grab a hockey stick over there."

"You sure?" Bianco asked Neris.

"Yeah. I got to get out of here. Hate confined places."

"Can you handle yourself?"

"Almost have my black belt."

"Nice," Bennett said, "Let's hope you can break some necks."

"Anything, Rachael?" Zarlapski asked

Rachael shook her head.

Zarlapski turned back to the boys.

"OK. Let's go. I want to retrace my steps and get my phone back. We need to let somebody know we're out there."

"You're going?"

"Yeah. We stay together."

"Might find them faster if we split up," Bianco said.

"Then what? They have guns," Z said angrily. "Our only chance is to overwhelm one or two of them. The odds aren't very good that way even."

He paused for a few seconds.

"You guys don't have to do this. Second thoughts?"

"Nope," Neris said.

"None here," said Bennett for himself and Bianco.

Ma shook his head.

"Anything, Rachael?" Zarlapski said as he walked over to the wall to grab his bat.

She shook her head. Other kids had joined in trying to call 911, but phones were now fading fast, and those that still had a charge were running slowly if at all, and no one seemed to be getting access to the school's wireless network anymore.

"We go left out the door, single file. Me first. Who wants the rear?"

"Got it," Ma said.

"I want to go back to up the steps to the second floor. I know I had the phone there. Whether or not we find it, we keep going to the second floor."

"That's going to be gruesome," Bennett said. "We saw bodies all over the place."

"We won't be there long. We'll head down the hallway past the shops, see if we can get out that way. We want to be out from under the bombs if they ever go off."

"And if we run into the shooters?" Bianco asked.

"If we spot them, without them seeing us, we go after them," Bennett offered.

"Take their heads off," Bianco said.

"Yeah. Remember they have guns. It'd better be quick," Zarlapski reiterated. "And the place is booby-trapped. If they see us, we run back here and barricade the place. Agreed?"

The small group looked around to see who would answer first.

"Agreed," said Ma.

Bennett had the belt loosened on the door closer.

"Tighten it when we leave," Bianco said. "If we want back in, we'll knock like this." He gave two quick claps, paused, and then one clap. "We may be in a hurry, so be quick."

"If we have to retreat, yell 'end zone,' and everybody comes back here," Zarlapski said.

Bennett cracked the door and listened.

The four boys each had a hockey stick. Zarlapski carried his bat in his right hand. Bennett and Bianco had placed screwdrivers in their back pockets. Ma was given the claw hammer to holster in his belt since he was the only one of the four boys wearing one.

"Have somebody arm the rest of these kids," Zarlapski said. "There're plenty of field hockey sticks left."

"I'll take care of it," Nikki piped up. She signaled for some of her AP classmates to join her.

"Careful," Snider urged.

"Always," Zarlapski replied. "It's been real."

40

The drone appeared again, hovering closer to the building, stayed for a couple of minutes, and then flew off toward the development north of the parking lot.

"I know the kid; Chad Thorn. Runs with us," fire chief Scott Brown said to Barry Greco and Frank Larabee in the command center as they discussed how to find the drone operator. "He knows about things like drones; he knows the area, graduated last year. This would be right up his alley."

"Let's just flood the area with cops," Larabee urged. "Knock down some doors."

"I want everybody to stay on scene. God knows what is going to happen next, and we don't need more chaos," Greco said. "The drone might just be some pain-in-the-ass kid."

"And if it is connected to the killers, we have a better shot by sneaking up on it. They might even be talking to the perps in the building. Give us some leverage," argued Brown. "Chad could walk down Main Street and into the development without attracting attention."

Greco agreed, and Brown went to find Chad Thorn and brought him back a minute later.

Greco waved Brown, Thorn, and officer John Abrams over to a monitor where a freeze frame of the drone was waiting.

"We think that's a drone," Greco said. "Whose is the question. Wondering if it is connected to the shooters. It flew off toward Heathergate."

"That's a Phantom 3," Thorn interrupted. "Nice. I've flown that one."

"Know anybody around here who has one?" Brown asked.

"Lots of people around here have drones. A Phantom? Don't know."

"How about if you go over to Heathergate," Brown said, "and try to spot the thing if it goes up again? It was heading that way. It's a longshot, but we're due for a break. Maybe they have a direct line to Ahmed."

"Jon," Greco said to Abrams, "change out of the uniform and take your car over toward Heathergate. Try to be invisible. We're going to have Chad here walk around. If he spots the drone, we want to be low profile for as long as we can."

"Got it," Abrams said starting for the door.

Greco stopped him. "Here," he said handing Midland walkies to Abrams and Thorn.

Abrams drove his Pennsville patrol car off the property.

Chad picked up his pace along the inside of the yellow police tape. He would communicate with Abrams once he got clear of the crowd. He stayed along the back end of the throng, acting like he was trying to get a better view, but gradually drifted to Main Street and walked past some media vans and other cars parked along the curbs on both sides of the street.

He walked past the mostly red brick houses that advertised the persona of the owners.

Number 820 belonged to the family of his ex-girlfriend. Her sister was a freshman or sophomore. He hoped she wasn't in the high school today.

Chad passed a sign that said "Heathergate: Heaven on Earth. Next Right" and turned as casually as he could at the neatest property on the block, the United Church of Pennsville at 3rd and Main. The outer green doors of the church were open, despite the chill of the morning. A couple of people had come to pray with the minister.

Chad put in his clear plastic earpiece and called Abrams, keeping the radio in his back pocket and the microphone clipped to his navy sweatshirt. He pulled his hoodie up and kept his head down.

"I'm going to park on 10th Street and walk the northern end. My Civic is black. Plate starts CBP," Abrams said.

"OK. I'm going up and down the streets on this end. I'll make my way to you."

Chad scanned the sky. Helicopters were hanging out over the reservoir, higher than they had been.

After a couple of minutes of fruitless strolling, Chad was already getting antsy. He nodded as he passed a mailman making his rounds in the development. Chad went about fifty more feet before an intuition turned him around.

"Excuse me, sir," Chad said. "Do you normally work this route?"

"Yes. Why?"

"Have you ever seen a drone flying around in the development?"

The mail carrier eyed Chad for a few seconds after he asked about a drone.

"Over on 4th between Laurel and Rose Lane. Last week. Followed me for a while and came within a couple of feet of my head."

"Do you remember the color of the drone?" Chad asked.

"White with red stripes."

It only took another minute for Chad to reach Laurel Street. He paused to look both ways at the intersection with 4th. Rose Lane was to his right. The whole area seemed deserted.

Chad slowed his pace and began trying to surreptitiously peer into yards and houses, looking for someone fiddling with a drone or telltale signs of a landing area. He knew that some "remote pilots" took their hobbies to the obsessive level, building landing pads and "hangars" for their beloved vehicles.

A gust of wind kicked up, and Chad caught movement in his peripheral vision. A windsock, attached to a wooden fence rail in the backyard of 472 4th St., had inflated. Nearby was a square, maybe four feet by four feet in the grass. A landing pad?

Chad pulled his hoodie tighter and continued toward Rose Lane. By the time he got to the intersection, he saw Abrams coming from the other direction. Chad gave Abrams a look and a tilt of the head and turned to walk up Rose. Abrams followed on the other side of the street. At 5th Street they both went left.

Abrams parked on Rose with a sightline to house address 472. Thorn joined him in the car and watched for a few minutes.

"Suppose this isn't the one?" Thorn speculated. "Maybe I should keep walking around."

Abrams glanced at Thorn. "Must be reading my mind. I'll stay here."

Thorn walked down 5th Street toward Poplar and then to the kiddie park at 7th and Poplar where he had a wider, less obstructed view and could see to the edge of the development down the backyards.

Chad gave the sky one last sweep before climbing down from a sliding board. He caught a flash of light off an object behind a house nearer the edge of Heathergate.

The drone was heading over him. He glanced back at the vicinity of the launch point. It had come up between two houses at the end of Poplar. Chad got out his phone and snapped a picture of the homes and then called Abrams as he watched the drone head for the high school.

"Our drone's up in the air," he told Abrams.

"Walk back here."

While Chad walked back, Abrams contacted Greco and told him about the latest development.

"I can't spare anybody right now," Greco said. "See what you can do. If you can find the operator, bring him over here. If it's too dangerous, wait. And keep the kid out of harm's way."

Chad climbed into the car as Abrams was finishing the conversation.

"Let's drive back the way you came, and you can point out the house," Abrams suggested.

Chad pointed out the two houses he had photographed. Both looked the same: two-story, beige siding, garage on the left at the top of fifty-foot blacktop driveways, concrete walk to the front door. Each sat on its quarter acre at the end of a cul-de-sac. Behind the backyards of the houses were remnants of the woods that had once extended for miles. A wide swath of trees separated Heathergate from an older development of eight houses built twenty-three years ago on the edge of an already established neighborhood. Beyond them were empty fields atop large, abandoned storm sewers that made it too tricky to build on.

Abrams drove up 10th Street. As they neared Poplar, Abrams slowed when they saw an individual in a backyard.

"I think I know him. Ethan Lutz. Used to work with him at Guiseppe's 'til he got fired."

"L-u-t-z?"

"Yeah."

Abrams called Greco on his radio and gave him the new information.

"If he's flying, I'll bet someone else is inside watching the stream," Thorn offered.

"Which house?"

"Good question. You could approach him and see which house he runs into."

"Or," Abrams countered, "You could distract him while I get behind him."

"I can do that."

"I'm going to get to the woods," Abrams said, pointing ahead, "and stay in the tree line. Give me a minute. No chances. If it doesn't feel right, get to hell out of there fast. What he get fired for?"

"Some kid came in just before we locked up and took ten minutes deciding on what to get. Then he didn't have enough money. Lutz grabbed him by his shirt and broke his nose with a punch. Blood everywhere."

"Oh yeah, I heard about that. Took two cops to subdue him."

"Well, Ethan was in an altered state of mind."

Abrams paused and eyed Thorn.

"I'll chat him up. We got along," Thorn said.

When Abrams got to the tree line, Chad got out of the Honda and headed down 10th toward Poplar. He pretended to do a double take as he spotted Ethan still focused on flying. Lutz did not notice Chad until the latter asked, "Flying a drone?"

Lutz glanced his way and went back to flying without a response.

"Is that you, Ethan?" Chad called.

Lutz gave him a brief, annoyed look. "Yeah, I'm flying a drone. What about it?"

"Cool," Chad said as he started walking toward him. He looked over his shoulder to see if he could spot the drone. When he looked back, he caught a glimpse of Abrams approaching Lutz from behind. "Flying over the high school?"

"No. What do you want?"

"Nothing man. I have a drone myself. What kind you flying?"

"Look, I'm busy. Need to concentrate, you know?"

Abrams was four steps away from Lutz, angled away from Chad in case he had to use his drawn gun.

"Police." Abrams announced loudly. "Don't move."

Lutz took a half-step right but thought better of it and froze in his tracks.

"Put the controller on the ground," Abrams commanded. "Slowly. Anyone else around?"

Lutz did not respond to Abrams as he bent down.

"Asshole," Lutz muttered.

"If you have anything to do with what's going on over there, I hope you get the fucking death penalty," Chad responded.

Lutz snorted.

"Anyone else around?" Abrams repeated.

"You figure it out," Lutz sneered.

Thorn recognized the controller. A minute later, he had the drone landed in the front yard of the house.

Abrams had Lutz on the ground, handcuffed, and was reading him his rights. Thorn grabbed the drone while Lutz was hauled to his feet and they all started up 10th Street. Lutz was put in the back seat.

"What about the other person in the house?" Thorn asked Abrams. "If there is another person."

"Drone suspect in custody," Abrams radioed Greco. "Heading to command post." He signaled Thorn to get into the car. Chad popped the mini-SD card out of its slot in the drone's camera and handed it to Abrams. He put the drone on the front seat.

"I'll keep an eye on the house," Chad said. "I'll call if I see anything."

"OK. No chances," Abrams warned after hesitating.

As he was heading down Main Street, Abrams passed a Channel 4 news van and watched it turn down 7th Street. A woman had her head out the passenger side window scanning the sky.

Abrams called Chad. "News van coming your way. Looks like they're trying to find the drone."

"Got it. Thanks."

"Anything?"

"Nope."

At the high school, Abrams held his badge out the window.

Abrams glanced at Lutz in the rearview mirror. The suspect was grinning as he took in the scene.

41

"Remember. 'End zone' if we have to get back here," Zarlapski reminded the boys the as they stood outside the storage area.

Zarlapski led the way toward the north stairwell. He opened the door and listened. He nodded in the direction of the steps and started through the doors. At the end of the line, Neris walked backward, holding the hockey stick out like a rifle, until he turned to go up the stairwell.

Z was confident his phone would be on the steps between the first and second floors. He was pretty sure he had dropped it there when those girls burst through the second-floor door. But it wasn't anywhere to be seen.

"Damn, damn, damn," he muttered into a handkerchief he put over his mouth and nose. Panic started to seep in. A familiar rhyme popped into his head: "Dear St. Anthony come around. Something's been lost and cannot be found." Z had been invoking the patron of lost objects more and more in the last year it seemed.

At the landing, Zarlapski waited for everyone else to catch up. He took a couple of steps up the flight toward the Penthouse and fruitlessly scanned for the phone. He came back to the landing.

"OK. We're going to make a left through the doors and then head down the hallway, past the shops. I'm assuming the outside door is still chained. If by some miracle, it's not, we go outside and get help."

Zarlapski steeled himself and put his hand on the door handle.

There was no miracle. The doors were still chained.

Nothing could have prepared Zarlapski for what he saw and smelled when he opened the door. The first thing he noticed was Baltz' body lying face up, left of center in the hallway. He knew it was Baltz only because of the once-impeccable blue suit. The facial features were blasted away. The gaping holes in his torso revealed internal organs.

Zarlapski had never encountered anything like this stench of blood, body fluids, and death.

"Don't look," he managed to gasp a whisper out to the four boys behind him, just now starting through the door.

Z could hear a couple of them gagging, stifling the noise as best they could; another wave of nausea came over him. He urged the group on.

At the T-intersection, he thought he heard some crying and a voice in 512, the room at the joining of the hallways.

Bennett was gesturing like he wanted to investigate. Zarlapski shook his head emphatically and mouthed, "No." He tapped an imaginary watch on his wrist.

Bennett shook his head slightly but rejoined the line as they formed up against the wall behind the teacher.

Zarlapski peered down the hallway and saw no one. He noted with disappointment that the two gray fire doors two-thirds of the way down the hall, past the Maker Space room, were chained with the same impervious locks and chains as the exit doors were. It made him briefly wonder how long the bad guys had planned this whole thing and how much money had they spent on chains, weapons, bombs, etc.

The wall on the left was lined with student lockers that ended at opaque glass. On the other side was the courtyard outside of the art rooms. An access door was cut into the wall but past the chained fire doors.

The shops were numbered in the 400's like the art classrooms. On the right was a large classroom with a hydroponics garden taking up half of the floor space. The space over the flora was still lit by a battery powered lighting system set up by the student group responsible for the semester-long project. Zarlapski wondered about

Blake Moyer, the teacher, before a new wave of nausea and lightheadedness overcame him, and Z went to one knee along the wall.

"I got it," Bennett said, stepping around him so he could peer through the window slit in the door. The room seemed empty. He waved everyone on. Ma looked deathly white and held a handkerchief to his face. Neris helped Zarlapski to his feet.

After a short stretch of lockers, the next room was a smaller classroom that had been converted to a robotics lab and a 3D printer room. It, too, was empty.

Next was the wood shop which resembled a mini-factory with a very high ceiling dangling, work lights, dust control hoses, and electrical cords. Ducts and pipes crisscrossed fifty feet off the ground. High on the parking lot side were large wooden letters that spelled out "TED^X Pennsville," left over from a day of TED speeches earlier in the school year. Large, unpainted pieces of furniture in various states of completeness were resting on some of the workbenches. Windows in the wall provided a line of sight. The limited look he had into the room did not reveal any people in the shop or the teacher's office in the corner.

"Looks like this is as far as we go," Bennett whispered, pointing at the chained fire doors.

"Aren't there doors from the shop to the parking lot?" Neris asked from the back of the formation.

"Yeah, right, there are," Bianco said. "Let me see if I can get a better look. Maybe they forgot about them."

He cautiously moved to the other side of the hallway to get an angle of sight into the shop. After a few seconds, he snapped his fingers to get everyone's attention and signaled for the group to move back down the hall.

Bianco pointed to the shop and put one finger up and used the hockey stick he was carrying to signify that the person in the shop had a gun.

Zarplapski squatted outside the robotics shop and signaled for everyone to go into the room. "Sit under the window," he whispered.

Once everyone was seated on the floor, Zarlapski risked closing the door. The lock clicked softly into place. The room was furnished with a rectangular table in the middle that could seat a dozen students. Other tables, with various projects and equipment resting on top, lined the walls. An inner door led into the hydroponics room, but there was no direct access to the wood shop.

"What do you have?" Zarlapski asked Bianco.

"One kid with an AK-47, or something, laying on a table. Kid was texting or whatever. He seemed pissed."

"Just one?"

"As far as I could see, and I couldn't see the whole room."

"Who?" asked Bennett.

"Maybe Brandyn Halinski. Or maybe that asshole, Caleb Stoltz. Built the same."

"Were the doors chained?" Zarlapski asked.

"Couldn't tell. View of the door was blocked."

"Maybe we could get out through the ducts that take the sawdust out," Ma offered. "I know there's a tall step ladder in there that maintenance uses all the time to clean sawdust out."

"Let's not forget there's a guy in there with a gun," Neris reminded everyone.

"Why don't they just drive a freaking tank through the wall and get this over with?" Ma said.

"I'm sure they thought of it. If it worked, they would do it," Zarlapski said.

"They don't have the whole damn building chained," Bianco said. "We know some people got out."

"If we can take the bad guy down without getting killed, can we try getting out through the ducts?" Zarlapski asked.

"I don't know if they would even hold us," Bennett said.

"Even if one of us can get out and get to the cops," Ma said.

"First things first," Zarlapski said. "If we can get the guns away from our bad guy in there, that would be a plus."

"How? He was on the other side of the room. He'd see us coming," Bianco observed.

"Lure him closer," Neris said.

"How?" responded Bianco.

"Then what?" added Bennett.

"Shh." Zarlapski ordered. "Let's think about this for a minute."

42

To avoid the news van that had turned down the street near the drone house, Chad Thorn deepened his path in the woods and positioned himself out of view behind an oak tree in the rear the 10th Street houses waiting to see if anyone exited.

It wasn't long before he observed some movement behind the sliding glass deck door on the first floor of the house to his right.

A few seconds after a van with a huge 4 on the side rolled past, the slider door to the deck opened, and a girl in a too big white hoodie emerged into the backyard. She darted to the left and peeked around the corner of the house and then ran to the other side and did the same.

Chad pulled out his phone and recorded video of the girl.

"Shit," Chad muttered as the girl started walking toward the woods, speeding up and slowing down as she occasionally glanced over her shoulder.

He put his phone away.

Her path was rapidly taking her away from Chad's position as she angled in an easterly direction away from Main Street. Chad pulled his head back when the girl, whom he judged to be about 5'6, looked over her shoulder. She brushed the hood from her head as she turned, and Chad caught a glimpse of the face of a late teen with shoulder-length dirty blond hair.

After a ten count, Chad peeked from behind the tree. The girl was now jogging through the brush, her hood back up. When she was far enough away, he radioed Abrams with a description and location as he started to head in her direction.

"OK, Chad. We'll be sending some people," Abrams replied. "I'm heading back now."

"OK, send them down 11th Street. By the way, she came out of the house to the right of where Lutz was. 1006 I think it was."

"Thanks. No chances. I'll be there in a minute."

The girl's tight jeans weren't doing her any favors. Chad heard the girl cry as she tripped to one knee, and he ducked behind another oak. She got up gingerly and started limping away without looking back.

Meanwhile, at the command post near the high school tennis courts, Abrams had parked as close to MC2 as he could and tried to shield Ethan Lutz from the view of reporters gathered across the street. Abrams practically ran Lutz into the mobile command center.

Greco met him at the door. "This Lutz? Take him back there." Greco directed him toward a corner where three chairs were arranged. A burly man in a dark blue suit stood next to the chair tapping a manilla folder in his left hand.

"Detective Clancy will conduct the interview."

"How's the fire?" Greco asked Rita Salvadore, who was monitoring fire communications, among other things.

"Seems to be contained, but they're only fighting from the outside. Don't want to get too close either."

"Got it," Greco said.

Knoll and Clancy rose from their chairs and stood to the side eyeballing Lutz as Abrams seated and cuffed him.

"Has he been read his rights?"

"Yes, sir," Abrams informed Clancy as he re-positioned the cuffed Lutz in one of the chairs.

"Do you understand your rights?" Clancy asked Lutz who was back to his screw-the-world countenance betrayed by several flicks of his tongue around his lips.

"Do you?" Clancy asked a second time

"Yeah," Lutz said looking past him.

Abrams returned to the car, retrieved the drone and wrapped it in a black plastic trash bag before carrying it into the command post.

"Who wants this?" he asked Greco, holding up the mini-card Thorn had removed.

"From the drone?" said Salvatore. "I'll take it."

Abrams unbagged the drone and gave it to Clancy who placed it on the table in front of Lutz.

"This yours?" asked the cop.

"Nope."

"Were you flying it?"

"Yep."

"Whose is it?"

"Don't know."

Clancy snorted. "So you just happened to find a drone and started flying it?"

"Somebody lent it to me."

"Who?"

"Guy I met at a party. Tom something."

That wasn't going where Clancy wanted. He resisted the impulse to grab this punk by the neck and extract the information he wanted by force.

"Excuse me," Abrams said after his radio squawked in his earbud.

Briggs nodded and began a different tack with Lutz.

"Where did you fly the drone?"

"Over the high school."

"Why?"

"Wanted to see what was going on just like everyone else."

"Anybody else with you at the house?"

"Nope."

"I'm going to head back," Abrams said to Greco as he headed out the door.

Lutz shifted in his seat.

Greco got Clancy's attention and signaled him to come over to a monitor. A frozen frame from the drone video showed someone waving or signaling to the drone from a classroom in the 500 wing.

"That's room 523," Greco said, checking the floor plan. "That's where we got reports of gunshots. All the rooms up there are empty now. As far as we know."

"Got it. Thanks."

Clancy went back talk to Lutz.

"Ethan, who was it who was waving to the drone from the building?"

Lutz hesitated before responding. "What do you mean?"

"Someone waved to the drone from a classroom."

"So?"

"I'm just wondering who that might be."

"How would I know?"

"You know, Ethan, a lot of people have died here today." Clancy paused when Lutz broke into a grin. The cop had to work to keep from punching this asshole in his arrogant face. He took a deep breath, looked at the wall behind Lutz, and counted to five before resuming, calmer now.

"That puts you on the hook for murder if you are helping these guys. Lots of murders. The public is going to want to see the killers suffer. That will include you unless you cooperate."

"I didn't kill anybody."

"In the eyes of the law, you might have."

"Maybe I should get a lawyer," Lutz responded, licking his lips. He crossed his arms and leaned back.

"Suit yourself," Clancy said. "But this is the best time to cooperate. A judge will look more kindly on you if you help us."

"I want to talk to a lawyer first," Lutz retorted. "And I need to take a leak."

Clancy double-checked Lutz' cuffed wrists and walked over to Salvatore who was still trolling through the video. "Anything else?"

"Definitely was focused on what the police and firemen were doing," Rita said. "Also flew out over the football field and toward the reservoir."

"Scouting an escape route?" Briggs offered.

"Hmmm. That's an interesting thought. Maybe we should check to see if any boats are waiting there. They could get cover through those pine trees."

"Where's the guy in charge?"

"Greco?"

"Yeah."

"Went back to the meeting with the suits."

"OK. Prick wants a lawyer," Clancy said, using his thumb to indicate Lutz, squirming in the chair.

"You guys got him?" Clancy called to Knoll. "I want to talk to Greco. Two minutes."

Knoll waved him on.

"Oh, and did I forgot to tell you he needs to piss? Yes, I did. Damn."

Rita snorted at her monitor.

"You owe me," Knoll said wearily.

Knoll yanked Lutz to his feet and guided him to the toilet where he unzipped the prisoner's pants and pulled them and his briefs to the knees.

43

While Lutz was being questioned inside the command center, Greco was outside, in the midst of answering questions from the bigwigs who had arrived.

He caught sight of a Pennsville Tours' bus rolling onto the property.

"An officer from Glennridge Area PD volunteered to drive. He has experience. Family owns a bus company," Greco explained to the group. "We have a couple of cameras concealed, but we're having internet issues. We have a mic under the dashboard and elsewhere."

Homeland Security and the FBI volunteered to coordinate on tracking the bus.

"I don't get it, though," said Bill Barnett the Homeland District Director from Philadelphia. "They can't be that stupid to think they are going to get away in a bus."

"Maybe they're stupid. Maybe not," snorted Larabee.

"Could it be for a suicide mission?" said Aloysius Dorney, the FBI Special Agent in Charge.

That caused some pause.

"For now, we're buying time. We'll figure it out as we go," said Greco finally. He could not resist looking at his watch a couple of times.

Detective Carol Donahue recapped again what the police had found at the Russo house. "Obviously, we are going on the assumption that the Russo boy is one of the shooters in the building. We are tracking down relatives; his mother lives in Philly, his brothers are military, and we have CIC scouring social media.

"Another possible shooter is a kid named Ackerman, Carey Ackerman," she said after checking her notes. "Officers went to his mother's house but found nothing out of the ordinary. According to a neighbor she is on an overseas business trip. We are working on contacting her. Same with him, though. We are looking at social media, cell phone records, etc."

"Also, this Ahmed guy appears to be someone named William Holder. In the last few minutes, we've found a couple of references on Instagram and Snapchat. One video appeared to show this guy in a field watching a bomb blow up. One of the others in the video might be the Lutz guy they just brought in."

"Motivation?" asked Dorney.

"Kicked out of Vista View. Criminal record. Settling scores?" Donahue replied. "Also has an interest in terrorist groups and extreme right leanings."

"And these other kids?" Barnett said.

"We're working with some reports that these kids all followed Holder like he was Jim Jones or Charles Manson," Greco said.

"The kids who have gotten out of the building know anything about these guys?" asked Barnett.

"So far not much, but we didn't know to ask until a little while ago. What we are getting is that Russo is a pain in the ass at times, but mostly typical stuff for a teenager. Some police contact on both sides of issues. Victim of domestic violence, caught vandalizing a car, shoplifting charge dropped, crap like that. We are re-interviewing now.

"Ackerman, more serious stuff, a couple of drug possessions, misdemeanor assault, harassment. Smart kid apparently, but so far nobody has much good to say. Nothing to indicate this level of violence, though, for either of them.

"An evacuation center is being established at the middle school, and the kids are being bused up there. That's where we will do more extensive interviewing."

Donahue continued reading from the notes on her phone.

"As for the bread truck that blew up, the route driver was Dmitri Kalinin according to ABC Bakery, which owns the truck. Russian; age 27; immigrated with mother at 13; no criminal record; worked for the company for three years; previously worked for a long-haul trucking firm, Haas-Kreiner; spotless work record at ABC; single. He made three stops before coming here. The last was at 7:20 at Pontiac Middle School in Jericho. Should have been here by 7:40. ABC has not heard from him since he left their depot. But that is not unusual. CIC is digging deeper on him."

"Give me the guy's other stops this morning; I'll get some people to visit, see if we come up with anything," Barnett said.

"Will do," Donahue said.

"Any other questions?" Greco asked. "No? Thank you for your help."

44

Zarlapski and the four students were still sitting in a row, backs against the wall, under the hallway window in the robotics room listening for sounds from the corridor and the rooms on either side.

"I'm just thinking about something here," Bianco said. "The dude in the shop was wearing a bulky coat. Like something was under it."

"What?" Ma asked

"Like a suicide vest," Bennett stated.

"You think?" Ma's eyes widened.

"I don't know. It reminded me of pictures I've seen of suicide bombers before they blow themselves up."

Jen-Mar Neris was rocking back and forth slightly and sporadically making the sign of the cross.

"You OK, man?" Matt Bianco asked him.

Neris shrugged his shoulders.

"The bodies?"

Neris took in a deep breath. "My cousin's laying out there. My girlfriend's brother is laying out there."

"That's rough, sorry," Bennett said, putting his hand on Neris' shoulder.

Jen-Mar blew out a long breath.

Bennett put his fingers to his lips and cocked his head to listen for sounds from the other room.

"You going to be OK?" Zarlapski asked. "We're going to have to go back that way."

Before Neris could respond, there was the sound of a door opening and voices in the hall. Another door opened; loud, indistinct voices; a yelp of pain; several screams; "Shut up."

The five in the room held their breaths, drew their legs in and flattened their backs against the wall behind them while readying their stick-weapons. Zarlapski faked his best "we got this" nod and fist pump.

It sounded like a procession was going past the window, the shuffling of feet, the squeak of sneakers on the linoleum tiles, stifled sobs. "Why are we going here?" a male whispered as he moved past.

A female wailed, "Oh my God."

A terse "Shut up."

A few "Shhhs."

"In there," a voice said above them. Bennett, closest to the door, quickly got to his knees, but "there" apparently meant the shop next door.

A different voice said, "Let's go. Move it."

Another door opened in the main hallway of the second floor.

Listening was the only thing the group in Robotics could do. Fists clenched and unclenched; weights shifted; Neris blessed himself more frequently; respiration consisted of sharp intakes of air followed by prolonged periods of breath-holding as they all tried to keep their worst fears at bay.

After a minute, the hall became relatively quiet. "Wait," Zarlapski whispered, and they listened for thirty more seconds. An angry voice carried into the room from the shop. The words were indecipherable.

Bianco asked, "Why?" Pointing his thumb toward the shop.

Zarlapski said, "Easier to control in one place? Who knows?"

"Or maybe everybody is going to get blown up and then the terrorists can live happily in heaven with their virgins or whatever to hell they believe," Bennett sneered.

"Voice down," Zarlapski whispered sharply.

"I counted at least two different 'shooter' voices, if you will," he continued. "That means at least three next door with guns. Nothing we can do now."

"What's the plan here?" Bianco asked.

"Head back to the Dungeon. Regroup."

"If they move again, maybe we can pick off the last guy. Get a gun."

A door squeaked open. Zarlapski put his fingers to his lips. The door squeaked again, and the latch clicked.

Zarlapski snapped his fingers lightly to get attention and pointed with two fingers to his eyes. He took a deep breath and slowly raised his upper body until he could see into the hallway. There was nobody in his field of vision.

"Clear as far as I can see," he whispered.

"I still say…" Bennett started.

"Enough," Zarlapski cut him off with a hoarse whisper. "We go back, and we think things through. Suppose they're going to blow 523; it's almost directly above us. We could get trapped here."

"The building could come down," Bianco agreed.

Bennett gave him a hostile look.

"I say we go," Ma said.

Neris nodded.

"Let me check the hall." Zarlapski knee-walked to the door and opened it slowly until he could fit his head through. No one in sight in either direction.

"You first, Steve. I'm last. Don't look," Z said, eyeing Neris as he went by him. "Ready?"

Bennett got into an athletic crouch and stepped cautiously through the doorway. He led the group to the T-intersection, looked both ways and turned left.

"Don't look," Zarlapski whispered loudly. By the time he got to the intersection, the first three students were coming back at him and Neris.

"Coming down the stairs," Bennett hissed.

"Run, run," Zarlapski said, pointing to the right. They rushed to the far end of the second floor, zigzagging or jumping over fallen bodies. The teacher was outside 513 when he heard the hall door behind him open.

"Hey," someone yelled.

"Go, go, go." Zarlapski urged. The plodding Neris was keeping Z from running as fast as he could, and as Neris finally turned through the hall door, Zarlapski heard two pops from behind.

Zarlapski felt his right leg cramp, and he stumbled into the outside wall, his right shoulder keeping his face and head from taking the brunt of the collision. The bat clattered to the floor. Two more pops and he felt a punch below his left shoulder blade that drove him to the floor. He grabbed for his bat as another shot pulverized a wall tile over his head. Rolling to his right, Z stumbled to his feet and went through the doors into the 400 wing.

The fire doors fifty feet away were chained

He tried the door to 422 on his left. Locked.

He hobbled across the hall to 423. Open. He entered.

Zarlapski hunched over, panting painfully. He straightened himself next to the door and held the bat aloft in his right hand.

A wave of pain brought him involuntarily to his knees. He crawled to the teacher desk and moved the chair back so he could hide in the opening underneath as he fought to stay conscious.

45

Phil Barlow was again calling about another Ahmed communication.

"Go," Tara said to Phil Barlow once he was on speaker.

"First of all," Barlow said. "I've been trying to get you for five minutes. It's getting harder and harder to get a connection.

"Anyway, Ahmed says that the bus does not have to be there until 11:30 now. Change in plans. He said only a driver should be on the bus, and if there was any, this is his word, 'deviation' he would blow the bus up. He said, hang on."

"Come on," Knoll said exasperatedly.

"I'll tell Greco," Tara said, leaving Knoll with the phone. The detective wrote, "Why the change?" on his notes as well as "DEVIATION," "11:30," "BOMB?"

"Tara?"

"Knoll here," the detective said to the phone. "Everything OK?"

"Yeah, well. Ahmed put a hostage on the phone. A girl. Uh, Ulrich, Leann Ulrich. He shot her while she was on the phone."

"Shot her," Knoll said, rising from his seat. Scofield came back to the table.

"Proving he had hostages. We heard a shot and screams. Ahmed comes back on and says he shot her in the foot. She was crying and screaming. Then he reminded us about the bus."

"Also, is, was, there something going on in the building a few minutes ago? Sounded like somebody was telling Ahmed about people in the shop?"

Knoll and Scofield exchanged looks.

"I'll have to check on that, Phil," Tara said.

"And something else…"

The call dropped.

46

The evacuees were bused to the middle school in a solemn ten-minute yellow caravan.

The Episcopal pastor of The Church of the Redeemer had called members of ministerium to be present at the school. Three ministers and two priests were now attempting to calm and console an agitated crowd of about two hundred who had gathered on the residential street in front of the school.

The superintendent had ordered the other schools in the district to close. Buses arriving at the middle school to start their premature end of day runs were creating gridlock. Anguished parents from the high school mingled with parents of middle schoolers who had shown up in droves to take their kids home. Some of the middle school students had siblings at the high school. The emotional temperature was approaching hysteria.

Two school board members, Gary McNichol and Barrett Kenny, walked through the crowd. Kenny was just out of his dentist's chair and still feeling the tingling effects of novocaine.

"What a mess," McNichol noted. "Did we have a plan for something like this? Where's Gilmore?"

"Don't know," Kenny said.

"Another conference?" McNichol asked. "Is she ever in the District?"

"What's going on, Gary?" asked a parent, stepping out of the crowd.

McNichol shook his hand and held it. "We're going to find out now. Is your kid OK?"

"That's what I'm trying to find out. We haven't heard from her in forty-five minutes."

"I'll see if I can find out anything. I'll call."

Kenny grabbed McNichol's jacket sleeve, and they headed up the steps of the middle school.

The buses carrying the first escapees from the high school were tangled in the traffic around the middle school. A couple of middle school teachers saw what was happening and stepped in to walk the yellow buses to the parking lot at the rear of the building so that the students could disembark in relative peace. Overwhelmed state police officers worked to hold the crowd back.

Shaken students were quickly ushered up the steps to the auditorium. Media members who had staked out the building rushed to the back of the school, and a few of the kids getting off the bus answered reporters' shouted questions. Others students told their peers and the reporters to "shut up" as a few parents formed a protective barrier between the students and press and shielded them as best they could.

Kids who had been in Ric's classroom filed in like zombies, some crying, some holding on to each other, or the shoulder of the person in front of them.

A few minutes later, the superintendents, Sarah Gilmore and Kris Horvath, showed up.

Gilmore's conversation with Greco had been terse. He gave her a brief update and asked her about procedures, but Gilmore had never really concerned herself with those kinds of things. Principals could handle their buildings, and there was a SRO. Greco had ended the call by saying he had to go.

Gilmore finally got through to the district maintenance director, Randy George, who was curt with Gilmore. He could not stand the woman, and he had things to do.

"I'll be there in a few minutes," Gilmore said.

"Great," George muttered, ending the call and left the command center to find the two surviving members of his four-person dayshift.

The media had gotten hold of Gilmore's cell phone number. At first, she ignored the calls, but the persistence began to annoy her. As she and her assistant superintendent, Horvath, were traveling back on the turnpike, Gilmore had written a statement: "The district staff is working closely with the police to resolve this situation as quickly and as safely as possible. We asked that the community remain patient. Students who have left the high school can be picked up at the Vista View Middle School. We ask for your continued prayers for those involved in this situation. The district will have no further comment until after the situation is resolved. Signed, Dr. Sarah Gilmore, Superintendent."

She texted the message to all the phone numbers that had been calling her cell.

Gilmore had barged into the command center. "I am in charge of this District, you know. I demand an update."

Greco resisted the urge to have her forcibly removed from the command center, put on his diplomatic face, and convinced Gilmore that at this point it would be best if she supervised at the middle school.

"It's important that you represent with a calm demeanor at the Middle School. The District needs you there," Greco said, stroking her ego.

Tara Scoffield stepped to the two administrators and politely but firmly guided them to the door. "We have your numbers." She watched as Gilmore and Horvath climbed into their car.

Greco made eye contact with Tara as she came through the door. They shook their heads.

With Horvath at the wheel, the two administrators headed toward the middle school. Gilmore ordered Horvath to park illegally in a handicap space a block from the school, and the two began picking their ways through the thickening crowd. A few who recognized the superintendent called out to her.

"When do we get our kids?"

"How did this happen?"

"You suck, Gilmore."

An incongruous smile froze on her face. She shrunk behind Horvath as they continued to walk.

"The plan is to get parents reunited with their children as quickly as possible," Principal Bedford told Gilmore who did not appear to be listening.

"I need to sit down. Call the lawyer," Gilmore ordered Horvath as she took the chair behind Bedford's desk.

"Get me some water, will you dear," she said to Bedford.

"I'll be back," Bedford responded.

Passing her secretary, the principal asked her to get "the queen" a bottle of water. The secretary had assumed a while ago that her boss despised the superintendent, but that was the first time she had heard open derision. Bedford headed for the auditorium.

The middle school students were still in their homerooms with their teachers. Bedford, after consultation with the principals at the two elementary schools, had decided that merely busing kids home was a not in the best interests of anybody. Parents needed more time to get home from work or make arrangements for the care of their children. Sending eleven, twelve, and thirteen-year-olds home to empty houses, especially if they lived anywhere near the high school, was not advisable at this time.

Bedford decided that buses would depart at 11:15 on their normal routes, but parents or guardians would have to come to the bus and present ID to get their children. Some buses were going to have to make multiple runs because the company was minus the buses being used to transport from the high school.

Individual house stops would be made, no mass corner stops. No child was to be let off at an empty house. No daycare stops were to be made. Parents and guardians only could claim their kids.

Middle school parents were advised via robocalls, social media, a bullhorn, and copies of a hastily typed memo distributed to the crowd about procedures.

Arriving high school students were ushered to the A Wing to wait to be interviewed and then sent to the auditorium.

Before she was called back to MC2, Detective Donahue had one of the state troopers on the scene stand in the hallway leading to the auditorium. Students who had been interviewed presented him with an index card indicating they could go. With Donahue's permission, hand-picked middle school staff at the front door began letting parents in to take seats in the auditorium.

Members of the ministerium circulated the auditorium consoling anxious parents. Bedford announced student names. She prefaced her remarks.

"We know you are all distraught. We are distraught. We are going to do the best we can to get you out of here quickly. If your child's name is not called immediately, we ask you to be patient. The police are still talking to many students in the A Wing. Just because we do not call a name, it does not mean that any harm has come to your child. Again, be patient."

The process was tedious. Tempers flared despite the presence of the clergy. Weeping was contagious.

Shannon Zimmerman was tearfully walking up the left aisle. Her mother squeezed her daughter's shoulder and cried through gasps. Shannon heard her name called from the middle of a row. She recognized the voice of her best friend's mother, Mrs. Lansing.

"Shannon, is Deanna here?" Mrs. Lansing asked as she moved toward the aisle, people getting out of their seats to let her pass. Shannon shook her head, trying to control herself.

"Shannon, is Deanna OK?" Mrs. Lansing asked in a higher pitch, fighting back her fears.

Shannon shook herself free from her mother and hugged Penny Lansing as hard as she could. Shannon's legs gave way and Mrs. Lansing managed to take the teen slowly to the floor.

She knelt in front of Shannon while Mrs. Zimmerman supported her daughter in a sitting position.

"Is Deanna hurt?"

A sob.

"Is she dead? Shannon?"

"I think so," Shannon managed to gasp. "She was laying in the hallway, and they told us to look away. I saw her though. I saw her."

Mrs. Zimmerman buried her face in her daughter's back.

"No. No. Damn it. No. I don't believe it. No." Mrs. Lansing tried to get up. A priest came over to help her to her feet. She shook him off.

"I'm sorry, Penny, I'm sorry."

"It's not true," Penny Lansing kept repeating as the priest took a firmer grip on her arm and led her out of the auditorium. "It's not true."

Amanda Zimmerman got her daughter to her feet, and they held each other tightly as they headed to the car to drive away from this nightmare.

47

The boys had turned left and went through the stairwell doors after the sprint from the shop. Steve Bennett hesitated on the landing between the first and second floors, the other three students on the steps above him.

"Where's Z?"

"Shot," Joe Ma reported.

"Keep moving," Matt Bianco ordered without hesitation. "End zone."

Bennett started back up the steps. Bianco grabbed his arm hard.

"Down. Now."

"Fuck." Bennett shook his arm loose from Bianco's grip. "Go, I'll be last."

The two friends stared at each other briefly.

The group turned to race down the steps. Bennett hesitated and started up, retracing his steps to the hallway.

Bianco opened the hall door on the first floor and looked down the corridor that led to the storage room.

"Move," he ordered. "End zone."

He glanced back. Bianco was not surprised that Bennett was not there at the end of the line.

The three raced for storage room door, halfway down the hallway.

A shooter appeared at the far end of the hall just as the group ducked into the alcove outside of the storage room.

Bianco used the practiced knock. "Hurry up," he yelled and then peeked into the hallway. The terrorist was about twenty yards away, tiptoeing on red sneakers along the wall. Bianco took a deep breath and stepped into view, aiming the hockey stick like it was a rifle. The ruse worked. The ducking shooter got off an unaimed shot that obliterated two ceiling tiles and turned and ran for the stairwell.

"You always were a pussy, Ackerman," Bianco smirked to himself.

The door opened, and Bianco, Neris, and Ma scrambled to safety into the storage room.

"Steve might be coming," Bianco said, turning back and keeping the "guards" from closing the door. He looked into the empty hallway.

"Lock it up and get away. Get in here, Bianco," Snider yelled, horse-collaring Matt into the room. McCreary and Perry worked swiftly to re-secure the door. Neris collapsed in a heap and crawled along the floor.

"Where's Steve?" Susan Snider asked. "And where's Z?" she asked after a few seconds.

Matt shook his head.

"What? What?" Snider said.

Rachael Megay joined the group.

"Z got shot. Apparently," Bianco said.

"Apparently? What do you mean apparently?" Rachael asked.

"That kid said he saw him get shot," Bianco said, pointing at Neris.

"How bad?" Snider said.

"Ask him. I don't know," Bianco responded.

"And you left him there?" Rachael snapped.

"It wasn't like that. I didn't even know it happened, and then we had to get back here. We all would have gotten shot," Bianco said testily.

"And Steve?" Snider said.

"Steve must have gone back."

"At least somebody around here has some balls," Rachael said before turning on her heel and following Snider over to the distraught Neris.

"What happened to Mr. Zarlapski?" Snider demanded, kneeling in front of Neris.

"He got shot. He was behind me. I turned and saw him hit the wall."

"And?"

"That's what I saw. I ran down the steps."

"Was he dead?"

"I don't know." Neris rubbed his face vigorously with his hands. "I can't believe this."

"Screw this," Rachael said to no one in particular and walked back to where most of the remaining members of Zarlapski's class were congregated. Meredith Clancy was helping with the injured. John Pagliano and Kyle Yarborough were on guard duty at the front door. Cassie Van Doren, Dan Streeter, Lauren Dougherty, and Nikki Bennington were sitting on the floor in a semi-circle staring into space. Behind them, Kelly Keiter was seated with Regina Himmelwright, holding her hand.

"Mr. Z got shot?" asked a tearful Cassie.

"That's what I hear," Rachael said angrily. "They had to come back without him, except for Steve."

"Steve got shot?"

"I didn't say that did I?" Rachael snapped.

"Now what?" Dan said.

"I say we start digging our way out through that elevator," Rachael said.

"How?" asked Lauren.

"I don't know. Use our hands. Whatever."

Streeter stood up. "I'll try."

Cassie and Lauren looked at each other and then stood up. Nikki reached behind for her crutches and climbed slowly to her feet. Kelly gave a tilt of the head toward Regina, who was staring blankly. Rachael indicated she understood.

"If anybody's looking for us, send them back there."

Snider returned to Bianco, Neris, and Ma after calming the growing hysteria in the middle of the room where most of the students from 502 and 503 were massed. Word had spread quickly.

Bianco sketched out what had happened. As he had turned to race in the other direction, Bianco related that he had gotten a glimpse of more frightened teens being led down the steps from the third floor of the 500's.

"We should have all gone back," he concluded.

Snider gave an unintentional scoffing laugh. "You'd all be KIA." She realized the implications of what she had said. "I'm sure Steve is fine. He's resourceful. No more excursions."

She pulled out her phone as she walked back to the triage area. The three boys headed deeper into the room, Neris and Ma to the makeshift toilet, Bianco to find his AP class.

"What's with Rachael?" Bianco asked John Pagliano.

Pagliano shrugged.

"Snider's right. We'd be dead," Bianco said.

"You think Steve?"

"No."

The shooters know where they are now, if they didn't before, Snider thought. Could they start shooting through the floor above them? Set a bomb off? 911 must have dropped off the face of the earth. Snider glanced at the group moving toward the elevator, Nikki taking up the rear.

Snider selected "Tess" from her Favorites, but nothing happened. She tried again. Snider looked at the strength of the signal indicator. There was no signal.

48

Rita Salvatore had set up a couple of easels with blow-ups of the floor plans outside the command center, in a tent shielded from the media. Barry Greco had hastily called a strategic meeting to make a final push to get into the building.

"We weren't able to get into the administration area here before the latest explosion," said Greco pointing. "We think a bomb in a backpack went off."

"For whatever their reasons, the 500 wing has been isolated. The outside doors in the wing, here and here, are inaccessible because of chains," Mann noted. "The fire doors, here in this hallway and here in this hallway, same thing."

"Why don't we just run that tank through the wall?" Bobby Matheson asked.

"Good question," interposed Frank Larabee, standing off to the side.

"A few reasons," Mann countered. "One, we have an engineer assessing the structural integrity and give us a safe place to breach if we have to. He hasn't gotten back to us yet. Two, we're not sure where all the students are. There was a threat to chain hostages to the doors, so we can't even consider plowing through them or setting off an explosive charge. And we don't want to go through a wall where a bunch of kids are sitting. Three, we are still in indirect communication with the shooters. Or, at least a shooter. Calls himself Ahmed. Ahmed says he has a room full of hostages." Mann sighed, and said, "And he says he'll waste one at a time if we try anything."

Larabee shook his head. "Ahmed," he muttered derisively. "We're just going to take this puke's word for it?"

"You willing to risk hostage lives?" Greco said.

Larabee shrugged.

Mann held up a hand to stop a couple of other about-to-be-asked questions. "Let me finish, and then we can clarify some things."

He looked down at his notes which had been prepared by Rita Salvatore as Carol Donahue joined the meeting.

"Ahmed also asked for a bus. He just extended the deadline from 10:35 to 11:15 and then to 11:30. Didn't say why. We'll come back to the bus in a minute."

Mann paused for a second and took a swig from a mini-bottle of water.

Salvatore turned the large map pages to a diagram of The Dungeon.

"Thanks, Rita. This is a large storage area. A lot of the people who were in the 500 wing are holed up there. This is one of the places we need to focus on. They have been asking to get some injured out of there for a while."

"Second floor," Greco said.

Salvatore found the map and flipped to the floor plan of the second floor again as Mann continued.

"Students and teachers are there still as far as we know. Haven't had any communication in the last ninety minutes."

"Cell phone communication has dropped significantly," Salvatore interjected. "It's never great to begin within this area, as you may have discovered, and a nearby tower went down mid-morning. Plus the volume of calls overwhelmed the system. And now batteries are dying. Don't rely on your phones."

Greco continued. "Ahmed warned us that there are bombs still ready to go in the building. Since the last parking lot explosion, dogs have been through all the parking areas and have not detected any explosives."

Tess Bennington came into the tent and stood unobtrusively behind the group, listening to the briefing.

Rita noticed her and gave a thumbs up. Tess smiled wanly.

"So, to sum up," Greco said, "we think we are clear in all wings except the 500. We estimate about two hundred people still in the 500 wing, most, if not all in the storage area and second floor classrooms. Those in the classrooms could be the hostages. The third floor might or might not be vacated, but we know we have/had a shooter up there, and there are alleged bombs in one of the rooms."

"Could be the stage for a grand finale," observed Larabee.

"Maybe," said Mann. "We are estimating there are between three and six shooters in the building."

"Questions?"

"What about the roof?" Scott Brown, the fire chief asked. "Could we cut a hole and drop into the shop. Get in position now?"

"We've talked about that," Mann said. "It's a long drop to the floor, plus we don't know if they have hostages in there now."

"Anybody here have experience rappelling, in case we do cut a hole in the roof?" asked Matheson.

"I think Steve Brown does," said Tom Morgan.

"Good," Mann said. "Find out if anyone else does."

"Getting desperate aren't we?" Larabee asked.

Mann changed the subject. "I forgot to mention we brought in the kid with the drone. We're talking to him now. There seems to be a connection between this kid, his name is Lutz, by the way, and the bombs."

"So how's that going to help us get into the building?" Larabee asked.

"We're tracking another person involved with the drone," Greco said. "A girl. We're following her right now. Maybe we can get some leverage to get these people out into the open, or find out what the plans are and set a trap."

"They related to this Ahmed?" Bobby Matheson asked.

"I can answer that," Tara Scoffield said coming up to the group in time to hear the question. "Just got some information. In short, yes, Lutz knows Ahmed, whom we are now ninety-nine percent certain is

William Holder. We think we have a line on the girl from the drone house, too. If she is who we think she is, it's Holder's girlfriend."

Rita Salvatore hustled in a man in a rumpled blue suit.

"This is Michael Jaso," Salvatore said. "I explained to him what the situation is."

After a nod from Mann, Jaso, an architect, went to the easel and took out a black marker. He looked at the diagram.

"It's my understanding that you are focused here," Jaso said, pointing to the 500 wing.

"Correct," Mann said.

"About the only relatively safe place to breach the wall on this side is here," Jaso said, putting an X on a spot along the recessed outside wall of the smaller shop classroom. This used to be a garage door. They walled it over. The other doors are relatively safe areas to knock down, but Rita here explained why you can't risk that. Or, I assume, you don't want to risk it.

"On the other side of the shop is a wall with lockers in it and about six by six feet of eight-inch thick opaque glass. That could be an entry point."

"What about the roof?" Mann asked

"There is an electrical attic here," Jaso responded adding another X on the floor plan. "This is an access door on the roof. It leads into a small room with electrical equipment and a set of steps goes down to the 400 wing proper. This is the inside access door in the janitor closet here," Jaso pointed.

"So that attic, as you called it, is inside the fire door, but the janitor's storage area is outside the chained fire doors," Greco noted as he pointed to the hallway that connected with the 500 wing several feet from room 515.

"Correct," Jaso said. "The stairway goes behind the fire doors about halfway down."

"What about other places of ingress from the roof?" Mann asked.

"In other places, the safest spots are over the hallways," Jaso explained.

"Questions?" Mann asked the group.

"What about going in through the ducts leading into the shop," Larabee asked. "There is definitely a big enough duct to crawl through. Do we know where it goes inside?"

Jaso took a close look at the floor plan. "My best guess is a standard dust control systems in a shop, what you see on the outside is what you get on the inside."

"It's worth the risk," Larabee said.

"Too much of a risk," Greco said.

"There is also possible entry through the elevator, here," Jaso resumed, indicating where the roof would have to be breached to access the elevator outside of 522. "The ground floor stop opens into a large storage area in the vicinity of, um, 503 and 502. The second-floor stop is across from this room in the shop suite and close to 512."

"We have students and teachers sheltering in storage; the teacher from the third floor was heading there before we lost contact," Greco said. "He also reported those wired propane tanks in 523, which is near the elevator."

Does anyone have any more questions for Mr. Jaso?" Mann asked.

"Thanks, Mr. Jaso," Mann said.

That was Salvatore's cue to take Jaso out of the planning session.

Greco grabbed Rita by the arm as she started to leave. "Have him look at the damage on the roof on the monitors. See if he can give us an idea about structural integrity," he said in Rita's ear. She nodded.

Greco got Mann's attention and whirled his right index finger in the air.

"We got to get moving," Mann told everyone. "We want to be in place in fifteen minutes. So here's the plan."

49

Bennett crept to the stairwell door on the second-floor of the 500 wing and peeked through the six-by-six window. At the T-intersection, the hall leading into the 400 wing had a blood trail. Steve opened the door slowly and stepped into the second-floor hallway. The now familiar potent odor hit him immediately. He saw fresh blood on the floor and wall to his left and the floor.

Bennett started across the hall when he saw movement to his right out of the corner of his eye. He turned his head to see a figure with a gun walking toward him.

"The great Steve Bennett."

"Brandyn Halinski," Steve responded.

The former baseball teammates stared at each other for a few seconds.

"You're involved in this?" Bennett asked matter-of-factly.

"I'm going to do you a favor for old times sake and not kill you here," Halinski said.

"So, I can go?"

"Not quite," Halinski said with a smirk. "This way." Halinski waved his Glock to the rear.

Halinski's eyes looked glazed and his speech had a slur to it. Drug issues, Bennett knew, had led to Halinski leaving the team. On the other hand, Halinski was bigger than Bennett and still powerfully built despite a beer gut.

Bennett considered rushing him and wrestling the gun from him.

"So what happened to your suicide vest?" Bennett asked.

"How do...? What do you mean?" Halinski said. Uncertainty creeping into his voice.

"Was that you in the shop a little while ago, Brandyn?" Bennett asked.

"How did you know that?"

"Do you really want to kill yourself, Brandyn? For what?" Bennett pried.

Halinski gave Bennett a glazed-over look, but didn't answer.

"You were a damn good pitcher, a shame..."

"Yeah? Then how come I got kicked off the team?"

Halinski moved back and signaled Bennett to walk toward him as he stayed at least ten feet away, haltingly backing down the hall, past bodies, until he got to the T-intersection that led to the shop. He hung several feet back as he waved Steve down the hallway.

"What's this all about?" Steve asked.

"All for the glory of Vista View," Halinski said, parroting a line from the alma mater.

"Did you help kill these people?"

Halinski shrugged.

"Don't you feel bad?"

Halinski shrugged again.

"You know..." Bennett began.

"Shut up," he said glancing down the hall, pulling a mask from his pocket

Once they got to the shop, Bennett was directed to open the door. Students were sprawled all over the floor of the shop while several masked individuals roamed among them.

Halinski, now with his face covered, pushed Bennett toward a side wall and told him to lie face down on the floor.

He complied, looking left into the terrified faces of fellow students.

At least he had distracted Halinski from Zarlapski's blood trail. If it was Zarlapski's.

Without warning, Steve felt a sharp pain in his ribs from a kick. He gasped for air as someone above him laughed derisively.

INTERNAL LOCKDOWN

Bennett turned painfully to see red sneakers walking away from him.

50

Zarlapski slowly came to consciousness in the darkness of room 423. From his vantage point under the desk he could see writing on the whiteboard, but the words were gibberish.

I guess that's the writing on the wall, he thought, trying to clear his head.

Why was he under the desk and where was his AP class? A cramp in his hamstring caused him to gasp in pain. The teacher reached down awkwardly to massage his thigh and was incredulous when his hand was covered in blood. He shook his head.

"Owww." The movement of his head shot pain through Zarlapski's left shoulder. He saw stars. His left arm felt numb, like it wasn't there. Z felt for it to reassure himself that it was still attached. Am I having a heart attack? He tried to take a deep breath but coughed painfully and tasted blood. By experimentation, he found that cocking his head to the side prevented the sharp pain in his shoulder. He fought down his panic by concentrating on regulating his breathing.

Zarlapski crawled out from under the desk and looked around. He was in Dieter Rasche's German classroom. Z got to his knees and tried to stand but dizziness sent him crashing back to the floor. Instinctively, he tried to brace with both arms, but his left was useless, and he partially face-planted on the floor. Nausea washed over him.

"God," he said aloud. "God." Everything came back to him. The race down the hall, the pops, the pain, stumbling into 423.

Z felt for his phone in his pocket, but then remembered he had lost it in the stairwell.

Think, think, he ordered himself. He crawled haltingly to the classroom door, noting that he had left a blood trail when he came in. Great. Might as well have made a sign "Here I Am." He looked around for a paper towel or a rag to clean the floor, but behind him, he saw that he was still leaking blood.

Zarlapski struggled into a sitting position against the wall to the left of the door. Breaths were harder to get. He closed his eyes and thought of his wife and kids and Tess and Sue. He asked his dead parents to watch over him. "Stop it," he said angrily to himself. "Think." He blessed himself and said an Act of Contrition before stealing a peek into the hall through the glass slit in the door.

His eye caught the EXIT sign hanging from the ceiling. Yeah, this may be the big exit; irony to the end. He coughed painfully and groaned.

Zarlapski heard a noise from the hallway. He leaned forward until he was on his knees and able to crawl back under Rasche's desk. Dull banging came from outside. An indistinct voice. He looked around for a weapon. His head was exploding with pain. For a brief second, Zarlapski wished it was over, and he was out of his misery. Screw that. He shifted out from under the desk into a kneeling position on the side. He started through another Act of Contrition but only got to "all my sins" before darkness descended. He had a sense he was on his back.

No, wait, he's having a catch with Michael. He's wearing a worn, black Ryne Sandberg-model glove, smelling the fragrance of the A1010 baseballs. Michael is using a similar glove, but tan with a basket weave. They are about fifty feet apart in a backyard still shaking off the effects of winter, tentative green here and there among the bare spots. The sun is bright in the sky, and it is warm. Michael stands where home plate used to be for the Wiffle Ball games. Dad is positioned near the second base bush, scraggly and forlorn, a faded plastic Rite Aid bag caught in the tangle of bare branches. They begin. The rhythm of the catch is established in a quiet broken only by that pleasurable thwack of ball meeting leather.

Michael tries a couple of curveballs. "I should have been a pitcher," Michael is saying. "I'm going to miss having a catch with you."

"What do you mean?" Dad asked. "You can always have a catch with me."

Michael shakes his head and turns to chase down a ball overthrown. Dad waits and waits for him to get back. It is getting dark. He's getting cold.

51

At Greco's request, the FBI's Jessica Villaneuva was tasked to accompany Jon Abrams to pursue the girl that Chad Thorn had located. They took the agent's car.

"You drive," Abrams said.

When they got to School Lane, Abrams directed Villanueva to pull into a parking area behind some trees.

It took three attempts for Abrams to reach Thorn on the radio.

"Chad, key your mic twice if you can't talk."

Two quick bursts came back.

"Call me when ready," Abrams said as he adjusted his earpiece.

"You there Abrams?" said a voice in his ear several seconds later.

"What do you have?"

"The girl is still walking down 11th about a block ahead of me. Wait, now she's turning onto the next street."

"Loney Street?"

"Hang on. She's getting into a white Beemer. License started with DST. I didn't get the rest."

"There," Villaneuva said, pointing to a white car speeding up 14th Street.

Abrams called Greco and quickly recapped what had happened.

"See where she goes," Greco ordered. "We think she might be one of the perpetrator's girlfriend. Maybe she knows what the plan is. But, first, let's find out if there are others involved."

The Beemer had gone right onto Main. By the time Villaneuva made the same turn, the Beemer was a quarter mile ahead and separating.

Villaneuva kept following but was still losing ground.

Greco ordered Abrams to break off pursuit. "Another FBI unit will handle. Pick up Thorn and go to 10th Street. Help secure that location."

By the time Villaneuva turned around in a bank parking lot, a black Suburban flashing blue and red lights flew past them in the direction of the white BMW.

"Pull out and block the road, now," Abrams ordered. The Channel 4 van was coming out of the slight bend near the post office.

Villaneuva complied and, with the help of a parked car, effectively cut off Main Street The van driver laid on the horn as he slowed. Villaneuva threw up her hands and smiled at the driver. She spent a long minute getting out of the way.

The state police helicopter that had brought the dignitaries from Harrisburg was now tasked to help with the pursuit of the BMW. However, Agents Max Piccone and Kurt Little in the black Suburban could not talk directly to the copter and updates had to be relayed to them through the command center.

"Vehicle has now turned left onto Astonville Pike," the helicopter advised the command center. "Suspect vehicle has pulled into a driveway to your right. Suspect is running into house."

Piccone made the turn onto Astonville and killed his lights. The agents could see the helicopter hovering. The white BMW was parked next to a black Ford van near the top of a long driveway. The van was backed up to an old stone farmhouse. The closest neighbor was a fenced-in junkyard a hundred yards up the road separated by overgrown fields. On the other side, an empty, neglected field extended to Upton Rd. A rusted John Deere tractor sat at the back of the property.

"What's our play?" Little asked as he wrote down the plate numbers of the BMW.

"Call for back-up. Wait. Pull over there behind that wall."

INTERNAL LOCKDOWN

Little called in the license plates and requested additional manpower while Piccone retrieved two 5.56mm Colt M16A2 burst-fire rifles from the back of the Suburban.

"You take this side; I'll head behind that big tree," Piccone pointed down the road.

52

At the high school meanwhile, as the FBI agents were deployed at the house, a muscular giant of a man in the brown uniform of a sheriff pulled Ethan Lutz up the steps of a white prison school bus parked near the command center and shoved him into the first row of seats behind a thick fence-like screen that separated the prisoners from the guards.

Lutz was indelicately manacled to a belt placed around his waist.

The giant sheriff kept pressure on Lutz's shoulders. Satisfied, he closed and locked the door in the separator. The defiant drone pilot's chest was heaving spasmodically.

"He'll break," the guard said to Will Clancy who was coming up to the bus. "He's a britney."

Clancy snorted at the slang term.

"Santangelo Rendon, Santa for short," the guard said.

Clancy snorted again.

"Clancy, Will."

"How can I help?"

"Our boy Ahmed is talking to channel whatever again," Clancy said. "More and more demands. We think this clown is a player and can tell us what the plan is.

"I'll tell you what, Officer Rendon. Mind sitting behind him while he and I chat? That should make him nervous."

"Pleasure."

Rendon climbed on first, "accidentally" brushing his elbow into Lutz's head as he sat behind the prisoner.

"Sorry," the huge guard said as he took his place, thick arms dangling over the empty seat on Lutz' right.

"What's your lawyer's name?" Clancy asked as he stood in the bus aisle.

Santa shifted in his seat behind the prisoner; Lutz turned his head to look behind and then cast his eyes to the floor.

"Lawyer?" Clancy repeated.

"Don't know. The last one I had was a public defender."

"Yeah, I see that," Clancy said. "You were a juvie then."

Lutz looked up to see what Clancy was reading.

"Well, Ethan. This is going to take a while. This gentleman will have to take you to Matsonford and hold you there until we can get a lawyer. You're a big boy now," Clancy said.

"Oh, and I know you don't want to rat anybody out, but the girl who was with you on 10th Street doesn't seem to have that same loyalty."

Lutz looked Clancy in the face now. His eyes were wide.

"First come, first served, buddy. As far as I know, she hasn't said anything about a lawyer yet."

"What'd she say about me?" Lutz asked.

Clancy shrugged. "Ready?" he said to Santa.

"Yep," Rendon said grabbing the seat back hard to steady his colossal frame.

"Wait. What do you want to know?" Lutz pleaded.

"Are you giving us permission to talk to you without a lawyer present?" Clancy said as he found the recording app on his phone. "And record the interview?"

"Yes."

"Say it in a complete sentence."

"You can talk to me without a lawyer present and record."

Rendon winked at Clancy and settled back.

"How many shooters are there in the building?"

"I don't know. Six, Seven. Look I tried to tell him this whole thing was not cool. I didn't want to be a part of it, but he's crazy. I don't know. He just gets people to do stuff."

"William Holder?"

"Yeah, yeah."

"Does he also go by Ahmed?"

"Sometimes. He says he wants to be a terrorist, and this'll give him street cred."

"So, he thinks he's getting out of this alive?"

"Yeah. I was supposed to be his eyes. You know, tell him where the cops were."

"And the other shooters? Are they supposed to get out alive too?"

"I guess, Anthony told me all this. I was out of the loop after I said I didn't want to kill people."

"Anthony Russo told you?" Knoll asked.

"Yeah."

"Who was the girl you were with?"

Lutz sighed. "Brandi something. Kimbrough. She's a piece of work."

"What were you guys doing with the drone."

Lutz licked his lips. "Showing them what the cops were doing as I said. Be his eyes."

"So they could see the feed?"

"Yeah, yeah. The Halinski kid is a hacker genius or something. He set it up. They got into the school's cameras."

"Brandyn Halinski?"

"Yeah. Did you know about him already?" Lutz asked.

Clancy ignored the question.

"Where do you think Brandi is now?"

"The bomb house."

That gave Clancy some pause.

"What bomb house?"

"Empty house in Green Hill. Ashtonville Road, I think."

"That's where they made the bombs they used?"

"Yeah."

"You involved in that, Ethan?"

"I know bombs, but like I told you, I didn't want to kill anyone. A couple of 'em were pissed at me. They got some other guy. Brandi knew him. One of her druggie friends."

"Name?"

"Every time I asked, he said screw you. I heard someone call him Toro once."

"Are there bombs still at the house?"

"Tons. The guy's a maniac. A genius, but a maniac. He's supposed to set up a diversion, so they can escape."

"What about the bus?"

Lutz paused, confused. "What bus?"

Knoll looked at Santa Rendon.

"I'll be right back. We have people heading for that house."

Clancy came back after a few minutes.

"Can I go now?" Lutz asked nervously, glancing back at Rendon.

Clancy looked at the guard who shrugged innocently.

"You've been great, Ethan. Thank you, but you'll have stay for now. One more question: why?"

"Why what?"

"What's the point of all this today?"

Lutz hesitated. "Will hates a lot of people here. They ruined his life. Said he was like that kid in *The Catcher in the Rye*. They ruined his innocence.

"And he wants to be a terrorist."

53

Rachael Megay led the AP students to the front corner of the storage area where the elevator shaft was now hidden behind a mountain of debris. Dust created an uncomfortable haze throughout the room.

"God knows what we're breathing in," Nikki Bennington commented.

The group could see that the shaft wall had fallen open, a large chunk of blocks toppling en masse and breaking apart. A slippery, oily substance made the floor treacherous in spots.

"Let's clear a path," Rachael said.

The students began grabbing at the pile and carrying materials to an open spot twenty feet to their right.

At the triage area, Jill Markos asked Miss Snider if she was going to answer her phone.

"What?" she said straightening up after examining the unconscious Barb Knaul.

"Isn't that your phone?" Jill said pointing to the aqua cased iPhone on a shelf cycling through an old school bell ring.

"Give it to me, please," she said to Margie Sweeney who was closer.

She stretched her arms in front to see who the caller was. "Hello?"

"Sue?"

"Tess, where are you?"

"Outside, with the police near the tennis courts. Is Nikki with you?"

"Yeah. She's here somewhere. She's fine."

Snider could hear a sharp intake of breath. "Thank, God." Sue could hear the tears in her voice.

"Listen, I want to talk to her, but Barry Greco wants to talk to Z. Is he with you, too? You guys are in that big storage room in The Dungeon, right?

"Yes, we are." She hesitated about what to tell her about Zarlapski.

"I'm going to get Greco. You get Z to the phone."

Snider heard background sounds of police activity as Bennington called for Greco. She signaled for Meredith Clancy to come over. "Get Bianco and Nikki over here right away. They're back there somewhere." Snider pointed toward the elevator. She knelt to check on Vince Stefanowicz who was unconscious and agitated, his lungs laboring. Ann-Marie Regan was keeping vigil even though her injured eye had swollen grotesquely and painfully. Maddie DiMarco sat with her.

Bianco joined the group at the elevator shaft.

"What are you doing?" Matt asked Rachael.

"What's it look like?"

Bianco looked at Dan Streeter who shrugged his shoulders.

"We're trying to get out through the elevator shaft," Nikki explained.

"That might not be safe," Bianco offered.

"Yeah. You have any better ideas?" Rachael hissed.

Bianco threw up his hands and glanced at Streeter. "What's with the heat?"

Rachael ignored him, struggling past Bianco dragging a rolled up carpet.

"It might be better if we started an assembly line and passed things. Maybe two lines," Streeter observed.

Meredith came up to the group, "Matt and Nikki, Miss Snider wants to see you now."

Bianco started to object, but Meredith had already started back toward Snider.

"We'll try to carry on," Rachael muttered.

"Mr. Zarlapski," Snider heard Greco's voice on her phone say as Bianco appeared, scowling. She waved him over.

"This is Sue Snider," she said into the phone. "Zarlapski's not here. We think he's been shot upstairs. We know he's on the second floor somewhere, but we don't know how he is. We are also missing a student who was with Zarlapski."

Greco told her to hang on, and Snider could hear him repeating the news about Zarlapski to someone.

"Go ahead," Greco said over the phone.

"I have a lot of injured here with me.," Snider continued. "They have to get to a hospital. When is that going to be possible?"

Bianco came up to Snider with Nikki Bennington using his shoulder to steady herself.

"We are working on it. Everything is focused on you guys," Greco responded.

Maddie DiMarco called for Snider.

"I'm going to give you to Matt Bianco. He was with Zarlapski and Bennett. Hang on." Snider handed the phone over.

"Let me talk to Mrs. Bennington when you're done. Don't hang up," she whispered to Matt before going to DeMarco.

"This is Matt Bianco." The junior student recapped what had happened on the excursion to the shop area. When he was done, he asked Greco to give the phone to Tess Bennington.

"Let me talk to Miss Snider first," Greco ordered.

Bianco hustled the phone to Snider., holding it out to her.

"Sue Snider."

"The boys told me…" was all she heard before the call dropped.

"Hello? Hello?"

She waited in vain for the callback.

"What did you want me for?" Nikki asked, hobbling over.

Snider hesitated. "Your mom wanted to talk to you."

"Is she OK?"

"Yes, yes. She's with the police. Stay here. I'll try calling back."

Three attempts got nowhere. Snider noted that the battery life was in single digits.

"I'm going back to help," Nikki said after a few seconds. "Let me know…"

Additional students had formed three lines working at clearing a path to the elevator.

They could now see the foot of the shaft. The remnants of the step ladder Bennett had used earlier helplessly protruded out from under the mangled car. Debris filled in on top of the vehicle and blocked the access to the doors on the next floor, outside of Admin.

"Anybody see a ladder?" Rachael called.

Three boys fanned out to look but came back empty-handed.

"How about using that thing?" Streeter pointed to strong looking oak shelving unit that had once held a place of honor in the main office until another secretary's cubicle had been needed.

"Good idea. Get all that stuff off it and bring it over," Rachael decided. Four boys awkwardly shuffled the heavy furniture over to the elevator.

"Get it closer and move it to the right," Rachael ordered. "I'll climb up and see what we got."

"Maybe one of us," Bianco began.

"I'm lighter," Rachael cut him off. "Dan and Kyle grab the sides. You, what's your name?"

"Ben."

"Help keep this steady. Can we lean this thing in?"

Bianco joined in steadying the "ladder."

"Don't start pulling stuff down. I don't want it landing on us," Streeter said.

"Just looking." Rachael made it up two shelves before losing her grip and falling to the floor, landing on her backside.

"You OK?" Cassie asked as Rachael popped up, brushed her hands on her jeans and climbed again. She reached for a flexible aluminum electrical conduit dangling from the ceiling, pulling on it tentatively.

"Don't electrocute yourself," Bianco warned.

This time she made it to the third "step" which put her above the semi-crushed car. There were cavities in the accumulated mess, but Rachael could not see the door on the next floor up.

Still gripping the conduit with her left hand, she reached for a broken cinderblock and worked it out of the debris pile. It came out reluctantly, and a shard of metal toppled toward the floor catching

Bianco on the shoulder, ripping his shirt and causing a laceration. He yelped in pain but kept his grip on the shelving.

"Get down, Rachael," Streeter said as Lauren Dougherty raced over to help Bianco.

Rachael hesitated and then tossed the cinderblock piece to the side as she gingerly descended.

"We're going to have to wait," Kyle Yarborough said.

54

Via radio, Barry Greco warned the FBI agents on site that the farmhouse at 2715 Astonville Pike might be a bomb factory.

"Be advised also that Northhampton SWAT and their bomb squad are en route to your position. ETA twenty minutes."

"No activity," agent Max Piccone responded. "Hang on, the front door just opened. An individual is coming out. Stand-by."

The same girl who had run into the house was now walking slowly with her hands raised. She was now wearing a long tan coat with something bulky underneath. They now knew her name was Brandi.

"Bomb vest?" his partner Kurt Little said into his radio.

"Could be, I guess," responded Piccone.

"Don't shoot." the girl yelled. "I'm wearing a bomb, and there is a rifle on me from in the house. I have a message for the police. Do you hear me?"

"We hear you. Stop there," Piccone yelled. The girl, now about halfway down the driveway, complied. "What is your message?"

"First, tell that helicopter to move out of sight."

Piccone hesitated.

"Tell it to move, or he will shoot it down," the girl yelled.

When Piccone was slow to respond, a shot into the sky erupted from the corner window of the second floor, apparently missing its target.

"Hold on," Piccone yelled. "This will take a minute. I can't talk to them directly."

But, the chopper detected the shot and initiated a climb and a turn. Piccone relayed the girl's order to the command center while the helicopter climbed out of his sight.

"OK?" Piccone yelled.

"Here are two messages," the girl replied after a moment.

"One, he will blow up the house if you try to enter. Did you hear me?"

"Yes."

"Also, Ahmed said to warn you that he has hostages wearing bomb vests and there is to be no delay in getting on the bus. Bombs will be on the bus. Did you hear me?"

"Yes," Piccone responded.

Without another word, the girl, hands still raised turned and walked back into the house.

"Who to hell is Ahmed?" Little asked over the radio. "What bus?"

"Don't know. Let me call this in."

55

Inside the high school, the teams were almost in place.

Alpha was assigned to gain entry through the electrical attic over the 400 wing, close to where the wing merged with the 500's. Bobby Matheson carried a fiberoptic camera that needed a hole only slightly more than an inch. Alpha was to assess in the hallway using the camera. If it was safe, they would breach and move into the 500 wing.

Bravo, minus two members, was assigned to check the elevator shaft that gave access to the storage room. Three team members had gone back into the building intending to enter the shaft outside the nurse's suite.

Charlie's and Delta's assignments were long shots. Charlie would cut through the roof over a hallway, and two members would rappel to the floor. Bolt cutters would be dropped to the two men although they were pretty sure that they needed more than bolt cutters to get through the chains. The men were also carrying explosive charges to use on the doors if no students were in danger. The rest of Charlie team would then head for the area outside the wood shop and support the Mine Resistant Ambush Protected vehicle if it was needed.

Like Charlie, Delta was to provide cover for the other teams as they prepped to enter the building through the ducts into the shop. They were also to provide cover and assistance as Antonio Garcia moved the MRAP vehicle to the North Parking Lot in case it was needed to break through the walls of the shop.

Matt Weiss was ordered to move his Advanced Weapons Vehicle to the parking lot outside the shop to provide protection.

The bomb-sniffing dogs and handlers were going through the lot again amid several smoking wrecks of cars that had been allowed to burn after the fire personnel and police had been killed.

Other bomb detectors rechecked for car bombs and scoured areas of the lot that had not been swept before the earlier IED's had detonated.

Delta began to prep for getting in through the ducts. The slight Skye Keaton had volunteered to crawl in.

But before the team got too far, Morgan signaled Keaton to abort the mission, swiping his hand under his chin. He indicated for her to climb off the ladder.

"People in the shop," he whispered to Keaton when she got on the ground.

"I still think…" Keaton began.

"Forget it."

They headed for the MRAP's and AWV's protection.

"Command post to all teams. Stand down. I repeat, stand down. Delta, move away from the shop now."

"Other teams hold your locations. Check-in," Mann ordered. After they had responded, Mann told them to "Stand-by for more information."

The command center caught the teams up on the intelligence provided by Bianco and Snider. Priorities were adjusted. Alpha was assigned to the 500 wing's second floor and then the first floor to see if they could make it to the storage area, all the while keeping an eye out for Zarlapski.

Bravo was advised that students were excavating from the bottom of the elevator shaft.

"Proceed with caution," Greco said.

Charlie was told to await further developments in the shop area.

While Delta was moving away from the shop, the Pennsville Tour bus drove into the lot and parked in front of the shop door. The driver, per instructions from Ahmed, parked with the open bus door facing the shop. Luggage compartments inside and outside were opened. The driver got off and moved away from the still-running vehicle.

56

The front door of 2715 Astonville Pike opened. The girl stood on the concrete slab, looking to her right and then left. She said something over her shoulder to someone in the house, and the door closed.

Five members of the Northampton Area Rapid Response Team had joined the FBI agents after a seventy-two-mile trek from the north-central area of the state. Their van and explosives disposal truck was parked at the foot of the driveway. The helicopter hovered in the distance, audible, but not visible.

After consulting with Max Piccone, the Northampton Site Commander sent two of his men into the woods behind the house to watch and wait. Another officer flanked the house from the front, selecting a large tree for protection. The bomb disposal experts deployed the robot to check on the two cars parked near the house. Even with tracked wheels, it had trouble negotiating the uneven, pothole infested stones.

"What do you think she is doing?" Al Dorney, the FBI Agent in Charge, asked from the command center after Piccone called in an update.

"Unknown. She did appear to talk to an unseen actor in the house," Piccone responded.

Kurt Little was studying the girl through binoculars. "She may have a vest on still," he told Piccone and the others. "Moving this way."

Brandi started slowly down the driveway. She staggered and had to brace herself with a hand on the Mustang. Brandi moved a couple of steps toward the robot and then turned and looked back at the home.

After several seconds, she gave the robot a wide berth and shuffled toward the road.

"Halt," Piccone yelled when she was within sixty feet. "Do not come any closer."

"He's going to kill me." While her voice was raised, her delivery was monotonal, rehearsed.

"Who's going to kill you?" Piccone yelled back.

A burst of semi-automatic fire sprayed from the house in response. The shots went high over the heads of everyone, bringing down debris from the trees behind them.

"Hold your fire." someone yelled.

"What's going on?" a SWAT member called over the radio from the woods behind the house.

"Taking fire from the second floor. Hold your position."

Brandi had remained standing during the fusillade.

"Help me," she called in a monotone.

"Stay there," Piccone yelled.

More fire from the house, this time the bullets flew lower. The shooter had changed positions on the second floor, moving to a corner window to the far left of the police position, removing Brandi from the line of fire.

"Help me," she called, arms outstretched.

"Get down on the ground," Piccone yelled.

The girl remained standing.

Northampton's commander ordered his men to pour suppressing fire onto the house. The three NARRT officers opened fire, splintering wood, chipping stone, and breaking glass.

"What do you want to do?" Kurt Little shouted in Piccone's ear.

"She's bait," Piccone said. "Nobody goes near her."

Shots rang out again, this time from a first-floor corner window, pinging off the bomb disposal truck and stitching several holes across the FBI vehicle. Brandi remained standing through it all swaying in the driveway.

The two officers behind the house rushed toward the edifice when the second round of shots started, each taking an end of the house. They broke windows and tossed tear gas canisters into the house.

More shots sent the three officers out front ducking. Brandi started to walk toward them, and the shooting subsided. An officer raced out to grab her despite Piccone yelling to stop.

As the officer grabbed Brandi's left arm, white flashes erupted from the girl and the house. The bomb disposal truck protected the NARRT commander and the two FBI agents from the nails, nuts, and bolts that rocketed from the vest around Brandi's now evaporated body.

However one of the Northampton team members was not so lucky. The officer, who had gone up to Brandi, was knocked fifty feet back even though his protective gear absorbed much of the blast. A nail penetrated between his helmet and his vest and ripped the carotid artery, rapidly draining the five liters of blood in his body.

The doomed officers at the back of the back of the house, which was now spewing flames from several windows, were caught in an avalanche of stone, wood, slate roofing, and pieces of furniture and appliances.

The helicopter moved in rapidly and called in a report as secondary explosions punctuated the horror.

57

"I still don't know what they think they're going to do with a bus," reiterated Homeland Security's Bill Barnett. "The end game could be to drive somewhere where there are a lot of people and blow themselves up. A mall or a busy highway."

"If the Lutz guy can be believed, the bus was not part of the original plan," said Barry Greco. "Maybe they think they can escape on a bus. They are getting desperate."

"Or maybe they are that stupid," Larabee added.

"But if they do intend to use it as a weapon?" Barnett persisted.

"Think your driver can keep that from happening?" FBI Special Agent Aloysius Dorney asked.

"We hope so," Greco said as he read a note Rita Salvatore had just handed him.

"Hope so? Then what's he doing on board? You're asking a lot of this guy," Frank Larabee chimed in.

"You have a better idea?" Mann interjected crossly.

"Yeah, why give them a bus at all?"

"They have hostages. They asked for a bus. Maybe we kept some people alive."

"They're going to kill everybody," Larabee insisted. "We're better off taking them out, even if a few innocent people might get hurt."

"If it comes to that, we'll do it, for now, we do it this way," said John Mann as he monitored communication from the teams at the north end of the building.

"The officer might be right," Barnett offered. "They may be stalling us. Do we know where they are exactly?"

"We're certain that the vast majority of the remaining hostages are in the shop," Mann responded. "We also have a group of non-captives sheltering in the basement below the shop. There are also some critically injured people there."

"Let's use stun grenades," Larabee interjected. "Roll a few in, stun everybody, and then pick off the bad guys."

"We don't know who the bad guys are," a frustrated Greco responded.

"The ones with the guns," Larabee jabbed.

"We're wasting time," Mann snarled while Greco glared at Larabee. "They're going to board the bus any second."

"Anything?" Greco called inside to Rita Salvatore.

"Bus is in place. Driver on sidewalk per directions. No sign of hostages. Can you come here for a minute?"

"They're late," Barnett announced.

"Anything new, Detective?" State Police commander Hardy Ramsey asked Carol Donahue as Greco went inside the command center.

"We've been talking to the perp who identifies himself as Ahmed, as you know. We are pretty certain that is Will Holder, but some students we've interviewed do know a kid named Hosni Afarini who goes by "Little Ahmed." Junior. Kids and teachers describe him as a loner. Little guy. Nobody believes he could mastermind this. Some complaints about bullying on social media, but nothing leading up to today. Could be a shooter though. We're still digging on him. Staying with a grandmother. We're searching the house now."

"Fall guy," Ramsey observed.

"Maybe," Donahue said. "Other than that, all the names that have been popping up are students or former students as Lutz said. Guess the headbands and crap were a way to try and throw us off."

"But they're trying to make us think it is terrorism?" Ramsey asked. "Why?"

"Good question. Aiming for a wider audience? Trying to deflect attention? Terrify the students? Acting out Holder's fantasy of being a terrorist?"

"You should also know that some of the evacuees think one of the shooters came out with them and walked off."

"How to hell did that happen?" Larabee, face flushed again, wanted to know.

"Well, sir, it's not like they're wearing uniforms or name tags," Donahue retorted.

"The kid who escaped joined the rush to get out of the building after the roof explosion. His name is, uh...," Donahue paused to check her notes. "His name is Tyler Yoder.

"Some kids said he was walking the halls with a gun before the evacuation. Showed ID that said he was eighteen-years-old. Did not need a parent to pick him up. Left on foot after arguing about being able to get his car."

"I assume you are searching," Barnett said.

"Yes, sir. We have his parents' house surveilled. We found his car. Nothing inside. We've ID'ed him to the media as a person of interest."

Greco came out to the group. He looked shaken.

"Ahmed's pushed back the deadline to 11:45. Says he is bringing people out at gunpoint and some will have bomb vests on. Anything happens he doesn't like, 'everybody dies.' His words."

Then Greco recapped the events at the bomb house. Dorney and Ramsey excused themselves and headed for the Ashtonville Pike house.

"At least we are disrupting their plans," Donahue offered.

"Yeah, but the more this gets out of their control, the more dangerous they become," Greco said. "I don't think they're going to be taken alive, and they'll take as many with them as they can."

58

Team Alpha's breach of the wall from the electrical attic had gone smoothly, and they were now inside the 500 wing doing a room-by-room search.

In their haste to get to the trapped students, the cops missed the faint blood trail outside room 423 and moved past Mike Zarlapski's position.

Alpha found room 515 unlocked and pristine. The neatly ordered classroom was untouched by the turmoil of the day.

Room 514 was a different story. Desks were strewn across the front of the room. Blood stained the floor and two walls. A female was on her side up against the divider in the rear of the room. A bloody sweatshirt was loosely wrapped around her arm. Bloody paper towels littered the floor among fragments of a shattered light.

"Check her," Bobby Matheson ordered as they entered the room.

"Don't shoot." the woman pleaded, without moving as the police trained their guns on her.

"Roll onto your back," Matheson commanded. "Hands where we can see them."

The woman painfully complied.

"Are you the teacher?"

"Yes. Yes. Lauren Chapman.

"Where's your class?"

Tears welled. "I don't know. They were here. I must've passed out."

"Were you shot?"

She nodded. "I think so. I think Hosni shot me. Hosni Afarini."

"Student?"

"Yes, yes."

"Can you walk?"

"I'll try." But as soon as Matheson and Sean Davidoff got the teacher to her feet, Chapman got dizzy. The two cops put her in a chair.

"I can do this," she told them. This time Matheson and Davidoff brought her up more slowly. She took a couple of tentative steps with support. "I'm good," she said unconvincingly.

"Take her out," Matheson said to Davidoff. "I'll radio ahead."

Matheson informed John Mann of the team's progress.

"No hostages chained to doors, correct?" Mann asked, trying to confirm the veracity of Ahmed's threat to prevent intrusion.

"Affirmative. No hostages chained to doors."

The team had finished checking the bodies. "All deceased," Vito Abbonizio reported, "and no trip wires that we could detect."

The team moved on.

The lavatories had blood stains on the floors and walls, but no injured or dead.

Room 513 was as gruesome as the hallway itself. The bloody body of a female teen lay against a wall. Her sweater was pulled up revealing exposed intestines—paper towels uselessly guarded her organs. A red handkerchief was perched on her shoulder.

Steve Brown skidded on the discharged contents of a fire extinguisher. The cylinder itself was lying next to the body of a big boy whose skull had been caved in, the teen's glasses shattered and askew on his face. The body of another male student was crumpled in a corner near the closet in the front of the room, part of the skull blown away.

"Jesus," Brown muttered, taking in the scene.

Greco called to remind the team about the propane bombs located in the rooms over their heads and to expedite.

"Next room," Matheson said.

Matheson pointed Abbonizio and Steve Brown to 511 while he and Sean Davidoff entered 512. Desks and books and bags and computers were strewn about as if an earthquake had struck. A couple of bodies lay in a puddle of commingled blood near the back.

"Careful," Matheson again reminded his partner as they moved toward the bodies. It was quickly evident that the female teacher was deceased, fragments of skull and brain matter obscenely apparent.

Davidoff pointed to the victim's left hand where a bullet had gone through.

"Saw it coming," Matheson offered.

An African-American male teen was contracted into the fetal position. Davidoff knew as soon as he touched the cold skin on the neck that the student was also gone.

Matheson waved everybody to a spot farther down the hall after they exited the room.

"What do you got?" Matheson asked the team members who had searched 511.

Vito Abbonizio reported that 511 was littered with empty cartridges, boxes of bullets, discarded clothing, and a toolkit. Two propane tanks like the kind used in outdoor grills stood in the corner. Boxes of nails, rolls of tape, bailing wire, and electrical wire were perched on a desk pulled up to the tanks.

Matheson called in a report to Mann and, after a thirty-second wait, Alpha was told to go down to the first floor and initiate a search of the classrooms.

"What about the room with the explosives?" Matheson inquired.

"Let it go for now. Could be a trap. We need manpower elsewhere. Do you see the storage area on your map?" Mann asked.

"Affirmative."

"If it is safe, begin evacuation of that 10-20. If not, provide support. Be advised they have injured in need of evac."

The men began moving after Matheson informed the team to be on the alert for Capitola Valley SWAT which would be entering the building and linking up with Alpha in about ten minutes.

Matheson led his team cautiously down the stairs and through the doors that opened into The Dungeon hallway. To the right were the classrooms. The left side was a beige, blue and white tiled wall interrupted by bathrooms and, farther down, the alcove that housed access to the student elevator, a janitor's room, and the large storage area where students and staff, including Sue Snider, were still bunkered.

The men dispersed to do their jobs as they had on the previous floor.

As Steve Brown pulled open the door to 504, there was a flash of light and a loud bang. Flames briefly mushroomed in the doorway. Sean Davidson was thrown up against the wall.

59

The floor in the storage area vibrated with the explosion down the hall. A few of the students whimpered in fear, but most were now traumatized into silence by the indignities they had suffered all morning.

Those nearest the hallway door moved deeper into the room at the sound of the explosion, dodging the toppled contents of athletic equipment boxes. The students working at the elevator moved back to the center of the room wary of an avalanche of loose debris and fearful of the noises they had heard from the elevator shaft a couple of minutes ago.

Sue Snider was leaning over the unconscious Barbara Knaul, checking for breathing when the explosion went off. Instinctively, she covered Knaul to keep dust and debris off her patient.

"What was that?" Kelly Keiter asked as Snider brushed the dust off her shoulders.

"I don't know," Snider responded. "See if everyone is OK," she said to Clancy.

Snider scanned the other people lying around her. Vince Stefanowicz was still agitated and breathing irregularly. Anne-Marie Regan was in obvious pain from her eye injury, crying intermittently.

Kelly was steadfastly comforting Regina Himmelwright who had been mostly expressionless for the last fifteen minutes. The previous blood sugar check had been within the tolerance range.

Katie McBurney was lying with her feet propped up, holding a T-shirt to her scalp wound. Alicia Goretti's slash wound needed stitches, but she was hanging in. Kevin O'Leary sat with her.

Other students with minor wounds, and those who just needed to be near an adult sat or reclined in the space cleared by Snider and her student helpers.

Clark Lewis rose unsteadily to his feet and staggered over to Snider. "We got to get out of here," he said. "Anything on Z?"

"Yes, I know we have to get out of here, and, no, I haven't heard anything about Z. Go sit back down before you fall on somebody."

Lewis started to respond, but Knaul gave a loud gasp and stiffened; her eyes rolled back in her head. Then she went limp.

"Shit," Snider exclaimed as she leaned in and felt for a pulse. "No breathing. No pulse," she said aloud.

Snider opened Knaul's mouth wider and gave two breaths. She positioned her hands correctly for the chest thrusts and began the first cycle, counting rapidly aloud.

Meredith Clancy knelt opposite Snider.

Lewis watched until Snider began the second cycle. He shook his head and went to check on the group working on the elevator shaft, supporting himself with whatever was in arm's reach.

60

Against protocol, a volunteer group from Vista View Fire and Rescue brought the jaws of life to the elevator outside the nurse's suite. They should not have been in an unsecured building, but four of the rescue personnel were there before Greco knew they were in the building.

The explosion on the roof had warped the frame around the elevator, but the door yielded after a few minutes of intense effort. A debris-filled shaft presented the next obstacle.

Bravo team's Jon Butler, J.J. Martin, and Bill McGinn studied the tangled deposit of cinder blocks, bricks, metal, plastic, and wires.

"Going to have to clear what we can reach and let the stuff on top fall and then clear that," Butler said the volunteer fire personnel were escorted back outside.

The others got to work on the shaft.

After tedious, difficult minutes, Butler though he heard noises from below.

"Yeah, yeah. I hear them," Bill McGinn confirmed.

"Anybody there?" a female voice called from below.

"Police," Butler called out. "Who are you?"

"Students. Help us."

"We're coming," Butler yelled into the debris-clogged shaft. "Stay back."

"Hurry," Rachael Megay said. "We have injured."

Farther back in the room, Susan Snider was exhausted and ached in her shoulders from doing extended CPR on Knaul. The other injured in Snider's "hospital" watched in horror. A few cried. A small group joined hands to pray.

"Mer, you think you can take over for a minute?"

"I'll try," Meredith Clancy replied tremulously.

Snider positioned Clancy's hands on Knaul's sternum. "Kneel up. Get your weight over your hands. Wait for me."

Snider gave two quick breaths. "Go," she told Clancy.

"Faster," she urged.

Snider picked up the rhythm of the count. "That's good."

At thirty, Snider breathed into Knaul's blue lips. "Go," she ordered.

Using her phone's flashlight, Snider noted the deepening bluish tinge to Knaul's fingernails and skin. She opened the eyelids and shined her light on pupils that were fixed and dilated.

She gave two more breaths. "I got it," she said to Clancy. "Stay here."

Snider already knew that her efforts to save Knaul were futile. Twice she had promised herself that this was the last round.

One more try.

She reached thirty, breathed for the stricken substitute teacher again, rechecked for a pulse, and rechecked the eyes. Dilated and fixed.

Snider sat back on her haunches. Clancy repeatedly looked from Snider to Knaul until Snider shook her head.

"She's dead?" Meredith wailed.

"Nothing else we can do," Snider said.

And on the floor next to her, Snider's drained phone died also.

Snider pulled the blanket up from Barbara Knaul's feet and covered her head and upper body.

"Dead?" Lewis asked incredulously as he came back to Snider. She nodded.

"What's going on over there?"

Lewis couldn't answer right away. "Uh, cops are digging us out. Hopefully."

"About time." Snider looked around at her charges. "Tell them we're going to need stretchers."

"Good idea. It's gonna be slow," Lewis said as he wobbled back toward the elevator after a final glance at Knaul's covered body.

Sadness unexpectedly descended on Snider as Lewis moved away. A tear ran down a dusty cheek leaving a trail. She rubbed her face vigorously with both hands.

She scanned the group of students around her. "Everybody OK?" A couple of nods in return. Snider didn't know how much more she could take, let alone these kids.

"Meredith?" Clancy shook her head. Snider sat next to her and hugged Meredith. "Me neither."

Snider pushed herself off the floor. "I'll be back in a minute." She considered the possibility of racing across the hall to 503. She was pretty sure that her phone charger was in her desk drawer.

"How are you guys doing?" she asked the scouts, still diligently manning the door but from farther into the room after the latest explosion.

"Shh." Thomas Perry put his fingers to his lips. "Voices." He pointed to the hallway.

Snider strained but didn't hear anything, but getting the charger was now out of the question.

Maybe someone in the room had a charger she could use. Was there even electricity to charge the phone?

The three listened a little longer but heard no voices.

"The police are trying to dig us out at the other end," she informed the boys.

"About time," Perry stated.

"That's what I said," Snider grunted wearily as she trudged back toward the injured.

61

Officer Andy Fitzgerald had been sent to find the recently arrived Capitola SWAT and bring them to join Alpha team in the basement of the 500's. They had heard the explosion, and the radio calls as they emerged through the wall breach made to get access to the 500 wing.

Fitzgerald hesitated, "Hang on. Let me call in," he said to Tony Paolone, the team's commander.

Paolone tapped Fitzgerald on the shoulder and pointed to a faint smeared blood trace on the floor of the corridor and pointed to room 423.

Fitzgerald shrugged in the darkened hallway; no one had noticed the blood in Alpha's haste to get into the 500 wing. Or maybe they had just started thinking of bloodstains as the new normal.

Paolone used hand signals to position a couple of men for room entry. Fitzgerald and two other SWAT members kept an eye on the doorway that opened into the 500 wing's second floor while monitoring his radio. He was anxious to get downstairs and help his stricken team.

Paolone was the first one into the room 423 which appeared empty except for a victim laying on his back on the far side of the teacher desk. While his men checked the closets, Paolone assessed the adult male lying in blood on the floor.

"Alive. Heavy blood loss," he announced. "Pulse feels weak. Let's get him out of here, now."

"Careful, check him. We were warned about booby-trapped bodies," Fitzgerald said.

"Thanks for telling me now," Paolone said. "Already moved him."

Paolone was careful as he patted down the injured man quickly. A Vista View ID fell out of a pants pocket. Paolone gave it to Fitzgerald.

"Michael Zarlapski. Teacher." Fitzgerald read, matching the picture to the blood-streaked face.

"How do we get him out?"

"Back to the roof. Only route," Fitzgerald said.

"This should be fun."

Paolone signaled the men in the room to lift and carry the body. They moved Zarlapski as gingerly, but as quickly, as they could up the steps to the roof while Fitzgerald notified the command center.

Greco responded and also told them to get moving to the basement.

The remaining members of Capitola SWAT began inching down both sides of the stairwell toward the bottom floor.

Fitzgerald opened the door a crack and saw Sean Davidoff sprawled on the floor up against the far wall. Steve Brown was seizing, his helmeted head banging on the ground.

The Capitola officers followed Fitzgerald into the hallway. "Check him," Bobby Matheson told Tony Paolone, pointing at Sean Davidoff.

Steve Brown was rolled onto his side as the seizure subsided, and he was checked for injuries. Matheson called in a report to the command center.

"How is he?" Matheson asked Paolone when he was done on the radio.

"Unconscious, but breathing. Looks like his vest took a beating. Bomb go off?"

"Yeah, and there's a couple of wired tanks down the hall. We need to evac."

Brown was quickly prepped for transport and lifted by two men, and they started up the steps.

Davidoff was taken care of in the same way.

Ten minutes later they were handing off the victims to paramedics on the roof. Matheson called in for instructions and was told to position inside the building near the shop area.

On the way back down, Alpha introduced themselves to Capitola SWAT.

62

Bravo worked quickly but cautiously to clear the elevator shaft and reach the students in the basement. It was slow going as they occasionally dodged debris slides and falling concrete chunks, and tried to ignore the rumblings and groans of the damaged building.

The stuff clogging the shaft had to be moved piece by piece and then tossed or carried to the wall near the steps. They had to move the nurse's body again, this time around the corner and into the lavatory alcove. Members took turns watching the halls in three different directions, cringing each time eyes caught the carnage evident in between the main office and guidance. They rotated every few minutes.

Jon Butler, the team leader, received an update from the command center that included a warning about the propane tanks wired to the doors in the basement hallway. He walked to the shaft and yelled a warning down to the students about not touching the doors at the other end of the storage area. Butler was also informed that he was getting help. Two additional officers arrived minutes later.

The team rigged a safety net with blankets from the nurse's suite to catch falling objects.

"Do we really need this?" J. J. Martin said.

"Maybe we don't," Butler said, rapping on his helmet. "But if we evacuate kids through there, they will." Martin shrugged and started shining his flashlight around the inside of the shaft.

Bill McGinn, in the meantime, had found a six-foot step ladder in the maintenance utility closet between the boys and girls bathrooms.

Soon Butler and Martin could see into the storage area.

"Stand back," Butler said to Rachael Megay, John Pagliano, and Matt Bianco who were staring up at him.

He and Martin began tossing materials with cautious rapidity into the basement until they had enough room to lower the step ladder to the floor.

63

The bus was waiting. Ahmed was late. The extra time allowed the police to enhance coverage of the parking lot. A bomb squad robot was slowly checking out a car that had been flagged by one of the dogs.

The MRAP was still parked in front to act as a blast shield. Police were positioned on the school's roof with unobstructed views of the parking lot, but careful not to be over the shop. The AWV, the other heavy vehicle, was parked at the corner of the parking lot and the entrance into the circular driveway. The driver, Matt Weiss, used the vehicle for cover. Police were deployed at numerous angles, but carefully, so as not to create crossfires.

Dwayne Bush, the police officer driving the bus, had been instructed to be cooperative but ready to intervene if hostage lives were threatened.

Teams were stationed on the roof. They were still hoping to cut a hole through the ceiling and use a ladder or rope to get near the shop. But, for now, the presence of hostages, and the threat of mass bomb casualties kept them from acting and off to the edges in case shots were fired through the roof. Or worse, a bomb went off below them.

At 11:50, the door to the shop opened, and a girl and a masked gunman, his left arm around the female's throat, a gun in his right hand, emerged.

"Move back," he snarled at Bush who was already twenty feet from the bus. Bush put his hands up and backed farther.

The gunman looked right and then left. "Move that thing out of here," he yelled to no one in particular when he spied the AWV at the parking lot driveway.

"Did you hear me?" the gunman said, tightening his grip on the girl's throat until she yelped and instinctively reached for his arm. In response, the gun was nudged painfully against her cheekbone.

Mann radioed Weiss to relocate the vehicle.

"Give us a minute," Harrison Knoll yelled. "Are you Ahmed? We'd like to talk to you."

The gunman ignored the question and invitation and waited as Weiss drove the AWV up the driveway out of sight.

"Who's in charge?" the gunman yelled.

"I am," responded Mann from behind a parked car in the first row of spaces.

"Come here. We need to talk."

"Put your gun down first," Mann ordered.

The gunman gave a derisive laugh. "I'm in charge now." He gave the girl a painful twist.

Mann spoke into the mouthpiece of his radio to advise his men that he was going to walk toward the gunman and reminded them of the standing order not to shoot without permission. If the intelligence about bombs and hostages was correct, the price of taking out one perpetrator, even if he was the leader, was too high.

Mann put his gun on the ground and put his hands in the air.

"Coming out," he yelled for everyone's benefit, slowly walking to within twenty feet of the gunman until he was told to stop.

Mann noted that the perpetrator was above average in height, maybe 6'1, 6'2. Every inch of skin was covered. He wore a black ski mask, a buttoned tan coat to mid-thigh possibly over a bulletproof black vest, black all-weather shooting gloves, military-style black cargo pants, black boots similar to what some of the SWAT team members were wearing. There was no sign of nervousness.

"I'll talk," he shouted in Knoll's direction. "You'll listen." His eyes shifted back to Mann. Mann could see tears leaking down the hostage's terrified face over a round red mark where the gun had been held. He tried to reassure with a slight nod. In response, the gunman tightened his grip on the shivering girl. The sun had gone behind a bank of clouds.

"What do you want?" Mann asked.

"I said, 'I'll talk,' not you. I'm going to take Gabby here on the bus with me. Anyone tries anything, the girl dies, and the shop blows up with all the people inside. Understand?"

"Yes, I do, but you need to understand..."

The gunman ignored Mann and backed into the bus, pulling the girl after him. The inspection was quick. Mann watched as the gunman dragged the hostage up and down the aisle as he looked under the seats and the storage bins above.

Without a word, the masked gunman exited the bus and went back into the shop, the girl in tow.

64

Jon Butler and a couple of others from Bravo had climbed cautiously down the elevator shaft and now stood in the storage room. Other members of the team stood waiting at the elevator door on the second floor.

"How many are down here?" Martin asked the students gathered in front of him.

"Fifty?" Bianco guessed.

"Where are your teachers?"

"Back there," Rachael Megay said. "I'll show you."

While she led Butler to Susan Snider, Rachael asked about Zarlapski. "Is he OK?"

"I don't know. I'll find out when I get a chance."

"What about Steve Bennett. He's a student?"

"I'll check, I promise," Butler said.

They came to the triage area Snider had improvised.

"This is Miss Snider," Rachael said.

"We have to get these people out of here," Snider said, pointing to Stefanowicz and Lewis.

Butler glanced at the covered corpse of Barb Knaul but didn't say anything. He called for a check of the nurse's suite to find stretchers and wheelchairs.

Butler studied the ceiling above the triage area. "That is the shop, right?" he asked pointing.

"I think so," Snider said.

The policeman pulled a floor plan from his pocket and oriented himself. He paced off several steps and placed a blue cafeteria chair several feet away.

"The chair marks outside of the shop," he told his fellow officers. "If those bombs go off in the shop, we don't want to be under it. Make sure everyone stays away from the door down there; start bringing them this way. Stay to the left of the chair. Start lining kids up near the elevator. We'll take the injured out first."

"I assume we're taking him first," Butler said, pointing to Stefanowicz, still unconscious.

"He needs to get to a hospital fast," Snider said.

John Pagliano and Kyle Yarborough lifted Stefanowicz onto the stretcher slowly and carefully and strapped him in before pulling him to the elevator.

"He's going to have to go out on a stretcher, too," said Snider, pointing to Lewis.

Some of the students lining up against the wall and facing the elevator gasped when they saw Stefanowicz's pale bluish face. He was lifted up and out of the shaft.

"You guys take him out of here," Butler said, joining the officers on the second floor.

Stefanowicz was quickly wheeled out for evacuation.

Snider went up to officer Butler and took a moment to explain the trussed up Brian Crawford, shivering even though he still had on his red hunting coat.

"He might know something," Snider said.

She also pointed out Donna Slowick.

"She might, too. Keep her away from this girl," Sue Snider said, patting Kellie Frasier on the back. "And her," she said, pointing at Rachael Megay who had avoided Slowick after coming to the basement.

Rachael and Snider had had a conversation similar to the one she held with Zarlapski about Rachael's brush with William Holder's cult.

The ambulatory injured were helped to the second floor and told to wait in the nurse's office until everyone else was brought up. The process was tedious. Some kids were not athletic enough to climb and needed boosting and steadying. Chivalrously, most of the boys stayed back and helped the girls go first.

Regina Himmelwright's legs failed her as she was boosted to the top of the elevator car; she had to be hoisted by rope to the second floor. Snider hung back at the end of the line. Rachael and Meredith Clancy stayed with her.

Jon Butler climbed back down and walked up and down the line of students waiting to get out. It was not outside the realm of possibilities that there was a conspirator in the room just waiting for the right moment.

Half the students had been evacuated when a loud boom shook the storage area from above. Everyone still left in the room instinctively crouched or hit the floor and covered their heads as some material from the ceiling fell. The shower of debris in the elevator increased in intensity for a moment.

Another ominous boom rattled through the basement from above, further fraying nerves.

"Move, move," Butler urged, but some debris shifted in the elevator shaft, and there was a delay as members of the teams who were not racing students out of the building waited for a few minutes before finishing the basement's evacuation.

Meredith Clancy was helped up the debris pile after Kellie Frazier leaving Rachael Megay and Miss Snider as the last two to be rescued.

Snider had a few minutes to contemplate the enormity of what was going on, and a few sobs escaped her chest. Rachael put her arm around Snider's shoulders, and they cried together until it was Rachael's turn to be brought up.

When Snider was helped up the shaft by Jon Butler, the storage room was finally empty, except for the late Barbara Knaul.

65

Several of the first responding EMS personnel were VVHS grads who still participated in the school community covering football games, giving guest lectures to classes, supporting fundraisers, etc. They knew the school nurse and the administrators and some of the teachers and occasionally responded to emergencies at the school.

There was some shock to be overcome at treating so many of their teachers, mentors, colleagues, and the children of neighbors, but they quickly focused on each "job" in front of them.

The exodus of the injured was a positive sign. They were alive. Not like the futile waiting around of emergency personnel in New York on 9/11.

The explosions in the parking lot created injuries that were more horrifying than the usual trauma treated by local rescue personnel. The tissue destruction from the high energy, heated projectiles carved jagged channels through protective clothing and flesh. Whether or not they had been stabilized, the gravest cases were whisked by air or ambulance to Lehigh Valley which was closed except for victims from the high school.

MedEvac helicopters were using the JV soccer field across the road from the baseball diamond as a landing area. Lehigh Valley's was the closest and the first to arrive. It was on the ground for only two minutes before transporting its first patient, a firefighter who caught shrapnel from the North Parking Lot explosion to the hospital.

Mike Zarlapski's blood pressure was dangerously low and his pulse thready from his wounds, and he was the first to receive blood from the impromptu blood bank that had assembled at St. Phillip's Catholic Church, a half-mile away. He had not regained consciousness and was still very unstable when taken by medevac to the trauma center.

Vince Stefanowicz arrested on the way down the ladder from the roof, and Vista paramedics had to use an AED to revive him on the ground. He, too, was rushed to the medevac site, but a warning light about a mechanical issue lit up in the chopper from Crossley Regional Hospital. He arrested and was revived again as he was loaded into an ambulance for the overland trip to the hospital.

Clark Lewis became combative with staff members from Carrollton Regional who were trying to treat him. He insisted on staying by Stefanowicz's side and had to be pulled from the Valley ambulance that was transporting his stricken partner. Lewis raised a fist to paramedic Nancy Crowley but passed out before throwing a punch. He was secured in the Valley unit and transported to Lehigh Valley five minutes behind Stefanowicz.

The triage center was busy stabilizing the less severely injured before dispatching them to area hospitals by ambulance. Conditions included broken bones, hypothermia, hypoglycemia, lacerations, shock, diabetic coma, sprained muscles, smoke inhalation, eye injuries, dental injuries, one severed finger, and mental meltdowns.

A makeshift morgue had also been established in an enclosed tent next to the triage center. At the moment only the covered body of special needs student Chloe Phipps' was inside. Her mother sat in Chloe's wheelchair rocking back and forth and crying quietly.

66

In the shop, the people with guns were screaming at the hostages to put their heads on the floor.

Cassidy Trumbauer, a student from Mrs. Chapman's class, was bemused despite her circumstances. She certainly knew what a gun could do, but she was not intimidated by the histrionics.

What an over-compensating mini-dick, she thought. The gunman closest to her was handling the weapon all wrong; if he did shoot, he would only hit random targets. But there were plenty of accidents-waiting-to-happen crowded on the floor.

The leader was different. He acted cold. If he wanted you dead, you'd be dead, Cassidy thought, as she watched him go outside.

When the door to the shop storage room had accidentally cracked open, Cassidy caught a glimpse of two other assholes putting on what must have been bomb vests. Several small pockets were stuffed with something clay-like and red and black wires were visible.

Clear baggies hung over some of the pockets. That scared Cassidy, and she worked to fight down panic. She was now determined to get a weapon. The movie about that plane that had been hijacked on 9/11 played in her head. The passengers, some of the passengers at least, knew they were going to die. They had nothing to lose. Neither did she now.

When Mini-Dick had moved on to yell at another group, Cassidy raised her head off the stained, cold concrete floor. All of the gunman, five or six as far as Cassidy could tell, were wearing black and carried guns hanging over their shoulders or cradled in crossed arms when they weren't waving them around.

One of the vest wearers was small and fidgeting like he was trying to escape his skin. His shoulders slumped, and he cautiously adjusted the jacket covering his vest several times. Cassidy figured it was that Hosni kid, the kid with the gun in 514. The one who had shot Mrs. Chapman. Cassidy wondered if Mrs. Chapman was dead. She hadn't moved for a long time in the classroom. Somebody had said she was still breathing, though.

Hosni was a weird kid. But nobody is this weird, Cassidy thought.

A few minutes ago, three of the shooter-morons had brought in a "prisoner" and thrown him roughly to the floor, leaving him in a heap several feet ahead and to Cassidy's right, next to her best friend, Robbie Quinn.

When the other kid raised his head to look around, she recognized Steve Bennett. Cassidy had been to the Bennett house many times to hang with Steve's sister, Devin, a sophomore at St. Thomas More High School. Cassidy had a crush on Steve, as did about a hundred other girls. She covertly watched Steve surveying the shop. He made eye contact with Cassidy and flashed a lopsided grin and gave her a thumbs up.

Cassidy mouthed the word "bombs" at Steve and tugged at her top to try and indicate the vests the bad guys were wearing. Steve looked quizzically at her but then nodded.

Robbie Quinn waved discreetly at Steve to put his head back down, making a barely perceptible nod toward the front of the room.

The gunmen guarding the room had stopped blustering and hung around the front of the shop near the outside door. Except for the little guy with the vest. He hung in the back corner walking small nervous circles now. The hostages on the floor near him had edged away as best they could.

The gun-toting hotshots at the door reminded Cassidy of her family dogs, Sparkle, Boyd, and Chester, after her dad went into the garage through the mudroom door. They stared and stared with anxiety until he came back into the house. Cassidy fought off a sudden wave of emotion that memory brought up. No time for that now if she wanted to snuggle with Sparkle again.

Even the other guy with the vest had calmed down. He had been the one to guide the hostages into the shop from the hallway. This gunman had pulled kids into the room and pushed them onto the floor, sometimes using his booted foot to the head of those too slow to comply or too fearful to function. He had practically goose-stepped among the hostages. A soldier in the douchebag army, Cassidy thought. That was over an hour ago. His enthusiasm must have waned.

When the Leader left to do whatever it is he's doing, with poor Katrina Leander as a shield, Douchebag dropped his act and leaned against a wall. He waved his weapon at people and yelled at them when their heads rose off the floor, but he did not see Cassidy scrutinizing him.

The room had been freezing when the hostages had been herded in, but it felt warmer now. And more malodorous. The native smells of sawdust and metal shavings were being overwhelmed by nervous perspiration and urine.

The guys with the guns and Cassidy was pretty sure they were all guys, must be getting hot. "Take off your masks," she messaged them telepathically, "so I know who to beat the shit out of later."

Cassidy looked over at Steve Bennett again. He had gotten closer to a workstation. Cassidy watched as Steve carefully looked around and reached a hand up to a tabletop. He kept his eyes on the shooters as he groped for the long screwdriver near the edge. Cassidy apprehensively glanced from guard to guard. When she looked back at Steve, he was safely prone on the ground, and the screwdriver was gone from the table.

Off to Cassidy's left was a similar table, a toolbox on the first shelf. A girl Cassidy didn't know was between Cassidy and the toolbox, however. The girl was crying into her sweatshirt-sleeved right arm.

"Hey," Cassidy whispered to get the girl's attention. Mini-Dick turned in their direction. Cassidy put her head down for a ten-count and looked again. Mini-Dick was now turned toward the entrance door. She caught sight of Robbie Quinn looking at her, his fingers to his lips.

Cassidy glanced at the guards once more and then moved closer to the girl who finally looked over at Cassidy.

Cassidy rechecked the room. "Switch with me," she ordered.

Cassidy got a befuddled look in return. She put her finger to her lips and crawled over the girl's back. The girl wriggled away, terrified that someone may have seen them. She put her face back into her sleeve.

Cassidy took a deep breath and reached for the toolbox. The latch was on the other side; she would have to turn the box around. Cassidy ducked her head in case anyone had been watching, and raised up again after counting to twenty-two, her favorite number. Cassidy motioned that the girl needed to put her head back down. She gently turned the box around. It had a padlock on it. She cursed again to herself.

Behind the box were several pieces of wood of various lengths and thicknesses. Project mistakes by students. She grabbed a thick piece about two-feet long from the top of the pile and brought it under her body just as the door opened.

The leader was back. He threw Katrina Leander to the floor. "Thanks, Gabby," he said sarcastically. Cassidy didn't know Katrina that well, but she had never heard her called "Gabby" before. The poor girl whimpered pathetically, cowering on her knees as if awaiting a blow.

Douchebag snapped back to his sadistic, arrogant posturing and heads that had been tentatively poking up hastily ducked back down. Cassidy, too, lowered her head but kept her eyes up.

67

Steve Bennett patiently moved forward on his belly a couple of inches at a time. He wanted to get as close to one of the gunmen as he could and grab a weapon. Red sneakers Carey Ackerman had carelessly left a rifle propped against a wall about thirty feet in front of Steve. That was doable along as there was time.

The obvious leader had vanished into the storage room to Steve's right. He reappeared now and went to each of the five other perpetrators and held brief conversations, the longest with Hosni. Hosni nodded his head and shuddered. A sob may have escaped as the leader patted Hosni on the back.

Steve cut the distance to the rifle by ten feet whispering a "hang in there" to students cowering on the floor as he passed them.

But when the leader was done talking with Hosni, he walked past Steve and grabbed Carey's propped rifle.

Damn it, Bennett thought. He gripped the screwdriver in his right hand for reassurance.

"This yours?" the leader said, pointing the gun at Carey. For a second he thought the leader was going to shoot Ackerman, who did not answer. Instead of giving it back, the leader carried the rifle into the storage room and came right back out without it.

"Line up ten people at the door," the leader commanded as he paced in the front of the room. "Now."

Two of the gunmen started going through the prone hostages nearest to the door, kicking and prodding with guns, randomly selecting, or maybe deliberating choosing those they knew. They seemed to disproportionately to be people of color.

Antoine Henry, a big JV football tackle, reflexively swung his arm at one of those ordering him off the floor, knocking the gunman off balance. Another ran over and slammed the butt of his gun against Henry's right temple. Antoine's chin crashed onto a workstation as he crumpled to the floor.

Now there were nine terrified students in line.

"Anybody else?" Ackerman snarled.

The leader ordered a skinny kid with a blond crew cut to put a black backpack on before grabbing Katrina Leander by her blond hair and hoisting her painfully to her feet. "I'll go out first with this bitch," he told Ackerman.

"This kid is wearing a bomb," the leader announced to the hostages in the shop, pointing at the male he had just given the backpack to. The blond kid began to cry.

"Stay behind me until I tell you to go," the leader told Ackerman. "Then put them on and guard the bus. Any shots fired, anybody runs, kill them all," he said loud enough for everyone to hear.

"But, Will…" Ackerman started to say.

"Shut up you idiot," the leader said. "Do what I say. Open the door and hold it," the leader ordered a heavy-set girl. The girl hesitated, and the leader raised his weapon. She moved clumsily to comply with the order.

Ackerman put a stranglehold on a female in the line. The girl gasped. Bennett had to refrain himself from rushing to the girl's aid forcibly. It would be suicide.

The leader went through the outside door and pivoted Katrina into the open while he stayed behind the door. "We're going to the bus," he yelled. "Try anything, and we kill everyone."

Ackerman got the signal to move to the bus. With his free hand, he prodded the first kid in line with the business end of his semi-automatic, and the line moved. "Hands up," the leader ordered as the procession passed him in the doorway.

Through the partially open door, Bennett watched Ackerman stay in the middle of the pack twisting and turning his human shield painfully. The hostages climbed on the bus, and Ackerman kept his hold on the frightened girl as he entered the vehicle.

No police were in Bennett's obstructed view, but they had to be out there. Right?

Satisfied, the leader came back inside with "Gabby" and ordered that ten more hostages be readied. He released the girl and went into the storage room.

Bennett heard a yelp of pain behind him and turned to look. One of the other shooters had grabbed Cassidy by the hair and was twisting it. She swung the piece of wood she had hidden under her body wildly and caught her tormentor on the thigh. He let out a grunt as he staggered back a couple of feet pulling Cassidy with him. In his peripheral vision, Bennett saw Robbie Quinn moving to help Cassidy.

"Get down," Steve hissed futilely at Robbie.

Robbie's wild overhand punch to the shooter's head forced him to release Cassidy's hair to ward off the blow.

At that moment, a loud roar erupted from Hosni's position in the back corner of the room as his vest went off prematurely maiming, but not killing, Hosni. The two people closest to him died instantly. Injured hostages screamed in primal agony and mortal fear.

Bennett ducked instinctively with everyone else as projectiles flew across the room in what sounded like a brief but ferocious hailstorm, and choking smoke filled the room. Those hit by shrapnel were moaning and writhing on the floor, or worse, went immediately still.

The people on the floor around Bennett had mostly escaped injury, but a girl to Steve's left was bleeding profusely from her head.

Before Steve could react, gunfire erupted a few seconds after the explosion and then stopped abruptly. Bennett glanced behind and saw Robbie on the floor next to Cassidy, his face grotesquely twisted in pain as he rolled protectively on top of Cassidy.

She struggled for a moment to free herself but caught sight of Steve motioning at her frantically. Cassidy went still and played dead.

INTERNAL LOCKDOWN

Bennett heard a crashing sound and shouts of "Police" shouted several times behind him. Somebody was yelling "This way. This way," from the front of the room.

Steve's first thought was to stay and help everyone else, including Cassidy, but when a screaming girl stumbled in front of him, he instinctively picked her up and practically carried her through the door in the wake of the cop who had yelled instructions to follow him. Others were stumbling out of the door behind Steve. He had no choice but to keep going behind the police and hope he didn't get shot.

68

A minute earlier a reconstituted, five-man police team had made its way to the hallway outside the shop and was awaiting orders when the team leader, Bobby Matheson, informed the command center that there was an explosion in the shop and shots had been fired, and he and his men were entering the shop. He did not wait for the reply.

Mike DiGennaro pulled the door open, and Vito Abbonizio and Stan Lara went in low. Tony Paolone broke to the left, and Joe Bosenhofer went right, moving behind two work tables.

The scene in the shop was chaotic and gruesome. A bomb vest had malfunctioned; the wearer was screaming in agony, blood gushing from two severed arms. Several hostages close-by were bloodied and wailed in pain. Bodies were on the floor.

Two gunmen were shooting sporadically as students frantically ran or crawled away or tried to cram under tables. A few of the hostages heard the call of "police," and ran at the officers in the back of the room inhibiting the cops from shooting back.

From his position behind a table, Matheson heard "This way." from the front of the room.

He only got a quick look as bullets chipped the wall behind him, but he caught a glimpse of a SWAT officer leading students out the front door of the shop and into the North Parking Lot.

Another explosion rocked the room; steel balls flew across the shop at nearly the speed of bullets. Some found soft targets.

Everyone fortunate enough to be shielded behind workstations stayed put for a long minute.

From the command center, Greco asked for an update.

"Stand-by," Matheson responded.

After an eternity, Matheson raised up slightly and scanned the room. Gunfire was coming from the parking lot but had ceased in the room. The smoking remains of the second suicide bomber lay across a workbench in the center. Agonized screaming and moaning filled the shop. Matheson wondered which one of the men had made it to the front of the room and if he had made it outside to safety.

One of the shooters dragged a screaming female toward the outside door. He had a vest on. The girl wriggled free and put space between her and the gunman. Gunfire erupted from Matheson's left. The shooter's head exploded in a red haze in the front of the room.

Matheson saw Abbonizio ahead and to the left, sweeping his smoking weapon across the room from a crouch. Lara was to the right, on one knee next to a girl bleeding profusely from an upper body wound. Paolone was behind Lara.

DiGennaro was ahead on the right; he and Matheson made eye contact. DiGennaro signaled he was moving to the front.

Abbonizio was waving at Matheson to come to him. Matheson swept the room and moved toward his teammate.

Officer Joe Boesenhofer was lying prone on the floor, Abbonizio crouching above him.

Boesenhofer groaned and tried to sit up. "Stay down," Matheson ordered.

"I'm good, I'm good," Boesenhofer said shaking his head.

"Stay with him," Matheson ordered Abbonizio.

Now all the officers were accounted for. Someone from another unit must have led the group to safety. Maybe a Capitola officer had led the students out the door.

An explosion from outside rocked the room. Everyone who stood hugged the floor again. After a few more precious seconds of waiting, four officers deployed across the room. Matheson signaled for them to hold their spots while he called in a quick report.

There was no reply from the command center, and Matheson repeated the call.

Greco finally replied and told him of an explosion in the parking lot.

Matheson signaled Paolone to stay behind and watch the back of the shop while the rest moved forward, picking through injured and terrified students.

"Stay down. Stay down," the police whispered as they moved.

From under Robbie Quinn's body, Cassidy made eye contact with Stan Lara as he walked past her. He put his fingers to his lips.

"I'll be back in a minute," he said.

69

A few minutes earlier, before the chaos in the shop broke out, the police outside the building were waiting impatiently for the order from command to end this nightmare. But they were forced to watch as hostages were herded onto the bus.

The heavily tinted windows hindered a clear view of what was going on, but the movements of the lone gunman on board were detectable. They could take him out. All the cops were itching for the order to shoot.

Then came the muffled boom of an explosion from inside the shop. Over the radio, Johnny Mann heard Bobby Matheson's frantic notification that they were entering the room. Semi-automatic gunfire erupted from inside, and shortly after the door burst open and students started running out of the shop accompanied by a SWAT officer who turned the escaping students, including Steve Bennett, toward the front of the campus and away from the building. The officer ran with the student escapees urging them to go faster

"Who to hell is that?" Larabee asked aloud.

"Greco. You know what's going on?" Mann called in.

"Negative," Greco responded. "We have people going into the shop now."

"About a dozen just came out the front door. They're headed toward Main Street.."

The policeman-driver, Dwayne Bush, climbed onto the tour bus. The hostages were cowering on the floor or scrunched on the seats. The gunman was at the back following the progress of the people who had run out of the building.

"Charlie 1, cover the bus," Mann said in a low voice over the radio. Two CIRT cops still on the roof both watched through their rifle scopes as Bush went into the vehicle. They saw the gunman turn toward Bush.

Bush drew his gun from inside a bus company windbreaker.

"Drop your weapon," Bush yelled.

The gunman pointed his weapon skyward with his left hand. Bush could see something in the gunman's right.

"Drop your…"

The explosion roared through the bus. Flames erupted from the middle section. Window glass and metal spewed in all directions sending small missiles into the parking lot. The negotiator, Harrison Knoll, caught one piece in the forehead and bounced off the hood of a car before landing face first on the parking lot. Two secondary explosions followed almost instantaneously.

Police on the roof and in the lot ducked away from the debris raining down.

Oily black smoke mixed with the flames quickly consumed the interior of the bus. The middle of the fiberglass body of the vehicle began melting. Agonized screaming subsided, but not entirely as the fire died down quickly.

While everyone else had focused on the bus before the explosion, state policeman Frank Larabee had started after the group that had exited the building. Something about the cop leading the students away from the parking lot did not seem right to Larabee, But, when the bus exploded, he broke off the pursuit and came back to help.

"Weiss, get your truck," Mann yelled, "Put it here. Larabee, be ready if more hostages come out." He alerted everyone to be very sure before any shots were fired.

Matt Weiss drove the AWV across the grass and parked the heavy vehicle between the smoldering bus and the exit door to the shop. The door was pitted with debris from the bus. Chipped masonry was strewn on the ground as were body parts. A small evergreen outside the door had been shredded.

"We are positioned outside the shop door, ready to enter," Mann called.

But Greco's voice over the radio advised all police to stand down and wait for further instruction.

"Evacuees will be coming to you momentarily. Repeat. Stand down."

Larabee's thoughts returned to the group that had run out of the building seconds before the bus exploded. He jogged forward to get a better view of the circular driveway at the top of the campus. Larabee could see the group of students now stretched, moving at various speeds. The biggest kid was trying to help the stragglers. The SWAT officer was nowhere in sight.

Another police officer and EMT's were running toward the group.

Mann came up behind Larabee. "Something wrong?"

Larabee explained his sense that something was off about the SWAT guy leading the students out.

Mann called into Greco to see if the command post knew who the cop was.

"Stand-by. Let me check," Greco said.

A minute later he was back.

"It wasn't any of the teams sent into the shop, and the other closest teams are accounted for. Sure it wasn't somebody with you guys?"

"Negative," Mann said. "We were all outside."

"What do you think?" Mann asked Larabee.

"I think that was our good buddy Ahmed dressed like a cop, and he is getting away."

"Talk to the kids," Mann said. "I have to stay here. Let me know. I'll call it in."

Larabee took off toward the escapees from the shop.

Mann advised Greco of their suspicions that the leader of the shooters was on the loose.

70

Steve Bennett had emerged from the shop about halfway in the pack of students who were following the policeman with SWAT on the back of his vest, his visor pulled down over his face, a semi-automatic rifle in his right hand. Bennett had taken the arm of the girl he picked up off the shop floor and was practically dragging her with him, throttling his speed.

They went left as soon they exited the shop and ran for the circular driveway in front of the school. They were about a football field away when the bus exploded.

A couple of the runners stumbled to the ground when they tried to look over their shoulders. Bennett released the girl he was running with and stopped to help those who had fallen.

"Hurry up," the cop leading them yelled from the top of the gradual slope of the driveway.

Bennett made sure everyone was moving and took up the rear. He glanced behind him to see the burning bus and the chaos in the lot. A trooper who had started after the group was now turning back to the parking lot.

"Hurry up," the SWAT guy yelled again. He had stepped aside at the bend in the driveway and was waving the students past him toward the southern end of the campus where the command post was located.

Three of the students were already winded and were barely running. "Take the lead," the cop said to Bennett through his dark visor. "I'll get them."

Bennett jogged ahead encouraging the students to keep moving. Steve looked back after going about fifty yards. Most of the line had kept up with his jogging pace, but the walking stragglers were far behind.

There was no sign of the SWAT guy who had led them out of the shop.

Bennett stopped.

"What to hell? Keep going," he said to the group behind him, pointing and waving them toward police officers and EMT's running across the grass toward them.

Bennett ran back to the three walkers. He had to support a male who was having trouble breathing.

"Inhaler?" the kid managed to gasp out.

"No. Sit here. You'll be fine. You did great." Bennett waved for the EMT as he helped the male to the curb. The other two walkers continued.

"You know where the SWAT guy went?" Bennett asked as they walked past.

"He said he had to go that way for something," a male wheezed in response, pointing toward Main Street and a thick stand of pine trees.

A dawning came over Bennett that something was amiss about the SWAT guy. How had he been at the front of the shop when the other cops had come in from behind? What was so crucial on Main Street that he didn't stay with the students?

Bennett intercepted one of the police officers who was coming to help the group and relayed his thoughts.

The policeman called into the command center and was told to bring Bennett there if he was uninjured.

"You OK?" the cop asked. "You have a pretty nasty bruise on the side of your face. Your arm is bleeding, too."

Bennett put his hand to the spot where Carey Ackerman had kicked him and only now was Steve beginning to feel some pain.

"I'm fine," he said.

Bennett and the police officer walked with the two other stragglers who were greeted by EMT's in the triage center. The policeman pointed Steve toward the command center.

Outside, Tess Bennington was tearfully hugging her daughter Nikki. When he arrived, Steve hugged each of them in turn, and then went inside where he joined Matt Bianco, Susan Snider, and Rachael Megay in another bittersweet reunion.

71

Hostages in the shop were evacuated immediately to the triage area, no matter their condition, for fear of more bombs going off in the building.

Except for those who wore the black tags placed by paramedics.

Each paramedic carried a wad of tags, each with an elastic band. At the bottom of each tag were four colored tear-off strips labeled, from the bottom: MINOR (green), DELAYED (yellow), IMMEDIATE (Red), DECEASED (Black). Assessment took less than thirty seconds in most cases.

The noise level in the room elevated with cries for help, moaning, sobbing, screaming, questions asked of no one, in particular, pleas to get out of the room.

And then there were those in shock who numbly stared at nothing in particular.

Among the injured, Cassidy Trumbauer was finally liberated from the corpse of Robbie Quinn. She passed out in the arms of a paramedic.

Bomb squads did preliminary surveys of the shop even as EMT's and volunteer doctors were supervising the evacuation and beginning treatments on the fly.

In the hour since the bus had blown up and the shop was cleared, teams had quickly, but systematically done a room-by-room search of the entire building.

Greco had authorized Larabee to organize the search for William Holder if that is who the SWAT officer was. The police had already done preliminary ID's of the bodies of the shooters on the bus and in the shop. Hosni's and Carey Ackerman's bodies were going to have to be positively ID'ed through DNA. Greco was confident they had all of the actual gunmen accounted for, except their leader, Holder. Greco was also assured by the staff in the command post and Detective Carol Donahue that, based on social media mining and interviews during the siege, including the questioning of drone flyer Ethan Lutz, they had everyone else involved in the massive plot, dead or alive. A student, Tyler Yoder, who had been suspected of being involved because he left the property without permission was located and cleared of any wrongdoing.

Sue Snider, Steve Bennett, Matt Bianco, Rachael Megay were relieved to hear from Greco that Zarlapski, Stefanowicz, and Lewis were alive and in hospitals. Greco held back on talking about their conditions, however.

The four were set up with detectives who gently, but thoroughly mined their experiences.

Rachael's thoughts on William Holder and his cult following were of particular interest to the police.

The students were then taken to reunite with the classmates they had started a normal day with in AP English, and then with their families.

Rachael's insights on, and Miss Snider's conversations with, Donna Slowick initiated a plan by the detectives to put Slowick and Lutz together and see if they could get information about where Holder might try to hide.

It worked, to an extent. Their faces dropped when Slowick walked into the room at the Pennsville police station where Ethan Lutz was being held after being escorted by the large guard from the prison bus, Santa Rendon. Then Slowick and Lutz were interviewed separately about William Holder.

Brian Crawford, who had been "arrested" by Snider in the basement, was a useless, blubbering mess who seemed to be more of a patsy than a participant.

Ethan Lutz revealed after ten intense minutes of grilling that Holder had several backup plans, including slipping into a SWAT uniform that he had Lutz purchase for him from an out-of-state contact. Lutz wasn't privy to all the details, he claimed, but this particular plan involved getting to a system of large storm sewer pipes that had been abandoned when the reservoir had been dug many years ago.

Holder had intimated to Lutz that he had a contact with members of a group loosely associated with domestic terrorists who would get him out of the country. Lutz did not know how or where, however. Lutz also said that if things went badly, as they did, he "knew that Will would have no qualms about sacrificing his 'friends'."

With the help of Tim Petit, the Pennsville council president, drawings of the sewer system were located, copied and rushed to Frank Larabee and the team he had hastily assembled to look for the SWAT impersonator. But the search had, so far, turned up nothing except some fresh incomplete footprints leading to a manhole cover, footprints from boots similar to what SWAT teams wear. That trail was lost quickly, however. The manhole appeared undisturbed, still half-hidden in weedy overgrowth.

After the preliminary sweep of the building declared it explosive free, a more painstaking approach began. Bomb squad teams again accompanied the teams, as did forensic teams who began what promised to be months of work. The first priority was to process the scenes involving the deceased so that they could be removed from the building.

A few hours later, a press conference was held in the Vista View Middle School gym. A prayer was said, condolences were expressed for everyone involved, including the killers' families.

"Let me run down the updated numbers," a weary Barry Greco began with several agency heads standing behind him. "We have confirmed that fifty-one students are deceased as are twelve staff members, five firemen, eight police officers, and five perpetrators. We are not releasing names until we have notified next of kin. We ask that you, please respect that process and do not cause further grief to the community through speculation or premature announcements.

"Additionally, twenty-three students, three staff members, one fireman, and four policemen have been admitted to area hospitals. Many other children and adults have been treated and released. We do not have an exact number yet."

"Five shooters were found dead, one on the bus that exploded, the others in the shop. This is domestic terrorism, and it appears that the actors tried to make it look like they were Middle Eastern.

"We are still searching for a person of interest, William Holder, also possibly known as Will Holder or Ahmed. You have his info in the packet we handed out. He is considered armed and dangerous. We believe he was the ringleader and may have escaped dressed as a policeman. The local search for him is continuing at this time and will go on as long as necessary.

"If you have information on this scum...on this person, call the hotline number behind me. A fifty thousand dollar reward is being offered for information leading to his arrest.

"We are asking residents to shelter in place, keep cars, trucks, windows locked. We know people want to come together for memorials, but, until we know where Mr. Holder is, large gatherings are prohibited.

"Three arrests have been made of associates who were helping the perpetrators. One is a former student. Two are current students.

"The residence on Astonville Pike was housing a bomb-making operation for the shooters. The State Police, Homeland Security, and ATF are investigating. I don't have any more information on that."

"We will be processing the scene all night and into tomorrow. School, of course, is canceled, and will be for at least the rest of this week."

The reporters questions for those on the podium mostly centered on the search for Ahmed and the motives for the massacre.

After ten minutes, Greco cut it short with a final statement

"It was the worst of days for many of us, but the day also brought out the best in those that responded for our children and adults who were victimized today by mindless terrorism.

"If there is any lesson to be drawn from this, it is that we hope that tomorrow schools across the country prepare or practice for a worst-case scenario like we saw unfold today and that our leaders take immediate action on solutions that will stop this madness before it happens again.

"Thank you."

EPILOGUE

When the shelter in place order was lifted after twenty-four hours of fruitless searching for Will Holder, most of the community members spent the week dealing with broken children, consoling each other, attending funerals and memorials, and fending off unwanted attention from the media.

The firehouses in the District were being staffed 24/7 with counselors and volunteers for anyone who needed emotional assistance. Sue Snider spent much of her time talking with drop-ins at the various firehouses. It was therapy for her, also. She also spent some time staffing the hotline that had been established.

Vince Stefanowicz had succumbed to his injuries on the operating table, twenty minutes after he arrived at the hospital. His funeral was pending.

Mike Zarlapski was still touch-and-go in a medically induced coma. Doctors were not sure if the severe blood loss had caused brain damage, but there had been hopeful signs of progress.

As a kind of therapy, the surviving AP students from Zarlapski's class decided to keep watch outside of Zarlapski's hospital room. Rachael Megay and Nikki Bennington organized the shifts. Tess Bennington arranged for some of the staff to also maintain a vigil. All the students participated except for Regina Himmelwright who had been admitted to a foundation for mental health. The boys in the class served as honorary pallbearers at Isaiah Shue's funeral.

INTERNAL LOCKDOWN

Matt Bianco and Steve Bennett tried to convince the interim superintendent to let the baseball team play out its schedule because they felt Coach Z would want that. The two conducted informal practices for the team while the decision was weighed. Attendance was one hundred percent. Snider occasionally dropped by to tend to any aches and pains.

All of the students who made it to the hospital survived, and most had been released. The mental trauma was, of course, something entirely different.

The search for Holder was even more intense. Two days after the shootings, a right-wing organization no one had ever heard of claimed responsibility for the attack. The boast was generally dismissed out of hand but did lend some credence to the terrorist connection Ethan Lutz contended that Will Holder had. International police agencies gave their resources and joined in the hunt for Holder. Tips were coming in at a steady rate, and a few were promising.

Lutz was being held without bail. Donna Slowick and Brian Crawford were also in adult prisons, but away from the general population. Slowick was on a suicide watch.

Plans were in place to conduct classes for the high school students at the middle school, using a split schedule, but no date had been set to restart classes. Retired teachers and other staff from Vista View School District and surrounding districts volunteered to fill the gaps left by the deaths or injuries suffered by VV District personnel during the shootings, at least until the end of the school year. The school board brought back a former, retired superintendent to guide the District for the remainder of the year while Dr. Sarah Gilmore was on a forced, paid leave. No plans had been announced about what to do with the high school building.

Barry Greco told close friends he was retiring after his active part in the investigation was wrapped up. If William Holder had not been apprehended by then, Greco vowed to spend "every minute of every day" bringing him to justice.

ERNIE QUATRANI